A MAPWALKER TRILOGY

MAP OF SHADOWS
MAP OF PLAGUES
MAP OF THE IMPOSSIBLE

J.F. PENN

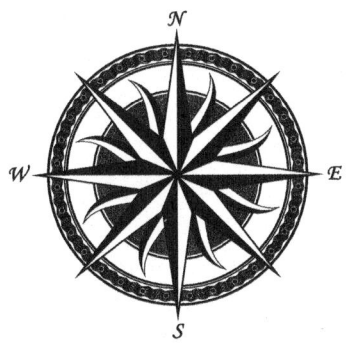

This book is a work of fiction. The characters, incidents and dialogue are drawn from the author's imagination and are not to be construed as real. Any resemblance to actual events or persons, living or dead, is fictionalized or coincidental.

A Mapwalker Trilogy: Map of Shadows,
Map of Plagues, Map of the Impossible

Copyright © J.F.Penn (2017, 2019, 2020, 2021). All rights reserved.

www.JFPenn.com

ISBN: 978-1-913321-46-8

The right of Joanna Penn to be identified as the authors of this work has been asserted by the authors in accordance with the Copyright, Designs and Patents Act,1988. All rights reserved. No part of this publication may be reproduced, stored in a retrieval system, or transmitted, in any form, or by any means, electronic, mechanical, photocopying, recording or otherwise, without the prior permission of the authors.

This book is sold subject to the condition that it shall not, by way of trade or otherwise, be lent, resold, hired out, or otherwise circulated without the author's prior consent in any form of binding or cover other than that in which it is published and without a similar condition being imposed on the subsequent purchaser.

Requests to publish work from this book should be sent to:
joanna@CurlUpPress.com

Cover and Interior Design: JD Smith Design
Printed by Amazon KDP

www.CurlUpPress.com

A place written out of history.

A world off the edge of the map.

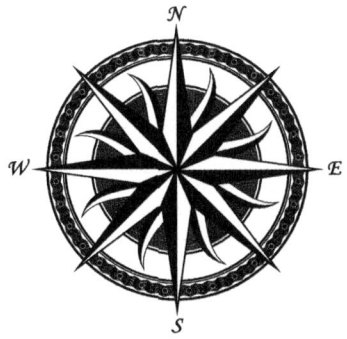

CONTENTS

Map of Shadows 1

Map of Plagues 191

Map of the Impossible 385

MAP of SHADOWS

A MAPWALKER NOVEL

J.F. PENN

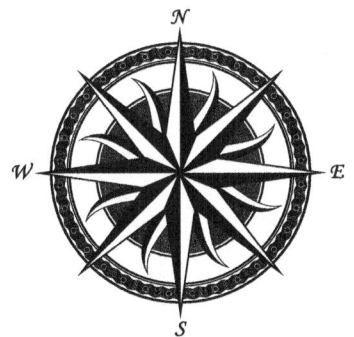

"It is not drawn on any map; true places never are."

Herman Melville, Moby Dick

PROLOGUE

MICHAEL FARREN SAT AT his desk in the old map shop, an antique parchment in front of him portraying the ancient city of Bath. An oversize globe sat on a low table nearby, its sepia tint displaying a seventeenth-century world that no longer existed. The borders had moved, the names of the countries had changed, and yet he kept it here to remind himself of what had once been. And what could be again.

His shop sat on Elizabeth Buildings, around the corner from The Circus, a circle of power built around one of the porous gates into the Borderlands. By day, he sold vintage maps to visiting tourists. By night, he watched and waited, performing the etching ritual. His gnarled hand held the fountain pen he had used for a lifetime of cartography as he traced over the fading lines on the map with a fine nib.

But tonight, Michael's hand shook as he etched the lines he knew so well with ink of blood and pitch. He tried to concentrate on the arc of the Royal Crescent, the straight line of Brock Street and the curves of The Circus. They were symbols of ancient Druids, a crescent moon attached to the sun by a narrow ley line, a power running deep under the earth.

The Circus was modeled on Stonehenge, the outer circumference matching the temple of Druidic power not far from here on Salisbury Plain. The Mapwalkers had protected the border for so long, but now, something was coming. It had been building in strength, biding its time, waiting until the Ministry was weak. Now there were only a few pure blood Mapwalkers left, and the Shadow Cartographers were rising.

The clock struck one and the cry of a night bird came from outside Michael's open window. The air smelled of summer, elderflower and honeysuckle … But then, something else.

Sulfur.

The air crackled, and the wind picked up, blowing into the shop. The maps on the walls lifted, their rustling sound speaking of change and borders redrawn.

"No, no," Michael whispered as he traced the lines faster, trying to restore the integrity of the carefully planned city. But his pen slipped as the ink began to rise off the page, a thick black ooze that obscured the precise Georgian streets. In the mirror of its shine, Michael saw the shapes of Borderland creatures, teeth bared as they slunk through the trees. The map began to change, the streets of Bath shifting as darkness crept into squares and gardens.

He reached for the phone, pressing a key code he'd only used once before back in darker days he had hoped never to see again.

"It's weakening," he said to the Ministry official who answered. "I'm going to perform the ritual. Send Bridget as soon as you can, but I'll get started. There's no time to wait."

Ignoring the protests on the other end of the line, Michael hung up. He grabbed his leather satchel and walked out of the door into the little pedestrianized street. Clouds scudded across the night sky above him, and a sudden freezing wind whipped his coat around his legs, blustering down between the buildings.

A howl rose up, a feral sound of wild creatures with no

place in this city. Michael quickened his pace, almost jogging to the end of the street, past the art gallery and left towards The Circus, only meters away.

A dense fog, a mist of undulating grey, obscured the circle of tall plane trees in the center of the Georgian terrace. The street-lamps flickered as Michael walked into the round, taking a breath as he tried to see within.

Thunder rolled overhead, and a flash of lightning lit up the sky, arching over the mist as it began to rain. There were shapes within the fog, slinking bodies with sharp teeth, pacing at the edges of the grey as it pushed out away from the inner circle.

Michael's heart raced. It had been a long time since he had faced Borderland creatures, since he had drawn this hard on his blood magic. He had hoped that the sacrifice of his family line was done with and that watching and renewing the lines would be enough. But now, the edges of the Earth-side map were blurring, and if they were to protect the city of Bath and this version of the world, then he had to go in there. It was one level of magic to etch lines on a map, but another to etch them into the earth itself.

He took a step towards the mist, clutching his leather satchel tight against his chest, the instruments of the Cartographer inside. He opened the flap and pulled his antique five-pointed compass from within. It was silver in a turned ivory pocket case, made in the seventeenth century, a time of explorers when the Cartographers were powerful men who carved up the earth, drawing the borders that would shape the political landscape. This compass had been present at the division of the Borderlands when his ancestors had shored up the boundary lines. Its needle had pointed to true north since that day.

Now Michael looked down as the needle spun around, wildly oscillating back and forth, unable to discern the right heading. He tucked it inside his waistcoat pocket, taking another step forward, steeling himself to enter the haze.

Tendrils of mist curled out towards him, wrapping around his feet, a subtle pressure, probing, testing. A chill ran through his bones and Michael gasped at its touch. He sensed the influence of a Shadow Cartographer here, one of those who sought to redraw the boundary and open the porous border to the feral horde beyond. He had to get to the center of the circle before it was too late.

Michael stepped into the mist, and the city of Bath receded, the curved terrace buildings disappearing as he walked further in. The circle of trees was only a few meters across, but it was as if he stepped into a forest. The heavy trunks loomed over him, leaves dripping with rain as it pelted down from above. The air was thick, and Michael's breathing became labored as he struggled to inhale the viscous atmosphere. It stank of the Borderlands beyond, a fetid soup of the diseased and dying, rotting flesh and the rubbish of those clustered in the camps without hope. So unlike the pristine civilization of Bath that he and the Ministry lived to protect.

A howl came from further in, echoed by another, calls from the wild wolves that had once roamed this land. They had been driven into the Borderlands, hunted to the edge of extinction like so many of the species in the realm beyond, waiting for their opportunity to roam free again. But they did not belong here, and he would not allow them to run loose in his city.

Michael caught a glimpse of one behind a tree, its powerful body still as it stared at him with yellow eyes. It growled, baring its teeth. The sound sent a shiver up Michael's spine, the call of the predator triggering ancient fear inside. But this was his realm, even though they were pushing at the boundary. He still held power here.

He pulled a ritual knife from his satchel, the yellowing ivory blade bound with a leather strap, tied into a series of knots around the end. Passed down from the time of the Druids, the blade had been used to sacrifice for many moons, and each drop of blood strengthened its power. The Blood Cartographers used such blades to mark the borders of Earth-side and tonight, Michael would use it once more.

He faced the wolf, drawing himself up to his full height, broadening his shoulders. He met its eyes, holding the knife out in front of him. The wolf sensed something wild within the man and backed away, slinking behind the tree. But Michael knew it would be back, along with its pack. These predators were only the forerunners of what lay beyond. They were sent as scouts, testing the boundaries of how far the Gate could be pushed open. This time, he feared it was wider than ever before.

He didn't have much time.

Michael walked to the center of the great trees, reciting the longitude and latitude of where he stood, the geographical coordinates that anchored the Gate to Earth-side. His voice grew stronger as he spoke, turning the numbers into an incantation. He planted his feet strongly upon the ground and rolled up his sleeve, baring his arm to the chill mist. The vapor curled around him, almost clawing at the scars that patterned his skin over faded tattoos. His veins ran with the pure magic of the Blood Cartographers, and now Michael knew he must call on it once again.

He put the knife against the flesh of his arm and began to carve the lines of the Gate, the circle and the crescent joined by a ley line of power as he chanted the numbers that bound this place to the physical realm. He fell to his knees, dropping the knife beside him as he dipped a finger in his wound and painted over the ground the ancient symbol of the five-pointed compass, the sigil of the Illuminated Cartographer. The storm broke overhead, the wind lashing the branches of the trees into whips that thrashed at the old man as his blood dripped upon the earth.

Michael felt his strength fading, a heaviness creeping over him as the chill mist descended. Dark powers swirled about him, and his voice faltered, hesitating as the numbers began to fade in his mind. His fingers paused over the ground, his blood dripping out. He was suddenly paralyzed, unable to speak.

A figure stepped from the trees, his features obscured by the tendrils of mist that wound around him. He wore a cloak of wolf pelt, an artifact from the Borderlands, but underneath, Michael could see he wore a suit cut from a cloth of earth. This man strode between worlds, a Shadow Cartographer, one of those who sought a new world order by remaking the maps. There was something about him, something familiar, but the mist pressed into Michael's mind, clouding his vision, making him forget.

A low growl came from behind him, and the wolf stepped from the shadows to stand by the Shadow Cartographer, its teeth bared. Behind it, the pack waited, eyes fixed on their prey.

"You're too weak this time, old man. Your kind is ending, and the Borderlanders will soon take what you have kept from them for too long."

Michael heard his words as if from afar, the sound muddled by the heavy atmosphere. In earlier times, this man would not have dared face him, but now he knew the truth. He was old and tired, his magic faded.

The wolves circled closer, sensing his weakness. Michael picked up the knife again, his movements slow as if he was underwater. The blade was heavy in his hand and strength drained from him as his blood ran onto the ground. One wolf darted in to lick at the growing pool. Michael spun with his knife, slicing at the beast but it ducked away unharmed. Another ran in to bite at his legs, its heavy body tipping him off balance. The pack formed a circle around him, teeth bared.

Two of them darted in behind, growling as they tore at his clothes, ripped through to his flesh. Michael spun again, but another two ran forward, worrying at him.

He was outnumbered.

Perhaps that had been the plan all along, after all, he was the watcher on this Gate. He thought of Bridget on her way up from the Ministry. He couldn't let her be taken as well.

He had one chance left to close the Gate, even though it would only hold a short while. But for now, it was the only way.

He looked up at the dark man watching from the shadows. He sensed triumph at the victory to come, but it would end here.

"For Galileo," Michael said, his voice strong as he spoke the words of the Illuminated Cartographer.

The wolves snarled and leapt towards their prey. Michael spun away from them, using the last of his strength to push through the pack.

He turned the blade, pressing it against his chest and hurled himself at the largest of the plane trees. Its hard trunk pushed the knife deep into his heart as Michael wrenched himself sideways, ripping himself open, falling to the ground.

Agony flashed through him as his blood pumped out, soaking the tree roots and the earth where he lay.

But the Gate was renewed by his sacrifice.

The mist curled into a vortex, and the wolves howled as they were sucked back inside the Borderlands. Michael lay panting with pain, trying to hold on long enough to watch the end.

The Shadow Cartographer stood watching him for a moment, resisting the swirl of the wind. "Your kind is ending," he whispered. "Your death only buys a little time before the change to come."

He bent to pick up Michael's five-pointed compass, then

slipped it into his pocket as he spun away, stepping back through the Gate of Shade, trailing the last of the mist behind him. The grand Georgian buildings emerged, and through the branches of the trees, Michael could see the stars above. This was his earth still, and Bath was safe.

For now.

As his blood pulsed more slowly, Michael thought of his granddaughter, Sienna. He hadn't seen her for so long, staying away in an attempt to shield her from a future he wouldn't wish on anyone. But now it seemed that she might be the only hope to close the borders for good.

CHAPTER 1

Sienna's footsteps echoed in the long corridor, acres of books in racks either side stretching into the shadows ahead of her. Dim lights came on as she walked, triggered by her movement.

It was like a bomb shelter down here. The world could be ending above ground in Oxford, but below the streets, she would be cushioned by the padding of ancient tomes. Sienna smiled, lost in thought. She could build a shelter down here in the underground stacks of the Bodleian Library. A den of ripped pages and a fire from words once considered special but now merely fuel. And she could read. Who could be lonely when there was so much to learn?

She passed into an older section of the library. The functional metal shelving changed to wooden stacks with carved lintels and wheels on the end to move them closer together. Sienna frowned. She didn't recognize this part of the library. She stopped and tugged on a cord to turn on a brighter light and bent to read the sign on the end of the nearest row. *Geopolitics of Borders and Boundaries*. She frowned and looked down at the retrieval slip in her hand. This was nowhere near where she was meant to be.

Sienna sighed. It was only her second week working in the library, and once again, she was lost. She should have turned left at Metaphysics, but she must have walked straight past the stack. By the time she retraced her steps and made it back over there, the Head Librarian would be tutting and looking at his watch, frown deepening in his furrowed brow. Books first, readers second, and lowly library clerks most definitely last. She turned and looked back the way she'd walked. The stacks stretched away, seemingly endless, darkening to shadow.

She sat down on the floor for a moment, leaning back against the shelf, sending up a cloud of dust into the air. The remains of crumbling pages, words written by those long dead, saved down here as if somehow, someone would recall them up to the rarefied air of the University once more.

She really needed to get a life.

It had been a year since leaving St Peter's College where Sienna had read Geography. Her friends had moved to jobs in London, but she hadn't been ready to leave Oxford. It had become her home over the years of study, a welcome escape from the suffocating cocoon of her mother's house. So she'd flitted around various short-term jobs and then finally landed this position, hoping it might be the right fit. But as she sat surrounded by old books, Sienna knew that this was over too.

Perhaps it was time to give in and move to London like everyone else. Perhaps she should even try again with Ben. They had been inseparable in her first two years at college, but he was a year older and got a job in the City after Finals. They'd held it together for the first year, but when she didn't move as he had expected, they began to drift apart. Right now, Sienna felt untethered, like a boat bobbing freely on the waves. She should be experiencing the exhilaration of freedom, but instead, she found herself longing for the shore. London hadn't felt like the right direction, but maybe it was time to give it another chance.

She looked at her watch and stood up again. Clutching

the retrieval slip, she retraced her steps, navigating by the signs at the end of the corridor until she found the book and hurried back to the Head Librarian's desk. He looked up as she emerged into the main vault of the Radcliffe Camera. His shaggy white eyebrows arched over his wire-rim glasses and Sienna felt his disdain rest upon her. He tapped his watch.

"Sorry," she whispered, as she placed the book on his desk. "I'm going out for my break now."

Sienna turned before he could stop her and hurried up the little stairs and out onto the steps of the Rad Cam. The air was fresh outside. Mid-June and still a little chilly, but there was a patch of sun on the other side of the square. Walking down the steps, Sienna turned on her phone, and within seconds, it started beeping with text messages and missed calls. Her mum had been calling on and off for the last hour. That was unusual. She was over-protective, but this was a lot even for her.

Sienna stood in the sun at the corner of the square by Brasenose Lane and called back.

"Hi, Mum. What's up?"

"Oh, sweetie. Something dreadful has happened. Your grandfather –" Her voice broke with a little sob.

Sienna frowned. Her mum's dad was already dead, mourned as a beloved granddad who had always shown her interesting things in the hedgerows and fields near their country house. Her father's dad was a distant memory, a man she hadn't seen or heard from since the year she started high school. He had been around after her father had disappeared, lost on a geographic survey to Antarctica, but then he'd faded into the background.

"What do you mean? What's happened?"

Her mum blew her nose. "Your grandfather's body was found this morning in Bath, just down the road from his map shop. They're saying it's some kind of ritual murder. A friend of his, Bridget, called me and told me the news. She wants to talk to you."

Shock slammed through Sienna at the words. Her grandfather murdered? It seemed impossible.

"Bridget said he left something for you, something your dad wanted you to have."

Sienna's breath caught in her throat. Ten years and the pain of losing her father still hurt, but curiosity rose at her mother's words. "Do you have her number?"

"She said you should go to Bath, to Grandad's old map shop and she would meet you there." A pause, then her mum's voice changed. "I don't think you should go, sweetie. You're working now, and you're busy. You don't want to go to that musty old map shop. It was always a complete mess when I went there with your dad back in the day. I'm sure this Bridget can send whatever it is."

Sienna half listened as she remembered being in the antique map shop as a child. The wonders of the world rendered in so many different ways. The smell of thick paper and ink, the weight and size of the maps on the wall, intricate tiny streets and imagined animals in the corners, cartouches of long-dead kings, calligraphy of names that no longer existed. Sienna remembered running her hands over the maps, feeling a vibration of energy, like they wanted her to step inside somehow. Then the concern on her dad's face, a sadness, like he wanted her to see only printed paper, not the worlds beyond the maps. After he disappeared, Mum had never taken her back there.

"I want to go," Sienna said, cutting off her mother's words.

"But what about your work?"

Sienna looked up at the dome of the Radcliffe Camera and the spires of All Souls College behind it. A gaggle of students burst from Brasenose College, chatting as they walked off to lectures.

"It's not really working out. So I'll go this afternoon. It's only a few hours on the bus to Bath."

"But I can't get down there, sweetie. You shouldn't go alone."

"I'm just going to the shop, Mum. I'm not going to visit the morgue or anything."

Her mum sighed. "Alright, but call me later. Your Grandfather was a meddler in life. I would expect him to be just as bad now he's gone."

* * *

As the bus drove through the outskirts of Bath a few hours later, Sienna gazed out the window at the fine Georgian terraces made from the distinctive honey-colored limestone that made the city famous for its architecture. Bath was smaller than Oxford, but there was a similar sense of historic weight about it. A World Heritage Site dominated by the ancient Roman Baths and a medieval Abbey, Bath had become a fashionable Georgian spa town, made famous in the books of Jane Austen.

Sienna remembered her dad talking about the background of the Farren family, how they had lived in Somerset for generations. He had only left the area because her mum had been set on London, the hub of politics surrounding their foreign aid work. But now Sienna was returning, without Dad, and with Granddad gone. The only Farren left in their line.

The bus stopped downtown, and Sienna walked up through the shops, navigating past the grand Abbey and up the hill towards The Circus. She passed a group of American tourists on the edge of Queen Square, their guide explaining loudly:

"This square marks the bottom of a key with The Circus at the top of the hill as the round end. Seen from above, it forms a Masonic shape built into the architecture of the city along with symbols of Druidic times."

His voice faded into the hubbub of the traffic as Sienna continued walking uphill towards the circle of trees visible on the rise at the end of the terrace.

As she reached the top, she paused to catch her breath, looking at the Georgian townhouses that curved around in a perfect circle. Three tiers of windows, each flanked by classical columns, rose up towards the blue sky. Stone acorn finials topped the buildings, and between each tier, a carved frieze of nautical elements, serpents and masonic symbols wove its way around. In the center of the circle, five huge plane trees stood tall on green grass, their leaves rustling in the breeze. It would have been a peaceful scene, a glimpse into a regal past, but today, bright yellow Crime Scene tape wound around the trees. Police officers stood on the perimeter, faces impassive, even as tourists took photos of the curious spectacle.

Sienna's heart thumped as she crossed the road and stood on the edge of the tape, as close as she dared go. Scene of Crime Officers still worked on the grass, but she could see between them to the trunk of the largest tree. Even from this distance, she could see it was stained with blood.

What had happened here last night? Her grandfather ran an antique map shop, so why would anyone want to hurt him? Perhaps his friend Bridget would be able to help.

Sienna turned and walked down Brock Street turning off before the Royal Crescent into Elizabeth Buildings. It was a short pedestrianized street, an eclectic mix of little shops and cafés punctuated by colorful flowers and wooden benches. She passed a curiosity shop with a maritime trunk in the window, alongside a carved wooden cross from one of the derelict churches in the nearby countryside. There was a shop selling crystals and fossils, next to a painting and craft store with glass jewelry in the window; an art gallery; a secondhand bookshop and there, in the middle, her grandfather's map shop.

While the other stores bustled with tourists, the map shop remained locked, its window in shadow. Sienna walked up and looked in at the window display. An old county map of Somerset stood in central position, its hills marked with green contoured shading. Next to it, her grandfather's book on the history of cartography, propped open by a tiny engraved globe in a wooden box. It was dark inside, but she could just make out his desk at the back, surrounded by racks of maps in plastic wrapping and the huge globe that had fascinated her as a child.

"You must be Sienna."

The voice made her jump and Sienna turned to see a woman with close-cropped dark hair standing behind. Her eyes were a piercing blue, and although the lines around them suggested the woman was over forty, she possessed an almost elfin look of mischief that made her appear younger. She wore a long dress of patchwork linen in shades of green, like the fields of the West Country in summer, interspersed with the bright yellow of rapeseed.

"I'm Bridget Ronan, a friend of your grandfather's. I recognize you from his photos. Michael had that same bright titian hair, although it looks better on you." Bridget's voice had a soft Irish lilt, and Sienna found herself immediately warming to the woman.

"Thanks for meeting me."

Bridget's welcoming smile faded. "I'm sorry for your loss, and for mine. Michael was a good friend and already sorely missed." She pulled a key from her bag. "Now, come inside." Bridget unlocked the door and pushed the door open.

Sienna walked, and as she breathed in the scent of the maps, she felt like she had come home. They called to her from the display racks, and she wanted to run her fingers over the lines, tracing the borders of the world. She walked to her grandfather's desk and turned the seventeenth-century globe a little, looking for the Barbary Coast, the area of North Africa that seemed so foreign to her when she was little. She found it and touched the picture of the apes sprawled over modern Algeria, a smile playing about her lips as she remembered the stories her grandfather told of times past.

She looked up at Bridget, who stood by the door watching her. "What happened to him?"

Bridget took a deep breath. "There's a lot we still don't know." She pulled an envelope from her bag. "But Michael gave me this to keep in case anything ever happened to him. He was nearly eighty, so he expected his time to come, although not as suddenly as this." Her eyes filled with tears as she handed Sienna the envelope. "I need to go deal with a couple of things in town, so I'll leave this with you, give you some time alone here, and I'll come back in an hour or so. Okay?"

Sienna nodded, and Bridget turned away, leaving the scent of flowers in her wake. Sienna looked down at the envelope, her name written on the front in her grandfather's spidery hand.

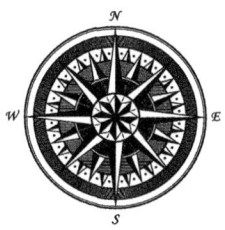

CHAPTER 2

THE DOORBELL TINKLED AS Bridget walked out and for a moment, Sienna just breathed in the air of the map shop. She sensed her grandfather's eye for detail in the angled lines of the wall displays, antique maps worth thousands of pounds hanging next to modern portrayals of emotional landscapes. After all, a map of the human heart is worth far more than the map of a city, she remembered him saying.

She looked down at his desk. An antique parchment map of Bath sat where he must have left it. It looked like something had spilled on the lines of The Circus, as if a red haze settled upon it. Why had he gone down there in the middle of the night?

Sienna sighed. She should have come to see him over the last years. After all, it wasn't so far to Bath, and even though her mother had kept them apart, there was no need to remain distant after going up to Oxford. He must have been lonely here, his only son dead, his only granddaughter estranged. A pang of guilt flushed through her. She should have been here for him, and now he was gone.

She opened the envelope to find one piece of cream paper inside, dated a year previously.

* * *

MAP OF SHADOWS

Dear Sienna,

As I write this, you are just finishing your degree at Oxford. I'm so proud of you, and I know your father would have been too. Geography was always his passion, as it has been mine, and I hope it can continue to be yours.

I'm sorry that we weren't able to be friends, but time and circumstance have stood between us. If you're reading this, I'm gone, and although I had hoped to spare you this, our family has always answered the call, and now it's your turn. Bridget will be able to explain more.

For now, the map shop is yours. I've arranged all the legal details, and it is in your name, along with the bank accounts and the flat above.

There will be those who try to part you from the shop, but the maps here are yours too. I hope you will remember how you felt their reality in your childhood. It's time to let that feeling emerge again, Sienna, because there is more at stake than you know.

For Galileo, and with much love,
Granddad Michael

* * *

Sienna frowned, her mind whirling with so many questions. She sat down heavily, looking up at the maps around her with new eyes. This was all hers.

She couldn't help the smile that spread across her face, even though loss resonated deep within her. It felt like coming home at last.

If she was honest, the memories of being here had driven her into studying Geography, the obsession with maps something her mother hadn't been able to remove despite emotional blackmail over the years. *Your father was lost over his obsession with maps. I won't have you go the same way.*

Her phone rang.

"Hi, Mum."

"Are you there, sweetie? Is it awful?"

"I'm here. It's fine. I met Granddad's friend, Bridget, and she gave me a letter."

A moment of silence and Sienna could sense her mother's dread. "What did it say?"

She took a deep breath. "He left me the map shop. The flat, the bank accounts. Even though I hadn't seen him for years. It's so strange."

"Well, that's wonderful news because you can sell it and use the money to pay off your loans and get a new start in London." Sienna tuned out as her mother rattled on about how much she could get for a place in central Bath and how lucky she was, and it was good because her father didn't leave anything and on and on.

Sienna looked around at the maps and felt them calling to her again. She stood and went to one of the racks, leafing through them as she made agreeable noises. On some of the maps, her fingers trembled against a kind of magnetic field from the paper even through the plastic sleeves that covered them. It was strange, and yet, it also felt natural. Some of the maps didn't have this effect. Maybe there was something in the paper? Perhaps Bridget would be able to help, as her grandfather had suggested.

"So, do you want me to contact the estate agents?" Her mother's voice broke through. "There's one just around the corner from you. I could get it sorted tomorrow."

"No, I need to wait a little, Mum. Let me sort this out myself."

"Well, don't wait too long. That street must look beautiful with the summer flowers out. It's a very good time to sell."

The doorbell tinkled again. Sienna turned to see a tall man enter, his frame erect, his back straight in an almost military fashion. He was distinguished, salt and pepper hair swept back from an angular face, with a patrician nose and thin lips. A vertical scar ran down from his right eye to his short beard, the skin pale and puckered around the old wound. He wore a tailored three-piece suit in English tweed and looked as if he'd just stepped out of one of the paintings from the Holburne Museum.

"I've got to go, Mum. I'll call you later." Sienna hung up and turned to the man. "Morning, can I help you?"

The man looked at her, eyes narrowing for a moment, then he smiled in recognition. "I was looking for Michael." His accent was impeccable Queen's English. "But you must be his granddaughter. I've seen pictures of you. Sienna, is it?" He reached out a hand. "I'm Sir Douglas Mercator."

Sienna stepped forward and shook his hand, meeting his grey eyes, the color of a wolf pelt. His grip was firm, his hand cool and although he was charming, there was something about him that made her take a step back. She felt rather than heard a rustle in the maps around her. "My grandfather isn't here. He … He died yesterday."

Saying the words aloud made Sienna flinch as if it made real something that had only been an idea before.

Sir Douglas' gaze didn't drop; his expression didn't falter. "Oh, I'm so sorry for your loss. You must have a lot to sort out here." He stepped forward and ran his hand over one of the maps displayed on the countertop. It was covered in glass, but Sienna thought she could smell burning, as if his touch singed the edges.

He turned back, pulled a business card from his jacket pocket and handed it to her. "I'm a dealer in antique maps, like your grandfather was." The card was embossed in gold, the word Mercator entwined with a projection of the globe.

"Oh, of course." Sienna shook her head in apology.

"Sorry, I didn't recognize your name at first. Are you related to the Flemish cartographer?"

Sir Douglas nodded. "Yes, I'm a direct descendant. Our family have been in the map trade since his day." He looked around the shop, his eyes alight with interest. "I knew your father as well. He was my contemporary when we studied Geography at Oxford. I believe it is your alma mater, too?"

Sienna nodded, a little in awe of the man. After all, he was cartographic royalty.

"With Michael gone, and your father too, perhaps the shop is yours now?" His voice changed, and Sienna sensed a covetousness behind his charm. "I've been trying to buy this shop from Michael for years. He was too old to run it well of late, and I have clients who would be interested in some of the maps. I can offer you a very good deal, Sienna. You'd have more money than you need and I'd handle everything for you. This is my world, after all." He smiled, but it didn't reach his eyes. "I'm sure you have a lot to think about, so keep my card and call me if you'd like to sell. Or even to offload some of this stock." He waved a hand around at the maps.

"Thank you. I'll definitely think about it."

Sir Douglas gave her a long look, then nodded and swept out of the shop. Sienna sensed the space exhale as if it had been holding itself in check while he was present. She went over to the map he had touched, and sure enough, around the edges, faint charring had appeared, dark patches of soot as if it had been burned. She shook her head. What was going on here?

Sienna went to the door and locked it, turning the sign to Closed. She didn't need any more unexpected visitors, and she wanted to look at the flat upstairs. Behind the desk at the back of the shop, a narrow wooden staircase wound up to the first floor. The stairs creaked as she walked up, the language of an old building, and she thought about her grandfather walking up here, footsteps heavy after a day's work.

At the top, a faded red wooden door etched with a curious five-pointed compass blocked the way. Sienna tried several of the keys until one fitted the lock and she walked in.

She had expected a musty old place, somewhere you'd expect an eighty-year-old to live, but her breath caught as she emerged into a wide open-plan living space. The walls had been opened up into archways, with picture windows looking out over the street on one side and a little courtyard at the back. A stylish kitchen and tasteful furniture made it into a modern flat, the type of place she'd only seen in magazines. Nothing like the chaos of her mother's house, packed to the gunnels with chests and boxes and bags. This was a haven and Sienna exhaled, relaxing into it.

One long wall of shelves was piled high with books, and she stepped closer to see what they were. *The Atlas of Improbable Places*, books of photos from abandoned cities, and a shelf of journals. They were all black, leather-bound hardbacks in the same A5 size, each with an elastic band to hold loose papers inside. They were dated on the spine, one per year going back to the 1950s.

Sienna's heart pounded as she considered them. They were her grandfather's private words, but he was gone, and after all, he'd left them here out in the open. She pulled one from the shelf and leafed through the pages. His handwriting was almost illegible, but it wasn't the words that caught her eye, it was the hand-drawn maps and sketches inside. The pencil lines were exact and confident, line drawings of temples next to a rough street map. She recognized the name of the place, but it didn't make sense. Babylon, a ruined city lost in time, but here, her grandfather had drawn it as if it were still alive, as if he had explored its streets.

The journals only added more questions to the many she already had. Sienna sat back and looked around her at the light and airy flat. It already felt like home. The job wasn't working out in Oxford anyway, so perhaps she should move here. Let Sir Douglas sell the shop and keep this part, or rent it, or something. There were suddenly so many options. She needed a coffee.

There was a little café over the street, so Sienna headed back downstairs, out the door and over to the Green Door. It bustled with customers, and the familiar smell of ground coffee filled the air. A young woman with pink curly hair and glitter in her eyebrows smiled in greeting as she arranged sweet pastries on the countertop.

"What can I get you, my lovely?" Her broad West Country accent made Sienna smile. Bath was in Somerset, after all, home of cider, rolling hills and Cheddar cheese.

"Just a black Americano, thanks."

As the young woman made the coffee, Sienna looked around at the place. Students worked on laptops as two men engaged in a heated business discussion in one corner, while a well-preserved older lady read the paper opposite them. Sienna wondered if her grandfather had sat here sometimes, and a pang of regret shot through her at opportunities lost.

She took her coffee out to the street and walked down Elizabeth Buildings towards Brock Street, wanting to catch the last rays of the sun. At the end, she turned towards the Royal Crescent where a group of tourists stood on the edge of the green lawn of Royal Victoria Park. Families sat enjoying the sun, playing games and laughing.

Sienna looked both ways and glimpsed a young, mixed-race woman walking a golden cocker spaniel on the opposite side of the road. The little dog looked up and started wagging its tail as it saw her just as a double-decker tourist bus turned the corner. It sped towards them, going too fast for the little streets. The spaniel ran out suddenly into the road, barking in excitement, its eyes fixed upon Sienna.

"Zippy! Come back!" the young woman shouted as the bus barreled down on them.

CHAPTER 3

Sienna dropped her coffee and stepped into the road.

She swept the little dog up into her arms as the bus horn blared and she darted back to the pavement. The spaniel licked her face, and she laughed, heart pounding at the near miss, wondering what the hell had made her step in front of a bus for a random dog.

The young woman crossed over the road. She was early twenties, similar to Sienna's age, but her features were a dark opposite. Her black curls were cropped close, her eyes almond-shaped with high arched eyebrows. She wore a plain black t-shirt and jeans, and she had tattoos down one arm. A globe intertwined with geographical symbols and a five-pointed compass, just like the one on her grandfather's door.

"I'm so sorry," the woman said. "He suddenly pulled out of my grip when he saw you." Sienna cuddled the little dog close as he nuzzled her neck. The woman frowned. "It's odd though, he doesn't do that with many people. Do we know you?"

Sienna shook her head. "I've just arrived." She pointed back down the street. "The map shop was my grandfather's."

The young woman's eyes widened in recognition. "You're Michael's granddaughter?"

"You knew him?"

She nodded. "Of course, yes. Oh, my goodness. I'm so sorry about his death." Sienna thought she could see more than just regret in the woman's eyes. Did she know something more? "Did you see Bridget already?"

"Yes, she gave me a key for the shop. Does everyone know everyone here?"

The young woman laughed. "It's a small city, and the map community is tight knit, for sure." She put out a hand. "I'm Mila Wendell."

Sienna put Zippy down and shook Mila's hand. "Sienna Farren."

"I helped your granddad out in the shop sometimes and often manned his stall at the map fairs in London if he was too tired to travel."

Her words cut through Sienna. She should have been the one helping. "I met Sir Douglas Mercator as well. You must know him?"

Mila's expression darkened. "Yes, of course. He's … Well, he doesn't usually come around this part of town much. He and your grandfather didn't get on. Actually, that's an understatement. What did he want?"

Sienna turned back towards Elizabeth Buildings. "To buy the shop."

Mila shook her head. "The old bastard's been trying to take it over for years. But before you make a decision, you should know a bit more about what Michael stood for. Did you find his compass?"

Sienna shook her head. "No, Bridget just gave me a letter."

"I know where it's kept. I can show you if you like. I know he'd want you to have it."

Together, they walked back to the map shop. Mila tied Zippy to a bench outside, and he lay down facing the shop, clearly used to the place. When they walked in, Sienna felt the maps warm to them both, and she sensed that Mila was welcome here. She didn't know how she knew it, and there were more questions piling up, but for now, Sienna was just glad to have someone around who knew her grandfather and seemed to love the shop.

Mila walked over to a chest of drawers with a glass display cabinet on top. "Michael kept some of the most precious maps here, away from sticky wandering fingers." She looked up. "Do you know anything about maps, about how much this is all worth?"

Sienna shook her head. "I studied Geography but it wasn't so much about maps, and I don't know anything about the antique or collectable side." She paused, looking around at what was left of her father's side of the family. "But I want to learn."

Mila met her eyes and then she nodded. "There's more to learn than you think." She knelt down and pulled a round wooden box out of the drawer, frowning as she felt its weight. She pulled the lid off to reveal an empty velvet case. Mila's face fell. "They must have taken it from him."

"Who? The people who killed Granddad?" Sienna knelt down next to her. "Do you know who it was?"

Mila took a deep breath. "It's complicated. I don't know what to tell you about his death, but a Cartographer's compass is his most treasured possession."

Sienna stood up. "This is all so crazy. This morning I woke up in Oxford and everything was fine, and now I'm here, and Granddad is gone. Murdered. I have this shop, but I also have an offer for it. Should I just take the money and run?"

Mila smiled softly. "If your life is elsewhere, then of course. I know Michael would understand. He would have wanted you to have a full life without the weight of family expectation. Bridget can help you sell the place if it's what you want."

Mila's words struck a chord because she didn't have a life

elsewhere. Not really. Sienna knew she'd been aimless and wandering for too long, unable to choose a path forward. Her father had made his choices and paid the ultimate price. Her grandfather too had met his end because of something to do with the maps. Her curiosity burned to know more, but there was a touch of fear there too. If she walked away now, she could go to London, patch things up with Ben, start anew with money in her pocket, student loans paid off, maybe even have enough to buy a place. And yet …

She touched the maps in the case before her, sensing a texture in the air around them, like running her hand through a field of wheat. There was something anchoring her here, and she wanted to know what the hell was going on, why Granddad died, and how there could possibly be sketches of long-dead cities in his journals upstairs.

Mila walked over to the globe and spun it around a little way. "Michael kept your ancestral history from you, but perhaps it's time for you to make your own map, Sienna."

The doorbell rang again. Bridget walked in and smiled to see Mila. "I'm glad you two found each other already."

"Zippy saw to that." Mila laughed, then she turned serious, indicating the empty case. "Michael's compass is gone."

Bridget frowned. "Then things are going to get worse. Sienna, I know you're confused. Michael tried to keep you away from all this, but now you have to know. Come with me to the Ministry of Maps. Come and see what your grandfather worked on. And your father too."

"My father? You knew him?"

Bridget nodded and her eyes softened in remembrance. "John and I trained together. We were … friends before he was lost. There are many things for you to know if you want to."

Sienna's phone buzzed. She pulled it out and looked at the name on the screen. It was her mother again. She wouldn't want her daughter getting involved. But something tugged at Sienna. She had to know.

She rejected the call. "I'll come with you. But I haven't made up my mind about keeping the shop yet."

Bridget nodded. "Of course."

Sienna grabbed her bag, and they left the shop. Zippy jumped around, nuzzling against Sienna's leg as Mila untied him. "He likes you. He adored Michael, too, but right now, I need to take him back to the boat. I'll meet you at the Ministry later." She headed off up the hill.

"So what is this Ministry?" Sienna asked.

"Suspend your rational side for a moment," Bridget said as they walked. "It can be hard to fathom, but we have to start somewhere." She took a deep breath. "Bath has two different sides. The city is a World Heritage Site with two thousand-year-old Roman Baths, the medieval Abbey, Georgian architecture and boutique shopping. That's what most people see. But it also has an unseen dimension you won't find on any terrestrial maps. It's a portal to the Borderlands, a place where this earth bleeds into another. There are other portals in ancient places where borders blur: Athens, Rome, Damascus, Varanasi, Jerusalem. Places where people have been written in and out of history. The Ministry protects the borders, and it keeps the Borderlands from slipping back over here."

They emerged into The Circus side by side, the police still working in the center. Bridget sighed. "Your grandfather worked for the Ministry, and this is where the border opened last night. He stopped whatever might have come through. He gave his life to protect the city, not that most people can ever know about it."

Sienna heard her words and saw the bloody tree, but how could this be real? Her mind reeled with questions. They walked around the edge and headed down the hill past the shops and the Bertinet bakery, past the Guildhall, until they reached the Abbey Church of Saint Peter and Saint Paul, known locally as Bath Abbey. Its Gothic presence dominated the central city, a hub for tourists and photographers for its carved facade of climbing angels and ornate wooden door. The Bath stone glowed with a golden light as the late sun touched the tower. Bridget paused as they reached the thick walls and they stood for a moment under the flying buttresses and magnificent stained glass windows.

"The Abbey was built on a pagan site, founded as a convent, then turned into a monastery in the seventh century. It's been rebuilt several times, grander with every incarnation. The Ministry is based in the levels beneath and in some of the surrounding buildings. We also have a training facility up at the University on the hill."

"Why here?" Sienna asked.

"Bath is an ancient energy center," Bridget explained. "With the confluence of ley lines that run across Britain, the river and the underground hot springs, it has drawn people through the ages. The Freemasons in the Georgian period concentrated the energy into The Circus and so the Ministry is here to protect the area."

"Is it part of the church?"

Bridget shook her head. "Not in a religious fashion, but our facility is wound into the structure of the Abbey. You'll see when we go below."

She lead Sienna round the back of the Abbey, past the inscription marking where the first king of all England, Edgar, was crowned in 973 AD. A statue of the risen Christ emerging from the grave, shroud bandages still around him, stood marking an entranceway with thick stone steps down to a tiny door.

"It doesn't look like much," Bridget said. "But wait until you get inside."

Sienna followed her down. At first, it seemed the stone steps must lead into some equally ancient crypt, but Bridget turned when they reached the bottom and faced the stone wall.

"You can walk on into the museum below the church, but the Ministry is this way."

She touched a groove in the wall, and the stone cracked open. The outline of a door emerged, and Bridget pushed against it. On the other side, there was a library, the walls lined with books of maps and easy chairs placed next to low tables for reading. Sienna didn't recognize many of the names on the spines and part of her longed to stay here and escape into the tomes. But Bridget marched straight through, entering a code on a door on the other side and leading her on.

They emerged into a long hallway with doors leading off it, each labeled with a different title. Antiquities, Restoration, Misinformation, Illustration. They passed one door stained a deep red with the words *Blood Gallery* etched into the wood.

Sienna took a step towards it, but Bridget held her arm. "That's not for you just yet. There will be time to learn it all if you choose, but first, you must meet the Illuminated Cartographer. This way."

The corridor walls were full of photographs, exuberant faces of explorers around the world. As they walked by, Sienna scanned them for a glimpse of her family. She stopped in front of one where her grandfather stood in front of the temple he had sketched in his journal. "Is it really Babylon?" she asked.

Bridget turned and came back to look. "Yes, I know it's hard to understand. But there are places that have been lost Earth-side, but remain in the Borderlands. Some of us cross those borders through special maps. We are Mapwalkers, Sienna. Mila and me. Your grandfather. Your father."

Sienna turned at her words. "Is there a picture of him?"

Bridget nodded and walked along a little, searching amongst the faces. "Here."

Sienna looked up at the picture. Her dad stood with four

others, two men and two women. His face was broad with a smile, his titian hair shining in the sun, his beard longer than she'd ever seen it. He wore khaki shorts and held a bulging backpack. Behind the group, what looked like a South American city stretched into green jungle. Sienna touched his face with a fingertip.

"I don't even have a grave to visit."

Bridget looked surprised. "Of course not. Your father isn't dead."

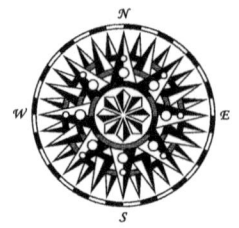

CHAPTER 4

MILA WALKED ALONG THE canal path, Zippy running along next to her, excited to be out in the warmth of the afternoon. He sniffed in the hedgerows and snuffled in the reeds as a pair of iridescent dragonflies flitted about his head. Mila thought about Sienna. The young woman didn't know anything about her Mapwalker heritage and it made Mila wonder what her own life would have been like if she'd never known.

A robin trilled in the hedgerows by her side, then the peep-peep of new ducklings came from the canal as the little balls of fluff paddled fast beside her hoping for a crumb. With every step, she was grateful. Grateful that she wasn't in London, in the tower block she grew up in, where she could barely walk a meter or so along the corridor. She used to run up and down the flights of stairs just to expend some of her energy, and to stay away from the other kids in her foster family. Although the word family barely applied, at least it was a roof over her head. She didn't know much about her birth parents, only hints that her father had been a student from war-torn Sierra Leone. In London, mixed-race was normal, but here in Bath, her darker skin and almond-shaped eyes stood out and sometimes, she liked being different.

Back then, Mila would escape to the canals of London, walking for hours alongside the slow-moving water. She longed to get in, to let the cool slide over her body. She wanted to open her mouth and let it flood into her lungs, to slit open her wrists and let her blood mingle with the canal, become one with it.

Sometimes she would go down to the Thames, past the great buildings of the old city, where the river swept towards the sea. It was wild and untamed and although she was drawn to it, Mila knew that if she were to dive into the water, she would lose herself. There were creatures in the ocean, beasts that would hurt her, whereas in the canal, there were only tiny fish, lithe water voles and diving ducks. A tamer form of escape.

After she left school, she traveled along the canal system, getting odd jobs now and then, helping out and learning the ropes from the other travelers, finding a new form of family among the canal boat people. She had saved up for her own boat and one day, found herself here in Bath, where she met Bridget who recognized her Mapwalker ability.

And now, every day she would walk here, along the Kennet and Avon Canal, away from Bath towards Bradford-on-Avon, a nature walk within hailing distance of the city. Seasons changed but the rhythm of the canal pulsed through her life. She knew this earth, this water and something was definitely wrong. Michael's murder had disturbed the equilibrium of the city, and Mila felt the tendrils of dark mist reach even here. She sighed and Zippy ran back to her, his dark eyes looking up with devotion.

"Good boy." She reached down to rub the soft fur around his ears. "Stay close now."

They walked on under a bridge built from thick blocks of stone, her footsteps echoing as she walked through. The coo of a wood pigeon boomed out as the sun dappled through the leaves of the horse chestnut trees at the waterside. A cloud of midges hung over the reeds next to a patch of purple clover and white flowers of wild garlic. The smell was a heady scent of summer as she walked along the bank next to sycamore trees and hedgerows of dog roses where blackberries would grow later in the autumn. Mila scanned the area, letting her senses spread out over the waterway, trying to pinpoint the source of her disturbance.

Water rippled as fish rose to feed on the midges. In the field above the canal, two great shire horses with shaggy feet stood grazing. A bell tinkled behind her and Mila moved to one side as a cyclist zoomed past. Zippy barked in greeting and ran alongside it a little way until returning to walk at her side. Mila smiled down at him. He gave her a reason to be on land, not mapwalking through the waterways all the time.

A friend on a boat further down the canal looked after him when she was away. A woodturner who roved the canal paths after storms, looking for branches to carve into animal shapes and bowls. Zippy was apparently a great helper in retrieving wood but Mila was always happiest when he was back with her. She loved being with Zippy, his quiet devotion, his lack of judgement for who she was or what she did. She missed him when she went into the Borderlands, but if he crossed over, he wouldn't make it back. He would be lost over there, as sometimes she felt she might be.

When Mila mapwalked the waterways, she became one with the canal and lost a part of herself. Sometimes she thought she would never emerge, that she could stay in there forever. Perhaps the water nymphs of old were born this way? Myths of women who lived in water and came out to tempt the sailors. She had read about them in a library book once. Perhaps her father had really been Neptune, great god of the sea. Mila smiled to herself to think she could actually be an ocean princess, rather than a poor foster child from a London tower block.

It was this search for identity that always drove her back

to the Ministry, even though she didn't really fit in there. The other trainees were from special families, those who understood their Mapwalking lineage. She was seen as some kind of throwback, a line that had branched off early. Mila wondered if perhaps back in Sierra Leone, she might find people like her. But she'd never been. She'd never left England, never gone to seek her father's heritage or find others like her, Africans who traveled by water. Perhaps that's what drew her to Sienna, who seemed to know even less about her own ability.

They walked on past a ginger cat lying in a patch of sun on a boat piled high with the detritus of living, a rusty wheelbarrow, logs of wood for the winter. It looked up sleepily as they passed, nonplussed by Zippy's exuberance. Mila nodded her head, acknowledging him as part of this world. In the Borderlands last time, she'd seen a cat there, but it had been misshapen, its eyes rheumy, weeping, diseased.

Mila walked on, past the graveyard next to the road, full of stone markers, Celtic crosses, and headstones marking the passing of time. The Bathampton Church was solid, squatting on the land like it would always be there. But Mila had seen others like it in the Borderlands, those where congregations had died and left the building derelict until the border had claimed it, rewriting it out of this history and into the alternate.

The rules were to always go into the Borderlands as a team. That was the official word, but Mila went over alone sometimes when she felt the need to be on the edge. The Mapwalkers went into the Borderlands to retrieve artifacts lost or deliberately written out but now needed back on Earth-side. The things they brought back were kept in the Ministry vaults. But when Mila sometimes traveled alone into those places, she brought back tiny things, shells or stones, coins sometimes, and she kept them on her boat, evidence of another place where perhaps she felt more at home.

Bridget had said she shouldn't keep things, shouldn't mark herself as a Mapwalker, that there were people who could track her because of those objects, that she left a part of herself behind if she went over too much. Maybe she was turning feral, turning Borderlander.

Mila passed a pair of swans with five cygnets nibbling at the grass at the side of the canal. The smell of elderflower lingered in the air, as the chirps of birds came from the hedgerows. She had walked in wild places in the Borderlands similar to this, but the foliage was different. It was as if the land there had crossed from the edges of the map in different cultures, growing strange plants, turning animals into different versions of themselves.

A thrush flew from the hedgerow, a snail in its beak, darting under the weeping willow on the opposite bank. The cluck-cluck of chickens came from one of the smallholdings just off the path. Mila passed a canal boat with a kneeling river goddess on top, her arms outstretched to welcome the day, a laughing Buddha by her side. A tangle of spiderwebs on the guide ropes glistened in the sun.

It seemed idyllic but something was definitely wrong.

Mila bent and put her hand down into the canal water, closing her eyes as she sensed the movement of the ripples and the deeper current as it swept towards the city and on to the river. Over time she had become attuned to the difference of the Borderlands, how her skin felt as she moved from bright sunlight to shade. And she sensed it now.

The border was being tested.

She stood up. "Zippy, come."

The spaniel darted to her side, bouncing up and down as they turned and walked quickly back towards town, back to where the canal ran alongside the manicured gardens of the Holburne Museum.

They kept walking until the canal emerged alongside allotments, little gardens where city dwellers grew vegetables and flowers. Their personalities were evident in the plots, some with colored buckets and different types of flowers, rows of runner beans on poles next to hollyhocks and poppies. One area had a blue gate with five bars, just a gate on two poles with no fence. It was unusual, but always made Mila smile as she passed. The pride people had in these little gardens in the heart of the city made her even more fiercely determined to protect it.

She walked on towards the lock, where the canal changed level. Water could be let in and out with heavy gates and the boat would move up or down as the canal rose and fell with the gradient of the land. The locks had scared her at first and she had avoided moving her own boat for fear of getting trapped in one, but now they were part of her life here. Mila heard a noise further on, a bubbling and boiling sound that filled her heart with dread.

The border was being breached.

A wild squawking of ducks came from up ahead and she raced towards the noise, Zippy by her side. They rounded a corner just past the end of the lock gate.

At the edge of the canal, the water bubbled ferociously. There was a smell in the air, the scent of a bombed-out city, spent ammunition and decay overpowering the earthy scent of nature. How could they breach here now? The thought flashed through Mila's mind as a man burst up out of the water. She could see by the half-moon tattoo on his face that he was one of the warlord's men, a Feral Borderlander. The man began to swim to shore.

CHAPTER 5

BRIDGET'S WORDS ROCKED THROUGH Sienna. Her heart pounded, her mind whirling. "What do you mean, he's not dead? My mum said he was lost on a mission to Antarctica."

Bridget sighed. "Your mother never knew what John really did. He kept his Mapwalking secret. He wanted to protect you both."

Sienna shook her head. "I can't believe it." That her father might still be alive was one thing, but that he purposefully let her believe him dead seemed unthinkable. She had so many questions but at least there was some hope she might see him again.

Bridget put a hand out and touched Sienna's arm. "It's true. I don't know what else to say. John was lost a month ago on the edge of the Uncharted, along with the rest of the Mapwalker team. It's a place of wild magic, beyond the Borderlands where the Shadow Cartographers rule." Bridget shook her head. "They should never have gone so far out, but there were rumors about a Map of Shadows being created there." She turned away. "They never came back. Time warps the further out you go in the Uncharted, so he could have been lost only yesterday in his time."

"So there's nothing I can do in order to find him?"

Bridget smiled. "We'll see." She turned away down the

hall. "You will know your path when the way forks before you."

Her words resounded in Sienna, an echo of something her father had said long ago. Words he had written on her heart. He had clearly wanted her to stay away from this place, but now she needed to know more. If he was still alive, she might somehow see him again. She hurried after Bridget.

They walked down a long corridor hung with tapestries. The maps were recognizable as European, but the contours were wrong, the lines off in some places. Bridget saw her looking. "These are maps of what was and perhaps what will be again."

"What do you mean?"

"People trust that the maps they see in books and pictures are true. They rarely question whether they match the real world. But what is more real? The map in your geography textbook or the world you walk upon with your own feet."

"But you can't know the shape of a land by walking it. You're too close to the ground," Sienna noted.

Bridget smiled. "Exactly, and the borders of these lands have been remade by those who draw the maps. The Cartographers. We make the borders and we have to keep redrawing the maps. There is no status quo. The Borderlanders are always shifting as new places are pushed through."

She pointed to the tapestries. "Maps are not an exact representation of the world, merely a worldview of the creator. For example, there are some maps that don't have Israel on them, others that have no Palestine. All you have to do is erase a name or change a line if you wish to wipe a nation off the map, or create a new one. Look at how the Sykes-Picot line changed the Middle East. Sykes drew his finger across a map, drawing a line that continues to shape modern day. Yet those lines didn't represent people's tribal allegiances, just an ideology."

Suddenly, a whooshing sound echoed down the corridor, like the explosive belch of air as a fire bursts from a furnace.

"Oh no, not again." Bridget ran towards the sound, Sienna following close behind. They reached a thick metal door, riveted with huge bolts and a reinforced glass window in the side. They peered inside.

A young man stood in the blackened room with his back turned, his clothes charred. His shoulders were slumped, and Sienna sensed his disappointment. He wore a blue t-shirt and jeans, but they were patchy with burned holes. He was tall and slender, his arms lightly muscled and now covered in ash. Before him on the table was a map that looked completely unharmed by the flames, if indeed there had been any, because there were none there now.

"Perry is struggling to harness his fire magic," Bridget explained as she knocked on the window.

The young man turned, his ice-blue eyes widening as he saw them. His face looked as if it had been carved from porcelain, so perfect were his features, his lips full with a patrician nose. His short blonde hair was singed and sooty. He made the okay signal with his finger and thumb and gave Sienna a wink as Bridget turned away.

"Luckily, the room is made for fire practice."

"What exactly is he doing?" Sienna asked as they continued to walk.

"There are different types of magic. The fire element enables the Mapwalker to destroy maps in order to remake them, so it's a blend of destruction and creation. Fire can rejuvenate, some seed pods open only in the heat of a flame, some species live only because others die. Those like Perry can walk in smoke and flame and travel in the seams of energy in the earth." Bridget sighed. "There's a strong fire faction in the Shadow Cartographers, so we're lucky to have Peregrine. Of course, as long as he can master it before the next mission."

"Mission?"

"We're training a new Mapwalker team. The Map of Shadows is a way to remake the borders, to write us out of history. The mission is to retrieve it from the Borderlands."

"So this team are going after my father?"

Bridget frowned. "Following his footsteps, for sure, but this time, we don't intend to lose anyone in the process."

They arrived at another door carved from a light ash inscribed with a globe. Bridget turned to Sienna. "What you see in here is as true as the maps in your grandfather's shop. Remember that."

Her words puzzled Sienna, and she frowned as Bridget pushed open the door and they stepped into the room.

For so deep under the ground, the room was incredibly bright, filled with mirrors reflecting light into even the farthest corners. It was a library of sorts, but instead of books, the shelves were full of rolled maps, some tiny and frayed, others the size of a rolled carpet. They spilt onto the floor in piles, like a hoarder's den. It smelled of cedar wood, tea and a hint of spices, of rose water and Turkish delight, like a Middle Eastern souk with an endless array of delight for the senses. There was a path through the maze of maps, and a rustling sound came from deeper inside the room.

"Is that you, Bridget?"

A man emerged from the pile as if he had been sleeping amongst the maps. His craggy face was etched with lines as deep as the caves under the Mendip hills, and as he moved, the maps moved with him. He was connected to them, they wound into him and through him, his blood inking the pages.

"They call me the Illuminated Cartographer," he said, and his voice crackled like the maps around him. "I am bound to this room, the beating heart of the maps. But once I walked as free as Bridget here." His dark eyes crinkled as he smiled. "I knew your father, Sienna, and I hope I will get to know you. After all, your place has always been here." He frowned. "Now there is something I have to give you." He spun around, the maps winding themselves around him. The colors changed as if the symbols morphed with his mood. "But I don't know quite where it is."

He walked away from them, pausing at a huge shelf with rows of rolled maps. A ladder leaned against it. "I'm getting too old for this." He looked back at Sienna. "Why don't you go up and get it, my dear?"

Sienna looked up at the miles of shelves. She thought she could spend forever in here, delving into interesting corners, but there was clearly something the Illuminated Cartographer wanted her to see.

She walked through the rustle of maps to the ladder and climbed up. Symbols marked each shelf she passed, the runes of the Mapwalkers. Some she recognized and others were foreign, evoking images of words whispered in forgotten places.

"A bit higher and to your right."

Sienna reached a shelf near the ceiling marked with a row of stars.

"Yours is there, child." There was a hint of regret in his voice as if he didn't want her to see whatever it was. And yet, she was here.

She leaned out to her right, looking down to the ground below. She had a fleeting thought that she could jump and land cushioned on the maps below, like a huge bouncy castle. Or she might just crack her head open on the floor. She turned back to the shelf.

The rolled maps had names written on them in tiny writing. Peregrine Mercator. Was he the guy in the fire room and was he related to Sir Douglas, the man who wanted her father's shop? Xander Temple. Mila Wendell. And then her name. Sienna Farren. What the hell?

"The children of the Mapwalkers," the Illuminated

Cartographer called up to her. "We map your star charts at birth and store them here. These charts go back generations, Sienna. You are here, as well as your father, your grandfather and those who came before."

"Why?"

"If you are lost, it is your last way home, back to the place where your stars aligned."

Sienna pulled her map from the shelf, wrapping one arm around the ladder to hold herself in place as she unrolled it. A star chart was tattooed on the smooth vellum, dots of stars anchoring her to a specific time and place. In the corner was a five-pointed compass rose, the decoration matching her father's compass that she remembered playing with as a child. Sienna looked down the rows of rolled vellum stretching into the distance. Who were all these other Mapwalkers and how far back did this lineage go?

Suddenly an alarm rang out, the lights around her flashing red, casting the room in a bloody glow.

* * *

Mila knew that where there was one Feral, more would follow. When these wild Borderlanders crossed over, they usually sent a scout first. If the scout didn't come back, well, there were plenty more where he came from. This one was young, only a teenager, younger than she was.

She stood back in the shadow of the lock gate, waiting, watching. As far as she knew, the warlord's men had never come through this far away from The Circus and that in itself was worrying. If they were finding new places, new rips in the border, then they could come through anywhere. Perhaps even further out in the countryside where no one was watching. Ministry protocol dictated that she should call this in right now and wait for backup, but the canal was her home, and she would not allow the Borderlanders through here.

The man swam towards the bank.

Mila knelt down and put her hand in the canal water at the side of the lock, feeling the cool flow touch her skin. It rippled through her body as her connection with the water expanded.

The man had almost reached the side. She had to stop him.

As his fingers touched the bank, Mila slipped into the water without so much as a ripple in her wake. She became one with the liquid, sliding sinuously through the darkness of the canal, her senses attuned to the invader. Slipping past him, Mila grabbed his leg, tugging him away from the lip of the canal before he could get out. His muffled cry came from above as she pulled him underwater, slipped on past, turned with an undulation and then came back for him.

In these moments, Mila felt like any hunter. The thrill of the chase, the knowledge of strength. The pity she might have felt for the Feral subsided under a need to protect what was hers. And this canal was hers, no doubt about it.

The man flailed in the water, trying to paddle to the shore again, his breath ragged. Mila slid past again and pulled him down under the water. He wrestled with her, his fingers sliding over her skin smooth as silk, part of the water.

She propelled herself down, dragging him towards a patch of weed that grew at the edge of the canal, taking him down. He kicked and flailed harder now, desperate for air. Silt rose around them in a cloud as Mila thrust him to the bottom. She took a handful of weed and wound it around his neck, anchoring him to the canal floor. His mouth pursed, desperate not to breathe and then he couldn't help himself. As she tightened the weed around his neck, he opened his mouth. The water poured in. He kicked and fought, eyes bulging.

Mila wondered if there was someone waiting for him

back in the Borderlands. What would they do when he didn't return? She hovered in the water above him, watched his eyes go blank, his body go limp.

He wasn't her first, and he wouldn't be her last. Mila would do this again and again to stop them coming through. She thought of the allotments above, the flowers and the hedgerows of the canal as she tightened the weed around the man's neck to keep his body down. The Ministry team would come and sort out the remains later. Ferals from the Borderland had no identity on this side, so it wasn't murder. It was defense.

This was war.

Mila slipped away and pulled herself out of the canal. She shook the water off like an animal as Zippy ran to her side, jumping up and barking in excitement. "It's okay, boy. We're alright."

She sat down on the bank to catch her breath, Zippy nuzzling into her lap. Mila watched the water go by as a heron fished in the quiet shade of a willow tree.

CHAPTER 6

The noise of the alarm echoed around the Illuminated Cartographer's library.

"Come down quickly," Bridget called up. "I need to get to the War Room."

Sienna hurried back down the ladder, clutching the star map to her chest. At the bottom, the Illuminated Cartographer held out a hand. "You can't take it with you now. It belongs here until such time as you go into the Borderlands."

"But I –"

"We need to go now." Bridget stood by the door, one hand holding it open as she beckoned.

Sienna hurried after her but turned at the door, looking back at the old man tethered to the map room, his life blood sustaining the core of the Ministry. He smiled at her, and in his eyes, she saw a promise of something she didn't quite grasp yet. Had those same eyes smiled at her father as he left?

"Let's go," Bridget said. "The alarm means there's been another breach. Stay close now."

Bridget hurried through the corridors, twisting left and right until Sienna was unsure how far they'd come or if they'd just doubled back on themselves multiple times.

They reached an open door leading into a wide room with a huge table in the middle. Above it spun a three-dimensional computer model of Bath, The Circus in the middle. It pulsed with a dim light as if some power hummed beneath. Mist hovered at its center while moving dots ranged out from the darkness. Another light flashed scarlet by the canal.

A group of people stood around the table, all talking at once, pointing at charts on the walls around them. The hum of voices coalesced into one, but Sienna heard snatches of the conversation.

"Multiple breaches …"

"Feral wolves …"

"Fatality on the canal …"

Bridget called for silence, and Sienna stood back a little, watching as the Irish woman took control of the situation. She turned to a man holding a tablet. It looked to be running some kind of mapping software. "Status update, please, Jerod."

The man adjusted his glasses. "There are multiple breaches this time. Mist descended on The Circus about twenty minutes ago, and the howling of feral wolves has been heard. Police investigators were already on the scene because of the murder." His eyes flicked to Sienna and then back to his screen. "Mila reported a Feral on the canal, but she closed the breach before anything else could come through."

"Where's Xander?"

"He's gone up to The Circus to deal with the wolves."

The door banged open. Perry stood in the doorway, his clothes burned full of holes, the scent of smoke on him. "Where do you need me, Bridget?"

She held up a hand to stop him, nodding to Jerod to continue.

"There are reports from Oxford as well as London. Multiple breach points."

"They're testing the defenses," Bridget said softly. "The canal is new. They haven't used water magic before. And so soon after Michael …" Her voice trailed off. "We can't wait any longer. We can't be on the defensive anymore." Bridget looked over at Perry and then to Sienna. "The new Mapwalker team must go into the Borderlands. We must have the Map of Shadows."

Sienna didn't understand why Bridget was looking at her in that way. She was overwhelmed by the things she had seen today; the existence of the Borderland and magic; her father's decision to leave her, and the possibility that he could still be alive. Her head reeled with it all.

And she was no Mapwalker – was she?

"Perry, take Sienna to the training room." Bridget's eyes narrowed. "We'll see what she can do."

Sienna took a step back. "No, I don't want this. My father and grandfather didn't even want me involved. I'm leaving."

She stared at Bridget with an unflinching gaze until the woman nodded.

"Go then, back to the map shop. But be aware, Sienna, there is no way you can escape this. The border is weakening, and if Bath falls, the rest of the country will follow. The maps will be rewritten and you may not have a choice in the days to come. Perry, escort Sienna back up to the Abbey level."

Perry turned, gesturing towards the door. "Let's go."

They walked back down the corridor as the sounds from the War Room faded behind them. Sienna felt an overwhelming sense of disappointment in herself and yet she wondered why. After all, she didn't ask for this. Perry walked by her side in companionable silence, but as they passed the room where he had been burning everything but the maps, he spoke.

"I know how you feel, Sienna, but Mapwalkers don't choose this life. We are born into it." He sighed. "Sometimes our parents are not the people we want them to be. Sometimes *we* are not the people we want to be. But if you're a Mapwalker, and Bridget believes you are, then I hope you might come with us into the Borderlands." He stopped and turned to her. Sienna looked up at his earnest face. "There are two sides, and we defend the border between them. Right now, we need all the help we can get."

He led her back through the winding corridors up to the Abbey level and held the door open for her to leave. "I hope to see you again."

Sienna emerged into the sun in the heart of Bath. A tourist group of Koreans wandered into the square, their guide talking into a tiny microphone as the huddle looked up at the Abbey. Sienna turned with them, trying to see it again with new eyes. The church loomed over the city, its ancient walls hiding something she had never known was beneath. She supposed that she wouldn't even be able to get back down there again unless she decided to join them. The best thing to do was forget this ever happened.

She walked back up towards the map shop, but the police now barred the way toward The Circus. Through the cordon, up the road, she could see mist hanging in the air around the Georgian buildings, obscuring the trees. She wondered who Xander was and what he could possibly be doing with the beasts. A smile ticked at the corner of her mouth. How could she even be thinking about these things?

Sienna took a detour around the edge of Royal Victoria Park and up past the Marlborough pub, then walked back towards the map shop. Mila sat on the doorstep, a puddle of water around her as she dried herself in the sun, her face turned up to the bright rays. Zippy wasn't with her this time.

She opened her eyes at Sienna's approach, arching one perfect eyebrow. "I heard you turned Bridget down."

Sienna smiled. "Word travels fast. But I don't have any Mapwalking skills, so I don't know what I could do to help even if I wanted to."

She pulled the key to the shop from her pocket. Mila stood up. "I drowned a Feral this afternoon." Her voice sounded strangely disconnected. "He looked like a man, but he didn't exist on this side of the border, so perhaps he wasn't real at all."

Sienna didn't know what to say. Perhaps this was all some kind of weird joke to scare her off so she would sell the map shop. She thought of Sir Douglas Mercator. All she had to do was call him, and she could move to London and forget all this.

Mila put her hand on Sienna's arm. "This is real and you must be curious. What if you *can* mapwalk? What if you could see your father again? Come with me back to the canal boat, and I'll help you try."

Sienna looked around the shop. The maps whispered to her, speaking of dormant power and far-off places. She had spent too much of her life not knowing what she wanted, aimless and wandering. Maybe it was time to make her own map.

She turned back to Mila. "Okay, I'll come for coffee, and we'll give it a go. But if nothing happens, I'm selling the shop."

They walked up through the back streets and out onto the towpath at Bathwick, emerging by the side of the canal. It felt like a different world to the teeming city they had left behind. Their footsteps crunched along the gravel, and the sound of birdsong rang from hedgerows wound through with dog roses and elderflower. Violet irises grew in the reeds along the edge of the water and ducks swam along, skimming for bugs. The afternoon sun shone through the canopy of trees, dappling the path as they passed narrowboats moored on the bank.

"I never liked the city much," Mila said as they walked. "I grew up in London and escaped onto the canals when I could. Turns out I can mapwalk through waterways, which explains why I've always been so drawn to them."

They turned a corner to where a boat was moored. It was the green of spring leaves painted with a five-pointed compass alongside a map of the sinuous canal waterway dotted with trees and intricate birds. Zippy lay on the bank in a patch of sun, guarding the entrance. He saw them coming and ran to meet them, barking happily as he bounced up and down. Sienna couldn't help but smile at his enthusiasm and bent to rub his fur.

"You are a lovely boy. Yes, you are."

Mila laughed. "See why I have him? No matter how the day goes, no matter what craziness the world throws at me, I arrive home to this bundle of joy. Come in. I'll put the kettle on."

The boat rocked a little as Sienna stepped aboard. It was long and narrow inside, like a gypsy caravan. There was a tiny kitchen area right by the door, a little stove, and a bench top with a few mismatched mugs in different patterns. A small table next to a window looked out on one side to the path and on the other side to the canal itself. Two foldable chairs sat stacked against the side. Further back, there was a bookshelf, then a little sleeping cabin with a curtain across. It was a tiny self-contained world and Sienna could see that it had everything a person might need. Mila seemed to have her life pretty sorted.

Zippy ran down the middle of the boat and back again, twisting around their legs, wagging his tail, his little face alive with happiness. Mila laughed and opened out the chairs. Zippy immediately jumped up onto one of them. "Welcome to our humble abode."

"Do you move the boat a lot?" Sienna asked.

Mila shook her head. "Sometimes if I need to escape, but I like it here. We have quite a community on the canal. I have friends, people who love Zippy. We are the misfits up here. Sometimes Bath likes to forget we exist because most people on the canal don't have normal jobs. There are craftsmen, artists, some barely eking out a living doing odd jobs here and there. But I like being free. I can just untether myself from the bank and go if I want to. Not very fast, of course. It takes forever to get through the locks, especially if you're on your own, but I love it."

Mila put the kettle on and pointed to the chair. "Have a seat. I'll make us some tea and then show you how my Mapwalking works."

As Mila brewed and poured the tea, Sienna felt a nervous energy, her anticipation building. After taking a sip, Mila knelt down and pulled away a rug from the floor, revealing a tiny trapdoor underneath, lined with a waterproof seal.

"This is not normal on a narrowboat," she said with a laugh. "But I find it easier to travel this way because otherwise people would be questioning why I was jumping in and out the water all the time. This way I can slip in and out and no one knows about it."

Mila tugged open the trapdoor to reveal the canal water beneath. The smell of weeds and rushes rose from the hatch. "So, I mapwalk through waterways," she said. "It's hard to explain how to do it, but I sensed you felt a pull towards the maps in the shop. For me, the pull is towards water. I haven't seen myself traveling, of course, but it feels like I'm some kind of water creature because I don't have to come up to breathe. Like being in a ripple, moving in the spaces between the waves as they cross the water. It's not so much swimming, more like a direction with my mind. I've become better at it over time." She grinned. "First time I tried it I ended up in a weir getting rolled over and over by the flow, wondering if I could get out. But sometimes you just have to just try things."

Mila put her hand down into the water, and her skin rippled as if her flesh had become liquid.

Sienna gasped. "That's incredible."

"Call it magic." Mila shrugged. "Call it a different kind of human. Call it what you want, but I was born with this. Your family are known as powerful Mapwalkers, so perhaps you have something too." She pulled her arm out of the water and closed the hatch. "I'm not going to take you into the water today. We don't want you gasping and panting as you try and breathe underwater."

Sienna frowned. "Does that mean you can take other people when you mapwalk?"

Mila nodded. "Yes, as long as you're connected somehow. Holding hands or tied together or something. How many people you can take with you is entirely dependent on the level of your control and your power. I've only taken one other person before, but I heard your grandfather once rescued a whole group of people from a prisoner-of-war camp, transporting them out through a map. There are rumors of Mapwalkers like me helping boats through storms." Mila's eyes shone with excitement. "I like the idea of being some kind of superhero." Then she frowned. "But most of our work is about protecting the border and artifact retrieval these days."

"So how would I mapwalk?" Sienna asked.

"It's like giving in to a sensation," Mila said. "Your body knows what it wants to do. You were born for it, so you just have to let it do what it knows deep inside." She walked to the bookshelf and pulled out a map of Bath. She opened it on the table in front of Sienna. "This is a good start." She pointed to a place on the canal path. "We're here. There's The Circus. That's where the shop is. Why don't you start by using this map to get us back to the shop?"

"How?" Sienna's heart pounded. She felt like she was about to cross a line. Her father and grandfather had wanted her to stay away from this, but something inside made her desperate to try.

"Just put your hand on the map."

Sienna placed her fingertips onto the paper. An electric

sensation of vibration traveled through her skin. She pulled her hand away quickly.

"It's okay." Mila smiled with encouragement. "Just relax."

"What does it look like to someone watching?" Sienna asked.

"I've seen your grandfather travel, and he just disappeared," Mila said. "Whereas I shimmer as I go into the water. That's what Perry told me anyway. I think you met him."

Sienna smiled. "Yeah, fire boy."

Mila grinned. "You need to meet Xander as well. He's way too good-looking, but he can do some pretty interesting things with illustration. He has earth magic. He can form creatures and animals on the vellum of maps. If he draws it, it can become real."

Sienna frowned. "What type of magic does my family have?"

Mila went to the window and paused a moment before speaking. "Your grandfather and your father both had blood magic."

"That doesn't sound good."

"Well, it's a mixed blessing. It's the most powerful magic, used to create the original maps. You can draw a new map, or reinforce the borders, whereas the rest of us can only travel through existing ones. Blood Cartographers can remake reality."

Sienna laughed nervously. "Doesn't quite sound like me."

"Well, if nothing happens, then you don't have to worry about it. Just try thinking of the map shop. Visualize the lines of the city. Think of the whispers of the maps. Let them speak to you."

Sienna placed her hand back on the map. "Do I need to close my eyes?"

Mila smiled. "Whatever feels most natural. Just relax."

Sienna closed her eyes and concentrated on the sensation

of the map, the feel of the paper beneath her fingertips. She could almost sense each individual molecule in it. Then it was as if she rose above her body, a sensation of weightlessness, of almost flying. Suddenly she could see into the map like a 3D image of the city below.

The sense of vertigo overwhelmed her. She opened her eyes, gasping for breath.

Mila put a hand on her shoulder. "You're still here, but you were definitely flickering just then."

"It was like flying." Sienna's breath caught in her throat. She wanted to go back there. She wanted to try again. If this was what her father had felt, she knew why he had left his family to pursue this life. It was intoxicating. "I want to try again."

Mila nodded. "I'm coming with you." She put her hand over Sienna's.

Sienna closed her eyes again, letting the feeling flood through her, unresisting this time. She rose above the map, above the canal and concentrated on the map shop, zooming down in her mind, wishing herself there.

CHAPTER 7

"Open your eyes." Mila's voice was delighted.

Sienna opened them to find a tiny garden surrounded by a brick wall.

Mila laughed. "Where the hell are we?"

Sienna spun around. Then she looked up. "I think that's the back of the map shop. This is the garden I saw from the flat earlier."

Mila pulled out her smart phone. "These don't work in the Borderlands, but here they can be useful." She looked at the GPS. "We're just behind the map shop, so you almost got it right."

They laughed together. "Back to the canal boat then?"

Sienna grinned. "Sure, this is fun!" And it was. It made her heart sing, an exhilaration she had never experienced before.

She took Mila's hand, ready to mapwalk again, then realized there was no map to concentrate on. "The map's back in the boat? How do I travel through it?"

"That's why Blood Cartographers are so special. Most of us travel with our star maps to orientate us home and our own compasses. But if you can see the map in your head, you can travel it. For now, just think back to the picture of the map you have in your head and take us back to the canal boat."

Sienna closed her eyes and concentrated. She smelled the lavender of the gardens as they soared above the city and then they were back on the canal boat, falling about laughing as they drank their tea together.

"That was amazing. I want to try again," Sienna said. "Could I find my father like this?"

Mila frowned. "That's pretty advanced stuff. Your grandfather could find missing people, but it takes a lot of training. I don't think you should do it without supervision, without Bridget. She's also a Blood Cartographer. Let's just practice around Bath if you want to do it again. How about trying to get back to the Abbey?"

Sienna felt a rising buzz in anticipation. It was a rush and she wanted to feel like she was flying again.

She looked down at the map in front of her with the streets of Bath laid out in deliberate ways. She thought of all the maps back in the shop, a way to travel wherever she wanted. How could her father have kept this from her? How could he have wanted her to remain ignorant of this ability?

"I want to do it again." Sienna put her hand on the map, and Mila put her hand on top. Sienna closed her eyes. She thought about the stone interior of the Abbey, the huge blocks that made up the walls of the ancient place of worship. In her mind, she conjured up the sense of space above and beneath her feet, the gravestones of those who died a thousand years ago. Her father would have walked these streets too and traveled above them.

She pictured where the Abbey was, the roads surrounding the river and the canal. She could see the square outside and the ancient Roman Baths, the main shopping area and the little tea rooms where tourists sat eating Bath buns. Maybe her father had sat there too, thinking of her over the years.

But as she mapwalked, it felt different this time. An overwhelming sense of cold stone and death. There was a sense of flying, but this time it was as if she had crossed a shadowy threshold.

"Where are we?" Mila's voice broke through her concentration.

Sienna opened her eyes. The sense of coldness she had felt just a minute ago was real, and she shivered as the chill permeated through her thin top. It looked like a castle dungeon. Great blocks of stone made up the walls and stagnant water trickled down, stinking of sewers and rotting flesh, metallic blood and the stench of suffering.

A scream rang out, echoing through the rooms beyond.

Mila pulled Sienna against the wall, and they huddled, cowering, backs pressed against the stone. "This isn't the Abbey," Mila whispered. "I don't know where we are."

Footsteps padded past in the corridor outside. They stayed huddled against the wall waiting until the steps passed. The agonized scream came again, a sound of agony and torture. Sienna imagined what might be happening down here and her skin goose-bumped in fear.

It fell silent, and that was somehow worse.

Mila stepped away from the wall, her eyes wide as she looked around. "Oh, no." Her hand flew to her mouth.

Sienna gradually realized what hung around them on the walls. The place was hung with maps, but not of paper or vellum. The maps were of flayed human skin with map lines tattooed on them, etched into the flesh. The acrid smell of dried blood permeated the room. Sienna fell to her knees, gagging and coughing.

Mila knelt by her. "You have to be quiet," she whispered. "They might hear us. I don't know exactly where we are, but we're definitely in the Borderlands."

"What are these ... things?" Sienna whispered as she gazed in horror at the gallery around them.

"Blood maps." Mila's eyes narrowed. "This is the dark side of your gift. Those with blood magic can create new places by etching maps with blood, and the most powerful method is to carve into human flesh. Each of the Blood Cartographers mark their skin over time, tattooing the places they care about most in order to protect them. Your grandfather, Michael, had The Circus and central Bath on his body. He protected the city with his blood." Mila frowned. "But the maps can be etched onto skin without permission. This is the work of the Shadow Cartographers."

Another scream rang out in the dungeon and Sienna had visions of someone strapped down as a knife carved lines of a map into warm flesh.

She understood now why her father wanted to keep her away from this world. Then a realization came to her. "Surely we can only be here if my father is here too? I was thinking about him as I began to mapwalk and this is where we ended up. What if he's here?" Sienna rose to her feet and went to the door. "I need to go and see."

Mila grabbed her arm, holding her back. "You can't go out there. The other side of being a Blood Cartographer is that *your* skin and *your* blood are the most powerful. If they mark you and skin you, they will have your power to remake maps." Mila pointed at the wall. "Do you want your flesh to hang here? Is this what your father would have wanted?"

Sienna sighed and stepped away from the door. Part of her was desperate to go and see whether it was her father screaming down the hall. But it was impossible. She shouldn't even hope that he was alive.

But she had to know for sure. She would go back to Bridget and join the Mapwalker team..

"We have to get back." Mila walked further into the room. "But before we go, we need to see what they have here."

Sienna looked more closely at one of the skin maps on the wall, her nostrils flaring at the fetid stench. The skin was from a woman, part of her breasts clearly visible, her legs hanging down like some disembodied jumpsuit. The skin had been tattooed with dark lines in black, marking out territory.

Mila leaned closer and then pointed her finger at a whorl-like shape. "This is the symbol for a mine, but it's a new minefield, for minerals or maybe coal or other kind of power generation. It's not a map to change the borders Earth-side. It's creating a new part of the Borderlands." She frowned. "They need power, so they need to mine, and if they can't go back over into Earth-side to get it, then they have to create it here."

Sienna took out her smart phone from her pocket to take some pictures but the screen was black, inert.

Mila looked over. "Technology doesn't work over here. Something about the way they created the border in the first place renders it unusable. Like a safety switch added to tip the balance in favor of Earth-side, I guess."

They walked around the room looking at the other maps tattooed on different shaped bodies. Some were still red and raw with droplets of blood dried in the lines of hills and cities. Some were older, more tanned, like an animal hide. And that is exactly what we are, Sienna thought. Just animals, in the end, our flesh rotted away, our skin merely leather. She shook her head at such a macabre thought.

Mila walked into the shadowed corner of the dungeon. "A five-pointed compass." Mila's voice was weak, her dark skin suddenly paler in the weak dungeon light. "It's only used by Mapwalkers. Each of us has a different compass rose, but all with five points. This one belonged to a woman who left with your father."

Sienna thought back to the picture on the wall, the team who were with him when he disappeared. "We have to check the rest of the bodies." Her voice was calm, cold as the air in the dungeon, but her skin prickled in anticipation for what they might find.

Was he hanging here?

They walked around slowly checking each of the hanging skins, but her father's wasn't there. Sienna exhaled sharply, relief flooding through her.

Then she noticed a small wooden door at the end of the dungeon. Sienna walked towards it and pushed it open. It creaked a little and she froze at the noise echoing through the dungeon.

But nobody came.

She walked inside, Mila close behind. A few oil lamps lit the room, casting red light around the walls. They were papered with maps of Earth-side, similar to those Sienna had seen in the library of the Illuminated Cartographer.

There was a huge map of Bath on one wall, with the Abbey in the center. Areas of the city had been stuck through with nails, hammered into the map next to razor slashes cut through streets. Burned houses had matches dug through them, smeared with soot. A small knife had been stuck into the heart of the Ministry, marking the site with blood.

"A fetish map," Mila whispered. "Blood Cartographers can change the shape of the world, but Bath is so well protected that they can't just destroy it and recreate it. But they *can* use a fetish map to bring pain and destruction to the city."

They looked around at the other maps on the wall. London, Jerusalem, Rome, and in the corner, Aleppo. The ancient city in Syria was littered with fetish marks, whole areas scratched out with razor blades and burnt matches thrust into ancient sites.

"Most of Old Aleppo is already in the Borderlands," Mila said softly. "Cities that are abandoned by so many, left in ruins, often are. Those who loved it enough to stay are either dead or forgotten and are pushed over into the Borderlands. This is why so many here are traumatized by war and disaster." Mila indicated the maps around them. "These maps are all cities with Ministry headquarters. Ancient places where the border has always been permeable, where it's easier to cross over." She turned back to the fetish map. "Whoever controls this map is planning on releasing hell into the city."

She reached out to pull it from the wall.

As she touched it, shouts rang out. The sound of feet running in their direction. Then another scream from down the hall.

Mila looked at Sienna. "We have to get out of here. There's no watercourse, so I can't do it myself. You have to do it."

They held hands and Sienna closed her eyes, desperately concentrating, trying to bring the image of the canal boat back to her mind. But the sound of screaming echoed through the dungeon, filling her mind with pain. She couldn't seem to lift herself into that three-dimensional world, out of her body, above wherever they were.

Mila pushed the door shut quietly, her eyes wide with fear. "It has to be now, Sienna. We don't have much time."

From outside the room, they heard footsteps enter into the hall of blood maps.

"They're almost here," Mila whispered. "Think of the map shop, think of your grandfather."

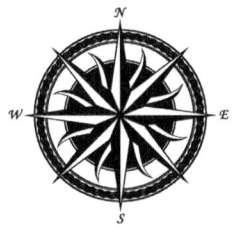

CHAPTER 8

Heart pounding, Sienna thought of the map shop, the pedestrian street that ran in front of it, the maps whispering inside, their texture on her skin. There was a whisper of breath on her cheek, and the sounds changed as the dungeon faded. Cool stone disappeared, and she opened her eyes to find them both back in the shop.

"That was close." Mila uncurled her hand from Sienna's. "We have to go down to the Ministry and tell Bridget what we saw. And what you can do."

Sienna suddenly felt dizzy and sat down on the chair by her grandfather's desk, her head in her hands. "What *can* I do?"

"You don't need to have a physical map or know it by heart to mapwalk. I've heard rumors of that kind of magic, but it's incredibly rare."

Sienna looked up at her. "But I don't know how to do it again. It was a fluke, and you realize that we almost got ourselves killed, right."

Mila grinned. "But we're still here. You got us back."

"But not whoever was in that dungeon." The memory of the screams rang around Sienna's mind. "We have to get back there."

Mila raised an eyebrow. "Does that mean you're joining us?"

Sienna met her gaze and nodded. "If there's a chance that my father is alive, I've got to try and find him."

They left the shop and walked down towards The Circus again. The mist still shrouded the trees in the center of the round, but it faded even as they watched. Police stood guard, turning people away, but Mila walked towards them. As she approached, they lifted the tape.

"Afternoon, Miss Wendell," one said with a respectful nod.

"Afternoon, Constable." Mila ducked under the tape and Sienna followed, curious as to what they might find within the mist.

"The Ministry has close links with the local police," Mila explained. "Sometimes they pick up Ferals who make it across, or there are incidents with Borderland creatures. Most of them think we operate some kind of weird zoo."

They approached the perimeter of the mist and stepped through. Bath faded around them, and Sienna felt a sudden sense of expansive space, far bigger than was possible in the tiny circle. It had the same darker vibration that she had felt in the dungeon, the touch of the Borderlands. But it was faint, further away now.

A roar came from deep within the mist.

"What the –?" Sienna's words were cut off as a huge lion padded towards them, its golden mane thick, keen eyes fixed upon them. Its huge powerful shoulders rippled with muscle and the fur around its mouth was stained with blood. It bared its teeth.

Sienna froze.

"Just stay still," Mila whispered.

The lion came closer and sniffed at Sienna's clothes. Then it purred like a big cat and rubbed its head against her, almost knocking her over.

"He likes you." A young man stepped out from behind a tree. His hair was a dark mop of loose curls, and his languid demeanor suggested that he'd just woken up from some debauched party. A few days of stubble highlighted his jawline and full mouth, and his eyes were a bright hazel-green. Mist swirled around him as he walked towards them, his gait confident and in control.

Mila introduced them. "Xander Temple, meet Sienna Farren. Hopefully our newest Mapwalker recruit."

Xander walked closer, his eyes appraising. Then he grinned and reached out his hand to shake hers. "Good to meet you, Sienna. We could use someone new to keep Mila out of trouble."

Mila nudged him in the ribs and they both laughed. Xander bent to kneel on the ground and wrapped his arms around the lion's neck, leaning his head against the soft fur. "This big softie is Asada. We've just been finishing off the last of the Ferals, and the border is now closed again."

He was so close to the powerful blood-stained jaws but there was no fear in Xander's eyes. Sienna noticed flecks of gold there, echoing the creature's golden gaze.

"You walk around Bath with a lion?" she asked.

Xander stood and pulled out a tattered map of the city on a scrap of leather from his pocket. The edges of the map were inked with creatures, a tentacled sea monster and a shark in one corner, a dragon in the opposite, a coiled serpent and then a space in the top right where it looked like something was missing.

"I'm an Illustrator," Xander explained. "On every map, there are decorative cartouches, and the corners of maps often feature monsters, demons and animals. Illustrators have earth magic. We draw creatures, and they live." He petted the lion once more and then placed the map on the ground. Asada stepped onto it, and for a moment, it looked as if his heavy body would tear through. Then he disappeared, and the inked image of a lion appeared in the previously empty corner. Sienna blinked in surprise, but the lion really had gone.

Xander picked up the map and folded it neatly before putting it back in his pocket. "We all have our different gifts." He smiled. "But I have the coolest."

Mila snorted. "You wish."

The mist dissipated around them and the outline of the Georgian buildings appeared through the haze. A ray of sunlight burst through, turning the leaves a brilliant green as a gust of wind made them rustle. The Circus was back to its usual self again.

Sienna's anticipation grew as the three of them walked down the hill back towards the Abbey. In a single day, the direction of her life had changed beyond recognition. By stepping back into the Ministry, by actively choosing to return with Mila and Xander, she was taking it even further – and she was ready for it.

As horrific as that dungeon had been, something had called to her there, something dark within her echoed to the heartbeat of the Borderlands. She craved that feeling again, but she needed backup next time. At least until she learned how to use her Mapwalking skills and could go alone.

They arrived back at the Ministry door, and this time, Sienna felt more at home. With Mila and Xander by her side, she could face Bridget.

They walked down the long corridor towards the War Room. Bridget stood looking at charts while Perry was deep in conversation with one of the other men. Bridget looked up as they entered, a smile dawning on her face.

"I'm glad you came back, Sienna."

Mila explained what they had seen in the dungeon within the Borderlands. Bridget's eyes widened at the five-pointed compass on one of the skins.

"Are you sure that's what it looked like?"

Mila nodded.

"Then it was Jenny, part of your father's team, Sienna. She was an Illustrator."

Xander turned away, cursing under his breath.

"The fetish map you saw is a version of our world twisted into something darker. It is not real yet – but it could be. Was there anything else that might help you get back there?"

Mila shook her head.

Bridget thought for a moment. "There might be something. Mila, help Perry and Xander prepare for the mission. Sienna, follow me."

They walked together back up the corridor to the wooden door marked Blood Gallery. Bridget stopped outside.

"Blood maps are part of Mapwalker heritage. Each Blood Cartographer tattoos themselves over a lifetime of magic. The tattooing is part ritual, part protecting that which we love." She rolled up the sleeve of her shirt to reveal a tattoo of Dublin, the lines of the port and the River Liffey, marks for the castle and the cathedral. Her eyes softened as she looked at Sienna. "Your grandfather tattooed these for me."

Bridget unlocked the door. "When a Blood Cartographer dies, their skin is kept as a powerful map. It might seem macabre, but the layers of blood and tattoos over generations have kept the border sealed and safe."

She pushed open the door. A cool blast of air rushed out and Sienna's skin goose-bumped in response. Bridget stepped inside. "Follow me."

Like the dungeon, this gallery was hung with skins, but they were displayed with respect here, rather than roughly nailed to the walls. Each was framed with the name of the dead inscribed beneath it, and a portrait or a photo of the Cartographer alongside their five-pointed compass rose. It smelled of tanned leather, of a museum, not of death. But the skins were the same macabre items they had seen in the dungeon.

"This is one of the oldest Blood Galleries," Bridget explained, "although there is one in every major Ministry location around the world. Each Blood Cartographer understands that this is where we will end up. Part of our responsibility is tattooing while we're alive in order to seal the borders with our blood."

Sienna shivered as she looked around at the skins. "So what were the skins we saw in the Borderlands?"

Bridget frowned. "They would have been forcibly tattooed. Jenny was only an Illustrator, her magic wasn't strong, but the Shadow Cartographers could have used her skin to inscribe with blood and pervert what we have done as a sacred rite for generations."

"Who are they?" Sienna whispered.

"Think of the border as the line between light and dark," Bridget explained. "Those who operate beyond it are known as Shadow Cartographers. They have the same magic as us, but it's stronger over there. It gets even more powerful the further out they go, beyond the Borderlands into the Uncharted." She turned and indicated the skins. "But we have the numbers. There are still more of us than them ... for now, at least."

"So why can't you just take control? Why are there so many incursions over the border?"

Bridget sighed. "Political events have tipped the balance in recent years. There are more people than ever pushed forcibly over the border, and they remember what it was like over here. Those people want to get home. But the border has been porous one way for generations, and only Mapwalkers have been able to cross both ways. Now we've heard that this Map of Shadows will remake the border in their favor."

"What will that mean?" Sienna asked. "I'm still not clear on how the border works."

Bridget smiled. "It's not like a hard border, patrolled by men with guns and dogs, where you need to present a passport to cross. Think of it more like a river, which acts as an ever-moving flow. When you cross it, you might enter at one point and emerge at another. And it can alter the banks on either side over time."

Bridget walked further into the room, stopping at one of the older skins set behind glass in a temperature-controlled environment. "This is a good example." She pointed at the lines, a group of islands off the eastern coast of Canada. "This is Newfoundland, and this is the Isle of Demons, which first appeared on maps in the sixteenth century, tattooed by one of the new world blood mages back then. But it disappeared in the mid-seventeenth century, and it's now part of the Borderlands. No one cared enough to keep it this side, so the darkness encroached and took it over."

Bridget turned, her eyes serious. "This could happen to Bath. This could happen to anywhere Earth-side."

"Why do the Shadow Cartographers want this land so much?" Sienna asked.

"Think about an olive tree planted in the soil that exists in the same place for a thousand years. The descendants of the original owner still think it belongs to them, but in later generations, as time passes and the man moves away, new owners come and resettle the land. The descendants of the new owners think it belongs to them too. There are many in the Borderlands who believe that Earth-side is still their home. But time moves differently over there and what they left behind often doesn't exist anymore."

"But who's to say which side is right?" Sienna asked.

Bridget smiled. "This is why you're meant to be with us. You see things differently because you haven't been brought up as a Mapwalker. Our mission is always to protect the border, to retain Earth-side as it has always been."

The door opened and Mila walked in, followed by Xander and Perry. Bridget turned to the four of them. "We don't have time to train you any further. Bath has the most ancient gate and the most well-fortified. If the border breaks here, England may fall. Make no mistake about it. We are at war. Some of you have seen what happens to slaves at the edges of the Borderlands. That could be our fate if you do not find the Map of Shadows."

Xander slouched against the doorframe. "No offense to Sienna, but why is she involved in this? She doesn't even know what ability she has."

He looked over at her and shrugged an apology. Sienna smiled back. "Oh, I understand. I didn't even know about this place until today, and now you're telling me I'm going into the Borderlands to find something I don't know anything about. It seems pretty crazy to me too."

Bridget raised a hand to silence them. "Mila mapwalked with Sienna today to a castle at the heart of the Borderlands. I've heard of it but never found it even though I looked, and I've ranged the Borderlands for twenty-five years. There is something that links Sienna to that dungeon, and the Blood Gallery suggests they might be creating the new map there, so you will need her. Your mission is to find the Map of Shadows and bring it back to the Ministry so the fire mages can burn it. Then we can re-strengthen the Border before it is weakened so much that the edges are frayed for ever."

"Why can't you come with us?" Sienna's voice was soft.

"I …" Bridget paused, her eyes full of regret and Sienna sensed she was hiding something. Then her voice hardened.

"It is your time. Your star charts overlap at this point in history. We have seen this conflict coming for many years, and we knew this day would come. Of course, we had hoped to prevent it. That's why the last Mapwalker team went over. But the prophecy speaks of the children of powerful mages coming together to defeat the shadow. The Illuminated Cartographer saw you would come, Sienna." Bridget shook her head. "I have been the one with unbelief. But now we don't have much time. You need to follow the footsteps of the last Mapwalker team."

"Why doesn't Sienna just mapwalk us back to this basement dungeon?" Perry asked. "Surely that would get us closer to where we need to be."

"I don't know how to get back there," Sienna said, acutely aware of how inadequate her ability was. "I don't even know how I did it the first time."

"Go easy on her," Mila said. "Remember how it was starting out for all of us."

Bridget nodded. "I know you're not a team yet, and if we had all the time in the world I would take you out into the Cotswolds, train you, build you into a team. But we don't have time now. I have to trust you will find it in yourselves to look after each other. This is your home. All of you stand to lose something if the Borderland bleeds through, and if the Shadow Cartographers take the Ministry…" Bridget trailed off, and in her silence, Sienna sensed what might happen, how the skins in the dungeon were created and what fate might await them if they failed.

"So how are we meant to find it?" Perry asked. "If you weren't able to locate the castle, how are we meant to?"

"There are many ways into the Borderlands, and you will go in through the same map the last team went through, a map that has the power to take you deeper into the Borderlands than any other, a map that has been protected for a thousand years."

CHAPTER 9

THE NEXT MORNING SIENNA rose early, excited to be off on the mission, anticipation rising within her. She had spent the night in her grandfather's flat. Although technically it was her flat now, she couldn't yet think of it that way. She had lain awake thinking of him last night, how she wished that she had got to know him while he was alive, but there was no time for regret now. She had eventually fallen asleep, dreaming of flayed skin and beasts from the edge of the map.

As she ate her breakfast, Sienna leafed through some of the journals, looking for anything that might mention a dungeon, a castle, anything her grandfather had written about the Borderlands. But the books were mostly sketches of what he had seen, strange enough, but nothing obvious to help them now. Did her father keep journals like this, and where might they be?

The bell rang, interrupting her thoughts. Sienna opened the door to find Mila standing outside, two takeaway coffees in her hands.

"Thanks. That's exactly what I need." Sienna smiled and took one. She indicated her small bag. "I've brought everything I have. It's not much. I didn't expect to stay long."

Mila laughed. "Don't worry, we have everything we need

in the military packs we take with us. There are also dead drops where we leave equipment, weapons, rations and other things over the border." She grinned. "I might also have some extra stashes the boys don't know about."

She pulled a small rolled-up leather map from her bag. "But you should keep this with you. It's your star chart. Just in case."

Sienna took it and put it deep within her pack as a horn beeped from the end of the road. Perry sat at the wheel of a four-wheel drive, Xander in the front next to him.

"Come on, you two," Perry called out. "We need to get going. Hereford awaits."

"Hereford was once Welsh," Xander said, as they drove out of town. "The border has changed multiple times. An early charter from 1189 had Hereford situated in Wales, as granted by Richard the First of England. But now it's English."

"And proudly so," Perry said in his impeccable accent, keeping his eyes on the road.

Sienna felt a little out of place in the car. She was an outsider but the other three didn't seem like a well-honed team either. They were more like a group of students going to a festival together. Xander turned up the radio as they headed west over the Severn Bridge and north through Wales. It wasn't long before they arrived in Hereford and pulled up near the cathedral.

Sienna looked up at the twelfth-century Romanesque church. "It's gorgeous."

Perry stretched as he got out of the car. "This was the Saxon capital of West Mercia in the eighth century, then the Welsh targeted the city in the eleventh century supported by the Vikings. There was once a castle here as big as Windsor in size and scale. The Welsh attacks were repelled, and it became a stronghold for the campaigns of English kings during the Welsh Marches. Pretty cool."

They walked towards the cathedral.

"We need to find a specific book in the chained library," Mila said. "Your father and his team came here before they went missing, Sienna."

"Sometimes I think a missing father might be better than any father at all," Perry muttered under his breath.

They walked into the cathedral and looked up at the decorative Norman columns and arches. Stone tombs with effigies of knights stood in alcoves off the nave and at the south end, there was a Norman font large enough to immerse a child. Knights Templar in chainmail armor decorated one of the tombs. The Bishop buried inside had been a Grand Master long ago. Underneath their feet were markers of the dead, those buried here for years, their bones resting under the flagstones, carved names fading under the footsteps of the faithful.

They walked past the choir, and Mila pointed to a bare patch on the wall. "The Mappa Mundi hung here for many years, but now it's kept safe in a separate building. That's what we're here to see."

"As well as the chained library," Perry said. "The last Mapwalker team used the Mappa Mundi to travel through, but it's big, and we need to know which part. There are many entrances to the Borderlands, and we need to make sure we take the right one."

They walked out of the church to the special center where the library and the map were held.

"Mappa Mundi means map of the world," Mila explained, as they walked across the forecourt. "It dates to around 1300AD and gives a view of how the medieval monks understood the world back then."

They entered the temperature-controlled room to find the Mappa Mundi lit with dim lights behind glass. Sienna walked closer to get a better look. It was truly incredible, a single piece of vellum illustrated by the hand of faith, with representations of myth and legend next to places that really existed. Perhaps this was the truth of maps. In part, they reflected the world as it actually was, and in part, they reflected the way the world could be, or as it was imagined. As Sienna looked at the Mappa Mundi, she began to understand why her father had gone on this quest.

At the very top, an enthroned Christ held his hands up to show the stigmata, the wounds of crucifixion. Next to him, believers rose from their graves and entered Heaven, while on the other side the damned were stripped, chained and dragged down to Hell where a great beast waited to devour them. Sienna shivered as she looked at the creature, imagining an Illustrator like Xander drawing it and calling it into existence. She looked over at his handsome profile. Was it possible that he and others like him could create something so terrible?

Sienna turned back to the map. An inaccessible circular island at the top of the world represented Eden, surrounded by a ring of fire and closed gates. A serpent waited while Eve held out her hand to accept the apple, ready to taste the fruit of the knowledge of good and evil. Sienna understood her temptation, her need to know, because that's just how she felt about the Borderlands right now.

There was a picture of Noah's Ark, the woven hull floating above a sea of red when God sent the great flood to wipe out the wickedness of humanity. The map showed a path through the Red Sea, the color still fresh after so many years, marking the wanderings of the Israelites from Egypt, out of slavery and into the Promised Land.

There were beasts on the map, a unicorn, a lynx slinking towards the southern coast of the Black Sea, a war elephant with a tower on its back, a strange parrot creature with a curled tail. There were strange-looking people too: a man with no head, only eyes on his chest holding a sword, another with one huge foot. There were troglodytes, cave dwellers in Africa, and men with heads of dogs.

"What is this map about?" Sienna asked. "It can't be real, surely?"

"A map is never truly real," Mila said. "It's only one aspect of the reality of the creator. But we need to pay attention to the cities on the map. Maybe your father took the team through one of those?"

Hereford was marked by a tiny building on the River Wye, almost rubbed off by pilgrims touching it over the years. Jerusalem was right in the center of the map, with a circular wall and a castle city with eight towers, marking the place of crucifixion.

Rome was shown as a towering cathedral with text next to it: 'Rome, head of the world, holds the bridle of the spherical earth.' Towers and pinnacles marked Paris, where the medieval University focused on philosophy and theology.

"The map is apparently a single piece of calfskin, but I think it's something different." Xander bent as close as he could get without the alarms going off. The map was drawn on the flesh side of the skin, not the hair side, making the map undulate as one was naturally more taut than the other. "I think it's the skin of an animal from the Borderlands. There's a vibration from it as if it calls to go home. Maybe something wandered over back then, but it's certainly more than just calfskin from Earth-side."

A labyrinth caught Sienna's eye, a circular maze, like the one in Crete with the Minotaur at the center. In the Middle Ages, many medieval cathedrals had labyrinths and pilgrims would walk around them looking for a way to the center, metaphorically searching for a way to God. She had visited Chartres Cathedral with her father years ago and they had walked the famous labyrinth together.

Mila pointed to a particular area of the map. "This is the camp of Alexander the Great. His conquest of the Persian Empire and domination of the known world was a popular theme, and there are several references on the map about

Alexander. This restraining wall was built to save the world from the destructive force of the Sons of Cain." She turned to Sienna. "Does anything here seem familiar?"

Sienna stared at the map, trying to see it with her father's eyes, trying to understand what he might have seen. He had traveled to many of the places portrayed but her eyes kept being drawn back to the labyrinth. "I'm not sure. Maybe we should look at the chained library. We can come back and check the map afterwards."

They walked through into the largest surviving chained library in the world. A librarian stood talking to a tourist group in front of them. "There are over 1500 books in the library and several hundred medieval manuscripts. There has been a library here since the year 800, and people still come from all over the world to examine them."

As the tourist group moved on, the librarian nodded in welcome, greeting the little group and then indicating the stacks. "Our most popular works are the Hereford Gospels, the Hereford Breviary and the sermons of St Bede."

She opened one of the books chained to a wooden lectern. "As you can see, there are miniature paintings and incredible illumination around the edges of many of the books. They were chained for their security, as there weren't very many books back in those days. We keep a few like this for historical accuracy." They walked through to the Hereford Gospels. "This is possibly the earliest surviving book made in Wales containing all four Gospels. It survived the sacking of the cathedral, and is revered as a relic for making it through the fire and destruction."

"Do you have any more illustrated books?" Xander asked.

The librarian nodded. "The Nuremberg Chronicle is one of the largest and most lavishly illustrated of the books dating from the fifteenth century. It tells the history of the world and has nearly two thousand woodcut illustrations."

Mila stepped forward. "Do you have a list of people who have visited and what they looked at?"

The librarian frowned. "Of course, but it's private information."

As she walked away, Mila turned to the others. "We need to come back later, after dark, so we can access those records."

* * *

It was after midnight when they crept back into the grounds of Hereford Cathedral, skirting around security lights and heading straight back to the library. Mila took a tiny piece of map parchment from her pocket and poured some water from a bottle over it. She laid it over the electronic locks and then used her magic to freeze it, cracking the locks from the inside. Sienna smiled. "Nice skill."

Mila grinned. "We all have our tricks." She looked over at Perry. "And it's less damaging than fire."

Inside, the library was quiet, and the four of them went straight to the librarian's station. Perry sat down at the computer. "I'm not all flames and fire, you know." He began tapping at the keyboard, looking for a way into the databases.

Sienna and Mila concentrated on the pile of old visitor books stacked in rows behind the desk. Xander stood watching for a moment, his eyes darting to the next room. "I think I'll go have a look at the Nuremberg Chronicle while we're here."

Mila raised an eyebrow as he walked off. "Xander is obsessed with illustrations."

The visitor books dated back over the last thirty years, so they pulled the older ones down first, flicking through the pages. It was strange to see the handwriting of people who'd visited many years ago. How many of them had passed on now? How many had found what they were looking for, and how many more had discovered new questions?

"Come and look at this," Perry said suddenly, his voice excited. Sienna and Mila went to stand behind him.

"Look, there was a break-in reported around the time the last team crossed over. They must have accessed the map then."

"But we still don't know which part they used to travel through," Mila said. "At least it gives us a narrower window to check the archives."

They turned back to the visitor books, pulling down one after the other.

Then Sienna saw her father's writing on the page, his distinctive sloped letters in purple ink. She touched the words with gentle fingers, thinking of him standing here in the library, a frown on his face as he concentrated. Did he think of her at all? She shook her head. She could only hope there would be time to ask him.

"He requested *Meditations on a Medieval Labyrinth*, so they must have gone through the labyrinth part of the map."

"Then that's the way we'll follow," Mila said. "Are you ready?"

Sienna nodded. "You put the books back, and I'll get Xander."

She left Mila re-stacking the shelves and walked through the library into the next room. Xander stood by a window, the light of the moon touching the book lying on the desk in front of him. It was chained to the wooden lectern, and she could see the detailed illustrations from across the room, the colors still bright after so many years. Xander sketched a dragon, a beast of scales and teeth and power, into the pocket journal he held. It was fat with extra notes and pages, and Sienna could only imagine what he drew in there, the creatures he held in his mind.

Xander looked up at her footsteps, his face taut with concern, then relaxing as he saw it was her. He indicated the page. "I've always wanted to illustrate a dragon, but Bridget asked where we'd put it and how we would hide it from the city." He shook his head with a sigh. "Such mundane questions when we should be using our abilities to the full, not hiding them."

Sienna walked closer and looked at the intricate lines on the page. "How do you create them?"

"The creatures can't come alive on any paper. I have to draw them on the edges of existing maps, preferably vellum or leather. I can't create maps from nothing as you can."

Sienna shrugged. "As I *supposedly* can. I haven't actually created a map yet."

Xander closed the book, his hand touching it lightly with respect. "The most powerful Illustrators have always worked closely with Blood Cartographers. Perhaps we could –"

Footsteps came from the corridor behind them, cutting off his words. Mila poked her head around the doorway.

"Come on, you two. Time to get going."

The four of them walked back to the Mappa Mundi, which lay within its protective case. Mila froze one of the panes of glass and made a hole big enough for Sienna to reach in and touch the map.

She hesitated, her heart beating faster. "So what do I do again?"

Mila took her hand. "Put your fingertips over the labyrinth and fix the image of it in your mind. Just think of the Borderlands as a country with multiple ways in. This map is one of the doors, but it should be where the last team went through and then we'll try to pick up their trail on the other side."

Sienna nodded. "And you can all come through with me?"

"We'll link hands," Perry said. "But it's a bit like a gate. You're opening it, and then we can come through after you. We're all Mapwalkers, remember that."

"I just don't want to leave anyone behind."

Perry smiled. "It's okay. We're coming too. We're not missing out on this adventure."

Sienna put her hand through the hole and touched the smooth skin of the map. It had a vibration under her fingers, a certain texture. She sensed that, as Xander had thought, it was not of Earth-side, but from the Borderlands originally. A creature that had once existed on the other side had somehow come through here, slaughtered away from its home and now revered as part of history.

Sienna placed her fingertips over the labyrinth and held out her other hand. The three others put their hands over hers, and Sienna closed her eyes, letting the sensation of lifting take her up and out of herself, over the city of Hereford. Spreading below her was the skin of the world with Jerusalem shining like a beacon further out on the horizon, but below her, she could see a form of the labyrinth. It called to her, and she dived back down into it.

CHAPTER 10

Sienna opened her eyes.

It was dark, but the air smelled different. Whereas the inside of the library had a sense of dust from the pages of old books, the air here smelled of smoke and ash. Sienna looked around.

They stood on a street, hemmed in on all sides by shelled-out buildings, towering close and dog-legging away so she couldn't see very far. It was a warren of narrow streets, not even big enough for a car to drive down, an urban labyrinth. Empty rooms looked down on them like vacant eyes, the stone crumbling, a place where nature had started to reclaim the emptiness.

"It's Old Aleppo," Mila said. "The part of the city pushed over the border."

Sienna felt the shadow as a visceral sense on this side. It was like a darkness pushed down inside her all her life, which had suddenly found its way to the surface. All the things she'd been told she couldn't have, or be, or do, suddenly welled up inside her like a rush.

A shadow rush.

She didn't have to be a good girl here. She could take what she wanted. She could *be* who she wanted. There seemed no limit on what was possible in the Borderlands. It was dizzying, intoxicating and Sienna felt the thrill of the dark side in her veins as they walked. A sense of losing control to a point but without having a drink, without taking drugs, without loosening the mind in a way she would have to do on Earth-side in order to feel this way.

Mila looked over with a half-smile on her face, recognition in her eyes. "That feeling is why the Ministry send us in teams. Because if you come over on your own, there's a chance you won't return. You could go native with the rush, and then you'd be lost."

"Have you ever been over on your own?" Sienna asked.

Mila raised an eyebrow. "What do you think?"

Sienna grinned. Together the four of them walked through the ruined city. It had the haunting echo of lives long forgotten, the beauty of decay inherent in the buildings left behind. Sienna glanced into one shattered space. The walls were a fresh orange color, and a blue frieze ran around the edges as if it had only been painted yesterday. But the doorframe was rotten and broken and the floor covered in sand and rocks blown in on a cruel wind.

Could there be any true beauty without the knowledge it would fade? Sienna thought of the flowers she sometimes took to her mother and how they were only fresh for a few days before dying. This place felt like that. Like it was once a blooming flower now fallen into decay. Entropy had taken it to dust, as it took us all eventually.

It started to rain. Sienna looked up at the dark clouds overhead. "How does the weather get here?"

Mila laughed. "The weather doesn't know the border, so the same rain falls on us and the Borderlanders alike. But natural events sometimes drive people over, like earthquakes and eruptions. Time is different the further out you go towards the Uncharted. There are still some out there who remember the destruction of Pompeii."

Sienna shook her head in amazement. It would be

fascinating to meet someone who had seen the eruption of Vesuvius, yet for them, it would have been the end of all they knew.

"How do you know what's here in the Borderlands?" she asked.

"It's a challenge as the edges are not entirely mapped," Mila said. "They move over time as people and places are driven off the edge of Earth-side. Those who are not wanted, who fall between the borders, find a place here. But, of course, there is a hierarchy between those who have been here the longest and those who arrive every day. There are refugees here too. Sometimes I think we are driving them over here on purpose." Mila sighed. "Sometimes I don't know which side we're on."

They walked down the cracked street under the arches of a ruined hall, the stone pockmarked by artillery shells. Sienna picked her way through the rubble, over fallen masonry and discarded furniture. There were signs of habitation in the rubble, a chipped cup and saucer, the tattered remains of a book, the springs of a bed frame.

Suddenly, they heard shouting up ahead.

The four of them huddled in a doorway, sheltered by a broken wall. The sound of running feet came closer and then a group of men passed, their faces set in determination, each with a half-moon tattoo.

"They have people here who can sense the border opening," Mila whispered. "They're looking for us."

After the men passed by, the group walked on with light feet, staying alert in the shadows. The smell of smoke from a fire wafted from a doorway and Sienna stopped to peek inside. A man lay on the ground, his face thin and drawn with pain, his limbs curled. A woman knelt by the fire boiling water in an old tin can, a baby next to her in the dust, a blanket wrapped around its thin body. The woman looked up with fearful eyes.

Sienna saw just another human there, someone who wanted to look after her family, someone who wanted to stay alive. She could understand why those in the Borderlands wanted to come back over to Earth-side. This place had been pushed out because nobody cared. The powers that be made their maps and decided what was important, *who* was important. The rest disappeared over here, cast adrift to survive alone.

The sound of shouting came from up ahead, deep voices raised, orders given. The woman turned back to the fire, not even flinching at the noise. Sienna walked on quickly after the others as they darted between alcoves in the buildings.

Perry turned around as she approached. "Try and keep up, we wouldn't want to lose you in here."

"Where are we heading?"

"The center of Old Aleppo. It's a souk, a trading market that stood for seven hundred years. At least it did stand until the war on Earth-side which now continues over here."

"Who's the fighting between here?" Sienna asked.

"The Borderlands are not just filled with one people," Perry said. "Factions fight each other for control of scarce resources." He stopped at a wall painted with a half-moon symbol in a dark ochre that could have been dried blood. "There are two factions in Old Aleppo. This symbol belongs to a warlord loyal to the Shadow Cartographers who sacrifices to the old gods. The price of human life is cheap Earth-side, but it's worth even less in the Borderlands. The Shadow Cartographers feed on the energy of violence, conflict and death, so they fan the flames to keep people in constant fear."

The stench of rotten flesh came on the air, a night breeze bringing it across the city. Sienna put her hand over her face, but they kept walking towards it, the smell intensifying.

"The warlord hangs the bodies of the rebels here," Perry said. "Around the labyrinth where the Resistance are known to be active."

The shadows shifted. Six bodies hung on the wall, hands tied behind their backs, hoods over their heads.

"We have contacts in the Resistance, those who trade for information. That's where we're going."

They walked past an abandoned temple. Holes in the roof let in shafts of moonlight. Sienna caught a glimpse of a mosaic on the back wall showing a god devouring his children.

Mila dropped back to walk next to her and pointed in at the statues of old gods. "Anything lost from Earth-side remains here in the shadows, including belief. There are people here who crawled over the border in the aftermath of ethnic cleansing. Those who escaped the massacres of Rwanda, of Srebrenica. The Borderlands claim those who would otherwise disappear on Earth-side." Mila shook her head.

"Is anyone born here?" Sienna asked.

Mila frowned. "Of course, there are children here, like anywhere. Some are Halbrasse, half-breeds. The Shadow Cartographers are trying to spawn a new generation of Mapwalkers, those who can cross the border like us. But to create such children, they risk creating abominations, those in whom magic twists into something that shouldn't live."

Sienna shivered. No wonder they needed to stop these people coming back over. For how could those on Earth-side stand against the inhumanity done here? The blood-soaked land did not forget what had been done to it, and the people who remained on the Borderland were the scars, the living tissue of what had gone before.

Mila stopped in front of the ruined building. "Things here are often not what they seem. You need to be careful. The Borderlands have a way of slipping inside you." She put her hand up, gesturing for them to stop and wait.

Sienna ducked into a doorway with Perry and Xander as Mila walked into the depths of the temple alone. The stones either side of the door were smashed, broken into pieces as if a gigantic hand had punched through them in anger. The thick beams stood out, charred and burned. It was a derelict skeleton, clouded with ash. Sienna looked down into the dust and noticed pieces of bone, shards of skull. They walked upon the bodies of the dead.

A few minutes later, Mila appeared at the broken door and beckoned them inside. Huge pillars dominated the space, rising to a roof that had been split asunder. A shaft of moonlight pierced down to the floor where carved spirals made the pattern of a labyrinth. There were sculptures in each of the alcoves around them, voluptuous goddesses with wreathes of dead flowers, the skeleton of a child in the lap of one. An offering to the dark goddess.

Mila stood with a tall man dressed in black leather. He turned at their approach.

"You didn't say you were bringing so many." His voice was deep and resonant. He stepped into a patch of moonlight and Sienna saw him more clearly. He had the regal bearing of an East African king, the limbs of a long-distance runner, the dark eyes of a moonless night. His head was closely shaved with stubble on his chin, highlighting a strong jaw.

"It's not safe here," he said. "We have to get moving."

Mila gestured towards him. "This is Finn Page. His father, Kosai, is the warlord here in Old Aleppo. Finn is the leader of the Resistance."

Finn turned to Mila. "If I do this, you'll keep your side of the bargain?"

She nodded.

"Then we must go now."

Finn led them out of the back of the temple, and they wound their way through the streets past the doorway that Sienna had glanced into before.

Finn turned around. "Wait here." He ducked into the room, and Sienna heard the rumble of his deep voice. He came back out a minute later, his face like thunder. "Follow me."

As Sienna walked past, she glanced into the room again. This time the woman had a loaf of bread, tearing at it hungrily as she shared it with her husband.

"My father has the relics with him tonight," Finn said, as they stalked through the ruined city. "The ritual is on the outskirts at the Tophet. We have a way to walk, then prepare yourself for Hell."

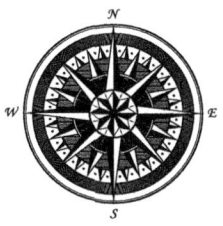

CHAPTER 11

Sometimes the landlocked city was so hot that the air dragged through Finn's lungs with each breath and even though they were miles from water, it made him feel like he was drowning. Tonight was one of those nights, and the cloying stink of smoke from the pyres made it worse. He loosened his shirt at the neck, breathing more deeply, trying to push down the fear rising within him as he led the Mapwalkers deeper into the city.

Twisted metal lay in piles against sandbags covered in dust from destroyed buildings, the faint smell of buried corpses beneath. Trees grew in the rubble at the side of cracked roads, their leaves mottled black with disease but Finn heard the coo of a pigeon as they passed, evidence of life in the ruins. Soft voices came from one of the skeletal buildings behind it, scarred by the bombing he had only heard about. There were no guns in the Borderlands, although his father and his men spoke of them often, their voices lowered in remembrance of what they had lost during the wars that had devastated their native lands. Finn had been born here, a child of the Borderlands, so it was hard to know what was truth and what was myth in the stories they told.

He led the group into the ruins of the souk, the old market where a maze of market stalls had once stood. They followed him, footsteps echoing under the medieval stone roofs. He turned briefly to check on them, his eyes darting to the willowy young woman with titian hair. She was new, he sensed it in her curiosity, the way she couldn't stop looking around her even as she stumbled over loose bricks on the ground. There was an innocence about her, and Finn wondered what the city looked like through her eyes. She turned and looked at him. He felt a jolt inside, as if she saw right to his heart.

Finn walked on, but not before he realized that his father would want this young woman for himself. Her fragile Celtic beauty made her a prize, and he could trade her for sorely needed provisions. Together with the rest of the Mapwalkers, this group was worth a great deal, both to his father and to the Shadow Cartographers.

A worthy trade for his sister.

The young woman caught up to him, walking faster by his side. "I'm Sienna," she said, softly. "Can I ask what this place used to be?"

"The markets," Finn said, his voice gruff. "Spices, meat, vegetables, fruit. But now …" He shrugged. "We do what we can. In the daytime, people sell what they have grown and one day perhaps this place will be fully alive again."

Sienna smiled. "I hope so. I've been to the markets in Jerusalem – stalls piled high with peaches and pomegranates, the sweet smell of oranges in the air mingling with the yeast of freshly baked bread. Shoppers haggling for the best price and market traders calling out their best prices."

Finn smiled as her words brought back memories of happier times. "There are markets like those in the outer villages where they grow produce on the hills, even though the soil is poor. I go there to trade and bring back what I can."

"Can people who come over the border bring things with them?"

Finn frowned as he looked over at her. "You don't know?"

Mila caught up and took Sienna's arm, shooting her a

warning look. "Sorry, she's new on our team. I haven't fully briefed her yet."

Finn raised an eyebrow. Mila blushed, and the two dropped back to walk behind him, voices low. It was the first time he'd met a Mapwalker who hadn't been superior in both attitude and knowledge, someone with a real hunger to learn about this land.

His land.

Perhaps she would answer his questions about what life was like on Earth-side, a way to verify some of his father's more outlandish claims and what he had read in books. Because books did cross the border intact, unlike anything mechanical. Ancient magic kept out any technology created after the border was put in place, but books had become a form of currency, smuggled, traded, an addiction Finn had discovered early, even though the Shadow Cartographers banned them. He led the Mapwalkers on, weaving his way around the ruins, becoming lost in his own thoughts as he traversed the familiar path.

For all his father's faults, the warlord had always encouraged Finn and his other children to read. He even kept some of the forbidden books in his citadel at the heart of Old Aleppo, seized in raids or smuggled in across the border. The smugglers knew to stop at the citadel first, or their goods would likely be seized anyway. Kosai liked fine clothes and sold much of it on at a profit but always kept the best for himself. Some would be given to his family, the women he favored at the time, and of course, to his children.

His library contained works banned and banished on Earth-side, appearing in smoldering piles where they had been burned, popping through the border as their existence was denied. There were often intact volumes under the ash, their pages still readable.

But books also brought darker knowledge. His father's favorite was Suetonius' *Lives of the Caesars*, and descriptions of things done to those who crossed the Emperor now found their way into Kosai's court. His father drew his sense of justice from the examples of tyrants, determined to paint himself as a demigod, as the Roman Emperors had once done.

Kosai's faith had become stronger over time, and it had shown itself in the rule of fear. For those who doubt do not slaughter in the way that true believers do. Only those who believe in an absolute idea will kill in the name of it. It had been the Shadow Cartographers who showed Kosai the way of Moloch, resurrecting the ancient god so they could benefit from the fear he evoked.

There had been a time when Finn adored his father, when they had gone on father-son hunting trips into the forests at the edge of the Borderland towards the Uncharted to find the giant boars roaming there. As a six-year-old, his father had taught him to use a knife for the first time. Finn remembered the weight of it in his hand, a bigger knife than he could handle, but his father said heavy blades would help him learn faster. Finn put his hand down, touching the pommel of his sword in a reflexive movement. Those early years had been hard, but his father had taught him well.

Finn's mother had fallen through, brought here in a slave band and favored by the warlord for a time. She had died of an infection after the birth of another child and he scarcely remembered her face, although his skin color mirrored hers, rather than his father's Middle Eastern heritage.

Growing up, Finn hadn't paid much attention to his siblings, leading his own pack of young warlord princes. Together, they raided the outer towns, patrolling the edge of the border, waiting for new people to be pushed through, then enslaving them, selling them on. His father claimed these new arrivals were not real people, that they didn't have any rights here. They had been pushed out from their home, and thus were ripe to be exploited.

Isabel had been born when Finn was twelve, and he had never seen anyone so precious. He remembered holding her in his arms and promising he would never let anything happen to his little sister. Her blonde hair and fair skin were so different to his own, but the shape of their noses, the way they used their hands when they talked, and their love for books, bonded them.

Finn would read to her in the library, smuggling pocketfuls of dried dates in, so they could both nibble on the sweetness as they read passages aloud. He had taught her to read early on and he had taught her to use a knife as well. His father didn't believe in teaching the girls, but Finn couldn't see why his sister shouldn't be able to protect herself. As she had reached her teens, he'd seen the way men looked at her. And how Kosai had looked at her too.

Then one day, they came for her.

Finn lashed out, fighting away the guards until five of them held him down. Her screams echoed as they bundled her into the back of a wagon and took her away to the castle of the Shadow Cartographers.

The Resistance had come to Finn that night, as he walked through the streets of Old Aleppo down to the ancient library where he and Isabel had always found a haven. He paced in the darkness, thumping his fists against each other, unable to contain his anger. He decided to go after her, to track the wagon at first light, then bring her back or set her free.

He had heard what happened at the castle. There were women who had come back, their eyes hollow, their bodies broken from birthing children who might have some usable magic, the Halbrasse, the half-breeds.

Back then, a woman had stepped from the shadows. "I know what happened to your sister, but you can't stop them now. You will only die in your quest. There will only be more women taken, more children sacrificed. But if you stay, you have a chance to change things. Your father trusts you. You can be the eyes and ears of the Resistance inside his camp. If you hear of a raid, we can get there before you. If you hear of who will be targeted for sacrifice, we can spirit them away. And in time, we will help you save your sister."

"I need to know when," Finn said. "I can't leave her there, knowing what will happen to her every day."

The woman put a hand on his arm. "She is strong, as I was. I have told her how to end the life that might grow inside. There are pits outside the castle walls for the bodies of the children. The unborn or those who made it into the world briefly, those too mutated or too broken to live. Secrets written out of even this history. I knelt at the pit when I left that stinking place, I cried for the life I lost, but it gave me a purpose. And if you join us, we can end the Halbrasse for good." She met his eyes.

"The Resistance is working with Mapwalkers on Earthside. There are those who want to make peace across our borders, those who want to release the hold of the Shadow Cartographers. They want to help us build the Borderlands into a place where life is worth living. We just need to throw off the yoke of oppression."

Her words echoed inside Finn's heart. This was a quest worth joining, a cause worth championing. He couldn't be part of his father's bloody campaign any longer.

He nodded. "Tell me what you want me to do."

As Finn strode through the rubble of Old Aleppo, the team of Mapwalkers behind him, he remembered that night and the promise he would now fulfill. He was part of the Resistance, but he was going to get his sister, whatever it took.

CHAPTER 12

Sienna tripped on a pile of rubble, cursing her clumsiness as she tried to catch up with the rangy Borderlander. Finn put his arm out to stop her falling, and she smiled up at him. "You said we were going to the Tophet. What is that?"

Finn's face darkened. "It's not something I would want you to see, but it's the only way to get to the relics." He met her eyes, and she saw anger there. "The gods pushed into the Borderlands demand blood, and the darkest rituals you Earth-siders banished now exist here. Chaos suits a certain type of person. Unfortunately one of those people is my father."

They walked out of the city, and the broken buildings soon gave way to the edge of a desert. The stars were high in the sky, and as Sienna looked up, she didn't recognize the constellations. It was a completely different view, as if the sky were inverted somehow. Finn led the way and as people passed on the road, many nodded at him, dipping their heads in respect.

Mila came back to walk beside Sienna. "Finn walks a fine line. Not for us, but for his people. He has respect as the son of his father, one of the most powerful warlords and certainly the most bloody. But now he works with the Resistance."

The sound of chanting came on a hot wind, a low rumble of voices repeating the name of a long-dead god.

They reached a sacred precinct, a circular area ringed with stones, topped with tiny skulls. At first, Sienna thought they might be animal bones. Some were so tiny that she could curl her fist around them. But as she looked closer, she realized they were babies and young children. A sense of foreboding filled her as they walked on.

In the center of the precinct, a crowd of people knelt in front of a large stone altar in the shape of the hungry god Moloch. His mouth was open to devour the sacrifice, and he held a basin of fire in his outstretched arms. The rhythmic chanting of the crowd grew stronger as a huge man walked forward, holding the wrist of a child of around four years old wearing a smiling mask.

"The mask hides their tears from the god," Mila said, her voice low.

The man dragged the child forward, and Sienna watched in rising horror, but they could do nothing as the place was surrounded by the warlord's men. They beat drums either side of the god to accompany the chants of the crowd.

"Why do the people allow this?" She looked up at Finn, shaking her head.

"They ask Moloch to grant them more than this life," he said. "They ask the god to break down the border. If you were trapped here in this hell, ruled by this tyrant, wouldn't you want that too? Besides, human sacrifice is a legacy from your Earth-side. Abraham was asked by God to sacrifice his own son, and in Homer's Iliad, King Agamemnon sacrifices his daughter Iphigenia for fair winds. Many of your ancient cultures had child sacrifice, and as it was banished, it ended up here."

Finn pointed around the back of the crowd. "This way. My father keeps the relics nearby, ready to be blessed with the fresh blood of the sacrifice. We have a little time before it's done."

They ducked down and ran around the edge of the crowd, keeping to the shadows amongst the grave markers.

A small temple stood out the back of the main complex. Two guards stood in front of it. They nodded their heads at Finn's approach.

"Stand aside," he said. "My father wishes me to take these pilgrims to the relics."

One of the guards looked confused. "I'm sorry, my Lord, but your father said not to let anyone in here tonight."

Finn stepped forward, pulling back his cloak to reveal a long sword at his side, the blade shining silver in the torchlight. "I'm not anyone."

The guard nodded and stepped aside. Finn led the Mapwalkers into the stone chamber. Sculptures of the god surrounded an altar where a number of objects lay on a white cloth. A ceremonial fire burned in front of the altar and Perry walked to it, putting his hand in the flames. He turned his hand as if coaxing the fire into his palm. His eyes reflected the fire, and it was as if his skin became burnished copper.

Mila walked to the altar. "These objects are considered relics, because they come from Earth-side. They have the energy of our civilization and act as anchors. Those Borderlanders with the right magic cross over using these objects. Do you recognize anything?"

Sienna looked closely and for a moment, she thought her father's compass lay on the cloth in front of her. Her heart beat faster, but then, she saw it had different engravings. She picked it up to look more closely.

Finn stepped close to her. "You can't touch it. Put it down." His voice was low and urgent. "The guards are watching, and we can't have them tell my father you were here. It jeopardizes my position."

Mila looked up at him. "It's a Mapwalker compass. You know we can't leave it here. We're taking it with us."

Finn's face turned to thunder. "You said you just wanted to look."

"I did, but it belonged to one of the group we're looking for." Mila shook her head. "It's time, Finn. You have to decide which side you're on."

The drums and chanting stopped. A single wail rose above the quiet, the piercing cry of a mother losing her child. The crowd roared as they celebrated the sacrifice. Sienna imagined the blood of the child shed for the hungry god, knowing it would never be enough.

The sound of running feet suddenly came from outside, then shouts as more guards arrived. Mila looked at the door and then over at Finn. "Time to make your choice."

Finn hesitated for a moment, then drew his sword.

Xander took the folded map from his pocket, laid it on the floor. The lion, Asada, stepped from the page. He roared, charging forward as guards ran into the room, swords held high, some with crossbows at the ready, arrows nocked.

Perry pulled his hand from the flame and threw a ball of fire at the guards. It exploded in the air above their heads, raining down shards of soot. The guards turned in pain, some of them on fire, running for the doorway. The lion leapt in with huge hooked paws, slicing at the guards nearest him.

"We can't hold them for long," Mila shouted. "We need to get out of here."

Sienna put the compass securely inside her jacket pocket, and they began to back away towards the far archway as Finn fought with the remaining guards.

A booming voice echoed out across the temple. "You dare to cross the god of the Tophet, my son? You would let these Earth-bastards take my relics like they have stolen our land?"

Finn turned towards his father's voice, momentarily distracted. One of the guards swooped in and slashed at him with a sword, drawing blood. Finn spun and with one sweep finished off the guard with a slice across his neck. He held his arm, blood running between his fingers, as the warlord spoke.

"You're a traitor. If you stay, I'll forgive you. But if you go with them, I will hunt you all down and your skulls will ring the pit along with the other firstborn."

Finn's face was set in a grim glare, his features carved from ebony. He took a deep breath, then turned and strode towards the Mapwalker team.

Perry summoned new life into the fire, creating a wall of flame between them and their pursuers.

"Asada, come." Xander put the map down and the lion leapt into it. Xander folded the scrap and put it back in his pocket.

Finn took the lead, running down the corridor as he shouted back at the team. "We need to get back to the souk. We'll lose them in the labyrinth. I have friends in the Resistance who will get us out the city, but we have a long way to go tonight."

They ran through narrow streets, surrounded on both sides by ruined buildings. Sounds of pursuit soon faded behind them. Finn ducked through the warren of tiny streets, turning left and right until Sienna wasn't sure which way they were going anymore, only that they had to trust this man who had turned against his father for them.

The compass seemed to pulse in her pocket. It occurred to her that she could put her hand on it and transport the Mapwalkers somewhere else. But then she looked at Finn running ahead. He had risked his life for them, walked away from his father and his life. She took her hand away from the compass.

Finn ducked into one of the many derelict houses, led them out the back and then down an underground passage. The walls dripped with water and smelled of rot and mold, the air chill. After walking for what seemed like too long in the cold darkness, they finally emerged into an ancient cistern. Two men and a woman greeted them, faces wrapped in scarves to cover their features, voices low as they talked in a language Sienna didn't recognize.

Finn turned back to the Mapwalkers. "We can stay here for now, lie low and eat. We'll continue the journey after some rest."

The woman brought them sleeping mats and a bowl of soup each. Mila took crackers from within her ration pack, handed them out, and they shared a meal together by the fire.

Perry gazed into the flames, the reflection turning his eyes a golden hue. Sienna wondered what he saw there. Could he find a way out through the fire?

Mila came and sat next to Sienna. "You still have the compass, right?"

"Of course." She looked over the fire at Finn. He was whittling a tiny horse from acacia wood, his movements graceful and precise. "What did you promise Finn in exchange for his help?"

Before Mila could speak, Finn looked over. "My sister was taken for the Halbrasse. My father exchanged her for power in this city. She's in the castle of the Shadow Cartographers." He narrowed his eyes at Mila. "And you will take me there as promised."

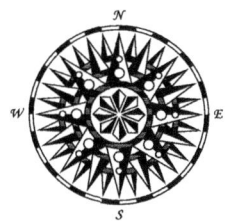

CHAPTER 13

Perry lay by the fire, looking into the flames. Sienna and Mila talked with the Borderlander, Finn, on the other side. Xander sat in the corner of the cistern, sketching in his notebook, absorbed in his drawing, like he seemed to do more and more these days. Perry cupped his hand and summoned a tiny flame in the center of his palm. He smiled. It seemed he was learning how to manage his magic at last. He thought back to the room in the citadel they had fled from. There was a moment when the fire had done his bidding. After so long struggling with control, he might finally be reaching a point where he knew how to use it.

But there was a darker current below his satisfaction.

When the flame kindled, he had felt a tug towards destruction. The difficulty in being a Fire Cartographer was walking the line between destruction and creation, between warming people and cooking food or burning everything to ash.

The marks of fire were everywhere in the Borderlands. People's homes burned down by regimes that didn't want them, the scars of burned cities on their skin. Perry wanted to be horrified, but as he had thrown the fire at those guards, their screams gave him a dark satisfaction. It disturbed him, because it was the edge of Shadow Cartography.

He remembered when he would sit with his father in the woods behind the Mercator estate gazing into the flames together. His father would light the fire with a flick of his fingers and make the flames dance as he told stories of his adventures in the Borderlands. Truth be told, his father loved the Borderlands more than he loved Earth-side and Perry was born because of his love for a Borderlander.

He was a Halbrasse.

Perry's eyes slid over to Finn, knowing the man's sister had been forced into creating half-breeds to feed the power of the Shadow Cartographers. But his own mother had not been forced into it.

Sir Douglas had met Morwenna on a mission when a Mapwalker team had come over looking for a certain artifact. His mother had been one of those guarding it, and the two had fallen in love. When the rest of the team had returned Earth-side, Sir Douglas had stayed, determined to live in the Borderlands, but the Illuminated Cartographer summoned him back. The way his father told it, the pair had been star-crossed lovers on either side of the border. Perry had been born in the Borderlands, but as he grew up, he discovered he could walk into Earth-side. Sir Douglas took him to live on the Mercator estate with all its luxury. A world away from his mother's camp.

Ten years ago, Morwenna had been killed, and one of the Mapwalkers from the Ministry was involved. His father had become distant, his trips into the Borderlands increasingly outside the rules of the Ministry.

Now Perry wrestled with where his allegiance should lie. He had friends on Earth-side, he went to school there and now he was a Mapwalker with the Ministry. He had a purpose and Perry was proud of that. And yet when he was over here, he saw the people in the Borderlands were no different. They loved, they wanted to provide for their children, they would fight for their families. And perhaps they needed more help than those who took life for granted on Earth-side.

Perry lay back and closed his eyes as his father's words echoed in memory. *The border is a construct, keeping two halves of a whole apart. Two halves which are one in you, my son.*

When the fire expanded under his skin, Perry thought he would rather live here in the Borderlands. On Earth-side, he couldn't even use the magic outside the Ministry. And what was he if not a Fire Cartographer? If he couldn't use his magic, what was the point?

* * *

After a few hours' sleep, Finn woke them up. Sienna jumped in the semi-darkness as his face loomed close to hers.

"It's okay. It's only me." He grinned. "I don't bite."

They packed up the bags and left the Resistance fighters in the cistern. They headed into the tunnels beyond and soon emerged into the far desert as dawn painted the horizon in shades of coral pink.

Sienna glanced over at Finn. He was only a few years older than she was, which meant his sister was a lot younger. No wonder he wanted to rescue her from the castle.

They walked through the desert, past scrub brushes and the ruins of old cities poking out through the sand, pieces of sculpture from lost civilizations. In the distance, a group of low mountains rose out of the sand where dunes had piled up over time. The mounds formed shapes of strange creatures as the sun rose higher. As they drew closer, a collection of small sandy dwellings could be seen nestled in the lee of the slope. They looked abandoned, used only by travelers to shelter from the scorching sun.

The detritus of those passing through littered the shack

inside. Old food tins and a tattered book, pages falling out from overuse. It was dusty and smelled like something had died and rotted there.

Finn walked to the back where a small second chamber led off the first, carved deeper into the sandstone. He beckoned, and they followed him in. He bent down and started to scrape away the sand. "I could use some help here."

Sienna and Perry got down next to him and began to sweep the dust and dirt away, revealing a trapdoor beneath. It seemed incongruous here in the middle of the desert as the trapdoor could only lead down to the sand below. Finn looked up, a smile on his face. "You won't believe what's down here."

He pulled it up. The hinges made no sound, clearly kept oiled and ready for use. The ruins and detritus were all for show.

"There are oil lamps once we get further in," Finn explained as he stepped down into the dark.

Sienna opened her mouth, ready to suggest they should just use a torch. Mila put her hand out and shook her head. "They don't have electricity here, so no batteries either. We have them just in case but we save them for emergencies."

The bright flare of a match came from down below and then the soft, warm light of an oil lamp. Sienna looked down into the trapdoor as Finn appeared at the bottom. He looked up, a lamp in his hand. "Come on down."

Sienna climbed down using stone handholds, each foot feeling for the next rung until she emerged into the passage below. She turned around, her fingers tracing chisel marks on the stone walls. The passage was narrow but tall enough so Finn could walk upright. He led them on into the dark.

"These caves were used a thousand years ago to escape the invasion of the Muslim Arabs. You know them on Earthside as part of the Derinkuyu caves. They could fit twenty thousand people down here, so the whole city could shelter in times of trouble. There were stables and cellars as well as chapels and meeting rooms." Finn smiled. "Even wine and oil presses. The important stuff."

"How were they built?" Sienna asked.

"It's soft volcanic rock, part of Cappadocia in Earth-side Turkey," Mila explained. "Pushed over the border when the caves were shut off to the public. I've heard you can cross directly here if you go through Turkey's Ministry."

Sienna found it hard to keep track of how the Borderlands related to Earth-side. Like the vellum map back in Hereford, it was as if the world had been scrunched up so the different parts touched at different points. The Borderlands were the negative space off the edges of Earth-side, constantly shifting as the world changed.

They walked on down narrow tunnels, passing places where the rooms opened out, held up by thick rock pillars. The cave walls were carved into functional shapes, places for animals to eat, alcoves to hold tiny statues of gods. The ceilings were low in some parts and Sienna couldn't help thinking of the weight of all that rock above them. But this place had stood for nearly a thousand years, so why would it fall now?

She just couldn't stop the thoughts from filling her mind. Some of the rooms were so tiny that they seemed like cells, but Sienna could see how the families felt safe down here while the world raged above. There were words carved into the rock, ancient graffiti from people who had lived and died here. She ran her fingers over the indentations, wondering about their lives.

"They had huge rocks to roll over the entrances, closing the city from inside," Finn explained. "Each separate level could be shut off. Like a castle in reverse."

"How deep is it?" Sienna asked.

"There are ten levels going all the way down to an underground river flowing beneath."

Mila turned at his words. "We need to go down there. The last team had a water walker like me, so perhaps they went that way."

They descended further, winding through the tunnels, air cooling as they went deeper. Sienna touched the water on the walls of the caves as they passed, trailing her fingers in the moisture.

They emerged into a chamber where four skeletons lay in what looked like a ritual pattern. Their heads all pointed to the center and one was propped up in the middle, one bony hand raised towards the roof.

"The five-pointed compass," Mila whispered. "It looks like Mapwalkers traveled here a long time ago. Perhaps these people sought to harness the magic somehow."

They walked into the next room.

Suddenly there was a sliding and slipping, the sound of sand washing through a chute.

"Watch out!" Finn stepped back, pushing Sienna behind him. Cracks in the ceiling opened up, dumping a huge load of rocks and sand in their path.

"I've heard there are traps down here," Finn said. "Ways to kill invaders. Things to keep people away."

They stood for a moment, listening, waiting, then walked carefully around the edge of the room and into another chamber. Fossils lined the walls, creatures that had once lived, trilobites and dinosaurs, their bones fossilized into the rock. This was a shrine to the long dead, but they stood like sentinels guarding the way.

Huge birds with sharp beaks and teeth like sharks stood either side of the doorway, their wing bones held high as if to stop anyone passing, their legs flexed ready to leap. A phalanx of fossilized sea spiders with huge articulated legs looked as if they could step out from the rock at any moment. Giant scorpions, triple the size Sienna had seen in the desert, their thick bodies full of venom, stood with arched tails ready to strike.

Around the fearsome fossils, there was a beautiful frieze of ammonites and sea creatures frozen into the rock, their colors still vibrant after so many years.

"These are amazing." Xander stepped closer and pulled out his sketchbook and pencil.

A crack of stone and crunch of rock split the air, a wrenching sound from the earth. A rumble shook the floor, sand and dust raining down on them from above. Two giant birds stepped out from the wall, articulated stone joints cracking as their empty eyes turned to look at their prey. Scorpions flicked themselves off the wall with their tails, scuttling to surround the group as spiders arched from the walls.

The creatures began to advance.

CHAPTER 14

ONE OF THE BIRDS darted in, teeth clacking together as it lunged at Finn. He spun away, pulling his sword and swinging it, taking the head of the bird off. It fell to the floor, but the bird kept coming, like a stone zombie intent on its prey.

One of the scorpions scuttled up Sienna's leg.

"How are you meant to kill a fossil?" Mila said, as she tugged the creature off, threw it to the ground and smashed it with a rock into tiny pieces until the scorpion stopped moving. Sienna picked up her own rock, and they stood back to back, fighting off the creatures together.

Xander took out his map and laid it on the ground. Nothing happened. Asada remained just an illustration on the page. Xander looked confused. "There's something different about this rock. I can't tap into earth magic."

"It's volcanic, made of lava," Finn shouted as he smashed the pommel of his sword down onto a spider, crushing its body to the floor.

Perry put his hand on the rock, trying to sense something that would help them. The birds advanced, bones clicking. The scorpions and spiders stalked across the floor towards them. He didn't have much time.

This rock had been made from fire, so maybe he could unmake it. He put his hand flat on the wall and concentrated on making the rock molten again. It softened and began to burn.

He pulled a ball of molten rock from the wall and threw it at one of the fossil birds. The fiery ball smashed through its head, and its bones began to melt in the flames. The others ducked away from the ash, falling back behind him.

Perry stepped forward and put his hands to the ground. Jets of flame came out of his hands, zoomed across the floor and soon the stone creatures were melting, becoming one with the volcanic rock again.

As the creatures melted into the floor, Perry watched the flames dance closer to his team. The Borderlander rose inside him and for a moment, he wanted to keep it burning.

He shook his head, lifting his hands from the floor as if they suddenly burned. These thoughts came every time he used his Mapwalker power. He had to be careful.

"We need to get going," Perry said. "I can sense there are more of these creatures down here. I can't melt them all."

They continued through the narrow stone passageway, down into the depths of the cave system. The dripping of water intensified and soon they could hear the quiet rush of a stream.

They emerged at the bottom of the cave system into a final chamber carved with images of a goddess. Tiamat of ancient Babylon, goddess of chaos and primordial creation, a sea serpent with curled tail wrapped around a sacrifice.

"The storm god Moloch killed her and the heavens and the earth formed from her slaughtered body." Mila ran her hand over the stone coils. "She's a powerful water goddess, ruling where the salt meets fresh." Mila turned to look into the dark waters flooding part of the chamber and led into the underground waterway. "There must be a reason she's worshipped down here." She pointed. "Look towards the back of the cave."

The coils of a great serpent rose from the water and then

sunk back down again. The creature of Tiamat was still here.

Mila walked to the water's edge and put her hand into the water. "This is where the sacrifice would be made to guarantee safe passage. I guess no one is volunteering." She looked around, one eyebrow raised. "I can go into the water. There must be a boat around here somewhere, something you can travel in as I propel you past."

Finn's dark skin seemed suddenly pale. "You didn't tell me we had to cross water."

"Why are you so scared?" Sienna asked.

"The sea and the rivers bleed into Earth-side. If I cross the border …" He shook his head.

"What would happen?" Sienna asked.

"I disappear into the shadow plane, cease to exist, although no one truly knows." Finn shrugged. "Many of us dream of crossing the border and seeing your side of the world, but it's just not possible."

"What if someone were to take you safely across?" Sienna asked.

"Who would do that?" Finn said.

"Here's a boat," Xander shouted from the corner of the cave. "It's old, but it might still be okay."

It was a coracle, a small round boat made of woven reeds and covered in pitch.

"Looks safe enough," Perry said, examining it closely.

Sienna couldn't imagine going too far in the bedraggled craft, but there was no other choice. "I guess we have to try."

They carried the coracle to the water. As they approached, the coils of the giant sea serpent came closer as if sensing their vibrations.

"Are you sure about this?" Sienna looked doubtfully towards the creature.

Mila nodded. "I know water." She gazed out over the darkness. "And I know her." Mila's skin already shimmered and she looked like she wanted to sink into the black.

There wasn't much room in the coracle, and they were all crushed together, Finn's hard body up against Sienna's. As Mila pushed the boat away from the shore, Sienna found herself leaning into him, finding solace in his warmth.

Perry held one of the lamps high as Mila slipped into the water behind them, her body shimmering as she became one with the liquid, disappearing beneath. The boat began to move through the cave system. Sienna looked down to see if she could see her friend, but the water was black and there was nothing but a ripple in their wake.

The great coils of the serpent dipped below the surface of the water and then disappeared. For a moment they looked around waiting for it to emerge but all was quiet, the lapping of water on the rocky sides of the cave system the only sound.

Stalactites hung down from the ceiling, great spikes of rock formed over the years dipping down to almost touch the water. The air smelled of minerals and salt. In some places the ceiling was so low they had to duck down, huddling together as the coracle edges bumped against the rocks. Sienna felt Finn tense at these moments, and she remembered his fear of being lost between worlds. She trailed her fingers in the water and thought of happy times on the beach. The waves were pleasure and freedom to her. How different it was in the Borderlands.

Time passed slowly as they moved through the deep waters of the cave system until finally, there was a shimmer of light in the distance that grew into a shaft of daylight beyond. As they came closer, a tall arch emerged from the darkness, carved from the rock, a portal to the outside. Beyond them, in the distance, blue water stretched to the horizon. Fruit-covered branches hung down over the entrance, and as they pushed through, the air was suddenly bright and filled with birdsong.

Finn reached up and grabbed one of the fruits, plucking it from the branch. "Do you have peaches Earth-side?"

"Of course." Sienna laughed.

Finn used the edge of his sword to cut the warm peach into four and shared it amongst them. Sweetness exploded on Sienna's tongue, a taste of summer. The boat edged towards a shoreline where stones made a tiny beach on the side of an island. The coracle pushed into the shallows and then Mila emerged from the water. She shivered, her skin still shimmering.

"You alright?" Sienna asked.

Mila nodded. "I just need a minute in the sun. It's the main problem with being a warm-blooded creature in a cold-blooded world. I haven't quite got the hang of staying warm while in the water." She looked around. "I wonder where we are. I don't recognize this place."

A path led up from the beach into dense forest. Crooked trees wound around each other, and parasitic plants on the trunks sapped their strength. The interior was an impenetrable dark green.

"We have two choices," Mila said. "We go back in the water, and I see where else I can take us." She turned and pointed to the water, where blue ocean stretched to the horizon. "Or we go up onto this island and see where the hell we are."

A screech came from the forest ahead of them. The sound of flapping wings and then a shadow fell upon the beach. Sienna looked up to see a huge silhouette against the sky, the bird's outstretched wings spanning thirty feet, much wider than any bird she had seen before. Its beak was a sharp hook as big as a scythe, and she could almost feel its gaze upon them, looking down from where it circled above. She wondered whether it could see through the border and how far away they were from its porous edge. It cried again, and there was an answering call in the distance.

Xander leaned back, his hand over his eyes as he focused on the bird. "Argentavis magnificens, extinct on Earth-side," he said with a smile. "We should discuss this at the forest's edge. They're hunters and big enough to carry one of us away."

CHAPTER 15

SIENNA FELT A TUG towards the interior of the island, through the darkness of the trees and onwards. She was sure the dark castle lay ahead of them on land, not by sea anymore.

"It's this way." Her voice was confident.

"Agreed," Finn said. "And I much prefer land to water." He took a few steps towards the trees and looked up at them. Sienna walked forward to join him. The dense foliage smelled of wet earth and moss, overlaid by the mold of dead leaves. A low buzz came from the semidarkness ahead, and Sienna caught sight of clouds of flying insects within.

"Looks like fun." Finn grinned.

Sienna pulled the sleeves of her top down, covering as much skin as possible as she smiled back. She was glad Finn was there. He was an outsider and as unsure of his place in the makeshift team as she was. They were a strange group, each with their own agenda. She turned to look back at the others. Mila stood facing the water, arms wrapped around herself as if she held herself back from diving into the blue and swimming away. Perry and Xander pulled the coracle further up away from the water's edge, bantering back and forth.

Sienna didn't know their individual reasons for being part of the Mapwalker team, but she understood Finn and his desire to free his sister. As long as they headed towards the castle, Finn would stay with them. And for that, she was glad.

Finn took a step into the forest and Sienna went after him, the others close behind. Within a few meters, the beach was out of sight. The canopy of trees rose above like a prison in shades of green with bars of thick tree trunks, hung with lianas, around them. The springy ground was dense with plants and entwined roots, tendrils wrapped around her ankles and seemed to drag back every step. The air had an intense humidity, every breath a gulp. Sweat trickled down Sienna's spine, and her clothes clung to her as moisture soaked through.

It was as if the land was decomposing, the body of the earth rotting, each footstep sinking into a bog of dead flesh. The ground opened like a huge dark mouth, roots of trees like decayed teeth waiting to devour any who stepped inside. The forest canopy cast a dark shadow, vines hanging down like sinister tentacles, a path of obstacles, an entangled world where chaos reigned.

Finn strode ahead, using his sword to chop down branches in their path. He was clearly used to the swing of it, his strokes confident. Sienna found herself mesmerized by the movement of the muscles on his back, his breath even as they pushed on.

"I think I came here a long time ago with my father," he called back. "We were on a hunt for wild pigs." His voice faltered. "But something else came out of the forest. I still don't know if we really saw it, or whether I just remember something that scared me as a child. But we didn't stay long after it had passed." He turned, and his eyes met Sienna's. "I'm sure it was nothing."

Sienna thought back to the warlord who ordered child sacrifice at the Tophet. What would scare a man like that?

It started to rain as they walked on and soon the ground

was slick with mud, their feet soaked through. The sound of rain dripping on leaves was a calm meditation, a welcome respite from the crazy pace of the last day. Sienna turned her face up so the cool drops touched her skin, glimpsing the sky through the canopy of leaves above. A sky that linked such diverse environments. On Earth-side, she would have to fly, drive, then trek huge distances to get between a buried Turkish city of lava and a jungle like this. Yet here in the Borderlands, they rubbed up against each other, pushed together by the ridges in the map.

Suddenly, Sienna thought she saw something move in the trees, a shadow swinging like a monkey, jumping from branch to branch. A hoot rang out, a low sound that echoed around them.

The group stopped, bunching together back to back as they faced out into the jungle. Finn held his sword in front of him, arms wide in a fighting stance. The hoot came again, and it sent a shiver down Sienna's spine.

"Any idea what it is?"

Finn shook his head. "But we need to keep moving. We have to be out of here before it gets dark."

They walked on, ducking under huge branches and climbing over logs.

"Keep an eye out as we walk," Finn said. "Look for slimy and scaly textures that stand out against the leaves. And don't touch anything. Try not to put your hand out even to help yourself over a log. That's when you're most likely to get bitten."

Sienna wondered what kind of first-aid knowledge the team had between them, what training they had in general. She was the newbie, and in the haste of the expedition, she had missed out on whatever passed for the standard training program. But she trusted Finn to keep them safe. He took the lead here, this was his land, after all.

She felt a sharp sting on her arm and slapped at a

mosquito the size of a coin. A splash of blood exploded from its body onto her skin. Sienna grimaced. It would be crazy to die of a mosquito bite in a jungle only miles from downtown Bath. She shook her head in wonder.

"Oh, that is cool." Xander's voice rang out.

Sienna turned to see him gazing at something on the trunk of a palm tree. A huge spider with a body as big as her hand and legs as long as her arm. It squatted on the bark, seemingly oblivious to their presence.

Xander pulled out his sketchbook and began to draw, sure strokes quickly recreating the shape of the spider on his page. He bent closer, and the spider reared up, fangs dripping venom. As Xander backed away, his eyes fixed on the creature, a smile on his face, Sienna couldn't help wondering what he did with his drawings. If he could only illustrate on maps created by others, did he have some pile of discarded maps with monsters on them ready to emerge into the world?

The rain grew heavier. The smell of the jungle intensified with the must of mold and the heavy fragrance of tropical flowers. Sienna felt suddenly alive. She had been slowly dying in the never-ending grind of her job back in Oxford. But this was adventure. This was geography made life.

She looked around with new eyes, noting the jungle seemed more Latin American than African. It was certainly as wet as the Amazon. A place where everything fought to survive, from the bugs biting through her shirt to the parasitic plants wound around the trees, up the food chain to the apex predators.

She tried not to think what they might be.

A skittering noise came from a log next to them. A giant centipede scurried across, its segmented body over a meter long in shades of ochre and orange. The striped legs all moved separately, and its head waved around as its antennae scanned ahead.

"This place is awesome," Xander said, with a wide grin.

A sharp cry rang out. They turned to see Perry wrapped in the coils of a huge snake, its muscled body completely encasing him.

"Titanoboa." Finn leapt forward, his sword outstretched to cut Perry free.

"Wait, don't harm it." Xander stepped in front. "It's a constrictor, so Perry has a moment. Let me try."

Xander reached out to touch the skin of the boa. Sienna recalled that such a creature, the largest snake ever discovered, had become extinct millions of years ago on Earthside. But these huge ancient creatures clearly thrived in the Borderlands.

Perry gasped as the coils tightened, his eyes wide with panic.

Xander stepped closer to the snake, its scales shining as rain dripped off them, rainbow colors on a copper skin marked with bands of black. The snake's head stretched out towards him, its tongue flickering. He stood there, letting the snake taste his skin, eyes closed as if he was communing with it. Sienna glimpsed the predator in him, a reflection of the reptile, perhaps.

Finn stepped closer, his sword raised. "Hurry."

Then, as suddenly as it had arrived, the boa unwrapped its coils from Perry's body. He dropped to the ground and the snake curled around the branch above.

Xander ran his hand along the boa's length, whispering something to it. When he turned, his eyes were as black as the snake's. Sienna blinked, and his eyes were green again.

"Time to go," he said. "It will be dark soon."

Mila put her arm around Perry's waist, supporting him until he caught his breath. They walked on through the jungle, stumbling over hidden branches as the light faded. It seemed like it would never end but then at last, there was a break in the trees ahead.

The quality of light changed from tropical green to a dull, cold grey as they approached. The edge of the jungle was a bright line where verdant foliage ended, and as they stepped out of the rainforest, Sienna could see derelict buildings clustered ahead of them, overgrown with weeds. The smell changed from lush jungle to the scent of smoke.

Tendrils of the forest reached out as if life wanted to encroach here but the green shoots curled up, dying on the black, brackish soil. The change in the landscape was disconcerting, like jumping through time and space all at once.

Finn bent and picked up handful of the soil, bringing it to his nose to smell. He rubbed it between his fingers before dropping it back to the ground, then wiped his hands on his clothes.

"I think this is Poveglia. I've heard rumors of it. They say the soil here is fifty percent human, made from burned and buried bodies." He frowned, looking ahead to the ruins. "They say it's cursed."

CHAPTER 16

Finn looked back into the forest. It was almost dark. He gestured ahead. "Whatever is here, it has to be safer than the jungle at night. Let's find a place to sleep."

They walked on, catching sight of a towering spire ahead, jutting out from the low buildings and stunted trees, and covered with twisted foliage. The sky was the shade of bruised plums, a sickening purple and black that barely lit the way ahead. The rain was gentler, but the ground was muddy underfoot and the wind a biting chill, as they walked on towards what had to be their haven for the night.

Finn dropped back to walk beside Sienna. "They say this was once an institution for the mentally ill and a quarantine island for those with the plague Earth-side. There are even rumors of experiments done on those the world wanted to forget."

They passed huge ovens with crumbling brick walls and metal doors hanging off rusty hinges. Sienna nodded towards them. "I suppose they needed to bake a lot of bread to feed all those people."

Finn shook his head with a half-smile. "Those are not for baking bread. The guards would shovel the dead into pits here, and when they were full, they would burn the bodies. Many of them weren't even dead, merely a step away from the end. My father thought about using this place as some kind of outpost." He looked up at the bell tower ahead of them. "But no one would stay here."

The path wound towards the bell tower around the edge of a deep pit. Sienna walked closer.

Finn put a hand on her arm. "Don't."

But she couldn't resist her curiosity. She walked closer and stared over the edge. Skeletons lay tangled together, their skulls facing in alternate directions on top of a jumble of long femurs, spines and pelvic bones.

There were so many.

The pit stretched as far as she could see in both directions. She raised a hand to her mouth, swallowing down the bile that rose. But she couldn't look away. Who were these people? Had they been pushed over into the Borderlands during life or only after death?

As she gazed at the bones, she could see they had been lying here for a very long time. There was no flesh left on them, and the pit smelled only of earth. Sienna frowned and bent closer as she noticed one of the skulls had a brick shoved between its teeth. What the –?

Finn came and stood by her side, noticing what she looked at. "It's a shroud eater," he said. "Some thought them to be vampires that fed on the bloody cloth surrounding the dead and then spread the plague to bring more victims. The brick forced into the vampire's mouth supposedly stopped it feeding and starved it to death." He shrugged. "Or maybe that's why they started burning people. To get rid of the food supply."

"It's horrible." Sienna pointed into the pit. "There are children in there."

Finn sighed. "There are places here in the Borderlands your people on Earth-side chose to forget. But you can't write people out of history, no matter what you do. There *are* witnesses, but they lie dead over here."

Sienna saw a hunger for justice on his face and a search for some kind of truth in this brutal place. Perhaps not all witnesses were in the grave.

Finn turned, and they walked on towards shelter. As they approached, details emerged from the semi-darkness. The bell tower had cracks through the stone, gaping holes and glassless windows, exposed bricks and broken walls, lichen crawling up its side. The crumbled state of the buildings reflected the fallen state of the world. This place had once been alive and beautiful, and now it was decayed and forgotten.

At the bell tower, they pushed open an old door hanging off its hinges. Inside at least there were walls and a roof, shelter from the cold wind and the rain.

They walked through an entrance hall with bars on the windows to keep those inside from escaping. The place was a strange juxtaposition of medieval plague pit and modern psychiatric hell. Vines grew through every window, and ceilings had collapsed in most of the rooms, rotted beams dropping down with the pervasive smell of mold and rot. The empty ruins had only a faint echo of the life that had once walked here.

They passed one room where jagged holes and lumps of metal riddled the walls, the edges still sharp.

"What happened here?" Sienna asked.

"A group of prisoners got hold of a hand grenade," Finn said. "They gathered tightly around it and pulled the pin. Their bodies were blown apart and the shrapnel embedded in the walls around us. That's one way out of hell, I suppose."

They walked on and found a room with a row of bed frames stacked against peeling wallpaper. The window was intact, there was no draught, and it felt warmer than the rest of the building. There was even a fireplace with decorative blue and white tiles covered in dust and ash. Underneath, birds flew over an expanse of ocean.

"Home, sweet home." Perry crossed to the fireplace. He grabbed a piece of discarded metal from a bed frame and poked around up the chimney. "Looks alright. I'll get the fire going. Then at least we can warm ourselves."

There was plenty of wooden furniture in the rooms around them. They collected rickety old chairs, breaking them against the walls to make smaller pieces. Perry conjured a flame, and soon they were warm and drying themselves in front of the fire. Perry got out his travel kettle and began boiling water. "Anyone else for tea?"

Sienna sipped the hot drink, considering how much better everything seemed to be inside a shelter with warmth. Perhaps things weren't so bad, after all.

As the others huddled around the fire, she suddenly had an acute desire to get away, craving some solitude after what had been a confusing and crazy twenty-four hours. Had it only been yesterday when she had heard of her grandfather's death?

She stood up. "I'm going to take a look around."

"I'll come with you," Mila said, standing up and dusting off her cargo pants.

"If you don't mind, I'd just like some space."

Mila paused and then nodded. "Of course, but don't go too far. Holler if you need us."

Sienna stepped outside the room and walked a little way in the semi-darkness, listening to the voices of the team fading behind her. She pulled her pack open and found the torch. Mila said it was only for emergencies, but she wouldn't be long.

She walked down the corridor, her footsteps an echo of the past, clouds of dust rising in her wake. She shone the torch into the rooms on either side, catching glimpses of broken furniture, desks and chairs, and then in one, the light glinted off a metal cage.

Sienna stepped into the room, playing the light over the

structure. As she walked closer, she saw a skeleton curled at the bottom, its arms wrapped around its head, a defensive posture it must have died in. She had read enough about the history of psychiatry to know about the atrocities committed in the name of science, but the cage was still disturbing.

A scratching sound came from the corner and Sienna spun around, her torchlight catching the thick tail of something furry as it scurried into a hole in the wall. A rat. Much bigger than anything she'd seen before. She shuddered to think of the food supply that would have sustained creatures here.

There was a door near the cage, and she opened it to find a small padded room beyond, the cushioned walls covered in lichen and mold. Rain dripped through a hole in the ceiling. Although the space was clearly man-made, it felt like nature was reclaiming this asylum, one room at a time. She shut the door and went back out to the corridor.

She turned to see the rosy glow of the fire coming from a doorway far back up where she had walked from. She considered returning to the team, but she was relishing this time alone. Sienna walked on and found a huge ballroom with a wooden floor that must have once been polished to a shine. Painted panels of flowers and fruit covered the walls. A pile of old suitcases in faded primary colors lay covered in dust and broken masonry from the partially caved-in ceiling.

A piano stood against one wall. She touched a key, and a dull note echoed in the room. A skittering noise came from within the instrument. She backed away and turned towards the end of the ballroom where another door led away from the main corridor. Sienna walked on into the heart of the institution.

In the middle of the next room, a dentist's chair sat, fully reclinable, but with thick leather straps for the wrists, ankles and head. A sink in the corner overflowed with ferns and moss, verdant life in the ruins. Next to it, a metal table with drawers covered in thick cobwebs. Sienna used her sleeve to brush them away and pulled the drawer open. A syringe with a thick needle lay next to a series of scalpels, the blades glinting in the light. The edges still looked sharp enough. She picked one up and wrapped the end in a piece of rag, slipping it into her pack before walking on. It made her feel better to have a makeshift weapon.

The next room had once been a morgue, the thick doors open wide to display racks of shelving behind. There were nine slots tapering into darkness and Sienna couldn't help thinking of who might have lain here last. They must have been important to avoid the grave pits outside.

Around the walls, there were racks of shelving with glass jars and test-tubes arrayed upon them. The jars were covered in dust, but there were shadows inside. Sienna reached up and brushed the front of one then recoiled as the side of a diseased face turned towards her in the liquid.

A rustling sound came from behind her.

She turned as a rat burst out from the shadows, running across the floor towards her. Sienna jumped, a gasp escaping her throat. The rat was big as a dog, its teeth bared as it approached, red eyes fixed on her.

Then out of the shadows, more emerged.

They moved as a pack, black-bristled fur over muscled bodies and thick pink tails like rope. The biggest rat darted in, teeth snapping. Sienna backed away and climbed quickly onto a gurney against the wall, pulling her feet out of its way just in time.

The pack ran forward, furry bodies clustering around the gurney, moving it on squeaky wheels as they swirled around the metal legs. A stench of feces and rotting flesh rose up from the pack and Sienna gagged as she looked down into the vortex of bodies. They looked up at her with the fixation of hungry animals desperate for a meal.

"Help!" she cried. "Finn! Mila? Anyone?"

She thumped on the gurney sending a metallic ringing sound out into the corridor. But there was no sound of running feet, no voices. She had wandered too far.

She was alone.

Sienna thought back to how she had sat in the stacks of the Bodleian, lost in the books, not knowing which way to go. Back then, she had to use someone else's map to escape, but Mila had said *anything* could be a map for a Blood Cartographer. She could create her own map and walk through it.

She looked down at the stinking rats with their sharp yellow teeth.

It was worth a try.

Sienna pulled the scalpel from her pack and looked at the blade, then down at the rats. She could use it as a weapon and try to get out of here. She could wait for someone to rescue her, or she could see what she was capable of.

She winced in anticipation of the pain. "It won't hurt, it won't hurt," she whispered, then sliced into her forearm.

It did hurt, and she didn't even want to consider the diseases she might have given herself with the dirty blade. But it was better than getting eaten by giant rats.

As blood welled up, she used the fingertips of her other hand to dab a little of the liquid and then started to paint on the wall. She visualized the asylum and the corridors she had walked through, sketching the lines of the area where the team waited.

She drew the dimensions of the room and the pathway to the outside where skeletons lay in their eternal rest. She sensed the orientation of the building on the earth beneath and drew her compass rose beside the sketch, with its true north an echo of what she felt inside. It was like a magnet pulling her closer and Sienna gasped as she glimpsed the intoxicating power of her blood.

But would it be enough? What if she couldn't make it work?

The rats snarled below, bumping against the gurney. As she rocked from side to side, she closed her eyes and placed her hand in the middle of the rough, bloody map.

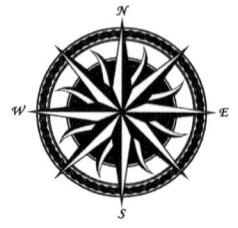

CHAPTER 17

SIENNA'S FINGERS TINGLED AS she thought of Perry and his kettle of tea, Finn whittling his running horse, Xander sketching and Mila staring into the flames. She brought life to the map in her mind and felt a lifting inside, the world as three-dimensional space below her.

Then she was back, sucked into the room where the fire burned and the team sat waiting. Sienna opened her eyes to see them all staring at her.

"Holy crap, you gave me a fright," Mila said. "Thought you were a ghost or something." She grinned. "Guess you're getting better at Mapwalking then."

Sienna nodded. "I … I got a bit lost." Her voice shook as the intensity of the experience rocked through her. Her breath came fast, and she sat down heavily by the fire.

Perry held out a mug of tea. "You look like you had a scare. This will help."

Sienna took it and sipped for a moment. She felt their eyes upon her.

"There were giant rats," Sienna said when she got her breath back.

Finn jumped up. "Mutant cloud rats." He began to pull the bed frames in front of the door. "Quickly, help me." Perry and Mila stacked the gaps with broken furniture as

Finn explained. "Supposedly, they escaped from some experimental lab on Earth-side, and they've found plenty to eat in the Borderlands. There are stories of them ravaging villages, swarming and devouring anything in their path. There can't be too many of them here though as there's not enough food to support a colony."

"There were enough of them," Sienna said.

Finn turned and met her eyes, nodding at her unspoken horror. "We'll watch in pairs while the others get some sleep. It's a few hours until dawn, and then we can be on our way when the rats sleep."

Xander yawned. "Wake me when it's my shift." He pulled his sleeping bag around himself and rolled over with his back to the fire.

Mila put a hand on Sienna's shoulder. "Get some rest. I'll take first watch with Finn."

* * *

Bristled bodies pinned her down and sharp teeth ripped at her flesh as she screamed for help. Sienna sat up sharply, gasping for breath.

"It's okay." Perry put a hand on her arm. "Must be a nightmare. You're safe."

His voice was calming, and he reached for the kettle, pouring her a steaming cup of tea. "Here you go."

"Is tea your answer to everything?" Sienna took a sip.

Perry gave a wry smile. "I have more questions than answers, to be honest, but I find tea helps me live with them."

Dawn filtered through the barred windows, casting a sickly pale light over the team. Mila lay curled next to the fire, sleeping bag pulled up over her head. Finn lay resting on his back, hand on his sword. His eyes were open, and he looked ready to spring into action. Xander sat on the pile of broken furniture, sketching.

"You should have woken me," Sienna said. "I would have taken my turn."

Perry shook his head. "Oh, don't worry. You're new, and Mapwalking takes it out of you. Surely Bridget told you about it?"

"She didn't tell me much really. It all happened so fast. What do you mean?"

Xander stopped sketching and looked over at her, his eyes wide. "You don't know?"

Mila turned inside her sleeping bag and sat up, rubbing her eyes. "I should have told you, but I thought we'd have more time before you used it properly." She took a deep breath. "Mapwalking comes with a cost. Every time you use it in the Borderlands, you exchange your blood for a drop of shadow and you begin to change. If you use it too much, you can't cross back into Earth-side."

Perry stirred the embers of the fire, his face troubled. "That's how Shadow Cartographers are born."

Mila continued. "And it's why Bridget can't come through anymore, or some of the older Mapwalkers. They can't risk it."

Her words echoed through Sienna's mind, and she imagined the taint of darkness seeping through her veins. Her skin prickled at the thought, and the cut throbbed on her arm. "How many times can I use it safely?"

"There's no way of knowing." Xander's hazel eyes fixed on hers. "Every Mapwalker is different, and the amount of blood needed depends on the journey ... and the number of people you carry with you."

"It's why we can't just use our magic all the time," Mila said. "And why we let you rest. We need you for the next part of the journey." She took a deep breath, looking at Sienna with an apology in her eyes. "You might as well know this too. The most powerful maps are all made from the skin of Blood Cartographers. They are most effective if they are used without a drop of shadow in them. Those are the master maps, the ones protecting the border."

"The younger the skin, the less traveled, the better the map," Xander said. "Your flesh and blood are the most precious thing we have."

"That's why the Shadow Cartographers are breeding Halbrasse." Finn sat up, his face contorted with anger. "They skin the children and use rare blood to make new maps."

"It's true." Mila nodded. "And we can't keep up on Earthside because we don't countenance breeding programs. They will soon outnumber us."

Finn looked at Sienna. "You have to leave the Borderlands. If they take you, they will –"

"I'm here for my father." She thought of him held captive, bled for the ink that the Shadow Cartographers would tattoo on the skins of half-breed children. Nausea churned her stomach. She stood up. "We need to go. It's light outside and time to move on."

"Wait, I think we might be back on charted territory now, so I might be able to navigate better." Mila unrolled a skin map from her bag and pointed to the labyrinth drawn upon it. "Bridget gave me this. When it was made, the labyrinth pushed right up against Poveglia. It can't have moved too far from here."

Sienna touched the edge of the map, finally understanding the pedigree of the leather. "Whose is it?" she said, softly.

"It's old." Mila stroked the edges. "But Bridget said it was given willingly." She looked up at Sienna. "It is the fate of Blood Cartographers to become the maps that guide us."

Sienna looked down at the twisting lines of the labyrinth, and for a moment, she felt like running. She could use her magic one last time, use the star map to get back to Bath, sell the shop to Sir Douglas Mercator and move to London. Live a normal life. But would she really be able to live with the knowledge of the Borderlands out here? And could she leave her father to be bled dry in a shadowy dungeon?

Finn bent to the map and traced a line to the side of Poveglia Island. "The greater part of the jungle is new in this area, pushed through recently, but if this is accurate, I think its incursion would have pushed the labyrinth to the southwest. Here." He pointed to an area of swampland, marked on the map by reed symbols. "It's a few hours on foot."

They packed up and walked into the dawn, silent except for the tread of their feet on the hard earth. Sienna looked up as the sun broke through the clouds, turning her face to the warmth of the rays. It was strange to think the same sun shone down on Earth-side and the Borderlands alike when so much was different over here.

This land was off the edge of the maps she had studied at school, its lines inverse to the borders she knew by heart. As a child, Sienna had learned the capital cities of every country, testing herself against the map of the world on her bedroom wall. After her father had disappeared, her mother tore it down and removed every atlas from the house. But the color-coded countries were so fixed in her brain she could recall them even now.

The Borderlands were on the other side, the fifth point of the compass, and as places from Earth-side were pushed through, they ended up here crushed up against each other, pushing older places towards the Uncharted. Its very name called to something in her, a desire to go deeper into this untamed land. She was starting to understand why the Shadow Cartographers fell so far.

"What's the difference between a labyrinth and a maze?" Perry asked, breaking the silence as they walked. "I mean, what are we expecting to find?"

"Technically, a labyrinth has only one way in and one way out," Mila said. "And one way to reach the center. It's not meant to be difficult to navigate."

Perry frowned. "What's the point then?"

"Most labyrinths are ritualistic or spiritually significant,"

Sienna explained. "So the path may be winding, but there is only one route to the center, or to God. The faithful walk to the middle of the labyrinth to ritually kill Satan in a triumph over death."

"Or the monster at the heart of the labyrinth," Xander noted. "Like the Minotaur, half-bull, half-man who devoured the tribute of young men and women in ancient Crete."

Sienna remembered going with her father to visit Chartres Cathedral one summer years ago, part of a father-daughter field trip to see some of France. But now she wondered what he was really doing there since clearly, he had kept so much about his life a secret.

They had stood in front of the rose labyrinth, set into the flagstones of the nave in the Gothic cathedral. Her father explained that pilgrims had walked this labyrinth for a thousand years. The site had originally been dedicated to a fertility goddess and the Church built upon it to honor the Virgin Mary, who gave birth to a god who would save mankind. Perhaps the obsession of the Shadow Cartographers stemmed from this myth, the birth of a powerful Mapwalker who would enable them to reshape the border.

"So what about a maze?" Perry asked. "Is it just more complicated?"

"There are multiple ways in and out, dead ends and choices where you might end up trapped." Mila looked at the map again. "I think where we're going is a labyrinth, so it should be simple enough."

Finn turned at her words. "My father has sent people here before. Two commanders who betrayed him were given the choice of the fire sacrifice or the labyrinth. They chose this way, but they never returned."

They walked on in silence. The sun rose higher in the sky, and the mist burned off. Before them, a vast wall of bright green stretched across the horizon.

"More jungle?" Mila asked. "Have we come the wrong way?"

Finn shook his head. "Look at the height. It's exactly the same all the way across. It has to be a man-made barrier."

They walked on and soon they could see a giant hedge rising above them with thick, impenetrable foliage stretching as far as the eye could see in either direction. Branches and leaves intertwined in layers, so it would take an age to hack their way through. Each branch had hooked thorns, like a barbed wire fence preventing anyone from passing.

Finn looked along the hedge in both directions. "I can't see where an entrance might be. Is it marked on your map, Mila?"

As they bent over to examine it, Sienna walked up close to the hedge. There was not a leaf out of place, and the top of it was neatly trimmed. She tried to imagine whose job it might be to keep it so pristine, but then again, things worked differently over here. It smelled of the wild highlands and native herbs but underneath, an animal note of musk.

There was something, perhaps someone, alive inside.

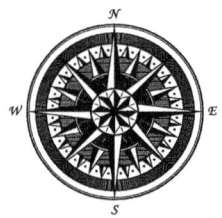

CHAPTER 18

SIENNA RAISED HER HAND and pressed it against the hedge, feeling the prickle of branches against her palm. Suddenly, she felt a pulse of energy from within the labyrinth, something pulling her forward.

Blood answering to blood.

This had to be the right direction. She pressed her palm more firmly and felt the prick of a thorn pierce her skin. She pulled her hand away sharply to see a trickle of blood running down the center.

But where the drop of ruby liquid touched them, the branches started unraveling, twisting away from each other with a creaking and rustling sound, opening up a hole in the wall. The others turned to watch as the space grew until there was an arch big enough for them to walk through in single file.

"If in doubt, bleed on it." Xander raised an eyebrow. "Are you okay?"

She nodded, rubbing at the tiny wound in her palm.

Finn stepped through the thick tangle of branches first, his sword raised, eyes darting to either side as he scouted for danger. He nodded back to them, and the others followed him inside. The animal smell was almost overpowering.

"Careful now," he whispered. "There's something here.

Keep your voices low." He looked at Sienna. "Which way?"

She glanced in either direction. Both ways were exactly the same, long corridors of green with towering hedges boxing both sides. How was she supposed to decide?

Her palm throbbed. Mila's words echoed back to her, about how each use of blood magic let a little shadow inside to take its place. But the minutes ticked by and she couldn't think of any other way, so she placed her palm against the hedge directly in front of the entrance they had made. Perhaps the maze itself would lead the way.

Once again, the branches untwisted, opening a space into the next corridor. But this time, the sound of breaking branches and a soft huffing noise came from beyond.

Xander poked his head around the corner before anyone could stop him and then ducked back quickly, his eyes bright with excitement. "Gigantopithecus," he whispered. "A giant ape. Extinct on Earth-side but this one looks like drawings I've seen."

Sienna walked into the gap in the hedge and peered around the side, Finn close behind her.

A giant ape stood on its hind legs picking off foliage from the top of the hedge, displaying its full height of over ten feet. Its meaty hands were the size of giant baseball mitts and its thigh muscles the width of tree trunks. It grabbed a handful of leaves and put them in its mouth, chewing as it dropped back onto its knuckles. Then it looked in their direction. Sienna felt a jolt of adrenalin as it met her eyes.

"Look down," Finn breathed. "Back away slowly."

They edged their way back into the branches as the ape lumbered along the corridor towards them, the thump of its great fists shaking the earth. Sienna's mind raced as she considered how in hell she was meant to shut the opening she had made. Her blood opened a path, but she couldn't take it back.

"Don't run or it will charge," Xander said quickly. "If it's like other apes, it won't attack if we're submissive. Bow your heads as it comes through. Don't meet its eyes."

The giant ape pushed through the branches. They cracked and ripped apart across its huge barrel chest as it emerged and stood tall. It slapped its chest and bared its teeth, roaring a challenge. Sienna kept her eyes down, her heart pounding as the vibrations of its call rippled through her. She saw Finn's hand tighten on its sword and willed him not to use it. Perhaps the ape would lose interest and move off.

But it took a huge step forward towards them and swung its giant fist.

Mila dove sideways, rolling away as the meaty arm slammed down where she had stood just a moment before.

"Guess submission doesn't work." Xander pulled the skin map from his pocket, dropped it to the ground as he bellowed, drawing the beast's attention away as Asada, his lion, stepped from the leather.

The lion roared and charged at the ape, barreling into its great body, knocking the beast to the ground. But the ape put its great arms around the lion and shoved it away enough to swing a giant fist into Asada's face. The lion rolled away, snarling, the roars of the two beasts combining into a fearsome cacophony.

They ran at each other, the ape howling as the lion attacked. Dust exploded into the air as the two gigantic creatures tussled, the lion slicing and biting, the ape thumping and rolling.

A slash of claws, and bright blood flew from the ape's chest.

It turned and bit deep into the lion's flank, and the big cat yelped with pain. They were well matched, but then the wound in the lion's side healed over, and its ferocity redoubled. It slashed and bit and tore at the ape, beating it down, tiring it until the great creature lay on the ground, chest heaving, its blood soaking the earth.

The lion bent its muzzle to the wound in the ape's chest and began to tear strips of flesh from it. The ape moaned in pain as it was eaten alive, the sound so similar to a human in distress that tears sprang to Sienna's eyes. The ape was some kind of distant ancestor, despite how wild this one was. Xander watched with a dark satisfaction on his face, almost as if he was the one feeding.

Then a throaty roar came from behind the maze wall in front of them.

The lion looked up, muzzle coated with blood. It stood motionless, and Finn drew his sword again. Another roar answered – and another. There were more giant apes, and they heard one of their own in pain.

They were coming.

"Run." Xander pushed Sienna ahead of him. "Get the path opened in front of us."

He dropped back, calling Asada to stand with him, Finn on his other side, sword drawn, Mila next to him.

"Come on." Perry dragged Sienna away. "We've got to find a way through. The others will follow."

They turned a corner, and Sienna felt a tug inwards. "Here." She stopped and pressed her bleeding palm against the wall. Again, it opened for her.

Perry pushed her through. "Just keep opening the way ahead. I'll signal the others."

Sienna crossed over the next corridor, trying to tune out the dull thud of fists against flesh, the snarl of the lion and the roaring of the apes behind her. At least there were no screams … yet. She had to hurry.

The maze began to twist more tightly, the tug inside calling her onwards. After four more walls, she reached a gate made of thick metal bars as tall as the woven branches around it.

"Here. I've found the center!" she called back through the thick walls of the maze. Had they heard her?

Then she saw Mila running through, Perry and the others close behind as they tried to outrun the giant apes.

The gate hung open on its hinges, the lock cracked by whoever had come before them. Sienna darted through and held it open. "Come on!"

Mila rushed through, panting as she tried to catch her breath. Perry and Finn darted ahead of Xander, who lingered as Asada the lion still fought. Sienna could almost feel the adrenalin of the fight through his powerful proxy. Xander's hands were raised, the muscles on his back tense as he drove the lion forward with his will. It savaged the first of the attacking apes as it tried to push through the narrow hedge, ripping into the thick neck. Blood spurted out, and the great ape collapsed, blocking the gap.

The beasts behind bellowed in anger and frustration, but they couldn't pass the wounded body. The lion darted in again, raking at the eyes of the giant ape as if it wanted to tear its face away.

"Come on!" Perry shouted. "Enough. Leave it now, or finish it off."

Xander spun, his eyes fixed on Perry, his face contorted like the lion who stood by his side. Almost as one with his illustrated beast. For a moment, it looked like he would send Asada to rip the other Mapwalker to shreds. Then the wildness left his eyes.

Xander took a breath and slumped forward. He placed the scrap of map leather on the ground, and the lion stalked into it.

Once they were all through, Mila pulled the gate shut and Perry wrapped a little piece of map leather around the broken lock. He conjured just enough flame to fuse the lock closed, so the gate shut firmly behind them.

The sound of the apes faded away as the other beasts moved off.

"There must be another way round," Finn said. "They won't give up."

"Then we better hurry up." Sienna turned to see where they were.

A circle of flat rocks formed a raised platform. In the middle, a pile of charred wood and human bones steamed in the sun.

"It's a pyre," Mila said. "Work of the Shadow Cartographers."

They clambered onto the pyre, the smell of burned wood and roasted flesh intensifying around them. Birds of prey circled above, beady eyes on the carrion below.

Mila used a partially burned branch to rake the pile of burned bones, looking for a sign of what might have happened here.

"You need to look at this, Sienna."

A small round object glinted in the afternoon sun. Sienna looked more closely and realized with a jolt what it was.

Her father's five-pointed compass.

She would recognize it anywhere. Engraved upon the face were the things her father valued, a book, the face of the goddess Aquae Sulis representing Bath, and enclosed within the glass, a lock of her baby hair. Tears welled in Sienna's eyes.

She fell to her knees in the ash. The grey dust billowed around her as she reached for the compass. She wiped it clean to reveal the patterns beneath.

"It's his, isn't it?" Mila said, softly.

Sienna nodded. "He was here." She looked at the pile of bones. "You don't think …?"

Mila shook her head. "He was too valuable to burn. The compass could have been stolen by someone else. These bodies might be rebels or smugglers."

Finn hunkered down to kneel next to Sienna. His closeness comforted her, and she could see a reflection of her loss in his dark eyes. "I know smugglers, and I know rebels. None of them would have left this here when they could get so much for it."

A roar sounded from just outside the gate.

They turned to see the giant apes gathered outside the bars, testing the strength as they eyed the enemy inside. One of the beasts slammed into the metal, its war cry ringing out. The gate shuddered and shook, but it held.

For now.

"We're not getting back out the maze that way," Xander said. "Even if we all fight, we can't hold them off for long. We need another way out of here."

One of the apes started to climb, pulling itself up the gate, hand over hand, baring its yellow teeth as it snarled at them.

Sienna clicked the button at the bottom of the compass, and it flicked open. Inside, the bronze was engraved with his name, John Farren. And on the opposite side, there was a carving, a tiny map inscribed on the inner surface with a castle at its center.

Sienna ran her fingers slowly over the carving, thinking of her father etching these lines. It was rough, but perhaps it was enough. Together with what they had learned before, together with Finn's desire to see his sister and her own to see her father, with Mila's knowledge of where the castle lay. Together they might be able to make it.

First one and then another ape dropped down on their side of the gate. They roared and lumbered towards the team.

"If in doubt …" Xander said. "Quickly now!"

Sienna's heart thumped as she considered the drip of shadow she would exchange for her blood. But they had no option.

She pulled the scalpel from her bag and used it to cut her hand slightly, dripping blood onto the map in the compass.

It filled the lines, scarlet and gold together with the rays of the sun forming a mesmerizing pool. All she had to do was fly into it.

Sienna felt lightness inside, even though they were surrounded by the stink of beasts with decaying flesh between their teeth, and the burned bones upon which they stood. This was a place of death, and they were going further towards darkness, but she could sense they were almost there. She would see her father again.

"Now would be good," Xander shouted as he turned to face the oncoming charge.

Sienna put one hand around the bloody compass and held her other hand out. The others gripped it and held each other, entwined together as the beasts bore down upon them.

Her heart pounded as she remembered Finn wasn't a Mapwalker. How could he come through? She looked over at him, eyes wide with fear. She didn't want to lose him now.

He nodded back at her. "It's okay, just do your part and I will follow through. And if you make it to the castle without me …" He looked over at Mila. "Then you *will* find my sister and set her free."

Mila nodded. "Quickly now."

Perry hurled a blast of flame, pushing the beasts back. They howled as flame caught fur and one rolled itself into the pile of ash, pieces of bone sticking to its flesh. Then it came for them, a thing of fury and ash, bone and flame.

Sienna closed her eyes, trying to tune out the roar of the beasts, and the expectation of her friends.

She thought of her father, fixing the map from the compass in her mind, and reached for blood in the darkness.

CHAPTER 19

One moment Sienna felt the sun on her skin and the next it was cold and clammy, the roar of the beasts replaced by quiet water dripping on stone.

"We made it." Finn's voice was filled with wonder.

Sienna opened her eyes to find them in a storage area with a low ceiling and walls of thick stone. They matched the dungeon she and Mila had visited before, and it certainly felt like the same castle. How many of these could there be in the Borderlands?

The sound of voices came from beyond a doorway, and the group melted into the shadows. The voices came closer and then passed by.

"They were talking about taking food up to the women," Finn said, his face set with anger. "I'm going after them."

Mila put a hand on his arm. "Wait a minute. We need to decide what the plan is first."

Finn shook her hand off, spinning towards her, his finger jabbing the air in front of her face.

"I am here for my sister, and you promised to help me."

Mila crossed her arms. "I promised to get you to the castle. I never said we would help you find her and take her home."

Sienna watched the two of them face off. They couldn't

find her father and Finn's sister at the same time, but the Borderlander had risked his life and his future to get here. They wouldn't have made it this far without him, and she couldn't leave him now.

"I'm going with Finn," she said. "We'll find his sister, then we'll come back and together, we'll find my father and the rest of the Mapwalker team. We won't be long. By the time we come back, you need to be ready to move."

* * *

Finn slipped through the corridor of the castle, Sienna close behind. He was surprised she'd chosen to come along, but he was glad of her help. They followed the servants at a distance through the twisting and turning corridors.

A scream came from up ahead, a primal sound of pain recognizable in any culture as a woman giving birth. Then the scream of a newborn, forced into a world they didn't choose. Finn could smell metallic blood soaked into straw, like an animal's den. He put his hand on the wall to steady himself as thoughts of his sister came to him.

The Shadow Cartographers had come to the citadel, taking those on the edge of womanhood. Isabel had only been fifteen, but already beautiful. She had an edge of magic, a mild gift she used to grow plants in the barren ground of the broken city. But with such a gift, other kinds of magic could be dormant, unlocked if she bred with another.

Finn had heard rumors of what came out of these halls over the years. The Elite Shadow Cartographers, wielding blood magic with precision, creating new worlds from their veins. But also the mutants, those whose magic coalesced into something twisted, tested and found wanting, fodder for sacrifice at the Tophet where the blood of children fueled the dark magic of the mages.

"Are you alright?" Sienna's whisper came from behind him.

Finn pushed away from the wall and nodded, leading her onwards. His heart pounded as he imagined what he might find ahead. Would Isabel even be here? She might be dead from childbirth, or he'd heard the girls who couldn't get pregnant were slaughtered, their blood used in ritual. Useless mouths weren't tolerated here.

He crept forward, peeking around a corner to check the way ahead.

A guard stood in front of a doorway, the edges decorated with horns of plenty, a bountiful harvest and phallic symbols. The fertility halls. A guard paced back and forth in front of the door, alert and ready.

"I'll distract him," Sienna whispered.

Before Finn could stop her, she walked out around the corner towards the guard, hands relaxed by her side. Finn remained in the shadows as the guard turned at her footsteps, his eyes widening at the sight of her. The man leered as Sienna exaggerated the swing of her hips, walking towards him with intent. He gripped the pommel of his sword tighter.

"What are you doing here?" the guard demanded.

Sienna rested against the wall next to him, angling her body so the guard turned, his back to Finn.

"I'm looking for someone." Sienna smiled. "I heard you might be able to help. I'm willing to do whatever it takes to find her." The guard stepped closer, his hand lifting from his sword to caress her cheek. Sienna leaned into him, pressing her body against his.

Finn slipped around the corner, and as the man reached to pull her body closer, Finn brought the pommel of his sword down hard on the back of the guard's head.

A dull thunk and the guard slumped to the ground. Finn would have finished him off, but Sienna stepped over him and bent to pull off the man's belt.

"We'll hogtie him and drag him into the tunnel," she whispered.

They worked quickly and soon had the unconscious guard back in the shadows. By the time he regained consciousness, they'd be long gone.

Sienna looked down at the guard and over at Finn. He felt her eyes appraising him, and he almost blushed under her gaze.

"There'll be more guards inside. It'll be tight, but you'll just fit this uniform."

"No." There was no way he was going to wear such an evil costume and drag Sienna like a captive around this unholy place. "There's too much that could go wrong."

She put her hand on his chest. "I'll be fine, Finn. I won't end up like your sister. We can't get rid of all the guards, so we need to walk unseen. This is the best way."

Finn took a deep breath. He had helped Sienna escape once, and now he felt responsible for her. There was no way he would put her back in danger again, especially here, where women only existed for one thing.

She bent to pull the guard's uniform off. "Help me." When he didn't move, she looked up at him. "Come on, we don't have much time. You want to find Isabel, don't you?"

His sister's name made Finn gasp. It had been so long since he had heard anyone else speak it, for once the girls were taken, they were dead to their families. It was ill-advised to speak of them again, except as the martyred dead. After all, it was an honor to be a vessel for a Halbrasse.

He might be so close to her now.

Finn bent to help Sienna pull off the guard's uniform and swapped his own clothes for the heavy armor of the guard. It shone, freshly polished, with the half-moon of the Shadow Cartographers. He wrapped a piece of rope around Sienna's wrists, tying them behind her back.

"Are you sure it's okay?" He whispered in her ear. "Not too tight?"

He was so close that he could smell the scent of her, a faint vanilla underneath sweat and the blood they had shed together. He had never thought a Mapwalker would look at him the way she did, but it seemed she saw past the external to his inner self.

"Push me ahead of you. Be a little rough. You won't hurt me."

Finn took a deep breath and then pushed Sienna forward a little. "Walk." His voice was stronger now, and he channeled his father as he assumed the swagger of authority.

They walked together into the tangle of winding passages beyond the archway, and as they passed, they peered through the barred windows of each of the cells. One woman lay crumpled on the floor, her body like a broken doll. Another banged on the door, yelling as she pulled at the bars. She screamed at them, pointing at Finn, calling him names Sienna recognized even though the woman spoke in a foreign language. It didn't matter what race you were here, only whether you could breed.

In another cell, a grunting sound and the rhythmic slap of flesh on flesh betrayed what occurred within, as the sound of weeping filled the corridors around them. It was a desolate, ugly place. Finn slowed his steps, wanting to help each one, but there were so many ...

Sienna turned, her eyes bright with anger, a flush of red on her cheeks. "We must go on. Your sister might still be here." She looked around her. "We can't help these women one by one. We have to change things at a more fundamental level. And I promise you that we will, Finn. But if we're caught, it's all over. For both of us."

He nodded and as they walked on, the cells changed in nature. Women in different stages of pregnancy paced inside or lay chained on their backs, bellies looming large, closer to term the further they went in.

Then suddenly, there were empty cells. Finn stopped,

looking inside of one, noting the crumpled blanket on the rickety bed, drops of blood on the floor. These women had gone to give birth and then they would be returned to the front cells ready to breed again.

Finn pounded his fist on the door of the last cell. "I'm too late."

A creak came from the end of the corridor.

Sienna slumped to the ground next to Finn's leg in a posture of submission, her head on one side, hair covering her face. A guard walked past, looking over with approval at what he presumed was another man's violent act.

After he passed by, his footsteps fading, Sienna looked towards the door. "There's something else behind there."

Finn took a step towards the door, sweat prickling his back, palms damp with fear of what he might find.

Sienna stood up and walked purposefully towards the door. Finn followed her. She pulled it open and immediately, a stench hit them from within. The smell of emptied bodies, disease and the rot of death. There were several bigger cells back here with up to ten women in each. They were thin and bedraggled, many of them lying on the floor or propped against the walls, some with bloody tunics. They were quiet, resigned to their fate.

"These are the ones they're finished with," Sienna whispered.

Finn frowned. "But some of the women return home. I know one in the Resistance, and she told me that when they've done their duty, they can leave. So why are these women here?"

"Perhaps they have to agree to something?" Sienna wondered aloud. "Maybe the ones who come back have promised to give up others, have promised to send other women. Maybe these are the ones who wouldn't agree."

Finn looked into the first cell, his eyes resting on each of the women in turn, each one a daughter, a mother, perhaps a sister or wife. Each one loved, and yet somehow, they ended up here. He wondered how many looked for them and his heart broke for those women who would never know they were loved. He wished he could help more, but even if they unlocked the doors to let these women out, they would perish on the journey home. They had no strength, and perhaps no will left to survive.

His anger at the Shadow Cartographers rose up inside. They needed to stop this. The only reason to breed Halbrasse was to invade and shift the border into Earth-side. But peace would mean that the Borderlands could develop into a better place. There must be a way. He looked over at Sienna. She wasn't like the other Mapwalkers, she could see both sides. Perhaps she could help.

Finn walked to the next prison door, gazing at each woman in turn. One woman had a shaved head, her face turned to the wall. But the shape of her nose, the set of her mouth were still recognizable.

"Isabel," he whispered.

CHAPTER 20

SOME OF THE WOMEN in the cell looked up with hollow eyes at his voice, but Isabel didn't move. Her chest rose and fell, but it was a faint movement. Her pale skin was almost translucent, and there was blood on her tunic.

"Isabel," he said again, louder this time.

She opened her eyes, and a half-smile played around her mouth as she saw him, but she didn't move, her body too weak.

Finn rattled at the door, but the lock held. Some of the women inside the cell began to moan, calling out to him in different languages. But Finn only had eyes for his sister.

"We need the key," Sienna said, softly. "It's the only way you're going to get to her. I'll stay here, and you go follow the guard."

Finn nodded, reining in his anger. There was no use trying to pick a fight with the guards when he needed to get into the cell as fast as possible. He jogged back down the corridor after the man who had passed them a little while ago.

He walked through into the main section and heard voices down the corridor. Two guards stood outside one of the women's cells. The one who had passed them told a dirty joke as the other man adjusted his uniform, a look of satisfaction on his face. Finn tuned out their words, determined not to get into a fight right now, even though he was desperate to pull out his sword and cut them both into pieces. There was a bunch of keys on the first guard's belt. The men looked up as he approached.

Finn smiled. "Hey there. I need the key for the holding cell in the back section."

The guard looked at him, eyes narrowing. "Haven't seen you around here before."

Finn nodded. "I'm new, just arrived from Old Aleppo with a girl of Mapwalker lineage. You saw her back in the corridor."

The guard nodded. "She looked fresh. Why are you putting her with the rejects?"

Finn sighed, affecting a look of resignation. "I might have sampled the merchandise on the journey, and I promised her a visit with her sister in exchange for her silence. She's a good girl. She'll behave, I promise."

The guard raised his eyebrows and laughed, the hollow noise echoing down the corridor. "Good girl? That's a riot. None of this lot are good, or at least they're only good enough for breeding." He paused, then smiled knowingly. "But we all sample the merchandise, friend. I'll pay her a visit myself later."

The guard shuffled the keys on his belt and pulled off a large brass one. "This will open the holding cells, but bring it back to the guard station as soon as you're done."

Finn took the key, nodded and turned away, walking back down the corridor. As soon as he was out of sight, he clenched his fists and exhaled sharply, pushing down his desire to kill something.

He walked through the final door and put the key in the lock, turning it with a click. As he opened it, some of the women crawled towards him, their arms outstretched as they moaned, asking for pity. Sienna slipped into the room after Finn and began talking to them, her eyes welling with tears.

Finn went to Isabel and pulled her into his arms, leaning back against the wall as he rocked her gently. She was so thin that her bones stuck out through her skin and she smelled of infection.

"It's okay, Izzy. I'm here now, I've come to take you home."

Her eyes flickered open, blue like the sky above the library when they had escaped the darkness of the city together to read in their haven. There was pain in her gaze, a deep suffering from months of torment and grief for what she had lost.

Her lips moved, and Finn bent his head so he could hear her.

"So good to see you." Her voice rasped, the breath of someone shut away from the light for too long.

He pulled out the little horse he had whittled and pushed it into her hand. "I made this for you. She's running like you always wanted to. It's time to run now, Izzy."

"It's too late." Isabel lifted her hand and placed it on her belly over the rust marks of dried blood.

Sienna came over and knelt next to them. She helped Isabel lift her tunic to reveal a deep wound, a yellow and black gash across her stomach oozing with pus and blood, an angry red infection around it. The stench rising from it made Finn gag.

"No," he gasped. "We have to get you out of here."

Isabel put her hand out and held his with the tiny bit of strength she had left.

"This is where we come to die." She took another breath. "But these women did not betray their families. These women are heroes. You have to stop this happening again, Finn. I have a daughter, Emily. Find her. Don't let her be raised by the Shadow Cartographers. Don't let this happen to her."

Tears streamed down Finn's cheeks. "I promise."

Isabel took another breath, and this time there was a rattle as she exhaled. Her head dropped back against Finn's chest, and he held her close as she groaned in pain.

Finn bent his head to hers. "Don't leave me, Izzy."

His sister took one last breath and then she was still.

Her weight sagged against him. His precious sister was lost, and her child was somewhere in this hellhole of a castle. Finn's tears slowed as his anger burned white-hot. He gently laid Isabel's body on the ground, knowing he could not bury her now. This dead flesh was not his sister, and she would want him to find her daughter, not wait here to be taken by the guards.

Finn stood, his body shaking with anger and grief as Sienna closed Isabel's eyes. The women moaned around them, most of them not far off death themselves. Finn clenched his fists and gripped the pommel of his sword. He stormed out of the cell, leaving the door wide open behind him.

"Finn, wait," Sienna shouted after him, but he ignored her. Those guards would be the first to go, and then he would see what other damage he could bring to this evil place.

He ran down the corridor. His blood was up, and he felt like a berserker from the Viking myths he and Izzy read about together. Family and blood were everything.

The two guards turned to face him, their faces confused as he ran towards them. They reached for their weapons, but Finn got there first, bringing his sword down in a heavy swipe cleaving the first man across the belly. He looked down in surprise, hands bloody as he held his stomach. Then his guts slithered out and the man crumpled to the floor.

The other guard pulled his sword and parried Finn, but he was no match for the better swordsman. Finn hacked down his sword, beating the man to his knees.

"Please, take whatever you want."

"I'll take you to Hell." Finn swung his sword, and the man's head separated from his body, rolling to Sienna's feet as she cautiously approached, hands outstretched to pacify him.

"You have to stop now, Finn. There will be more guards coming with all the noise. You can't help Isabel's daughter – your niece – if you're captured."

Sienna came closer, and Finn looked at her, taking in the laughter lines at the corners of her eyes. Laughter seemed so far away right now. He couldn't let her be taken.

"You shouldn't be here." He took her hands in his. "The Borderlands are not your place. I wouldn't wish this life on anyone, and certainly not on you." He slowly lifted a finger to stroke her cheek. He wanted to kiss her, to lose himself in her.

The sound of running feet and the shouts of guards came from the corridors ahead.

Finn grabbed Sienna's hand. "We need to get back to the others, find your father and Emily."

He took one last look at the cells behind, the women trapped inside. He would avenge his sister, and then he would stop this evil trade. He would find whoever ran this place and bring it down. If it took him the rest of his life.

Together, they ran back through the corridors, down to the storeroom where the others waited.

Mila looked up as they came in, noting the blood on Finn's clothes. "What the hell?"

"Finn's sister is dead," Sienna said. "But he has a niece, and there are more children here, born from enforced slavery."

Finn stepped forward. "You need to find Sienna's father, but I'm going after the children. I wish you all the best for your journey onwards."

He nodded at them all. At the door, he took one last look back at Sienna, wondering if he would ever see her again. She would soon be returning Earth-side, and his path was here in the Borderlands. He turned and walked out of the door.

* * *

Sienna watched Finn go. What she had seen in the fertility halls had shocked her to the core. Like him, she wanted to free all the women, tear down this hated castle. But there weren't enough of them to win the war now. She had to find her father first, but she swore to return here. She could only hope that Finn would make it. He had fulfilled his part of the bargain, and now, of course, he had to try to save his family. But her heart ached as he walked out and she suddenly realized the Borderlander meant more than she had thought. Their little team was incomplete without him.

"We did some investigating," Mila said, interrupting her thoughts. "The dungeons where we saw the flesh maps are another level down."

Sienna nodded her head. "Let's go." Her voice was strong, but inside she wondered whether her father could possibly still be alive.

As they walked down the corridor and descended the stairs to the level of the dungeons, a sense of foreboding rose inside her. A copper smell of dried blood hung in the air mingled with smoke from torches held in brackets against the wall.

They heard the sound of running feet as they walked, but all were heading away from them. Finn's rampage had drawn the guards away from them and Sienna hoped that somehow he would be able to escape.

They came to a partially open door. Sienna pushed it open to find a man, or what had once been a man, chained face down on a thick wooden table. His back had been carved with the lines of a city, his ruined flesh still wet with blood. His hair was matted and stuck to his head, his face turned away. But the shape of his shoulders, the curve of his neck were familiar. Could it possibly be him?

CHAPTER 21

"Careful." Mila walked in beside Sienna. Perry and Xander followed behind, keeping an eye out for the guards.

The room was dimly lit by the flicker of flames in a stone fireplace and torches in brackets around the walls. Rushes covered the floor by the table, dark with blood.

Sienna walked to the man's head. With a shaking hand, she gently pulled back the hair around his face. Her hand flew to her mouth and tears welled in her eyes as she saw his features. His eyes were shut and swollen from a beating, his lips cracked and bleeding, but it was her father.

"Dad," she whispered, kneeling next to him, her fingers brushing his temple. His body must be a mass of agony, and yet somehow he still lived.

The man's eyes flickered open, a piercing blue, and when he saw her a flash of recognition lit up his face and then a deep despair came over him.

"Sienna," he whispered. "You shouldn't be here."

"I came to take you home." She looked around desperately for a way to get him out of the bonds. Perry and Mila searched the room for a way to unlock the shackles. Xander stood by the door, his body tense and alert.

"Here." Mila held up a key and then returned to the

table, unlocking the shackles at John's wrists and ankles. He groaned, flinching as he arched away from the wood. Blood ran from the wounds on his back, revealing the city in more detail.

Mila's eyes widened. "It's Old Aleppo." Her eyes met Sienna's. "They're drawing the city of the warlord into Earthside. They're going to shift the Borderlands."

John nodded. "My skin is the Map of Shadows. They lured us here –" His words were cut off as he coughed, blood trickling from the side of his mouth.

Perry and Sienna helped John sit up, his face a mask of agony as he tried to speak again. "They needed more power, a map made from the skin of a Blood Cartographer, a map that would remake the border in their favor and start the invasion."

He paled, eyes closing as his head lolled to one side.

"No, Dad, please," Sienna whispered as his body slumped against hers.

Perry helped her lift him, blood soaking into his shirt. "Usually the Blood Cartographers are tattooed over a long period of time, often slowly for years." He frowned. "This has been done in a hurry. Each drop of his blood makes the map stronger, but it may cost him everything."

"We have to get him back to the Ministry."

John's eyes fluttered open. "Don't let them use my body, Sienna. Destroy the map. Finish me so they can't use it." He reached out a hand in desperation.

Sienna took it in hers. "You're coming home with me." Tears welled in her eyes, and she thought of Finn losing Isabel, and of the skins in the nearby dungeon. Was this land only one of loss, a dark reflection of the world she had left behind? "I need you, Dad. Besides, I don't know how to get us all home. I need you to show me."

John's head dropped again, his eyes rolling back in his head as he passed out.

"We need to get him to a doctor," Sienna said.

Mila looked grave. "The only way is to get him back to the Ministry. Can you take us all through?"

Sienna nodded. "I'll try." But in her heart, she worried that she wasn't strong enough.

Suddenly from outside the door came the double-time step of a patrol heading towards them.

"Shut the door, Xander," Mila called. "You can't let them in. Sienna will be able to get us all out of here soon enough."

Xander turned, and his face was as Sienna had glimpsed it in the jungle and again in the torture of the beasts in the labyrinth. His hazel-gold eyes were now black.

"I don't think so." Xander's voice was quiet, and he stepped aside as a group of guards arrived. They filed into the room, weapons pointed at the team, forming a phalanx of sharp spears. Xander stood with them facing the Mapwalker team.

Footsteps echoed down the hall and a tall man walked in, a wolf pelt cloak over his tailored suit.

Perry did a double take, his face a mask of confusion. "Dad?"

Sienna recognized Sir Douglas Mercator, the man who tried to buy her grandfather's map shop. Cartographic royalty and it would seem – a Shadow Cartographer.

"Good to see you all." Sir Douglas smiled. "Especially you, son. This map –" He pointed at John. "Is the last map we need before the invasion." He inclined his head towards Sienna. "And her blood will help make it more powerful."

Perry shook his head. "No, I didn't bring her for that." Perry looked over at Sienna and Mila, shaking his head. "I didn't know, I promise."

"But I did." Xander stepped forward,

"Why are you doing this?" Mila said, her fists clenched. Sienna put a hand on her arm to hold her friend's anger back.

"It's time for a change," Xander answered. "I'm sick of hiding our magic as we do Earth-side, pretending we are nothing. Here in the Borderlands, I can use my powers as much as I like. I can create anything. My future lies here."

Sir Douglas put his hand on Xander's shoulder, nodding his head with pride. "You've done well." He looked over at Perry. "And now you, my son. It's time to stand with us. The balance is shifting. You can embrace who you truly are, a Halbrasse of great power."

"But ... I can't –"

"That man killed Morwenna." Sir Douglas spat the words as he pointed at John. "He murdered your mother."

"No." Sienna turned to Perry, pleading with them. "There must be some mistake or a reason why. Please –"

Perry looked over at John and hung his head, his body crumpling in on itself, defeated. The guards took a step forward, weapons threatening, faces set with a lust for blood.

But Perry's head snapped up as they moved towards his friends.

He reached into the fireplace behind him and pulled out a burning coal, holding in front with a shaking hand. It burned with ferocity. "Don't come any closer."

Sir Douglas put a hand out to stop the guards. They halted, weapons drawn, ready to charge on his word.

"Don't fight this, son. These three are nothing to you. We can use the skin of the two Blood Cartographers to create even more powerful maps, and the girl of water will go to the breeding room. Perhaps her magic will combine to produce a powerful child."

"I'll take her as part of my reward," Xander said, his eyes raking down Mila's body.

Mila spat at him. "I wouldn't come anywhere near you."

"No one said you had a choice. I take what's mine." Xander pulled his map from his pocket and placed it on the ground. This time, instead of the lion, Asada, a hybrid beast emerged, one created from his sketches along the journey. It had the powerful limbs of the giant ape, rising to the height of the ceiling, but it had scales and a snout like a dragon and when it opened its jaws to roar, its teeth were razor sharp.

Perry took a step back.

Sir Douglas smiled with a look of triumph. "It's over. Join us, Sienna. Use your blood willingly for the Map of Shadows, for real power, or I will bleed it from you as I have from your father."

Mila took a step closer to Sienna and put her hand out. Sienna took it, and they stood in front of John's body together, Perry by their side.

Sir Douglas shook his head at their defiance. "Then it's over." He dropped his hand. The guards and the hybrid beast started forward.

Perry threw the burning coal down to the floor in front of them and stepped back behind it, concentrating his power. Fire burst from the coal, and a wall of flame rose up between them and their attackers.

"Don't be stupid, son," Sir Douglas shouted over the crackling of the flames. "End this now and join me."

Perry reached out his hands, urging the flames higher, feeding off the coals in the grate. The hybrid beast screeched as it tried to push through, its dragon scales protecting it but the great ape limbs burned. The stench of singed flesh filled the room. Xander urged it on, his face contorted with anger. "Attack!"

"Hurry," Perry called back to Sienna, his body taut with the effort of commanding the flames. "I can't hold them too long."

Mila and Sienna dragged John's body back to the stone wall behind the flames.

John's eyes flickered open. "I don't have long, Sienna. Leave me here to burn and get away. Please."

"It's no use," Xander called over the flames. "Even if you go back, it will be too late. When I repaired the rent Michael made in the border, I left a back door. The warlord of Old

Aleppo will be entering Bath even now, and your rebel friend won't be there to stop him this time. The Ministry is finished, so you have nothing to go back for." He held up a small rolled-up parchment. "And besides, I have your star map, Sienna. You're trapped here."

* * *

Finn ran through the castle corridors, glancing into rooms as he passed, trying to see where they might keep the children. He came upon a couple of guards playing dice in a murky side room. They looked up as he entered, faces guilty at being caught before changing to alarm as Finn reached for his sword, shutting the door behind him.

A swift slash and one of the guards lay gurgling on the ground, clutching at his bloody throat. The other backed away, hands outstretched in supplication.

"Please, what do you want? I can help you."

Finn stalked towards the cowering man. "Where are the Halbrasse children kept?"

The man paled. "I … You can't –"

Finn pointed at the now-dead guard. "You want to join him?"

The man slumped. "The children are held in the east wing. There are dormitories and a school where they learn to use their abilities." He shook his head. "But none of us go there. We don't need to. They guard themselves."

"Which way?"

"Follow the corridor to the end and then cross the courtyard into the east wing. It has its own door."

Finn leaned in and thumped the man on the side of the head with the pommel of his sword. The guard collapsed on the floor, unconscious. Finn turned and walked out of the storeroom, hurrying east.

He reached a wide courtyard, open to the sky above. It was dark and Finn could see the stars above, a serenity that calmed his pounding heart. He looked up at the tower in front of him, a huge wooden door the final barrier to the children's wing.

It was strangely quiet. The rest of the castle had plenty of guards but there seemed to be none here. He walked around the edge of the courtyard, staying in the shadows in case anyone was watching. But it was silent except for his quiet footsteps on the gravel.

The hair on the back of his neck prickled as he reached the door. It was carved with the half-moon of the Shadow Cartographers.

He pushed it open, and it creaked on heavy hinges. As Finn stepped inside, he heard the rustle of clothes and the giggle of children. There was a lamp further down the hall, but it was semi-darkness by the door. He caught a glimpse of little shadows moving around, hiding behind the furniture.

"Hello," Finn whispered. "Anybody here?"

A giggle to his right and he turned to see a little girl peeking out from behind a chair. She wore a white nightdress, and her blonde hair was tied in two pigtails.

"Hi there." Finn knelt down and smiled, stretching out his hand towards her. "I'm Finn, a friend. I'm not going to hurt you."

Soft footsteps echoed in the corridor, and he looked up to see a group of children coming towards him, the littlest toddling along holding hands with an older child. They were angelic in the moonlight streaming through the high windows, all of them in white nightgowns, all different races, a picture of the diversity of the Borderlands.

But as they drew closer, he could see their faces weren't welcoming. They weren't scared. They were ready to attack.

The first little boy pointed at Finn. "Stranger," he whispered, softly at first.

They all joined in. "Stranger. Stranger." Marching towards

him, fingers outstretched, voices growing louder as they approached. "Stranger."

Finn held his hands out wide. "It's okay. I'm not here to hurt you. I'm –"

The blow came from nowhere.

A sudden burning explosion in his side and Finn fell sideways with the force of it. He cried out in pain, looking at the little girl by the chair. She had one hand out, her head tilted sideways as she looked at him.

"Stranger," she said along with the others and blasted him again. A ball of fire leapt from her fingers and smashed into Finn. He flew backwards, hitting the wall behind him. The smell of burning metal came from his body armor. He wouldn't last long against her onslaught.

The march of little feet came closer, the children's chanting getting louder as they approached, hands held out ready to attack.

CHAPTER 22

Finn gripped the pommel of his sword, but he couldn't bring himself to attack or even threaten the children. They didn't know what they were and they had been taught to hate. There was no chance of finding Emily now, and if he stayed, they would kill him.

He took one last look at the children and then scrambled back towards the door.

"Stranger." The little girl blasted him again, and Finn was knocked sideways, banging his head against the metal rivets. He pulled himself on, legs like jelly from the attack as he hauled himself out of the door. He rolled back into the courtyard, lying on the gravel, panting with pain. If they came out now, they would finish him.

But the door slammed shut, and he was left alone, staring up at the stars.

Finn lay there for a moment, his breath returning to normal as the pain eased. It was like the little girl had electrocuted him. What the hell kind of power did she have? He had heard Mila say that every use of magic in the Borderlands meant a little more shadow in the Mapwalker who used it. But what did that mean for these little Halbrasse? His niece, Emily, was only a newborn so it would be years before her talents could be exploited.

He had time – but he needed the help of the Mapwalkers. He needed Sienna. The others were already set in their prejudice against the Borderlanders, but she had seen a different side of his people. She was hope for a shared future.

Finn rolled over and pushed himself up onto his knees, then staggered to his feet. His whole body felt weak with the aftermath of the attack, but he had to get back to Sienna before she mapwalked back to Earth-side. He might never have this chance again.

* * *

Sienna heard Xander's words through the roar of the flames. She looked at Mila, saw in her eyes that it could be true, that he could have left a gap in the border ready to be exploited when the time was right. She remembered the fetish map she'd seen in the first visit to the dungeons of the castle, where Bath lay broken, a burnt-out shell, its inhabitants slaughtered by feral invaders.

"We have to get back." She looked at her father. "And we're not leaving anyone behind."

Sienna's mind raced as she considered the star map Xander held. It was supposedly the only reliable way to get home, to orientate across the border, but she had created a map from nothing before. She had to do it again.

She turned to Perry. "Can you hold them a little longer?"

He grimaced, his face ruddy from the flames and she saw the flicker of shadow in his eyes. There was a chance he had used too much magic in a short time, that he would tip over to his father's side, but she had to believe he would hold the line.

"For Galileo," he said, steel in his voice.

Sienna took the scalpel from her bag and cut into her arm. As blood welled, she closed her eyes and began to sketch the lines of Bath on the stone wall in front of her. She tuned out the throb of pain, the roar of the beast and the flames at her back. She fixed her imagination on the city she had only just begun to know, the map shop on the little street with the coffee shop opposite, Mila's canal boat and Zippy waiting alongside, the Abbey and the Baths. She painted them on the wall with her blood, and as she drew it, she felt a tug towards home, the pull of the map.

Her father looked up, and Sienna saw pride mixed with fear in his eyes. Fear, not for himself, but for her future now he saw what she could do. But there was no time to think about what might happen. They had to go.

Beyond the fire, the guards redoubled their efforts, thrusting long pikes through the flames towards Perry. Sir Douglas shouted something, and one of them ran through, bellowing his rage.

Perry blasted a stream of flame at him, and the guard tottered forward, his body alight. He slammed into the wooden table, flames consuming his body, but the height of the main wall ebbed a little with the distraction.

Xander urged his great beast forward, and it reached through the flames, screaming as it lit afire, but this time, it kept coming.

Perry fell back as it advanced. "We need to get out of here."

Sienna placed her hands on the wall, letting her mind sink into the lines, opening the portal back to the shop, back to where the rustle of her grandfather's maps called her.

Mila dragged John towards the wall, ready to cross over behind her. Perry edged back, trying to keep the beast far enough away but still ready to join them.

"Sienna!" Finn's voice suddenly came across the flames.

She turned to see him dart into the room, slashing at the guards as he moved towards the wall of flame. The beast lunged for him, but he rolled underneath it, angling his sword across its belly, cutting it deeply as he sprang away on the other side.

For a moment, Sienna faltered, the intensity of the map fading as she was drawn back towards Finn. If they left him, he would certainly be killed. But he couldn't cross into Earth-side, could he?

"Go now," Mila urged. "We have to."

Sienna took one last look back at Finn, as he fought with two guards on the other side of the wall of flame. She opened the map again, felt the expansion of the world beneath her.

She reached out her hands, touching Perry with one and her father with the other, felt Mila's hand on her arm and closed her eyes.

"No!"

Sienna opened her eyes to see Finn dart through the flames just as they died out – as Perry grasped her hand – as the guards surged forward with a roar – as the beast stormed at them, jaws gaping wide.

Finn reached out his arm and wrapped it around Sienna's waist. She buried her head against his chest as she took them through the map.

* * *

The air cooled, and the sound of chaos abated. It smelled of parchment and the faint tang of ink. Sienna opened her eyes to find them all back in the map shop, her father on the floor, Mila at his side, Perry dazed from the fight as he sat down, his face pale from the exertion of using so much magic.

Sienna stood wrapped in Finn's arms, feeling the beating of his heart against her body. She rested there, safe in his arms, a moment of calm after the escape.

Sienna looked up at him. "You're here."

Finn smiled, his dark eyes betraying his wonder. "You can bring Borderlanders across."

"It's only because the border is open right now." Mila stood up and brushed the ash from her clothes. She looked over at Finn. "You'd be gone otherwise, lost in whatever darkness holds our two worlds apart."

Sienna pulled away from him. "I'm sorry. I didn't know."

Finn shook his head. "You couldn't have stopped me trying to come after you."

Mila opened the door. The night was calm, just the sounds of friendly banter from the pub down the road and the soft patter of rain against the windows. For a moment, it seemed as if everything was normal.

Then they heard the howl of a wolf … and screaming.

"They've broken through," Mila said. "I need to get down to The Circus. The Ministry team will be there, or at least on their way. We need to shut the Gate, so the Borderlanders are sucked back through."

Finn gripped the pommel of his sword. "I'm coming too. You need someone to watch your back, and it's my father out there. I know how he works."

Mila nodded and then looked down at John, broken and bleeding on the floor, then over at Perry, collapsed against one of the map cabinets. "You need to get to the Ministry, Sienna. Get to the Blood Gallery and renew the lines of the border. Your blood is powerful, and you can send them back. Bridget will show you how."

Sienna bent down to her father and stroked the matted hair back from his forehead. His chest rose and fell in a jerky movement, but he still lived. He needed medical help, but there would be no chance if the city fell. She clenched her fists. She would not lose her father again.

"I'll renew the lines, and then I'll come and help you close that Gate."

She looked up at Finn and met his eyes. His gaze softened,

and then he nodded. Sienna took hold of her father and Perry and traveled into the map of Bath, her mind fixed on the Ministry below the Abbey.

* * *

Finn watched Sienna fade, marveling at the magic of Mapwalking.

"Let's go, lover boy," Mila snapped as she darted out of the map shop into the rain. Finn headed after her, and as he emerged into the night, he couldn't help but stare at the buildings around him. His home in Old Aleppo was broken and crumbling, a shade of its former glory, but this city was intact, its buildings commanding the eye with beautiful stone facades. Flowers bloomed in window boxes, and as they passed a shop on the end, Finn gaped to see paintings of the ocean and sculptures of birds. This was a place where people made art, a city of life, not death, and he desperately wanted more of it. Could the Borderlands ever be like this?

A woman screamed and ran past the end of the road. A huge grey wolf loped behind, barreling into her and taking her down, its teeth sinking into the flesh of her neck, cutting off her scream as the beast shook her.

Finn ran forward, swinging his sword in a low arc, using the flat of the blade to smash into the wolf's face, sending it twisting away. It let the woman go, and she lay unmoving on the ground. The creature turned and snarled, slinking back towards them. Finn stood in front of the woman's body, sword raised, ready to fight, Mila beside him.

Then deep growls came from the shadows in every direction. The wolf pack surrounded them.

"I've got this," Mila said. She held out her hands to the rain, and where the water touched her skin, she rippled with power as she channeled the element. She began to spin one hand, whirling the drops into a tornado of water and then spun it out like a whip at the nearest wolf.

It smashed the beast backwards, lifting it against the stone wall behind. It fell limp to the ground. Mila whirled the tornado on, using it to send the wolves flying away. With two more badly injured, the others slunk off, running off to find easier prey.

"Nicely done," Finn said, hefting his sword.

"We're not done yet. We have to get to the center of that." Mila pointed down the road towards a dense mist forming around The Circus.

A few Borderlanders staggered out of it, disorientated by the buildings around them, mouths gaping open as if they couldn't believe what they saw around them. "Looks like the full force hasn't come through yet."

Then the beating of drums came from within the mist, a rhythmic pounding that echoed through the streets.

"War drums," Finn said. "My father is coming."

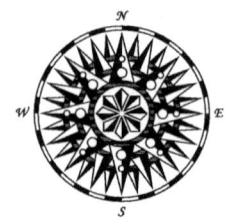

CHAPTER 23

A RUSH OF COOL air touched her skin and Sienna opened her eyes to find herself surrounded by the skins of the Blood Gallery, her father and Perry slumped at her feet. The flesh here was respectfully displayed and honored as a critical part of the Ministry, but in the end, they were still skin maps etched with the blood of people like her father.

And herself.

For a moment, all she could hear was their breathing. Then the sound of a blaring alarm rang out within the Ministry. The attack must have started.

John groaned, and Sienna leaned down to brush his hair from his face. She shuddered to think that he had almost ended up in the Blood Gallery of the Shadow Cartographers.

The door opened with a creak.

"Sienna?" Bridget came through the door, followed by one of her clerks. She looked down at the two men on the floor. "John?" She turned to the clerk. "Get the medics down here."

The man rushed back out, and Bridget came to kneel by her friend. John's blood had dried a little, but he was still a mess of cut and bruised flesh, barely recognizable.

Bridget put out a hand on his arm, lightly touching the skin between his wounds. "You're home now, my love," she whispered, tears welling in her eyes, then she looked up. "Where are Mila and Xander?"

Sienna quickly filled Bridget in, and the Irish woman's eyes darkened as she heard of Xander's betrayal.

"We have to strengthen the borders again and close the Gate." Bridget looked at Sienna. "Are you ready?"

Three medics burst through the door, two carrying a stretcher. Between them, they rolled John gently onto the support and carried him out, the other man supporting Perry as they headed out to the Ministry hospital.

Bridget turned to Sienna as the door closed behind them. "John is strong, he should make it through, but he can't help us now. We have to do this together. We are the only Blood Cartographers left now, but we do have the help of one who loved you very much." She walked to a circular wooden table set in the middle of the room.

Sienna frowned as she approached it, suddenly seeing the new skin mounted there, the edges pegged out so the torso and limbs could be clearly seen. The leather was wrinkled and tanned in parts, but the tattoos were finely drawn, the lines of the ancient city of Bath visible with the Borderlands beyond.

Then she realized whose skin it was.

Sienna's hand flew to her mouth. "Grandfather," she whispered. Nausea rushed over her, and she clutched at her throat. "No."

Bridget put out a hand. "It's what Michael wanted. It's why he inked himself like this. His skin and his blood magic helped define and strengthen the border here. He lived to protect it, and in death, he protects it still. But because Xander left a back door, it needs fresh blood, Sienna. It has to be yours." Bridget hung her head. "My blood magic is weak now, I've used it too much in recent times and the shadow has grown strong in me. I ... I feel its dark pull."

"I felt a glimmer of it in the Borderlands," Sienna said,

stepping closer to the table. "It was powerful, like the edge of addiction."

Bridget nodded. "Yes, and the feeling will grow every time you use your magic. If I use mine now, I'm afraid I won't be strong enough. It will pull me too far into the shadow side, and they will win."

Bridget picked up the ritual knife from beside the map and held it out. "This was Michael's. Blood Cartographers have used it for generations, and I know he would have wanted you to have it now."

She held it out towards Sienna.

* * *

The rhythmic thump of drums beat through Finn's chest. The deep notes echoed within him, bringing back memories of joining his father on raids at the edge of the Uncharted where they would gather slaves to sell to the Shadow Cartographers. Slave women he now knew became forced vessels for the Halbrasse, and men they used for sacrifice to the gods of the once dead.

The warlord's men would drink a special concoction before forming their ranks, downing a sharp alcohol spiked with hallucinogenic plants and flavorful herbs. It gave them an edge in battle, a belief that they were superhuman in strength and power. It made them uncaring of physical pain, separating their rational minds from willing bodies. These were the men who would cross into Earth-side through the gathered mist, a vanguard for the warlord's hand-picked warriors.

Finn ran down the road towards The Circus as tendrils of mist stretched further out from the great plane trees in the center.

"Wait," Mila shouted after him. "We need backup."

"No time," Finn called back. Up ahead, he could see a gathering crowd of tourists and locals, staring with interest at the mist, some with devices they held up to capture images of the strange sight. The wolves were running in the side streets, but here, people were entranced, unheeding of the danger.

"Move away from the area," a police officer shouted, waving people back as he stood on the edge of the mist.

Suddenly, a huge axe came out of the grey above him, hacking into the man's shoulder, cleaving his arm away. The officer dropped to his knees as the attacker emerged, face tattooed with the half-moon, teeth bared in a bloody grimace. The crowd backed away in horror and turned to run, tripping over each other, screaming as they tried to escape.

The Borderlander launched into a flurry of death-dealing blows, wielding the axe in a frenzied, drug-fueled state.

Finn didn't falter, he ran straight at the axe-man, swinging his sword as he approached from behind. He thrust his weapon into the man's back, angling the sharp blade so it pierced the man's heart, tugging him closer with a neck hold as the murderer died. Then Finn pushed the body forward, pulling his blade out.

"Run!" he bellowed at the people still there. Those remaining ran or crawled away as Finn picked up the man's fallen axe and turned to face the swirling mist.

The drums beat faster.

Mila stood by Finn's side, her hands lifted to the falling rain as she called it to her, twisting the water into tornado whips. The mist parted, and a horde of Borderlanders strode through in filed ranks. These were not the Ferals those on Earth-side talked of, these were the warriors of the warlord of Old Aleppo come to take what was rightfully theirs. They were dressed in the cast-off, mismatched uniforms of dead soldiers, those who slipped through the border, but they walked in unison.

They were an army.

In the middle of the men, Finn saw his father. Kosai held up a hand to halt the company. His soldiers stood to attention, eyes fixed forward, disciplined enough not to break ranks when faced with this strange environment.

"Have you come to welcome me, son?" The warlord walked forward. "Or beg for mercy after you took what was mine?" He looked Mila up and down, lingering on the curves of her body. "Have you brought me tribute?"

Finn lifted his weapons and took a fighting stance.

The soldiers either side immediately stepped forward, swords raised, blocking his path to their warlord.

Kosai laughed and shook his head. "Do you think you can stop this, Finn? It is beyond time that we took Earthside for our home." He turned around, his arms raised as he looked up at the stunning architecture. "Look at this place. Wouldn't you rather live here than in the ruins of Old Aleppo or in one of their cast-off forgotten cities?"

"There are people here already," Finn said, his voice controlled.

Kosai spun round, eyes blazing with anger. "People who will take our place in the Borderlands. People who deserve to suffer for what they have done to those of us pushed out of this earth." His voice softened. "Join me, son. Rule with me in this new world, and help me build a better life for *our* people."

Finn thought of the castle and Isabel's death, the way Sienna had helped him, the possibilities for a future where both sides of the border could be better somehow. He sighed. "I know the Mapwalkers on this side will help us. If you would just talk with them, Father, I –"

"Take them." Kosai's voice cut off Finn's words and the guards either side swarmed in, blocking Finn's blows and taking him swiftly to the ground. Mila spun out a tornado whip, cutting one of the soldiers down but then she too was overcome.

"I can't trust you, Finn. You've clearly spent too much time with these lying Earth-siders." Kosai nodded to the men. "Hold him."

Two of the biggest guards forced Finn to his knees. Another pulled his head back, exposing his throat to the warlord.

"You were my son once," Kosai said, "but now you will be the first sacrifice to Moloch on Earth-side soil for thousands of years, the first of many offered in the days to come as Borderlanders take all of it back."

"No!" Mila shouted. The man holding her wrapped an arm around her neck, choking her into silence.

The warlord smiled. "Don't worry, beautiful. We won't take your head. You're going to the breeding rooms of the Halbrasse." He turned back to Finn. "But this one …"

Kosai pulled a knife from his belt and stepped closer to his son.

* * *

Sienna looked at the ritual knife in Bridget's outstretched hand. It had an ivory blade bound with a leather strap tied into a series of knots around the end. The border had to be closed, but she couldn't bring herself to touch it.

She looked down at her grandfather's skin, trying to equate the tanned leather with the living man she once knew. This was the fate her father had tried to keep her from, because he would eventually hang in this gallery … and so would she.

But if she ran from the Ministry now, she would find a changed city, and the border could be redrawn in other places too.

Sienna reached out and took the ritual knife. "What do I do?"

"Your blood knows its power," Bridget said. "Just let it out."

Sienna cut into her arm, letting ruby drops drip onto her grandfather's skin. Bridget used a fine brush to paint it over the lines of the ancient city, the circle and the half-moon of The Circus and Royal Crescent, down to the Abbey and around the Baths, along the border around the city.

As her blood sank into the leather, Sienna felt a pulsing as if her heart beat inside the city itself. Screams echoed in her mind as the shadows began to be sucked back inside the border.

* * *

The earth shook, and the warlord stumbled, his knife slicing to one side as he was thrown off balance, hitting one of his own men with a glancing blow.

"What the –?"

Finn took his chance and rolled out of the grip of the men holding him, springing to one side, grabbing the blade from one of the soldiers. He turned swiftly, slicing the man's throat.

Mila ducked under the arm of the man who held her, clawing the rain down into a whip and then spinning it around her, cutting through the soldiers as they looked about in horror.

A howl came from the shadowed streets, the animal sound of beasts in pain. The soldiers fell from their tight formation as the mist swirled about them, the ground shaking as they began to be sucked back into the vortex of the gate.

"The border is closing," Mila shouted in triumph. "Sienna must have made it!"

Finn heard her words and despair shot through him, for it meant that he must go too. He couldn't be on this side when the gate finally shut, or he would dissipate into shadow, and somehow, he had to see Sienna again.

The soldiers scattered, some going willingly back into the mist. Others tried to run, but tendrils of grey reached out for them, dragging them back into the copse of trees and then through the Shadow Gate.

The warlord stood, legs akimbo, bracing himself against the moving earth. He looked at Finn. "This isn't over. I'll be waiting for you on the other side."

He strode back into the mist.

* * *

Bridget looked at Sienna. "The gate must be closed properly, so you need to go back up to The Circus. The Ferals will be swept back through as the border closes and you can use your blood to seal it."

Finn.

Sienna thought of the last look they had shared, the things that remained unsaid. She had to get to him.

"I'll go right now." She picked up the ritual knife and laid her hand on her grandfather's skin. A pulse arced where she touched it and she smiled to think of some part of him wishing her well. She closed her eyes and used the map to travel to The Circus, lifting away in her mind.

* * *

She opened her eyes to find herself in the Georgian circular terrace, but instead of pristine pavements, injured and dying Borderlanders, tourists and police littered the streets. Two wolves tore at one body, ripping chunks of flesh as they worried at it with bloody jaws even as they were sucked back towards the vortex of the mist. The smell of death lingered in the air, and the fetid stench of the Borderlands swirled in the mist around her.

But it receded even as she watched, slowly swirling back towards the copse of plane trees, circling the gate between them.

Was she too late?

Sienna ran into the mist. "Finn!"

Tears ran down her cheeks as she tore into the grey, clammy air sticking to her skin as she tried to see through the shadows to where he might be.

The circle of trees emerged, and suddenly she saw him. He stood next to one of the great plane trees, right on the edge of the border. The mist chased at her heels, and she knew that as soon as it disappeared, the border would go too, the gate would close, and he would be sucked into the darkness.

"Sienna!"

She ran into his arms, and Finn pulled her close, dipping his head down to meet her lips. They clung to one another, lost in a kiss where borders meant nothing.

The wind picked up around them. Sienna pulled away. "I'll come to you. I'll find you again."

Finn took a deep breath and walked towards the shadow gate. As the mist swirled closer, he turned and looked at her, an unspoken promise in his eyes.

Then he stepped through.

As the last of the mist dissipated into the air, Sienna drew the knife along her arm once more. With tears running down her cheeks, she used her blood to paint ancient runes on the trees, following the lines her grandfather had carved before her.

EPILOGUE

Two days later.

SIENNA SAT AT THE old desk in the map shop, her grandfather's parchment in front of her portraying the ancient city of Bath. The oversize globe sat next to her, in pride of place at her right hand, a reminder of how borders had shifted over time. The door to the shop was open, and the smell of freshly roasted coffee came from the café over the road. A light breeze whispered across the maps with a rustle.

The sounds and smells of normality.

Sienna breathed a sigh of relief. Her father recovered in the Ministry hospital, his back healing from his physical wounds even as he drifted in and out of consciousness, muttering of nightmares. On Bridget's urging, Sienna hadn't told her mother about what had happened or about John being back. That was one conversation she would tackle when her father was ready. If he ever was.

Perry was back in the chambers of the Ministry, practicing his fire magic with newfound confidence, driving flames into his targets again and again. Sienna knew he saw Xander's face there alongside his father's and she had no doubt that Perry would want to be on the next mission into the Borderlands. Mila had taken her canal boat east, escaping onto the water, Zippy by her side as she recovered in her own way.

Sienna had no way of knowing what had happened to Finn after the border closed. She could only hope that he had joined the underground Resistance and escaped Old Aleppo, away from the wrath of his father.

She picked up the fountain pen and began to trace over the lines of central Bath with deep red ink, new drops of her blood mingling with her grandfather's. Each stroke of the pen was a line of power, strengthening the border as she traced the arch of the Royal Crescent, the straight line of Brock Street and the curves of The Circus.

For now, the border was closed again, and Finn's world was separate from hers. But Sienna was counting the hours until she could go back into the Borderlands again. She remembered the other blood maps in the castle dungeon, the world remade. The Shadow Cartographers had many more plans, and one setback would not stop them.

Before Bath, Sienna had been drifting through life, unable to see the path ahead. But now she would make her own map and this was only the beginning.

***

AUTHOR'S NOTE

I hope you enjoyed this fantasy as an escapist story, but perhaps you also glimpsed something of the themes beneath as you read. Here's how the idea came into being.

The antique map shop

I moved to Bath, England, in 2015 and discovered an antique map shop in a little pedestrianized street between The Royal Crescent and The Circus.

I walked past it almost every day when I went to the café to write, and one day, I went in and bought some books. It sparked my research around cartography, maps, and the obsession that humans seem to have with finding our physical place in the world.

Bath can seem perfect at times, with its Roman Baths, medieval Abbey, Georgian architecture and tasteful shops and restaurants. I love living here, but the darker edge of my imagination invented a shadow side to the city, a place just off the edge of the map, and the Borderlands were born.

You can find more of my thoughts and pictures at
www.BooksAndTravel.page/unusual-bath

Borders

In November 2016, we visited Israel on a research trip for my ARKANE thriller, *End of Days*.

Borders are a big deal in Israel, surrounded as it is by nations who want to destroy it, and split internally by occupied territory. When we traveled to the West Bank, through checkpoints that Palestinians couldn't cross, I began to think about what it meant to be born on the other side, to be locked into a certain place, unable to leave, to be left with the land no one wanted.

As I write this in 2017, borders and walls have become part of the international conversation. Refugees find themselves crossing borders, and perhaps some of them have wandered into the Borderlands, pushed over by those countries who don't welcome them.

Here in Europe, Brexit fills the news. I voted Remain, but at this point, it seems certain that the passport I hold as a European Citizen will be revoked. I won't be able to cross borders as easily as I have done for most of my adult life and the international landscape I value so much is gradually disappearing beneath rampant nationalism.

I haven't chosen to give up being European – that identity is being taken from me.

So perhaps this is, in fact, a political book, a way I can deal with the complicated and unsolvable problems of borders.

There are no answers, but there are always stories.

Places in the book

As usual with my fiction, I have set the story in real places and modeled the Borderland locations on reality too. You can see some of the pictures that inspired the story at Pinterest.com/jfpenn/map-of-shadows.

Bibliography

I read a lot of books as part of my research. Some of them include:

The Mapmakers' World - Marjo T. Nurminen

Maps: Their Untold Stories - Rose Mitchell & Andrew Janes

Collecting Antique Maps: An Introduction to the History of Cartography - Jonathan Potter

Great Maps: The World's Masterpieces Explored and Explained - Jerry Brotton

The Phantom Atlas: The Greatest Myths, Lies and Blunders on Maps - Edward Brooke-Hitching

The Un-Discovered Islands - Malachy Tallack

Tragic Shores: A Memoir of Dark Travel - Thomas H. Cook

Atlas of Cursed Places: A Travel Guide to Dangerous and Frightful Destinations - Olivier Le Carrer

You Are Here: Personal Geographies and Other Maps of the Imagination - Katharine Harmon

MAP of PLAGUES

A MAPWALKER NOVEL

J.F. PENN

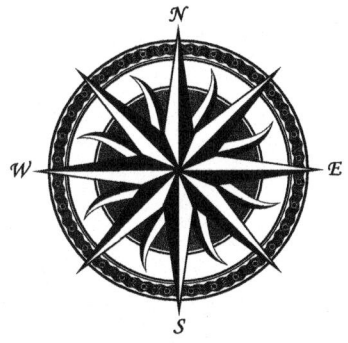

"We are a plague on the Earth."

David Attenborough

"Anyone who was alive during the outbreak of the bubonic plague in the 14th century experienced something terrifyingly close to the widespread death and chaos of an apocalyptic event."

Alan Huffman, International Business Times

PROLOGUE

THE STORM BROKE OVER London in the early hours of the morning. Rain crashed down onto the cobbled street that ran past Traitor's Gate, the passage to death in the Tower above. Lightning flashed, forking across the city, illuminating the skyscrapers that reached heavenward. A confident city, secure in its power, with no heed of the threat below.

Beneath the gate, the murky river Thames began to boil. A fetid stench bubbled from the depths as four men swam up from below. As they reached for the shore, another flash of lightning caught their faces in profile. Hard ridges of bone, thick jaws set in determination and the half-moon tattoo of the Warlord that painted their faces in shadow.

As the Feral Borderlanders climbed from the water, pulling their muscled bodies easily up the side of the wall, a man stepped from the shelter of the Tower. He wore a plague doctor's mask, the hooked beak of an ibis, the Egyptian bird of the dead. Two bags lay at his feet.

He called softly down to the climbing men. "Quickly now. We don't have much time."

The four men changed into dry clothes, pulling up hoods to hide their faces in this city of ever-present cameras. Two hefted the bags onto their backs. The plague doctor pulled a long cloak around him, set his face against the storm and led the men around the perimeter of the Tower. He glanced up at the symbol of a once-great empire. Fragile flesh would rot away but these stones would remain even as a new power took this city in the days to come.

The men crossed Smithfield within sight of what had once been the Royal Mint, the white imperial facade of what was now the Chinese Embassy lit with spotlights from below. They skirted the edge of the light, staying in the shadows, until they reached a door on the building beyond marked with No Entry signs. It was bolted and padlocked, set with multiple alarms. The plague doctor stood in front of the door and the four men ranged around him, alert for danger.

A spark of flame from his fingers, a flash of electrics. The bolts fell off, the padlock dropped, the door clicked. He held his breath for a moment, half expecting the high-pitched squeal of alarms. But it remained silent.

The plague doctor pushed the door open and the men stepped inside. They turned on torches, revealing stone steps that wound down into darkness. Water dripped from their clothes onto the stone, droplets as dark as blood. It smelled of damp earth and decay.

They headed down with heavy footsteps, their boots marking time like the inevitable march of history.

At the bottom, they emerged into a wide cavern, the roof supported by metal reinforcing pillars so as not to disturb the graves beneath. The excavation was just one of many in London, part of the ever-expanding development of the transport network. This site had once been a Cistercian Abbey and in 1349, during the Black Death, it had become a plague cemetery, a mass grave for the diseased bodies of parishioners.

Pieces of rope bisected the site, dividing the plot into specific areas and orange flags marked the bodies beneath. Skeletons embedded in the dirt reached for freedom, bony fingers clutching at the air as if they tried to rise again even as their remains crumbled to dust.

The plague doctor ignored these common dead, his cloak swirling about him as he strode to the back of the cavern where a stone wall barred the way. It was made from mismatched blocks, some of the stones weathered as if they had once stood against ferocious storms like the one raging outside. The plague doctor ran his fingertips over the blocks, leaning close to them as if he could sense their history through his skin.

According to ancient texts, these stones had been carried from Jerusalem, taken from the rubble of the Second Temple, borne across plague-ravaged Europe to stand guard at the entrance to the knights' final resting place.

After years of research, the plague doctor suspected that the graves of those who fought the plague also rested here. A secret order of knights who believed that the contagion ravaging the continent had been sent by the Devil himself, a curse that could somehow be lifted by those of faith — and power. Secret annals suggested that they had achieved their goal, pushing the last of the plague out of this world — and into another.

But after years of searching in the Borderlands, the plague island was still out of his reach, lost as the borders continued to morph over time until the original contours disappeared. The only chance to find it now was the map that the knights had made, a map of skin made from plague victims that linked to the island of the dead, a portal back from that lost world to this one.

The plague doctor thought of the gleaming skyscrapers in the city above, the millions who slept secure in their beds. They had no idea what was coming for them.

He stood back from the wall. "Take it down."

The four men with half-moon tattoos put down the bags and pulled out lump hammers, shovels and picks. One man hefted the weight of a hammer, a grin spreading across his face as his meaty hands dwarfed the handle.

He stepped toward the wall and smashed the weapon into the stone. The sound echoed through the chamber but the blow made scarcely a dent. The man swung again. Another stepped beside him and together they pounded the ancient wall, muscles flexing.

The striking of metal on stone rang through the plague pit but the plague doctor was confident that the thick walls of the old Cistercian Abbey would shield the noise from above. By the time the workers arrived in the morning, his team would be long gone.

The men hammered away until they made a hole in the wall big enough to step through, then stepped back, panting with exertion. Sweat ran down their faces, carving a path through the dust that had settled on their skin. The plague doctor held his torch high and stepped through the hole into the chamber beyond.

The mass grave of the outer room was crammed full of the dead, but this inner tomb was spacious. Intricately carved arches rose to a dome overhead painted with faded images of demons devouring plague victims beneath the watchful eye of a vengeful god. Around the walls, deep niches held the remains of the band of brothers, but the plague doctor ignored them and stalked toward the centerpiece of the vault.

A huge stone sarcophagus sat in pride of place in the middle of the chamber topped with the effigy of the knight who slept beneath. He lay resplendent in full armor, the pommel of a longsword clutched between his hands. Lichen covered his craggy face, eating away at the features of a man who had been feared once, but was now forgotten in time. The plague doctor pointed, his finger shaking just a little as he considered what might be inside.

"Open it."

Two of the men hefted the lid from the top of the stone sarcophagus, grunting with effort as they pushed it to one side revealing darkness within. The smell of rotted leather with a metallic edge filled the air, permeating even the plague doctor's mask as the men pushed again. The stone crashed to the floor.

The plague doctor walked to the edge of the sarcophagus and peered in. A suit of armor lay with its hands on its chest, sunken in death, the patina of age turning the once shiny metal to rust red. A yellowed skull grimaced from within the helmet, bones held together by metal hundreds of years after death. This knight had died fighting a foe that could not be beaten by any sword, a creeping invisible enemy that slaughtered loved ones with no hope of reprieve. The plague doctor could only imagine what this man had done to try and rid Europe of the devastation.

In his skeletal hand, the knight clutched a rough box fashioned from lead with rivets at the edges. The plague doctor reached for it, his heart pounding. He had searched for so long, could this finally be the moment?

As he touched the knight's hands, the bones turned to dust, leaving the box resting on top of the armor. He lifted it from the remains and beckoned for light. One of the men shone a torch at the box while the plague doctor gently levered the top open.

A folded piece of parchment lay inside, grimy with the dust of generations but still intact. The plague doctor lifted the tattered piece of parchment from its resting place with care, placing it lightly on the stone beneath. He unfurled it, revealing a piece of an ancient map, the edges rough where it had been ripped into quarters. It was only one fragment, but it was the beginning of the end for Earthside.

"The plague wreaked havoc on Europe," he whispered. "Some say it killed six in every ten people. It heralded the end of civilization." He looked more closely at the tattered map, a silver-grey gleam in his eyes, like a wolf identifying its prey. "It can do so once again."

CHAPTER 1

MORNING SUN LANCED THROUGH the windows of the flat above the old map shop, lighting on the walnut wood bookshelves laden with notebooks and leather-bound journals. The cry of seagulls wafted in as they hung on the breeze above the Georgian streets of Bath, tasting the ocean on the air as it blew inland from the Bristol Channel.

Sienna Farren sat cross-legged on a cushion by the bookshelves, a tendril of titian hair escaping from her blue striped headscarf as she pulled down another of her grandfather's journals. The cover was grey leather, faded in parts, marked by the sun of another time. It looked like elephant skin, but as she ran her fingers over the whorls and lines, she sensed a different vibration. It was from a creature of the Borderlands, lost to Earthside but hunted over there, brought back in death.

The journals captured fleeting moments from the years that Michael Farren had spent as a Mapwalker on missions off the edge of the map. That world was lost in time, but the moments he had spent watching were captured here on the page, passed from his memory to hers across the generations. Sienna had not really known her grandfather in the years before he was murdered, sacrificing himself to save the city of Bath from Borderland invasion. She had inherited his map shop as well as his lifelong mission and in many ways, she was still trying to come to terms with the new direction of her life. These journals were an insight into the mind of a man she wished she had known better in life, but perhaps could still help her even in death.

She flicked through the pages of the journal, past line drawings in thick black ink, some highlighted with color. A bright kingfisher sketched on the edge of a sparkling stream with feathers of burnt orange and turquoise, his spiked beak slightly open. A mountain range with numbered passes, a thin line to show the path of the Mapwalker team. Red-hot lava spilling over the top of a volcanic cone, trailing a path of destruction toward a village that lay beneath.

The face of a young Nubian woman gazed out from another page, loving lines and delicate shading betraying a deeper connection. Sienna wondered who the woman was, and how long ago her grandfather had loved her.

She read on past pages of temples and buildings and ruins, some overrun with vines, others as pristine as if they had been built yesterday. He had noted the sounds and smells of the jungle next to the sketches, the call of monkeys, the fecund aroma of tropical flowers. The scent of berries rose from the page, the purple ink made from the juice of some unusual Borderland fruit that Sienna didn't recognize.

The journals were numbered with tiny Roman numerals etched into the spine. They were ordered on the shelves, but number twenty-four was missing. Her grandfather's compass was still missing too, stolen by a Shadow Cartographer just round the corner from the map shop where she now sat. Sienna wondered where the notebook was now.

She understood that the sketchbooks weren't absolute truth, they were her grandfather's perception of a moment of time. But who's to say where art, truth and history intersected? The notes he made and the drawings he sketched told his version of the tale, even if the annals of the Mapwalkers told something different. None of those who traveled there could take pictures. The boundaries of the Borderlands turned all technology to dead metal. When the borders were formed in the days of stronger blood magic, only the old ways remained off the edge of the map. So Michael had used pen and ink, paint when he could. Charcoal, ash, dust.

Blood.

Sienna pulled up her shirt sleeve to reveal her healing scars, tattooed ley lines of The Circus and the Royal Crescent. Her grandfather's skin had the same lines, his own blood map providing protection for the city of Bath and the portal that they guarded here. Now it was Sienna's turn to be the guardian of the gate. But she wanted more than that. She wanted to be fighting the Shadow Cartographers, trying to build a future for the Borderlanders.

Alongside Finn.

She flicked through more of the pages, pulling down the journals faster now. Her grandfather had traveled all over the Borderlands. He must have visited the trader town on the edge of the Uncharted, he must have known a way to get back there. Sienna thought of Finn's face as he stepped back through the gate as the border closed around him. It had only been a month ago, but it felt like forever. He had said his mother came from the slave markets there and after the battle with his warlord father, it made sense that he would flee to the edge of Borderlander civilization, where there were plenty of places to hide.

But it was hard to find and she couldn't just walk back there through a map of her own creation. She had no context, no anchor, and as with all locations in the Borderlands, its position changed as new places were pushed off the edge of Earthside. As the landscape of the Borderlands shifted, it pushed the trader town even further into the Uncharted. Few dared stay too long, as time moved differently out there.

Sienna wondered if Finn thought of her. She saw his face

every night when she closed her eyes, and she longed to go to him.

But there was also a darker thread to her desire.

When she had cut into her skin and used her blood to create a powerful map, she had let the shadow inside. Now it beat within her, drawing her back to the dark magic of the Borderlands, pulsing deep within her heart.

She had to go back there, but she didn't want to go alone. There was one person who understood this craving, one person she could trust. Sienna picked up her phone and texted Mila.

* * *

The low thrum of the engine beat time as the canal boat moved slowly through the water under the shade of overhanging trees. As her phone buzzed, Mila Wendell kept one hand on the tiller while she read the text from Sienna.

When are you back?

A bark of excitement made Mila look up as Zippy, her golden cocker spaniel, greeted the local ducks as they turned toward the aqueduct at Dundas, just a few miles out from Bath. Sunlight dappled the water with shades of green and the smell of elderflower rose from the hedgerows as they passed.

After the battle with the Borderlanders, Mila had fled the city, needing time to let her body return to its Earthside physicality. She could travel in the ripples between waves, spin liquid into weapons, turn her body to water. It was freedom, but every time the Mapwalkers used their magic, a sliver of shadow weaved its way inside — and Mila knew that she had used too much of it in those last days.

And yet every day for the last month, she had fought the desire to go back to the Borderlands alone. She held Zippy close in the night, weeping into his fur as she resisted the pull to darkness. It was an addiction that only grew worse with time. Their mentor, Bridget, had warned of this and it was why Mapwalkers must always travel in teams into the Borderlands. If they had too much shadow, they could no longer cross over for fear of losing themselves. Too many of their kind had been lost over the years, too many had shifted into Shadow Cartography.

Like Xander had done on the last mission.

Once the golden child of Mapwalker lineage, his skill as an Illustrator had marked him out for greatness, but he had betrayed them all for a chance to use his magic every day. To stop resisting the dark.

Mila understood why he had made that choice, but she hoped that she could resist it long enough to help Sienna find Finn and maybe, just maybe, there was a chance for peace between Earthside and the Borderlands.

Zippy ran up and down the roof of the canal boat, happiness on his doggy face. He knew the smells of this place, and they both had friends here, friends who would look after the little spaniel when she had to travel alone. It was time to moor up again, to settle for a time in a place she had come to call home.

Mila texted back. *Soon.*

* * *

In the stone corridors beneath Bath Abbey, the whoosh of fire echoed before ending in a metallic slam. The sounds repeated again and again, faster now, until suddenly it stopped. Peregrine Mercator leaned over, hands on his knees, panting with effort, his t-shirt damp with sweat in the over-heated room.

As his breath slowed, Perry stood again and pulled the

human-shaped target back toward him across the wide expanse of the practice room. It was made of thick metal, but its heart had burned clean through with his repeated attack. Perry nodded, pleased at his improved precision. He was not the same man who had faced his father a month ago. He was stronger now, his muscles more defined, his magic under control.

He sent the target back once again, opened his palms and conjured the fire once more. While the other Mapwalkers had to be careful of using their magic on Earthside, he was a Halbrasse, a half-breed, able to move between the realms, born with shadow already in his veins, choosing to stay and fight for the world he had grown up in. This was his home and when they came for it again, he would be ready.

He slammed flame into the head of the metal target once more, seeing his father's face melt away with every blow.

* * *

Outside the door of the training room, John Farren sighed as he watched Perry's anger explode. He leaned heavily on his cane, the barely healed scars on his back preventing him from standing upright, part of his mind still chained in the bloody dungeon of the Borderlands. He understood the depth of the young man's pain, and he saw a reckoning ahead with the man who had wounded them both so deeply. Sir Douglas Mercator, Perry's father — and the Shadow Cartographer who had tried to make a blood map from John's own skin.

An alarm sounded suddenly, a deep note of warning.

John turned from the window and limped away down the corridor. In years past, the sound had been unusual but these days, it seemed the borders were tested several times a day, the Borderlanders pushing against the limits of their world, finding ways back into Earthside. For generations, the magic of the border had been taken for granted, but now it seemed, it was beginning to crumble. It was only a matter of time before they faced a proper invasion and this world would have to face a truth hidden for too long.

He reached the War Room. Bridget Ronan stood before a computer screen showing a map of the south of England, a red light pulsing above the City of London. A deep frown creased her beautiful face, and as she leaned to look more closely, her multi-colored patchwork dress swirled around her legs. As it shifted, John remembered one night when they had danced together under the full moon on a ruined terrace above a forgotten river deep within the Borderlands. The scent of spring blossom hung in the balmy air and the sound of the water splashing below drowned their cries of pleasure as they lost themselves in one another. That night they had left their responsibilities behind, a stolen moment off the edge of the map. But they had returned to real life soon after, the memories fading as he returned to his Earthside family, and she took on a different role in the Ministry. It had been their last mission together.

Bridget looked up, her expression softening as she saw him standing there. Perhaps the memories hadn't faded after all. Perhaps there was still a chance for them. But with the amount of shadow now within him, John knew he could never go into the Borderlands again. He was stuck on Earthside, as Bridget was too, both of them tainted by the magic they had used on the other side of the map.

Bridget turned back to the screen and zoomed in on the map to show a plague pit behind the City of London.

"A small group of Ferals breached one of the secondary gates under the Thames. It seems they only had one goal." She pulled up pictures of a tomb surrounded by security tape, then a sarcophagus, an empty box upon the remains of a knight. Above it, the painting of a demon devouring plague victims as the dead piled up in mounds around it. She clicked through to security footage of a man in a plague doctor's mask.

Bridget frowned, biting her lip in concern. "I think they found the first piece."

John reached for her hand. "It's not over, then?"

Bridget shook her head. "It's only just beginning."

CHAPTER 2

The rocky beach was busy even in the small hours of the morning. Fishermen readied their boats and traders joked with one another as they warmed their hands by braziers, beacons of flame against the dark. A woman in a black headscarf squatted on her haunches on the stones in front of a fire, her hands shaping balls of dough into smooth round shapes which she threw on the coals with practiced skill. The smell of fresh flatbreads mingled with the tang of smoke and salt in the air.

Finn Page wrapped his thick cloak more tightly around himself, scant protection against the cold wind blowing in from the sea, but more as a shield against anyone recognizing him. His face was on Wanted posters all over the northern Borderland towns but down here, on the very edge of the Uncharted, he should be safe. People here tended to turn a blind eye, since many were also amongst the wanted themselves. He had escaped through the network of the Resistance, but he couldn't stay anywhere for long, not wanting to draw down the wrath of his father on those who sheltered him.

Finn leaned back against the wooden spars of the jetty, gazing toward the horizon and the faint glimmer of dawn. The sun would rise whatever happened to him. The world turned regardless of whether his life ended in the dungeons of the Shadow Cartographers.

He thought of Sienna on the other side of the map and wondered whether she thought of him at all. Time moved differently out here and the kiss they had shared as the border closed had begun to fade in his memory now. It was crazy to think that he could love an Earthsider, that they could ever find common ground. But Sienna gave him hope that things could be mended somehow, her optimism as yet unshaken by the Shadow.

A light flashed out in the gloom, a lamp held aloft by new arrivals. Another lifeboat filled with refugees rejected from Earthside. They had chosen to leave their homeland for fear of death and chaos, but they were not wanted by anyone else. As each nation turned them away, they became lost on the seas and flickered over the border. These last few months, they had arrived in their thousands, spirits broken by the journey and constant rejection from those who should have let them stay.

Finn understood the feeling of loss. Since he had stepped through the portal in Bath, turned his back on that glorious city and Sienna, he had been running from his father, the Warlord of Old Aleppo. His father threatened death for his betrayal, but more than punishment, Finn regretted the loss of his home. The sweet smell of oranges from the market as he sipped strong coffee with his friends, the stacks of his father's library filled with contraband books, walking for hours through the streets of a city he had grown up in and knew every corner of. He even missed his father's laugh as he played with his younger children. The Warlord was a pleasure-loving family man when he was not away slaughtering his enemies — and perhaps now there was hope.

In the last few days, Finn had heard through his Resistance contacts that the Warlord talked of amnesty, a willingness to trade. Finn could live safely in one of the lesser Borderland cities, his niece, Emily, would be returned to him, rescued from the Halbrasse training camps. They would be left alone to live in peace. It sounded like an impossible dream, a tranquil life where he could raise his niece in memory of her mother, Isabel. He had promised to keep Emily safe as his sister took her dying breath, but now that promise haunted him. Finn gripped his sword, knuckles white with tension. He was a warrior, always had been, always would be. While he wanted a better life for Emily than the halls of the Halbrasse, he also couldn't see himself tending orchards in the outer cities for the rest of his life.

But he had to know more about his possible future, so he was here, ready to meet with a messenger from his father. The rocky beach served well as a public place where he could slip into the shadows if it looked like a trap. The bounty on his head was still worth collecting, after all.

The sound of oars paddling grew louder than the waves as the lifeboat drew closer to the shore, hollow-cheeked men onboard still rowing with tired arms. They wore layers of stained and ragged clothes, pockets filled with what little they could carry from their homeland. Some wore hats pulled low over their eyes as if to shield the world from their sight. Finn glimpsed the drawn face of a beautiful young woman clutching a silent baby boy in her arms, her big dark eyes staring toward an unknown shore.

The traders readied themselves on the rocks, jostling for position, ready to guide the travelers to what they thought was safety.

But Finn knew what really awaited these people.

This was not the coast of some welcoming haven where refugees would be helped into a new life. This was the Borderlands, where those pushed off the edge of the map ended up in forgotten places, where history remained in the present, and the extinct lived on. It was ruled by the Shadow Cartographers, those who could wield dark magic, who bred a new generation focused on taking back the land they believed was theirs. Earthside, where Sienna lived, where a whole world of people lived their lives with no idea that the Borderlands or the Uncharted even existed.

Finn watched the new arrivals. They would learn soon enough.

The boat beached on the shore with the grating sound of metal over stone. The traders helped people out, guiding them up the bank, funneling them toward the soldiers who waited on the crest of the hill above, faces painted with the half-moon of the Shadow. The new arrivals spoke the names of their home towns, the places they had fled for fear of their lives, hoping for news of home, of family, of those who had left before them. Those on the beach merely shook their heads, denying any knowledge.

Soldiers singled out the ones who might be especially useful. One pointed at the beautiful young woman, proof of her ability to breed held in her arms. One of the traders pulled her away from the group.

She turned, calling out to an older man. "Papa!"

The man started up the beach toward his daughter. "Wait, what are you doing?"

He pulled papers from his jeans, the sodden pages almost legible. He thrust them at the soldier, but the man brushed them away, the papers fluttering to the floor. "These are worthless now."

One of the traders pulled the old man roughly back. "Leave her. She is no longer yours."

"No!" The old man struggled but more of the traders piled in, punched him to the ground, kicked him as the girl was dragged away screaming, the baby crying, the sound of lamentation in the air.

Finn closed his eyes against their suffering and clenched his fists as he tried to hold himself back. There were too many for him to fight alone and he had no friends here. The girl would probably end up in the breeding halls where his sister had died in a bloody dungeon not so long ago, buried in the mass grave behind the Castle of the Shadow. The girl's father would probably die in the mines of the Uncharted. This is what the Resistance fought against, but they needed a whole lot more help to overthrow the power of the Shadow Cartographers and he could not fight this battle alone.

As the traders stripped the boat for parts, the refugees were herded away. By the time the sun rose above the horizon, the only thing left on the beach was a child's doll, choked with seaweed, trampled into the sand.

Finn turned to see the willowy figure of a woman standing alone on the jetty, black hair loose, swirling about her in the wind like the snakes of Medusa. She carried twin crossed swords on her back and her face was marked with the half-moon. As the rays of dawn touched the jetty with a golden glow, Finn recognized her. Jari, one of the Warlord's trusted bodyguards, renowned for her skill with the sword and her brutality in battle. They had trained together in their younger days, matched in skill on the battlefield — and in their passion afterwards. She was even more beautiful now with the scars she wore with pride. Finn remembered the shape of her muscled body beneath that cloak. He could still recall the warmth of her. He shook his head. His father knew him too well.

He watched Jari from the shadows, waiting for any sense that she wasn't alone. Minutes passed and she stared resolutely out to sea, her cloak flapping in the breeze.

Finn stepped out into the open, hand on his sword, checking around him for danger.

Jari looked over. "I came alone, as promised." Her eyes flashed with a dark smile. "Besides, if I wanted to take you, I would. I hear you're out of practice, Finn."

She sat down, long legs swinging off the edge of the jetty. She seemed relaxed but Finn was still wary. She was right, he had been running and hiding for too long, and his sword arm was out of practice. Jari could probably even beat him in hand-to-hand combat, but he hoped they wouldn't have to try that right here.

"What does my father want?"

Jari paused for a moment, her dark eyes raking over his body as if she remembered those nights years ago as well as he did.

"The Shadow Cartographers seek pieces of an ancient map that show the way to an island lost in time, pushed out into the far Uncharted."

"What does that have to do with me?"

Jari raised an eyebrow. "The Warlord knows of your love for Earthsiders and they will come soon looking for your help to find the pieces of this map. We have one fragment already and they will do anything to find the rest."

Finn's heart raced at the thought of Sienna coming over the border again. He would see her once more. But he could not betray her. If the Mapwalkers needed the ancient map, then it must have power to destroy something on Earthside. He turned toward the ocean, the frown deepening between his eyes.

"I can't—"

Jari cut him off. "Your baby niece has no magic."

Finn spun back to face her. "What? How do you know? She is too young to face the test."

Jari jumped off the jetty and walked toward him, her gait swaying slightly as if she danced across the rocks. Finn grasped the pommel of his sword and she gave a half-smile at his gesture, like a cat toying with its prey.

"There is one whose magic is knowing gifts early, reading the blood of the newborns to see where their talents lie. To see who is worth keeping."

Finn flinched at the thought of little Emily's blood taken for a dark purpose.

Jari walked closer. "Do you know what they do with those who have no magic in the Castle of the Shadow?"

Her words were soft, menacing.

Finn closed his eyes, recalling the thick stone walls of the dungeon, the bodies of the dead, the Blood Gallery, the torture chambers — and the mass graves of those considered worthless to the cause.

He sighed and nodded slowly.

Jari put her hand on his arm and looked up at him with a half-smile on her lips. "She is safe, looked after by the wet nurses, kept from the blood pits — for now. She'll be returned to your care if you bring the three missing pieces of the Map of Plagues to your father in Old Aleppo by the end of the next half-moon. You can raise her in peace, your transgressions forgiven." She shrugged. "Who knows, maybe Kosai will want to play happy families. After all, she is his granddaughter."

Finn spun round, shaking off her hand, his face contorted with anger. "That bastard sent his own daughter to the Castle of the Shadow. Do you know what happens to women in those breeding halls? Women like you?"

Jari laughed in his face. "Not like me. Your sister was weak, easily broken. The question is whether you are, too."

She was so close that Finn could smell the mint tea on her breath, see the pores of her skin, sense the latent strength of her body. How he wished to fight her now, see her proud face in the dust, but what she offered would fulfill the vow he had made to Isabel as she lay in a pool of her own blood. He promised to look after Emily and he could not storm the castle by force. He had tried before and been vanquished by mere children trying out their newfound magic.

Finn stepped back, giving ground before meeting her eyes. "If I do this, then I want safe passage for the Mapwalker team. I will find the pieces of the map but they must be allowed to return to Earthside afterwards."

Jari hesitated a moment, then nodded. "The Shadow Cartographers want the Map of Plagues, not the people you have a fondness for. Their fate is sealed, regardless, like all those on Earthside."

Finn could only hope that her words were empty, that there would be a way to prevent disaster, but for now, he had to move toward saving Emily. He would figure out the rest later, with Sienna by his side.

"Then I'll do it."

Jari smiled again. "There is just one more condition."

CHAPTER 3

Sienna turned the sign on the door of the shop to Closed. The maps behind her rustled, their pages calling to her as portals to adventure, or a warning of places lost in time. She hadn't even been through the entire inventory yet, the wonders that her grandfather had preserved in a lifetime of cartographical collecting. Each map was potential in paper form, a way into another world, and Sienna longed to place her fingertips on the ink and step through, no matter the price she would have to pay.

She sighed and stepped outside, locking the door with her grandfather's key. Sienna still thought of it as his even though he had left everything to her, along with the legacy of protecting the city he had loved all his life. Now it seemed it was threatened once again. Bridget's voice had sounded tense on the phone as she summoned the Mapwalker team to the Ministry.

As Sienna walked along, the bright sun lit up the pedestrianized street of Elizabeth Buildings, colorful with flowering window boxes. The smell of freshly roasted coffee filled the air from the cafe across the way. It was difficult to imagine that these streets had run with blood not long ago as feral wolves ran through the gate followed by the Warlord's soldiers threatening far worse. They had been vanquished that day, but they still strained at the gates between the worlds.

Sienna turned onto Brock Street, the giant plane trees of The Circus looming ahead. When all was well in the city, red double-decker buses cruised these streets filled with eager tourists listening to the glittering history of the Roman spa and Georgian elite. The buttery Bath stone glowed in the sun, and for the first time, Sienna considered that this could be her home. Her grandfather had loved Bath so deeply that he had given his life to save the city. She had never formed that kind of attachment before, but perhaps now, it might be possible.

Thoughts of Finn intruded. She had promised to help him bring down the dark regime of the Shadow Cartographers, to free the children and enslaved women. That world seemed so far away from this perfection of a city where life was easy and free.

Sienna walked down through the busy streets, past the independent shops, packed restaurants, and the faces of happy families with no idea of that other place.

She turned into the paved square of the Abbey Churchyard and looked up at the facade of the great church, the vaulted stained glass windows flanked by Jacob's ladder carved in stone on which angels climbed heavenwards. Her eyes were drawn to the sinister angel that crawled down, its contorted body more like a demon. Most never noticed the anomaly, but then most didn't know of what lay below this ancient place. The winding halls of the Ministry of Maps lay buffered up against Roman ruins, wound amongst the remains of an ancient city, powered by the ley lines that the Druids of old had known so well.

Sienna walked around the back of the Abbey to the doorway she had run from the first time she had been confronted with the truth of the Mapwalkers. Now she entered again willingly, hoping that this was her way back to Finn.

"Wait for me!"

Sienna turned to see Mila in the alley, walking toward her with confident strides. Her dark curls were tied back with a red scarf patterned with grinning sugar skulls that matched her goth t-shirt, pulled tight over lithe curves and the web of tattoos on her arms.

Sienna smiled. "I'm so glad you're back. I've been going nuts here without you. How was your escape?"

Mila shook her head. "Not long enough. What's going on?"

Sienna shrugged. "Not sure. But Bridget said it was urgent."

Together they walked down the steps and entered the corridors of the Ministry. They passed doorways for the main departments: Antiquities, Restoration, Misinformation, Illustration. The Blood Gallery.

Sienna clenched her fists as they passed, a cord of emotion pulling her toward what would one day be her own resting place. As a Blood Mapwalker, the most powerful magic flowed through her family line, and one day she would have to pay the ultimate sacrifice.

By the time they reached the War Room, it was busy with Mapwalker staff talking in smaller groups, gathered around a framed image of giant rats devouring a corpse.

Bridget raised her arms and calm descended on the room. She nodded to the screen behind her. "Last night, a tomb was uncovered behind a plague pit in London." The screen flicked to images of a sarcophagus, the stone lid broken next to it, then a group of men, one wearing a plague doctor's mask, four with half-moon tattoos.

"These men broke in and we believe they found something, something we thought lost many generations ago."

The image on the screen changed to a woodblock carving, hard black lines revealing a grim tableau. A man lay dying, his face contorted with pain, bulbous black growths under his arms. Rats gathered under his bed, his family gathered behind him, and beyond them, a hooded figure stood with a scythe.

Bridget closed her eyes for a second, as if gathering strength, then opened them again, the brilliant blue as hard as sapphires. "We don't have any pictures of the Map of Plagues, but we think a part of it was found last night by these men."

Questions came thick and fast across the room, the noise growing louder until Bridget held up her hand for quiet. "I'll tell you all we know from the histories. As the Black Plague ravaged Europe, a group of Mapwalker knights tried to save what was left by opening a portal and pushing the badly infected onto a forgotten island in the Borderlands, effectively quarantining them from Earthside."

Perry frowned. "And damning those on the other side. They're people too, you know."

Bridget nodded. "We can't escape the sins of the past, but regardless of what was right, that's what they did. After they pushed the final plague villages into the Borderlands, they used the skin of victims to create a map marking the resting place of the cursed island. The Map of Plagues."

As Bridget spoke, Sienna touched the scars on her arm, her own skin an evolving map of Bath. Had those men been distant relations of her own blood? She felt her father's eyes upon her, and she turned to smile at him. His face was old beyond his years now, marked by the passage of time he had spent as a tortured prisoner of the Shadow Cartographers. She had barely recognized him when they found his carved up body shackled to a table and Sienna knew his scars ran deeper than the wounds that scarred his flesh.

Her father's blue eyes were filled with concern, his knuckles white around his cane with worry, but he wouldn't hold her back from this mission. He had spent years protecting her from the secret of their bloodline but now she was here, now she had taken her place on the Mapwalker team, she knew he was proud of her.

Mila pointed at the woodcut of the plague victim on the screen. "Can a medieval plague really have an impact on the world these days?"

Bridget tapped on her tablet computer to bring up recent news reports of a plague outbreak. Health workers in white plastic clothing and face masks tended to living victims while the dead lay in body bags in neat rows waiting for cremation.

"It's not medieval. The plague still emerges every year in Madagascar, and has been present in Congo, and even the western states of America."

Perry stepped forward. "Don't we have vaccines or ways to stop it?"

"There is no vaccination for bubonic plague but it can be treated with antibiotics, so it's controllable. The problem comes when the plague goes pneumonic and becomes airborne, spreading through coughing and contact." She paused, her frown deepening. "We think the Shadow Cartographers will use the Map of Plagues to find the most virulent strain, the one that the knights banished over the border, and then somehow send it back over to Earthside. Coordinated attacks have been increasing. They're testing our defenses."

Bridget pointed at the map again as the red dots of plague overran the stricken continent, leaving millions dead. "This is what the Shadow Cartographers mean to bring back. We can't let it happen. We have to find the Map of Plagues before they do and destroy it."

"Where do we start?" Mila asked. "Are there any clues in the archives?"

Bridget shook her head. "The knights didn't trust anyone, even their own kind. They split the map into four pieces and separated them. There have been fragments supposedly sighted over the years, notes in the annals but nothing concrete." She hesitated. "There is someone who might know more but she is deep in the Uncharted."

John stepped forward, shaking his head. "You can't send them there, Bridget. It's too dangerous. The Librarian hasn't been seen since …" His voice trailed off.

"Since the last time we sought her out," Bridget finished for him, and a moment of understanding passed between them. "Time passes differently out there. She may yet help us again."

Perry walked up to the screen and examined the plague doctor. He zoomed in and tapped on the man's face. "I can't be sure but I think this is my father's work. He won't stop until Earthside is destroyed and the Borderlanders retake what they think is theirs." He spun around, face set in determination. "When do we leave?"

Bridget frowned. "You need a guide to the outer Borderlands and possibly even into the Uncharted. The trader town on its northern edge is the best option. We've found many guides there over the years, people willing to risk traveling with us. It has no name so it cannot be found easily and its position shifts, of course, but there is one way you can get there quickly. Follow me."

Sienna's heart beat faster at the mention of the trader town. Could it be the same place Finn had run to? As she followed the others toward the door, her father stopped her with a gentle hand.

"Be careful," he said softly. "I know how the shadow feels." His eyes were haunted, like an addict remembering the early days before magic ravaged his body. He shook his head. "I'm sorry, I should have prepared you—"

"It's okay, Dad. I'll be fine. We can talk when I come home again."

He nodded and waved her on with a smile. "Go then. Be safe with your friends."

The others were way up the corridor now, waiting outside a locked door, one of the many hidden beneath the ancient city. Sienna hadn't noticed this one before. It was nothing special, just a wooden door, stained and varnished to enhance the natural grain. But as she drew closer, Sienna noted the intricate locking mechanism that held it shut. Carved runes surrounded a silver keyhole and she could sense magic wound within, as if it would only open to those chosen for a purpose.

Bridget pulled a silver key from her pocket and placed it within the lock, whispering words under her breath as she turned it. She pushed open the door, her blue eyes sparkling with a love for adventure. "Welcome to the Gallery of Geographical Maps."

Sienna couldn't help but gasp as Bridget turned the lights on overhead. The gallery stretched ahead of her, the length of a football field, with bright colors of earth and sea on either side and above her, a vaulted ceiling of gold extravagance.

Each painted map was as big as the wall, a bird's-eye view of a region of the world, shaded with detail of the land. Olive groves and mountains, white-capped sea and calm turquoise lakes. Walled cities of grandeur, rural villages and sea ports with ships that headed out into the blue. A tingling in her fingers made Sienna lean in more closely to one of the cities. She sensed that she could use these to travel through, a shorthand version of the more detailed maps held within the vaults, or those she could make herself. This was some kind of Mapwalker portal room, with access to places the team had traveled to in the past — and perhaps had still to visit.

Bridget led them down the gallery and stopped in front of a fresco of Italy. "The way that leads to the trader town is hidden in the map of Rome itself." She traced the lines of the city with a gentle fingertip. "See, this quarter is not of the ancient city on Earthside. You can enter through here."

Sienna reached out a hand and caressed the lines as she imagined diving down into those streets. Would Finn be there?

Bridget stepped back to allow Mila and Perry to stand close to Sienna. "Be careful out there, but remember, we need those pieces of the Map of Plagues, whatever it takes."

Sienna sensed the pull of the Borderlands and as it pulsed through her, she closed her eyes. She held out her other hand to Perry and Mila and as they touched her palm, she led them through the map.

* * *

The energy in the room shifted as the team passed through. The wall of maps seemed to ripple in their wake and Bridget put out a hand to catch the air that passed through. Was that the salt of the ocean she could smell? The smoke from cooking fires?

She remembered traveling to the trader town years ago, the thrill of being on the edge of adventure as her team passed through on their way to the Uncharted. Bridget sighed. She could never walk there again. She could never swim in the forgotten lakes of sparkling emerald or walk in the hanging gardens. She could never again visit the lost cities of legend. She could not feel the dark thrill of shadow in her veins, the intensity of the rush that came from crossing over.

She wrapped her arms around herself, clutching her body tightly, holding herself back. Because of course, she *could* travel again. She was a Blood Mapwalker, all she had to do was walk through the map.

But Bridget could barely contain the throb of shadow as it called to its home. Every time she had used her magic, the darkness burrowed deeper within her, its tendrils wrapped round her heart. She could cross over again but one more drop might be enough to tip her over. She thought of Sir Douglas Mercator, Perry's father, once her colleague — once her friend — fighting alongside the Mapwalker team to maintain the border in times gone by.

Until the drops of shadow grew too strong in him, and he turned.

Bridget took a step closer to the detailed map, her fingers tracing the lines that represented the border. Would this desire remain in her for the rest of her life? Would she have to resist it every single day?

She rested her forehead against the wall, closed her eyes, allowed the need to rise up within her. She could leave, forget all that held her here, forget John and her responsibilities, forget the fight over the border. It would be simpler to just let go. The tug of shadow throbbed within her and Bridget let it rise …

She stepped back from the wall quickly, heart hammering as she realized how close she had come.

She took a deep breath.

She could not give in. She could never use her blood magic ever again, for it would cost her everything.

CHAPTER 4

The castle smelled of damp and decay and Xander could never quite get his clothes completely dry. He huddled on his bed, pulled the blankets tighter about his shoulders and leaned back against the wooden headboard, carved with intricate designs of poisonous plants. Mold grew in the corners of his room and despite covering the flagstones with thick rugs, it was always cold. There was a fireplace surrounded by fancy metal scrollwork but nothing to burn and no way to start the flame anyway.

Xander sighed. This was *not* what he had signed up for.

His access to the hidden libraries had been refused until he could prove himself a true follower of the Shadow. He didn't have any friends because the castle was full of guards below his station and feral children with no control over their magic. He had tried to get into their hall but the little freaks had driven him away with fireballs and cruel laughter. He was allowed — even encouraged — to visit the Fertility Halls but the place made his skin crawl. He was truly an outsider here.

When Sir Douglas Mercator had first talked of the glories of the shadow side, he had spoken of unlimited magic, of a forbidden library full of books of beasts that Xander could illustrate and skin maps he could use to conjure them into being. He promised a fulfilling life in the Borderlands, the life of a prince, no longer subject to the demands of the Ministry, no need to restrict his magic. All he had to do was deliver the daughter of John Farren, so her skin alongside her father's would complete the Map of Shadows, and Xander would have his new life.

He had fulfilled his promise and brought Sienna to the castle but somehow, the Mapwalker team had made it out. Xander still remembered her face as he had revealed his true allegiance, how Perry had lost his father that day and how he had lost his friends.

He'd also lost his prize and so Xander found himself consigned to the castle, living not the princely life he'd been promised, but a limbo existence unwanted by all. Sir Douglas hadn't mentioned the bleak living conditions here in the castle or that the forbidden library would still be forbidden, or that the skin maps he had been promised were kept locked up to be used for more important things than conjuring beasts.

On top of all that, Xander had been without his phone for missions into the Borderlands but he had never really considered a life without technology altogether. It pretty much sucked.

Despite his annoyance at Bridget and the Ministry and the dire warnings of what would happen if they gave in to the shadow side, he found himself missing Bath. The way the stone turned to honey-gold in the late afternoons, the birdsong along the canal where he had walked with Mila sometimes, Zippy her spaniel running ahead. Right now he even missed Perry. He could start a fire anywhere and right now, the warmth of the flames would go a long way to making this place bearable. Xander wasn't even getting a chance to use his magic, since Sir Douglas was holed up in his study at the top of the north tower and hadn't been seen for days.

Enough.

Xander unwrapped himself from the blanket and grabbed the satchel containing his sketchbook and pens. He would just go knock on the door and ask — no, demand — access to the forbidden library. That would be a start until there was something more interesting to do. Like summon the cool beasts he'd soon be drawing. After all, what was the point of being an Illustrator when you couldn't illustrate? He would prove himself to the Shadow if it took all his magic to get there.

* * *

Xander stalked through the corridors of the castle, the stone tunnels lit with lamps in iron brackets, the cold permeating his bones. He passed soldiers along the way, some staring at him with searching eyes, assessing his status. He met their gaze, noting their features, determined to seek them out once he was given his rightful place here. They would respect him when they faced the creatures he conjured.

As their footsteps faded into the distance, Xander reached the bottom of the staircase to the north tower. It was flanked by two pillars carved with occult symbols on one side and the crest of the Mercators' on the other. Xander put his foot on the first step, hesitating as the cold seemed to permeate deep into his blood, filling his veins with ice. He looked up, a sudden doubt filling him. What was really up there?

Perhaps he should come back another time? Perhaps Sir Douglas was too busy to see him right now?

Footsteps echoed behind him as the soldiers marched back down the corridor.

Xander walked on, taking the steps two at a time, unwilling to face them as he retreated. His heart pounded as he climbed, the welcome exertion of physical movement combined with one concern.

He had not been invited.

Xander slowed his steps to stop on the curve of the stair and pulled a scrap of leather from his pocket. Placing it on the ground, he smoothed out the edges around the beasts drawn there: a tentacled sea monster and a shark in one corner, a dragon in the opposite, next to a coiled serpent and a powerful lion.

Xander summoned his Illustrator magic and channeled it into the leather. Asada, the lion, stepped from the map, shaking his thick golden mane as if waking from sleep. He rolled his powerful shoulders and nuzzled against Xander's side, his purr a deep sound that echoed in the corridor. Xander put his face in Asada's mane, closed his eyes and breathed in the animal scent mingled with the leather of the map. This was about as close to home as he could get and for now, it was enough. With Asada by his side, Xander's confidence returned. Together they padded quietly up the stairs.

As the staircase spiraled up into the upper reaches of the tower, Xander looked out of the slits in the rock which opened to the castle and lands below. On one side, guards trained in the quadrangle in front of huge double doors leading to the children's wing. On another, a group of women in rags stood around a pile of bloody shrouds, those who didn't make it out of the Breeding Halls alive. Carrion birds swooped low over the burial pit, their cries a haunting ululation to honor the silence of the suffering victims. Xander looked away and redoubled his pace, Asada at his heel.

As they reached the top of the tower, Xander slowed, taking quiet steps toward the giant wooden door which stood open a fraction. He could hear voices from further inside, although they were faint. Sir Douglas had a whole suite of rooms up here in the tower, so Xander pushed the first door open with a gentle hand and stepped inside.

The plush apartment was cosy, warm with a crackling

log fire and animal skins on the walls for insulation. Xander reached for Asada's mane as he noticed a lion pelt next to a rare leopardskin. Life was cheap here, even more so for animals.

Sir Douglas's wide mahogany desk dominated the space, a map of the Borderlands placed on top, the corners weighed down with the tiny skulls of children.

Xander started as the voices rose in argument, now clearly coming from the next room. He knew that he should leave now but something about the map drew him in.

The Ministry had many maps of the Borderlands but all were of different parts and they shifted over time. As new places were pushed over the border, the very shape of the Borderlands changed as it squashed some cities closer, pulled apart mountain ranges, and nudged rivers off course.

But this map was a recent survey, a bird's-eye view of the whole expanse all the way to the Uncharted with the addition of tent cities that Xander had never seen before, each drawn close to portals that he definitely did know about. The biggest tent city near the shadow gate that led into Bath through the portal at The Circus — right in the heart of the city he had left behind.

As Asada lay down by the fire, licking his paws and enjoying its warmth, Xander walked around the other side of the desk. Rounding the corner, his foot knocked against something leaning on the side. A plague doctor's mask with a long beak once stuffed full of medicinal herbs. Xander frowned at the curious thing. He wasn't aware of Sir Douglas's interest in medieval times, but then there was a lot he didn't know about this side of the border.

The argument grew louder still on the other side of the door, and Sir Douglas's voice became clear.

"The plague could spread further than we can control. It's too dangerous. Our people—"

His words turned into a scream, an agonizing sound of terror and pain.

Asada stood, hackles raised, and bared his teeth as the scream trailed off. Xander clutched the table, eyes wide as he stood looking at the door. He wanted to go in there, he wanted to help, but something stopped him, something cold and dark that pierced his heart with a lance of shadow. He didn't want to face what lay behind that door.

A broken voice stuttered, faint through the door, "I'm sorry, my lord. Please …"

The scream came again.

Xander fled, Asada on his heels as they ran for the safety of the lower halls.

Even as he reached his room and barred the door, Xander knew that something had sensed his presence, something knew what he had seen and heard, something was out there waiting for him.

He sat on the floor, his back against the wooden door. He put his arms around Asada's neck and buried his face in the lion's mane once more. Tears welled in his eyes as he wished he could take back the decisions he'd made. How had he ended up here? Was there any way he could fix this terrible mistake?

CHAPTER 5

S**IENNA LEANED INTO THE** sense of weightlessness as she flew above a world that shifted along an ever-changing boundary. The lines of the walled map morphed into three-dimensional streets next to an ocean that stretched into the distance. The world curved into the horizon and for a moment, she couldn't tell whether she was in the map or above it. Could she keep traveling up here, far beyond the border?

She swallowed the exhilaration and dived down into the city, giddy with sensation.

The smell of rotting fish and the salty tang of the ocean greeted Sienna as she opened her eyes. They were in a street behind a food market, the shouts of stallholders blending with the call of seabirds above them as they dived down to snatch pieces of discarded produce. Sienna could just make out the ocean beyond the maze of stalls, the clean blue a stark contrast to the riot of color and movement within the market.

Perry crouched on the ground retching.

"I don't know if I'll ever get used to that," he groaned.

Mila pulled him up by one arm. "Come on, we have to get moving. The Shadow guards will sense the breach in the border and we don't want to be here if they come looking."

They skirted the edge of the market and headed into the warren of dirt streets that led away from the waterfront. They were dense with makeshift shelters, shacks made of rusted iron sheets tied together with rope leaning up against each other and hung with plastic tarpaulin to keep out the rain. Some were sturdy, reinforced with planks of wood and metal rivets, others cobbled together with flotsam from the ocean.

An old woman sat on a low plastic chair smoking a hand-rolled cigarette, the sweet smell of smoke hanging in the air around her, disguising the stink of the open sewer nearby. She watched them pass with glassy eyes, no trace of curiosity left in her.

A chicken strutted past, pecking at the dust. Dried fish hung in strips from one shelter, pungent with salt. A makeshift kite of rags flew high above, a glimpse of red against the blue, a sign that perhaps there was still some hope here.

"I've heard that this place has no name because no one stays long enough to call it home," Perry said as they walked on. "Thousands of people pass through but none stay to build anything."

Mila walked faster. "Well, we're not staying long either."

They passed people of all cultures along the way. Veiled women of Middle Eastern origin, Africans in bright colored headpieces, and men with the tall blonde features of Slavs.

"How do all these people get here?" Sienna asked.

"If they're lost on water, they end up here," Mila said. "The lucky ones might find a place to call home."

Sienna frowned. "And the unlucky ones?"

Shouting and the sound of drums came from the streets ahead. People on the streets faded quickly into the shadows, alert to danger.

Mila looked ahead, her eyes narrowing. "The unlucky ones find out this is a slave trader town."

They headed in the direction of the drums, harsh beats

that reverberated in the narrow lanes, and soon joined a throng of people heading in the same direction. There were merchants in the crowd, and soldiers too, those who could use slaves perhaps, as well as those in need of entertainment.

The Mapwalker team kept their heads down, merging with the pack as the streets opened out into a large square. The smell of roasting nuts and hot sugar filled the air, and a folk band played in the corner, the atmosphere almost like a carnival as the late afternoon sun lit the square with a golden glow. Sienna looked around at the excitement on the faces around her. Humanity had ever loved to watch a spectacle of suffering.

A raised dais stood in the middle of the square covered in colored streamers, a long metal cage in its center. Soldiers of the Shadow stood around it, their posture relaxed but alert and ready to act should the crowd surge forward. Sienna rose up on her tiptoes to see better. A chill washed over her as she saw what lay within.

The cage contained seven people, five adults and two children, faces desperate as they clutched at the bars. From their clothes, they had only recently crossed from Earthside, refugees lost on the ocean or perhaps they had wandered over the border during some desperate situation. War drove people over here, escaping from one life only to enter another just as dangerous.

The crowd cheered as a muscled hulk of a man stood up on the stage, a wooden cosh in one hand. The weapon was dented and stained with blood and sweat. The slave trader had the ruddy face of someone who enjoyed life too much but the cruel look in his eyes made it clear that his enjoyment involved the suffering of others.

"Are you ready?" he called across the heads of the crowd.

The baying of voices rose to the sky as the mob clamored for spectacle and drama, a moment of escape from their own pitiful lives. Sienna tried to crush down the nausea that rose within as the slave trader pulled a young boy from the cage, his meaty hand wrapped around the scrawny wrist of a nine-year-old with the olive skin of the Mediterranean and the dark eyes of Hispanic descent.

"This one is something special. Found him myself in the camps lighting fires with his magic." He shook the boy. "Show them."

The boy cowered away from the man as tears ran down his cheeks, his face frozen in fear. The slave master pushed the boy to the ground and raised the wooden cosh, ready to strike. "Show them, boy!"

Sienna couldn't bear to watch any longer. She took a step forward, raising her arm in a bid to catch the attention of the slave master.

A strong hand pushed her arm back down, holding her wrist in a tight grip.

She spun around. "What are you …?"

Her words trailed off as she looked up into the face of the man who stood behind her. Dark eyes and the regal features of an African prince.

Finn.

He pulled her away, shielding her body with his own as he led her out of the central area to the edge of the market.

"Are you trying to get yourself captured?" he demanded as soon as they were out of sight of the slave master. He shook his head in frustration. "This place is crawling with Shadow guards and spies who will betray you for a loaf of bread."

She looked up at him, heart thumping. "Hi."

Finn took a deep breath. His eyes softened and he lifted a hand to stroke her cheek. "Hi." He shook his head. "I'm sorry. I saw you there and I couldn't let you draw attention to yourself."

"But those people—"

"You can't help them. You saw the soldiers guarding

them, the crowd waiting to see them fall. It's the same as the Castle of the Shadow. We couldn't save all those women in the breeding halls, we couldn't save the children either." Finn hung his head. "I don't know who we can save anymore."

Sienna reached up and cupped his face in her hand. "I missed you."

"I missed you too." Finn wrapped his arms around her, pulling her close so their hearts beat together. He bent his head to kiss her, his lips just touching hers.

"Don't mind me."

Finn pulled back at the mocking voice, leaving Sienna bereft. She opened her eyes to see a willowy woman with black hair tied back with a leather strap, twin crossed-swords on her back. Scars snaked up her lean muscled arms and her face was marked with the half-moon tattoo of the Warlord. Her tawny eyes raked over Sienna.

"This is the one you turned your back on your family for?" The woman raised an eyebrow. "She must be good."

Sienna blushed.

Finn cleared his throat. "Sienna, this is Jari. We're … working together at the moment."

Mila and Perry pushed through the crowd, emerging at the edge just in time to hear Finn's words. Jari took a step back, hands hovering near her swords now she was outnumbered.

Mila glanced over at her then directed her question at Finn. "We need a guide to the library and we need to go tonight. We don't have much time. You know of anyone who might be able to help?"

Finn hesitated and Sienna thought she saw a flicker of uncertainty cross his face, as if he had to make a choice in that moment. She desperately wanted him to say he would come but what did she know of his life now — and who was this Jari, with her stark beauty that was so intimidating?

Jari stepped forward, hands resting by her side now, a

half-smile on her face. "We're free, actually, and we were just talking about a possible journey. It's been a while since we've traveled together, isn't it, Finn?"

Sienna heard a possessive edge in her words, a hint of an intimate history that made her burn inside.

Finn took a deep breath. "What do you need?"

Mila explained a little about the Map of Plagues. "We need to get to the Library of Alexandria, or what's left of it."

Jari laughed. "When you push places out of Earthside, they thrive here. You destroy and write them off your maps, but here, they live again. The library is far greater than it once was. And it's not too far from here — *if* you know the mountain passes."

Her words hung in the air.

Mila looked directly at Finn. "We only need one guide."

Finn glanced over at Jari and a look passed between them. He sighed. "We travel together. It's both of us, or none at all."

Sienna sensed that there was something going on, something that trapped Finn into this arrangement somehow. She could only hope that he would tell her at some point, but for now, they needed to get moving and she didn't want to leave him behind.

"We don't have much time," Sienna said, putting her hand on Mila's arm. "And we do need a guide."

Mila bit her lip, narrowing her eyes at the warrior woman. "I don't like it. Even our friends have betrayed us before."

Jari shrugged. "Your loss." She began to walk away.

Finn took a step back, his eyes darting between Jari and the Mapwalker team. "I … have to go with her."

Mila put a hand out. "Wait. If you vouch for her, Finn, then we'll accept the terms."

Jari stopped and turned back. A beat of silence before Finn spoke. "We have fought beside each other in many battles. Jari will keep her side of the bargain, as I will keep mine."

Sienna couldn't help feeling that his words had a deeper level of meaning and there was a sadness beneath his tone that she couldn't quite put her finger on. But at least now they would have time together and she could find out what was going on.

Mila nodded. "Alright, let's get moving before night falls." Her eyes didn't leave Jari's back as the warrior woman led them out of town in the gathering dark.

They soon passed a queue of ragged people lining up for a soup kitchen. There were splashes of color but most were dressed in the brown and green and grey of dirt and mud and broken earth. The smell of roasted vegetables filled the air, the promise of a full belly drawing people here from all over the makeshift city.

A young woman, belly swollen with late pregnancy, leaned against the wall. She smoked a hand-rolled cigarette and as they walked by, Sienna caught the almost sweet smell of marijuana but with a taint of something else underneath.

Finn noticed her confusion. "People will do anything to escape for a while, but the drugs here are often laced with other things — experimental compounds aimed at mutation."

Sienna shook her head in horror. "Why would anyone do such a thing?"

"Mapwalkers are born, not made, you know that as well as I do. The Shadow Cartographers seek new strains of magic and they don't have any restraints on how that's achieved."

Mila joined in the conversation. "Unlike on Earthside where the Mapwalkers are dying out."

"Because we don't force people to breed like they do here," Sienna snapped, remembering the Fertility Halls of the Castle of the Shadow.

Finn's jaw tightened. "Your people on Earthside are not at war. At least they don't know they are yet, but over here, the drums beat harder every day for invasion, and wars need people to fight them."

As they walked on, his words echoed in Sienna's mind. Back in Bath, it was hard to imagine what war might look like, how Earthside could be changed by invaders from the Borderlands, but Finn was right. Mapwalkers dwindled on Earthside, but here they bred new blood every day and each birth was a chance that more powerful magic would emerge. Even if they found and destroyed the Map of Plagues now, what did it all mean for the future? She had promised Finn she would help him fight for peace between their worlds, but suddenly that seemed so far out of reach.

The densely packed makeshift housing grew more sparse as the team walked south, past the edge of the shanty town as it spilled into the desert. The night air smelled fresh out here and Sienna took some huge breaths, suddenly aware that she had been shallow breathing in the city to avoid inhaling the stench.

The cry of a night bird called from above, the silhouette of a raptor hovering overhead. Sienna shuddered to think of it swooping down to pick at the carcasses of the dead from the city behind them.

Undulating dunes rose as they walked toward a distant ridge far ahead, the rising moonlight casting a silver glint on its slopes where a path wound up into darkness.

As Finn led them out into the desert, they saw a column of refugees heading over the hill in the opposite direction. Families huddled together carrying what they could, bent shoulders, slow steps.

"Where are they going?" Sienna asked.

Mila glanced back at them. "I heard talk in the market of a refugee camp in that direction, a place where the sick are cared for, with enough food and even protection from slave traders."

Jari gave a harsh laugh and shook her head. "This is the Borderlands. You think there'd be something like that here? I don't know what's out there but there's no way it's some paradise. Those people are marked by the shadow. They have no future."

The warrior woman strode ahead, her words leaving the team in silence as they walked into the night.

At the edge of the desert, just before the land rose sharply into the escarpment, a ruined temple rose out of the valley floor.

"We'll stop there briefly before we journey on," Finn said.

They reached it as the moon rose high above the ruined temple, casting a silver light upon the statuesque figures of long-dead gods.

Finn knelt by the altar, his dark head bent in respect, his lips moving in silent prayer. His fingers caressed the pommel of his sword, held in front of him like a rosary.

Sienna watched him from the side of the ruined temple. She had never had a faith like his, perhaps she never had cause to. Faith helped in the darkest of times and even when her father had gone missing years ago, she had relied on books and learning, rather than God to answer her questions. Of course, the holy books on Earthside had no light to cast on the split world. There was no place for Borderlanders in their singular history.

She wondered how the priests and shamans here explained the split. Perhaps she could study their holy books and find out. Perhaps that way she might understand more of Finn's world, the way he thought.

Sometimes it was as if there was no barrier between them, not even a whisper of difference in who they were. In those moments, Sienna believed that somehow they could have a possible future. She dreamed of fixing the border, solving the problem of the Warlord's bloodlust and the power-hungry Shadow Cartographers, bringing peace to both sides. Surely that was possible?

A ray of light from the moon caught the silver handle of Finn's sword, the intricate patterns reminding her of his allegiances, of how little she really knew him.

She sighed softly and turned to see Jari leaning against the wall, twin swords never far from her hands. A warrior woman, more than Finn's equal here. Jari met Sienna's eyes, her cool gaze an appraisal that found her wanting.

CHAPTER 6

It was still dark when Sienna awakened. Her thick cloak was scant protection against the cold stone but for a moment, she lay motionless, listening to Mila's gentle breath and the deeper sounds of Perry's snoring in the corner of the cave. Jari lay silent a little further away. They had found the cave by starlight after hours of walking and sunk quickly into sleep the night before, muscles aching from the long trek.

The sound of cloth shifting on stony ground came from the entrance. Sienna could just make out Finn's faint silhouette. She slowly unwrapped herself, careful not to wake the others and tiptoed out to join him.

It was cold and foggy, the clouds still dense above them but in the distance, the coral fingers of dawn crept over the horizon, the promise of a new day. Sienna sat down on the outer ledge next to Finn, aware that they had not been alone in too long. There was so much to say, so much she wanted to ask him.

"Morning," he whispered.

Sienna grinned. "Morning." That was as good a start as any.

Finn pointed out into the blackness of the valley below, at the faint shimmer of a river and the outlines of buildings.

"That's the library." His voice was reverential as if he spoke of a temple or another place of worship. "I haven't been here in a long time. Part of me thought perhaps I had dreamed it even existed."

"What's it like?"

Finn reached for her hand in the dark and she took it, holding onto his strength. "It is everything I think the best of Earthside must be. Knowledge, truth ..." He turned to look in her eyes. "Beauty."

Sienna could hardly breathe as tension mounted between them. He dipped his head to kiss her—

"Not interrupting anything, am I?" Jari stepped across them, her words mocking as she sat down on the edge, legs swinging out into the canyon below. She had her pack by her side, her two swords strapped and ready to go. She seemed effortlessly poised.

Finn pulled away and dropped Sienna's hand. The imprint of his palm remained and she wrapped her arms around herself, trying to hold onto the moment.

"Not at all." Finn was brusque once more and just like that, the barrier was back between them.

Jari pulled some leftover bread from her pack, tearing off tiny pieces as she gazed out. "It's a hell of a view."

A ray of sun broke through the clouds and lit upon a towering spire of white marble that rose up from a classical courtyard beneath surrounded by a small town of houses and market squares.

Sienna had imagined the ruins of Alexandria laid out before them, evidence of neglect and the burnt-out remains of what had been destroyed by Christians in the fourth century. But of course, life didn't stop when a place ended up here in the Borderlands. Time passed and life would always find a way.

She looked sideways at Finn, his face staunch. In the same way, the sun rose and set every day they were not together, life taking them in different directions.

Finn stretched and stood up. "We should descend the gorge before the sun is high and it gets too hot to walk. I'll wake the others."

He stepped around Sienna, avoiding her eyes and went back into the cave. Mila's groan of annoyance and Perry's low rumble of a voice echoed from within, followed by the sound of laughter.

"He's not for you." Jari's voice was low, as gentle as the sharpest blade that cuts deep to the bone before you even notice. "Finn is a Borderlander, this is his home, we are his people. Remember that."

Before Sienna could reply, Mila came out of the cave entrance, yawning and stretching. "Oh wow, this place is incredible. How did we possibly let this go from Earthside?"

Jari stood up and brushed off her clothes. "You drove it away. You denied its existence. You burned it down and killed its people. You don't deserve it."

She spun on her heel and set off down the steep path, sure-footed on the rocky ground. She didn't look back.

Mila raised an eyebrow. "Okay, then. Someone's grumpy this morning." She looked down at Sienna with a cheeky grin. "You two been fighting over something?"

Sienna blushed as she stood up and flicked the dirt from her clothes.

Perry hefted his pack up onto his shoulders. "Jari's right, though. The grand destruction of the Library of Alexandria is a romantic myth. It declined over several hundred years, the scholars expelled before some of it was burned during the time of Caesar and later under the Christian Pope. But after Alexandria lost its preeminence in the classical world, the library disappeared from history."

Finn laughed. "It disappeared from *your* history, but it began a new chapter right here. Let's go see the Librarian." He set off down the track, Mila following, then Sienna and Perry bringing up the rear.

The path was clear, well-worn by travelers, and the group strung out, giving each other space as they descended into the valley. Sienna looked up as the cry of a falcon rang out, the bird of prey hanging in the updraft as the sun warmed the land. The Library of Alexandria stretched out below, its central buildings like a classical temple winding down to a river with stepped terraces. Around it, the town awakened in the morning light, and Sienna could just make out tiny figures walking through the streets. She wondered about their lives here. How much did they even know of Earthside?

Distracted, she stumbled a little, her feet slipping on loose rocks, her heart pounding as she clutched the stony cliff behind her. Life was fragile on both sides of the border and no magic would save her if she fell off the edge, dashed on the rocks below. She laughed to herself. That would be a really stupid way to die. She stopped looking at the view and placed her feet more carefully as she descended.

The sun was high by the time they regrouped at the bottom of the escarpment by the banks of a sparkling river. Jari lay on a rock, eyes closed, relaxing in the sun. At least she looked relaxed, but Sienna had no doubt that the warrior woman could leap to her feet, swords at the ready, if she sensed a threat.

Finn crouched on the bank and drew in the dirt with a stick, sketching a long rectangle marked with a central box. "The Librarian works in the central hall here." He marked an X in the box. "But we can't just waltz in there, especially with you two." He looked at Perry and Mila. "Fire magic and water magic are forbidden, for obvious reasons with all those books. But more than that, the security is run by a branch of the Shadow Cartographers — the Scryers."

Mila sighed. "They can sense what magic we have."

Finn nodded. "They recruit from here, and when I say recruit—"

"You actually mean force into slavery or worse," Perry cut

in. "I've heard of these Scryers. My father said …" He shuddered as his words trailed off. He shook his head to clear the memory. "We can just stay out here and wait for you."

Jari sat up. "Don't be a baby. We can get past a few Scryers."

Sienna crouched down next to Finn. "And besides, we have to go together." She pointed at the X in the center. "If the Librarian knows a way to get to the pieces of the map, it's likely that we'll travel from there straight away. I'll need you all with me because I can't come back for you."

Finn nodded. "Exactly." He drew lines around three sides of the main library hall. "The Scryers have outposts here, here, and here and the rumor is that they have some kind of net under the river protecting the water entrance. We can get past them." He looked up at Jari with a dark smile. "We just need a diversion."

Jari jumped down from her rock. "I'm sure I'll think of something by the time we get there."

The group walked along the bank of the river past humble dwellings that soon gave way to grander mansions and then became the bustling hub of the city. The river widened, forded by pedestrian bridges and ferry boats that carried people and animals alike. Street vendors called from market stalls as they passed, hawkers tried to sell them library trinkets. Sienna slowed down to look at some tiny books bound with real leather before Mila pulled her away.

"You can't take anything back, remember. It creates a link back to you, a way for the Shadow Cartographers to find you on Earthside."

Sienna thought of Mila's canal boat, the objects she had on her shelf. "But you—"

Mila rolled her eyes. "I didn't know any better and besides, mine were taken through ages ago." She pointed at the others moving further into the crowd. They funneled toward one of the main gates into the library complex where people moved through a turnstile flanked by guards. "Come on, we have to catch them up."

When they reached Finn and Perry, Jari was nowhere to be seen.

"Where's she gone?" Mila asked, her tone as suspicious as ever of the Borderlander warrior.

"She'll be ready when we need her." Finn pulled them into the shadows of a temple wall within sight of the turnstile. People queued to get through, chatting and relaxed, the gate clicking as each passed. Guards stood on either side looking out into the crowd, paying no obvious attention to what was clearly an everyday occurrence.

Finn leaned down, his voice low. "We need to get through that gate. Each one of us has to pass through the turnstile separately. They keep it moving pretty fast. Watch how the regular folk behave. You can spot the tourists."

Sienna followed his gaze toward a small group of travellers in the long robes of a religious order, eyes wide as they gazed up at the library ahead. One of them hung back, a young man in his twenties. He had a scar down the side of his neck as if something had been carved from his skin. Sienna frowned as she noticed his white knuckles, his clenched fists. He looked as if he was going to run, but then he stopped himself, took a deep breath and stepped toward the gate, waiting his turn at the end of his group.

As the turnstile clicked and the young man stood between the gatehouses, a harsh sound like the caw of a crow burst out. The guards either side moved in a flash, thrusting their spears out, barricading the young man between them.

An audible gasp spread through the crowd and people surged forward to see what was happening.

Sienna moved with them. As she ducked under one man's arm, she caught a glimpse of an impossibly long bony arm with fingers like spider's legs darting out of the gatehouse, wrapping around the young man before dragging him inside.

He screamed, a sound of terror that was cut off almost as soon as it began.

As silence fell again, the guards stepped back, opening their spears once more. One of them nodded at the next person in the queue, a local woman by the looks of the basket of bread on her hip. She stepped forward with confidence, approached the turnstile and moved through. The rhythmic clicking began again as others followed.

Sienna turned back to see that Perry's face had gone white.

"There's a Scryer in that gatehouse," he whispered, eyes wide with fear. "My father told me stories of them when I was young. They take people down into their den, they suck the magic from you, they leave you a broken husk."

Sienna put her hand on his arm. "It's okay, we'll be fine. Jari's going to make a distraction, right?" She looked at Finn.

He nodded. "Absolutely. And we should go now while that Scryer is busy."

Perry backed away. "No, no, not me. You guys go. I'm staying right here."

Mila took Perry's arm. "You can't go back now. If you don't come with us, you'd better learn to love it here. So, man up and get moving. Look like a genuine tourist and they might not even notice how sweaty you are."

Perry clenched his fists, nodded sharply and together, the group stepped into the crowd. Finn waved the others ahead of him as they approached the gate.

"Whatever happens, don't stop, don't turn around. Stay in a line and just keep moving. Wait for us by the statue of the Muses near the main steps."

Mila walked forward, shoulders back, flirtatious smile on her face as she sashayed up to the guards, Sienna behind her, then Perry.

Just as she reached the turnstile, an explosion boomed out across the surrounding rooftops. Smoke billowed out of a nearby house and the crowd surged forward to the gate. Several pushed in front of Mila in their haste to escape the crush. The guards lost their calm composure and stepped back to allow them all through.

Mila went with the flow, surging through with a group of locals.

A little girl burst into tears near Sienna and she grabbed the child's hand, lifting her up into a hug and carrying her through the gate. "It's alright. We'll find your mommy, sweetheart."

Sienna lost sight of Perry in the crowd but she didn't look back, stepping through the gate quickly. As she crossed into a classical forecourt, a woman's voice called out in desperation, "Jasmine, where are you?"

The little girl struggled at the sound of her voice. "Mama."

Sienna spun and handed the little girl over, then turned back to the gate just as Perry stepped between the gatehouses. His face was determined and he looked straight ahead, meeting Sienna's eyes. A smile of relief crossed his face as the turnstile clicked. He was almost through.

Suddenly, the harsh caw of a crow. The metallic slam of spears.

The guards stepped in front and behind, blocking his path.

"No!" Sienna cried out as the bony hand of the Scryer reached out and dragged Perry away.

CHAPTER 7

As the harsh cry of the crow sounded, Perry tried to summon his magic, reaching for the flame inside. But the bony hand reached out like a pincer and snapped tight shut around him. As it crushed his body and dragged him inside the gatehouse, it snuffed out the flicker of light inside, his scream cut off before it erupted from his throat.

The gatehouse was pitch black inside. Perry couldn't see the Scryer but he could smell its breath, like wet body parts, as rank as a drowned corpse. Its bones creaked as it moved toward him, the sandpaper scrape of its skin on stone. It raked its bony fingers over his body and the violation cut deep into his muscles, into his heart.

He couldn't move. He couldn't breathe.

His father's words came back to him, as they sat by the fire on the Mercator estate so many years ago. *If you ever get caught by the Scryers, you'll wish you'd never been born. Better to die by the fire of your own hand than have them feed on you and suck the marrow from your bones. They don't answer to anyone but the Shadow itself.*

Perhaps it would let him go. Perhaps his magic wasn't strong enough for them to take. Perhaps—

A trapdoor below his feet opened and Perry fell through, his body still immobilized by the curious power of the Scryer.

He landed on straw, soft enough to break his fall but still crackly and sharp. The clang of metal and spikes rose up from the ground beneath, forming a cage around him. The trapdoor snapped shut above, leaving him in darkness.

Perry grabbed the bars, suddenly released from his paralysis. "Help! Let me out of here."

His words echoed back to him. It sounded like he was in a long corridor but he could sense no one else there. It smelled of minerals and water on rock like an abandoned mine and he could hear the faint skitter of a thousand tiny legs. Perry couldn't help imagining what kind of insects collected the pieces of the dead down here. He stood up sharply, pulling himself away from the floor, his skin crawling at the thought of them feeding on him.

Suddenly, a clank of gears resounded. His cage began to move on rails that took him deeper into darkness before light flickered up ahead. Perry gulped as he considered what he would face, whether the light was a blessing or whether darkness would be better.

The cage entered a long hall lit by flaming torches high up in curved brackets. It clanked to a halt next to another, the bars bumping up against its neighbor.

In the dim light, Perry could see a body lying on the straw, head turned toward him. It was the young man who had been taken just a few minutes before.

"Hey, are you alright?"

The man didn't move. As Perry looked closer, he noticed dark patches on the man's skin. They pulsed rhythmically, like a sinister heartbeat and as he watched, one of them moved, crawling slowly, leaving a trail of black blood behind.

This time, there was no stopping Perry's scream as it erupted from his throat.

* * *

Up above, the crowd surged on toward the grand marble facade of the library. Sienna turned to run back to the gate, desperate to get to Perry. A strong hand reached out to hold her back, tight fingers wrapped around her arm.

"Don't draw attention to yourself," Jari's rough voice whispered. "Or you'll be down there with him."

Sienna shook her hand off. "We have to get Perry out of there. You saw how terrified he was."

She remembered the hunt for the Map of Shadows and how Perry hadn't been scared back then, how he had faced skeletal birds and fire-breathing dragons with no fear. How much worse could the Scryers be? She imagined him down there, buried beneath the city. They had to find him.

Finn came through the turnstile and joined them, his expression like thunder. "I saw what happened. There's nothing we can do."

Mila stepped forward and took Sienna's hand. "We're not going on without him. Perry is one of our team and besides, he saved us in the Castle of the Shadow, remember? You can't proceed without Sienna, so I guess we all have to find a way down there."

Finn looked at Jari. "Any ideas?"

The warrior woman rolled her eyes. "Seriously, no one told me this was a babysitting job." She paused. "But there are some tunnels I've heard about. I'll need to go see a contact of mine. Wait by the statue. I'll be back soon."

As Sienna watched her go, Mila led her over to the marble statue of the Muses, nine beautiful sisters joyous in their celebration of music, poetry, song and dance. They sat on its edge watching the sun-dappled square in front of them as locals and pilgrims alike gathered to approach the monumental entrance of the library.

This was a place Sienna had dreamed of, the prototype of the Bodleian in Oxford, a temple to knowledge, a never-ending stream of learning. She should be entering these halls as joyous as the Muses immortalized above them. Yet all she could think about was Perry, broken and empty somewhere beneath.

It seemed impossible that this bright world existed above and yet below lay only terror and darkness.

* * *

Perry stopped screaming. He panted and retched, tears springing to his eyes as he tried to control the panic rising within him. He looked up to the flickering torches above, reaching inside for his fire magic. He would summon it and turn this place into a fiery hell.

But once again, the strange dampening effect crushed the spark, some power that the Scryers used to keep magic at bay down here, a way to control their victims. Perry slumped in defeat.

The sound of rustling and then limping footsteps came from the shadows at the side of the hall.

A spindly figure, nearly as tall as the torch brackets, hobbled out of the gloom. A Scryer wrapped in layers of ragged cloth that covered it from head to toe, dragging in the dust as it moved toward Perry.

He backed away as far as he could into the corner of the cage. "I'm Halbrasse. Please. My father is one with the Shadow. Stop! I'll do anything."

A pressure built in his head as the Scryer moved closer. It didn't need words. It had a presence he couldn't resist, a way to reach into his very soul.

The Scryers had been human once but generations of old magic had wound into their flesh and now they were scraps of skin and bone held together by pure shadow. Annals of the Mapwalkers said that they lived below some of the oldest cities pushed through from Earthside, sustained by the blood that seeped down through the earth and the magic they could drain from those they captured.

As the Scryer reached the bars, Perry couldn't help but fall to his knees as if it pushed him down with overwhelming force. It pulled back its hood and he raised his eyes to look into the face of abomination. Empty eye sockets in a skull covered with rotting flesh. It opened its mouth to reveal a pulsating mass of Shadow leeches oozing over each other in search of food.

The Scryer lifted one bony arm with its long fingers and picked a leech from within its maw. It writhed, tiny rows of teeth searching for something to latch onto. The Scryer stretched through the bars and placed the leech on Perry's neck. He moaned as the foul creature began to bite into his skin, latching on, sucking the life out of him as weakness spread through his body.

The Scryer reached back into its mouth for more of the parasites.

* * *

Sienna couldn't stand it any longer. She paced back and forth in front of the statue of the Muses. "We're wasting time. What if I just draw a map here and now, go down there, get Perry and bring him back?"

Mila sighed. "You know what happens after you use your blood magic. You'll be exhausted and we need you to get us out of here. Plus, what if they capture you as well?"

Finn looked out at the crowds. "She'll be back soon. Jari's good at what she does."

"I bet she is," Sienna whispered.

Even as she spoke, the lithe warrior woman walked swiftly toward them, weaving around people with an unerring sense of her place in the world. Sienna could only wish for such confidence.

Jari pulled a map from her bag, scrawled with chalk marks. She laid it at the feet of the Muses as Finn, Mila and Sienna gathered round.

"There's a gate here near the graveyard that leads into their compound. The Scryers take what they can from corpses in exchange for processing the dead."

"What the hell does that mean?" Mila said sharply.

"You don't have death rituals on Earthside?" Jari spat back. "A lot of people die here. The townspeople of course, and those who travel to see the library. Some religious sects believe that if they die here, they will make it into some Illuminated afterlife. Someone has to deal with the sheer volume of the dead."

"Why not expel the Scryers?" Sienna asked. "Move them somewhere else."

Finn picked up the map, looking at it closely. "They were here first." He looked down at Sienna, his eyes suddenly distant. "And besides, that's an Earthsider attitude. If you don't like something, expel it. As if everything could be so simple."

Sienna flushed at his words, acutely aware of the truth he spoke. But Perry wasn't dead and she wasn't leaving without him.

"So we go in, get Perry and carry on with our mission."

Finn put his hand on the pommel of his sword. He nodded at Jari. "Okay, but we're in charge. Follow our lead." He leaned in close, so she could smell the cinnamon spice of his skin. "No blood magic, I mean it. I don't want to lose you down there."

He pulled away and she nodded.

Jari scowled. "Let's get this over with." She pointed at the main gates of the library beyond, a marble archway covered in flowers, constantly renewed by the pilgrims who placed them as they passed. "The gate of flowers is sanctuary. If in doubt, run for that. The Scryers are forbidden from entering."

They skirted the edge of the library buildings beyond

the grand edifice to the service area. As with any sprawling public complex, it needed an army of people to run it. They lived and died behind the beauty of marble sculptures and hushed enlightenment.

They passed kitchens, the smell of roasting meat wafting from within, reminding Sienna of how long it had been since they'd eaten a meager breakfast on the escarpment above. Steam hissed out of vents and she glimpsed abundant storerooms through half-open doors, terracotta jars full of wine and oil, dried chilis and other spices she didn't recognize.

Behind the kitchens, rows of sleeping huts stretched back, becoming more humble toward the cliff face where the worst of them backed onto the graveyard. At least that's what Sienna supposed it was, but this place was unlike any she'd seen before.

Tiny shrines of different faiths sat around the edges of a raised platform on which three trapdoors sat, two open, one closed.

Jari hopped up on the platform and knelt by one of the open doors. She leaned in and knocked gently against the wooden panel within. "They must take the bodies down this way."

Sienna walked to the nearest shrine upon which trinkets lay in devotion, some carved with the names of those who had passed. In a sense, this practice was no different to the sky burial of Tibetan Buddhism or the Towers of Silence of Zoroastrianism where the body was left out for birds of prey to devour. The difference here was that the Scryers took the living as well as the dead.

She walked back to the platform and climbed up onto it. "Let's go."

Mila tilted her head to one side. "But how do we actually get in there?"

Jari gingerly stepped down onto the other trapdoor. As she put her whole weight on it, the door dropped and she fell into blackness. The door shut behind her.

"Guess that's how," Finn said, stepping forward and dropping through after her.

Mila and Sienna followed suit.

They regrouped in the tunnel beneath the trapdoors. It was colder down here and the air smelled of decay and something else — something that made Sienna's stomach turn. But it wasn't the dead they came for.

Jari and Finn pulled their swords and together, they walked slowly down the tunnel into the heart of the Scryers' domain.

CHAPTER 8

PERRY LAY ON THE straw, his breath weak and ragged as the Scryer placed one final Shadow leech on his outstretched arm. It made a soft caw, then turned to shuffle back into the darkness. He watched it go with heavy eyes, wanting desperately to close them and sink into oblivion but a sliver of hope kept him awake. Sienna and Mila would not leave him down here to die. He just had to hold on a little longer …

The pain was a pulsating wound, his magic draining away with every heartbeat. A death of a thousand cuts as the leeches sucked the fire from him. When the Scryer gulped down the creatures again, it would absorb his magic with their flesh, perfect parasites existing in symbiosis.

There was no reasoning with them, no moral argument that could be made to stop their malevolent consumption. They sought out and devoured magic and somehow, Perry guessed, it made its way back to wherever the source of the Shadow lay. It was strangely comforting to know that a part of him would go back to its origin after he breathed his last. He would give much to see where it lay.

His vision began to narrow, the flicker of the torches dimming as he closed his eyes, a sense of the tide washing over him, cold spreading through his veins.

Then a sound came from the corridor beyond. A scuffle of footsteps.

Too late ...

* * *

Flaming torches in brackets lit the hall beyond, giving the cages around the edge a sinister red glow. Finn and Jari entered first in fighting stances, swords held at the ready. Sienna walked in behind them, Mila at her side.

The corridors from the graveyard had been empty, and there had been no challenge to the team's progress so far — no watchers, no soldiers, no protection for those within.

But Sienna did feel a weight pressing upon her, a heaviness that drew her down with every step.

"Do you feel that?" Mila asked quietly. "I just want to lie down and sleep. It's exhausting."

Jari turned. "The Scryers have a dampening effect on magic. They sense it, they drain it. Don't let them touch you." She walked quickly to the first cage. "Perry must be in one of these."

Sienna looked down the line at hundreds of cages, each holding a captive, lying prone on bloody straw beneath. The figure that lay in the closest cage was just a husk of a person, unrecognizable, drained of all life and magic. A sense of hopelessness rose up within her. Were they already too late for Perry?

A clank of machinery sounded in the hall and the cages shunted forward.

"The far end," Finn whispered. "As each drop through, they move along. Perry will be in the more recent cages."

They ran together, footsteps ringing out in the hall. A new cage came through from the tunnel beyond, a little girl this time, her eyes wide with fear, her face streaked with tears. Sienna reached through the bars. "It's okay, we'll get you out of here."

Jari knocked away her hand. "Stop that. We're not here for her, or any of them." She pointed to the hundreds of other cages. "You want to let them all go? Find your friend quickly before we end up like these poor wretches."

Tears sprang to Sienna's eyes as she turned away. Jari was right, of course, they couldn't save every soul.

"He's here," Mila called out from a few cages further up, her voice desperate with concern.

Sienna rushed to her side and Finn joined them. Perry lay unmoving on the straw, dark creatures pulsating on his skin.

"Shadow leeches," Finn said as he tugged at the bars, searching for a way to get inside. "Get them off him. Mila, help me loosen these."

Sienna bent down to kneel next to Perry's head. She reached through the bars, shuddering as she touched one of the fleshy creatures.

"Perry, we're here. Hang on now."

Sienna grasped the leech and pulled. As she tugged, it tore and ripped at Perry's flesh, burrowing deeper. It was part of his body now, no longer just a parasite.

Mila handed her a knife. "Here, try cutting it off."

Sienna edged the blade under the leech, black ooze running from it along with the dark stain of Perry's blood. She pried it off, cutting through its flesh.

A cry of agony rang from the darkened arches beyond the cage, like a wounded bird keening for its mate. A Scryer stumbled from the gloom, its long limbs and ragged clothes brushing the floor. Its skeletal visage of bone and shadow screamed at them, the same black and red blood running over its chin that wept from the leech.

"You're hurting it," Mila said in wonder, then her voice hardened. "Do it again."

Finn stepped forward, his sword held high. "Quickly."

Jari spun away from the cage of the little girl, ready to fight alongside him.

The Scryer rushed them, long limbs flailing as its avian lament echoed through the hall, the screech making the hair on Sienna's arms rise up at the terrible noise. She stabbed at the leeches on Perry's skin, slashing at them, hacking them off.

The Scryer screamed with pain as the leeches shriveled up in bloody clumps, its agony linked to the tiny parasites. Finn swung his sword at it and the blade went right through as if it were just air, trailing wreaths of shadow behind its arc. Finn spun with the weight of the blade and tried again, just as Jari darted in with her weapon. But neither of them could touch the wraith.

It staggered closer to Sienna, long fingers reaching out, its features flickering in pain. Jari ran back to help and together, they scraped the last of the leeches from Perry's skin. They withered on the straw, plump blood-filled bodies shrinking to empty sacs. As the last one dried up, the Scryer gave a final cry and sank to the ground. Finn stabbed at the pile of rags with his sword but it went straight through, ringing on the stone beneath.

As the Scryer disappeared, a click sounded in the hallway and the gates of the cages fell open. Sienna darted forward. She bent to Perry, touched his cheek. "It's okay now. Wake up. It's gone."

His eyelids flickered and slowly, he opened his eyes, his gaze weakened but the Perry they knew was still in there. He opened his mouth to speak—

Just as the loud caw of a crow echoed through the darkened halls joined by another and another until the whole place was a splintering cacophony.

More Scryers coming to defend their home — and their food.

"We need to get out of here." Finn bent to the cage and hauled Perry out, lifting him over his shoulder in a fireman's lift. "Run!"

As Mila headed for the exit, Sienna turned to see Jari lifting the little girl from the cage next to Perry's. The warrior woman scowled and shook her head. "I'm not leaving her. Now run!"

Together they raced back the way they had come, through the tunnels toward the graveyard. But this time, the harsh cawing followed them, the incensed sound of Scryers stumbling, their towering bodies unused to moving so fast.

The team pulled ahead and made it back to the trapdoors in the graveyard. Finn placed Perry gently down on the ground before pulling down the hatch and boosting Mila up into the daylight, followed by Sienna. He lifted Perry and pushed him up into their waiting arms, helping Jari and the little girl next and then finally, pulling himself out of the hole.

They stood panting on the raised platform, the bustle of the library city before them, willfully oblivious to the horrors beneath.

"We made it," Mila panted, bending over to catch her breath—

Just as a long, bony arm reached out from the last trapdoor, catching her hair and tugging her to her knees. From below, the sound of triumphant cawing rose from the darkness.

"To sanctuary!" Jari shouted as she jumped off the platform, the little girl in her arms, tiny face buried in her neck.

Finn used his sword to cut through Mila's hair and Sienna pulled her friend away. Finn picked up Perry again and together they ran back past the kitchens and service areas toward the gate of flowers. Panicked screams rose up behind them along with angry caws as the Scryers pursued their prey.

The group turned into the main plaza, the orderly stream of pilgrims entering through the gate turning to look in the direction of the commotion. Soldiers moved forward with their lances outstretched, faces aghast at the creatures chasing behind.

"Out of the way!" Finn bellowed as they ran for the gate of flowers. Something in the pilgrim mass responded and the crowd parted, allowing them to surge forward. They were so close now.

The Scryer in the gatehouse emerged and the crowd gasped at its soaring monstrosity, the power it exuded as it stalked forward, joining its brethren in pursuit of the escapees.

Sienna stumbled, tripping on the stone steps, falling forward.

She cried out and rolled quickly, just as the long fingers of the Scryer behind reached down for her, raking across her flesh. She looked up into the darkness of its hooded visage and saw something like surprise in its depths, a recognition of her magic. Its caw this time was primal, a deep sound of yearning for her powerful blood.

Mila darted back, grabbed Sienna's hand and pulled her up, onward to the gate, an arch of flowers, a haze of scent and color marking the boundary.

A group of pilgrims stood watching the chase. Some urged the team on, beckoning them to safety. Others were silent, watching with hungry eyes, eager to witness the magical victims dragged back down to the catacombs.

A slender Nubian woman stood in the middle of the flowering arch, her hair white as spun sugar, her face ageless, her eyes deep pools of an unusual sapphire blue that stood out against her black skin. Even as she ran for her life, Sienna sensed the woman saw further than this realm, and weighed greater matters than just their lives in her hands.

The Librarian.

Jari ran through the arch first, falling to her knees, hugging the little girl to her chest. Finn crossed the line next, placing Perry on the ground before turning to reach for Sienna's hand, pulling her over with Mila just as the gatehouse Scryer reached them. It stopped outside the gate of flowers as its brethren gathered behind, tall wraith-like creatures wrapped in rags, long skeletal fingers brushing the ground. They exuded menace, their presence causing a hush to fall over the gathered crowd.

Finn went down on his knees before the Librarian. "Please, give us sanctuary. We need your help for a terror far greater than these can bring. A terror that threatens us all."

The Librarian looked over his head at the ragged Scryers beyond, her blue eyes raking over them with an edge of steel in the depths. It was clear that she hated the devourers of magic and abhorred their power in the outer limits of her realm, but she had little choice.

The gatehouse Scryer took a step forward, right up to the flower gate, only millimeters from the bright fallen petals strewn over the earth. It gave a rough caw like a crow over carrion, a reminder of the balance that must be kept according to the laws of the Shadow.

The Librarian's shoulders slumped and she looked around at the Mapwalker team with a sigh. "I'm sorry, I must …"

CHAPTER 9

THE LIBRARIAN'S WORDS TRAILED off as her eyes alighted on Sienna and the sapphire blue sparkled as she smiled in recognition. She lifted one regal hand and pointed away from the gate speaking in the rough caw of the Scryer tongue. It was clearly a dismissal.

The Scryers stood for a long second, then turned as one and stalked away, back to the darkness beneath and the hidden inner gatehouse beyond.

The crowd drifted away now the conflict was over, leaving the Mapwalker team kneeling on the ground before the Librarian.

"Thank you," Sienna said. "Why did you change your mind?"

The Librarian smiled. "Your grandfather was my … friend … when he was your age. I would know that titian hair anywhere and I can sense an echo of his power in your blood."

Her eyes grew soft at the mention of the past and Sienna wondered how much more than friends they had really been. She remembered the young woman sketched in her grandfather's journal with such love. Time passed differently out here at the edge of the Uncharted but could this really be the same woman? If it was, she had barely aged a day.

The Librarian waved her arm toward the inner courts. "Welcome to the library. Now, come inside and tell me why you're here. It had better be worth the fury of the Scryers." She looked down at Jari, her arms still wrapped around the little girl. "Leave her with the Sisters of Grace in the forecourt. She will not be sent back down there, I give you my word."

Jari nodded and darted away with the child without a second glance. Finn watched her go and Sienna noticed a smile playing around his lips as he witnessed the warrior woman's long-hidden kindness. It seemed she was not so cold after all.

The Librarian led them inside the classical library, a grand edifice of marble columns with decorative Corinthian scrolls, like a stylized forest of learning. The atmosphere was hushed, reverent, and Sienna glimpsed rooms beyond the columns where scholars studied and pilgrims worshipped at the shrine of the book. Part of her wished she could stay awhile, with nothing to concern herself except the number of pages read each day. But would a quiet life of contemplation really satisfy her now after all she had seen in the Borderlands — and all that was yet to come?

Jari emerged from a side corridor as they passed by. She was alone now, the hand that had clutched that of the little girl now wrapped around the pommel of her sword.

She met Sienna's questioning gaze with a hard look. "Don't even think about saying anything."

They stopped by a pool of crystal water surrounded by ornate fountains with sculptures of ancient Egyptian gods at their center. The high ceiling opened up to the sky above, allowing dappled light to play across the stream. Tropical flowers blossomed, casting their heavy scent into the air and tiny birds flitted between the leaves, their song a sweet note.

The Librarian indicated marble benches under a bower of flowering cherry blossom that provided privacy from the bustling pilgrims. Mila and Finn helped Perry to a long bench and healers came to tend to his wounds. He lay unmoving as they coated his lesions with a salve that smelled of honey and spice.

Servers brought fruit and tea with the fragrance of high mountains and the team sat together with the Librarian as Sienna explained their mission to find the Map of Plagues.

"The Mapwalker annals mention that one of the knights may have crossed over here to the Library of Alexandria. Perhaps he hid a piece in the archives amongst the many manuscripts? Perhaps he sought help from the Librarian of the time?"

The Librarian frowned. "It's possible. We have our own annals, passed down over the centuries, notes about what really happened since history written by men of power portrays only one version of the truth. Those scrolls rest in the oldest part of the library." She took Sienna's hand. "I'll take you to them because of your grandfather."

Sienna smiled. "I know he would have loved to see you once again."

The healers finished patching up Perry, providing a staff for him to lean upon until he recovered full strength. He was pale and drawn, his shoulders slumped, but his eyes had regained a glimmer of their old sparkle.

He shrugged off the help that Finn and Mila tried to provide. "I'm fine, honestly. Just let me walk."

The Librarian led them away from the sanctuary of the pool toward the center of the collection. The architecture changed as they wound their way through corridors of stone, becoming less ornate, more functional. Age had worn down the flagstones they walked upon, leaving imprints of footsteps from the long dead. Ash and the dust of millennia blackened the walls. These inner halls were almost deserted, just a few quiet figures slipping behind columns as they passed.

"There's not much left of Alexandria now," the Librarian said as she led them deeper within, light fading as the windows grew smaller until they were only chinks that let in a sliver of light. "What is left we keep in darkness to protect from the damage of time."

The inner library became a labyrinth of twists and turns until finally, they reached a central room constructed from huge blocks of stone. Shelves hacked from the rock were piled high with hundreds, perhaps thousands, of scrolls. Some were thick, as long as carpets, rolled on the lower shelves, and others light and airy heaped nearer the ceiling. Many looked fragile, like they would crumble to the touch. It was reminiscent of the Illuminated Cartographer's study, but where that was alive and vibrant, lit by reflected sunbeams, this room was cold and barren.

The past could be alive in the Borderlands after it had been pushed out from Earthside, but only if people made it their own. These scrolls were the dead parts of Alexandria, discarded history that the descendants of those Egyptians chose to leave behind. But Sienna also sensed power lying in maps of skin somewhere here, maps made from Blood Mapwalkers like herself.

Jari spun around in the center of the room, shaking her head. "How are we meant to find a tiny piece of a map in here?"

The Librarian gave a knowing smile. "If the map is to be found, I trust it will be." She turned to Sienna. "Your grandfather renewed the pact with the library and I hold you now to the same promise. The dark clouds of war gather overhead and we want no part of it. Leave us be. Take your fragment and then forget you were ever here. Do not mark us on your new maps, do not report us to the Ministry. Let us continue to be forgotten as a piece of a once glorious past so that we can live on for centuries more."

As Sienna looked into the deep blue of the Librarian's

eyes, she caught a glimpse of ancient Egypt, palm trees and pyramids, then the slow death of a civilization that thought it would rule forever. A sense of foreboding washed over her, a realization that everything must die, that every great society must crumble.

"Promise me," the Librarian urged.

Sienna nodded. "I promise."

The Librarian squeezed her hand, then turned to the group. "I'll leave you now. Go with my blessing."

Jari looked confused. "But you can't leave us in here. There's no way we'll make it out of this labyrinth without help."

Finn put his hand on her shoulder. "We're not leaving that way."

Jari flushed, shook her head. "Of course, I didn't … let's just start looking." She walked to a stack of scrolls and began to search.

The Librarian walked to the door and turned one last time as if to fix them all in her memory, then she left, leaving only the scent of flowers in her wake.

Perry sank to the floor with exhaustion and leaned back against one of the pillars. Sienna bent and tucked his jacket around his shoulders. "Just rest until it's time to go."

Mila turned around in the center of the room, hands on her hips, as she examined the racks of scrolls. "There's something here, something more than just vellum and papyrus." She met Sienna's eyes. "Something of skin."

Sienna nodded. "I feel it, too."

She stood and together they walked slowly around the chamber, becoming attuned to the vibrations of the library and each scroll within it. Finn and Jari went to sit next to Perry, watching the women in silence.

Sienna felt a pulse in her blood quicken as they drew closer to one section and Mila stopped next to her with a puzzled expression. They both turned to the shelf and examined the pile of scrolls. They had fused together with time, a tangle of lost knowledge. Mila bent and blew off the dust. It rose into the air, making them sneeze.

"Bless you," Perry said instinctively from across the room before falling into an awkward silence. The phrase stemmed from plague times when the blessing of God was called down on potential sufferers, a ward against disease. Sienna hoped they wouldn't need that protection themselves.

"Let's go carefully and try not to inhale too much ancient dust," Mila joked, breaking the tension. She pulled out each scroll carefully, edging the top ones off the pile and Sienna placed them on the floor. Jari and Finn came to help and together, they emptied the rack, laying out the scrolls in rows.

Sienna noticed that one in particular seemed to emanate with an inner light. It was dirty brown on the outside, as dusty as the rest, nothing special, and yet she felt an urge to touch it. She stepped gingerly around the other scrolls and bent down, brushing her fingertips over the skin.

She gasped as a jolt of energy rushed through her.

She unrolled it carefully on the stone floor. Inside the outer scroll lay a piece of tattered skin, a patchwork of different colors and lines. It was not the skin of an animal and it wasn't like the blood maps that hung in the gallery of the Ministry. This was something hybrid, something knitted from the skin of many and inscribed with powerful blood.

"Is that it?" Jari asked. "Is it a fragment from the Map of Plagues?"

Sienna nodded. "It must be. It's knitted together from pieces of skin, some from plague sufferers and some from a Blood Mapwalker. The knights must have sewn them together, entwining magic with the plague itself to keep it hidden."

As she looked at it, Sienna had the sense of something uncurling deep within the earth, something long buried from ancient times. It fed from the mass graves of genocide and the horrors of war. It devoured the plague-ridden bodies of the diseased and dying.

And now it was awake.

CHAPTER 10

Finn knelt next to Sienna and placed a hand on her shoulder. "Are you alright? You've gone pale."

Sienna took a deep breath. "There's more going on here than we know."

He nodded. "But that's always been true and we just have to keep going. So, where next?"

Sienna lifted the ragged piece of the Map of Plagues away from its protective outer scroll. It too had lines inscribed upon it, a simple sketch showing waterways and islands. There was a drop of dried blood on the page, the color of rust partially obscuring the lines of a death's head skull. "The knight had to travel somewhere when he left this place. He must have drawn this and then stepped through it to escape Alexandria. The Librarian kept it with the piece of the map he left behind."

Mila examined it more closely. "It looks like Venice. Does the trail take us back to Earthside?"

Perry pulled himself up from the wall and limped over. "That's not Venice in Italy. That's the Venice of Africa. It's part of Benin on Earthside, on the northern shore of Lake Nokoué."

Finn laughed. "Of course, it's Ganvié Island, the floating city. Like Old Aleppo, it straddles the border, half pushed out from your world into ours. The local Fon tribespeople helped Portuguese slave traders by raiding the villages of other tribes hundreds of years ago. But their religious beliefs prevented them from attacking those who dwelled on water, so the floating city grew out of the homes of those early escapees."

"You know it?" Mila asked.

Finn shook his head. "I've never been but I've heard stories. We'll have to be careful. Its waters cross the border and people are lost between the worlds there all the time."

Sienna folded the piece of the Map of Plagues and placed it inside a waterproof pouch within her jacket. She pulled out the ritual knife that she kept close to her heart, the knife that had spilled the blood of her grandfather. Any blade would do to make the cut, it was her blood that held the power, but the reminder gave her strength. He had never retreated from his duty, and neither would she.

She ran her fingers over the map of Ganvié, calling on the tendrils of her magic as she strengthened herself for what was to come. Every time she spilled her blood and traveled through the maps, a drop of Shadow entered her — a tiny speck, but still, it built up over years and eventually, could turn the Mapwalker to the Shadow side. Some chose never to use their magic after a certain point, trapped on Earthside or in the Borderlands at the point of turning, like Bridget and now her own father. Others chose to give in and become a Shadow Cartographer, embracing their magic in all its glory.

Sienna looked up at Perry. His father had chosen that path, as had Xander, who had been with them on the hunt for the Map of Shadows. She had thought he was a friend but he had betrayed them all.

There were no limits to the use of magic if you gave in to the Shadow and Sienna sometimes dreamed of the possibilities. Back at Oxford, she had always felt so lost and yet over here in the Borderlands, she could be much more than she ever thought possible. She wanted to give in to the rush. A taste of it was never enough, but it was all she could have right now.

Sienna looked up at Finn and Jari. "Make sure you keep hold of my hand." She purposefully met Finn's gaze. "I don't want to lose you."

She bent over the map and cut into her palm with the knife, letting a single drop of blood drip down onto the lines, pooling with the knight's from so long ago. She reached out with the other hand so the team could hold onto her, then she closed her eyes and dived into the map.

In Sienna's mind, the lines became three-dimensional, lifting from the page to form a city stretched out below. This was the moment she craved and Sienna longed to stay right here in the lines between the map and the physical world. If she traveled alone, perhaps she could prolong the time between, but the others were a heavy weight upon her, forcing her back down to the physical world. She could make out boats below on turquoise water, fisherman casting their nets and a tangle of islands that made up the watery city.

The border appeared as a shimmering line and Sienna made sure to come down on the Borderland side. Finn and Jari would disappear if they crossed back into Earthside without traveling through an open portal. No one really knew what happened to those who disappeared but she wasn't about to find out now.

She picked one of the huts on stilts that looked like a place of worship rather than a dwelling and dived down into it.

The wooden hut was hot after the cool inner sanctum of the library. The smell of salt water and drying fish wafted through the air. Sienna heard a slithering sound of scales on wood, then the rapid breath of panic as the team landed beside her.

She opened her eyes, trying to focus even as the nausea

receded. Traveling this way left her weak, especially when she carried this many people. The tiny wound on her palm throbbed and she could almost feel the drop of shadow suffusing her blood as it healed.

She lay inside a wooden hut with a tin roof, the others on the floor around her. The planks on the floor had gaps between them that showed the water beneath. Around the edges of the hut were wooden crates, stacked three high. The slithering sound came from within.

Jari sat up, a half-smile on her face. She looked at Sienna with renewed respect and an edge of fear. "That was crazy. What a way to travel. You must jump around like that all the time."

Mila stood up, recovering quickly. "There's a price she must pay for it."

Jari shrugged. "We all pay, in this lifetime or the next."

As the team recovered, pulling themselves up to sit against the walls of the hut, a hissing came from within the stacked crates.

Finn went to look inside, pressing his face against the slats before pulling back sharply. "That's a lot of snakes."

"Voodoo," Perry said, his voice stronger now. "It's the state religion in Benin and I imagine that's continued over here in the Borderlands. Pythons are revered. There's even a python temple in Ouidah on Earthside. Other kinds of snakes are used in ceremonies."

Finn nodded. "I've heard of these minor sacrifices. They are nothing compared to those performed in the name of Moloch." He glanced over at Jari who had gone still at his words. "But I'd rather not stay in here longer than we need to. Where do we go next?"

Sienna took a deep breath and pulled herself upright using the wall as support. "Let's see if we can pick up the trail of where the knight went next."

* * *

Mila's heart pounded as she put her hand against the door of the hut. She wanted to be out there first, barely able to contain the excitement that had been building since Perry mentioned the Venice of Africa. She had grown up in a London tower-block, a mixed-race foster kid with little knowledge of her birth parents except that her father had been a student from war-torn Sierra Leone. It was further west in Africa than Benin but this was much closer than she had ever been to her possible ancestors.

Waterwalkers, those who could become one with the waterways, were born rarely and many of them disappeared without trace, choosing to remain beneath the waves rather than return to the air. Mila understood that choice. Even now as she looked down between the slats of the hut, she wanted to be in the water below. The channels around the stilts were the real roads and she craved the freedom of traveling at her own speed, darting alongside the sea creatures below.

As she gazed down into the water, Mila suddenly saw movement. Not the shimmer of schooling fish, but something larger, its edges blurred by the ripples of the seabed. Mila frowned. It looked like the outline of a person — could there be Waterwalkers here?

"What are you waiting for?" Sienna's words interrupted her reverie.

Mila shook her head. "I saw something under the— It doesn't matter. Let's go."

She pushed open the door, barely catching a glimpse of the city on the water before a shout of challenge rang out, deep voices blending together as a group of Ganvié tribesmen thrust sharp spears toward her, their scarified faces fixed in a challenge.

Mila reeled back into the hut, knocking into the others as the tribesmen advanced.

"Wait," Finn said, backing away, his hands held out in surrender. "We're on a mission from the Warlord of Aleppo. We have safe passage." He pointed at Jari's facial tattoo of the half-moon. "See, his emissary is with us."

Mila wondered what he was talking about and noted Sienna's look of puzzlement too. That was more than Finn had told them so far and the idea that he might be working with his father was troubling. But there was no time to find out more as the tribesmen quickly bound their hands behind their backs.

The sound of heavy footsteps came from outside on the boardwalk and an obese man waddled into the room. He wiped the sweat from his bald head with a corner of his tunic. It was tied around his waist with a rope from which hung dried pieces of sea creatures interspersed with shark's teeth, pervading the room with a rank smell. The tribesmen deferred to him, shrinking away as if he wielded cruel power over them. Mila supposed he was a priest of some kind.

He squinted at Jari in the semi-darkness of the hut. "You're Aleppo filth. You die first." He looked around at the others. "The rest will be a grand offering to Requin Géant."

Sienna stepped forward. "Please, we don't want trouble. We're here to find traces of a medieval knight, a man in armor who might have come here a long time ago with a piece of a map. It's a danger to us all. Please let us go. We mean no harm."

Mila was sure that a flicker of recognition crossed the man's face at the mention of the knight, and she definitely recognized the name of their god. Requin Géant. French for giant shark.

CHAPTER 11

XANDER SAT SKETCHING ON the edge of the castle wall, looking out at carrion birds as they swooped low over the burial pits. He could look at them now without flinching, ignoring the women who wept below, an unceasing roll-call of death. But the birds ... well, the birds were life and Xander could bring life to the beasts he illustrated. If he could only get a skin to draw on. For now, he had to make do with his sketchbook and as his hand moved across the page, he brought the birds to life on the wing, their feathers ruffled by the wind, their beaks open to snatch insects from the air.

He completed one bird and on the opposite page, he began to draw again, using the template of its shape to extend the wings, add talons to its feet and make the beak more like a scythe, the feathers more like blades. Sir Douglas had tasked him with creating weapons from the creatures he could illustrate and with nothing else to occupy his time, Xander filled his sketchbooks with creatures of the imagination.

From his perch this high up, he could see into the walled garden behind the double doors of the children's wing, a quadrangle of green flanked by trees and bushes with colorful flowers to brighten it. A movement caught his eye and Xander watched as a slight young woman with cropped, almost silver hair ran on tiptoes over the grass, her arms raised high as she spun around, her red dress billowing out around her. She turned her face to the sun and smiled. Xander couldn't help smiling with her, the simple joy of a sunny morning. He wished life could always be so simple.

The young woman pulled something from her pocket and bent to the ground, digging a little hole and placing whatever it was within. Xander strained to focus, a frown on his face as he tried to see what she was burying.

She covered the hole with earth, patted it down, then placed her right palm upon it and stretched out her left toward one of the other trees, an apple tree with white blossoms. She closed her eyes and lifted her face again, her mouth set in determination.

A few blossoms fell from the tree as if a gust of wind had caught it.

Then they rained down in a thick cloud, leaving the boughs of the apple tree empty. It began to wither even as the girl lifted her hand from the earth, revealing a tiny sapling underneath that stretched toward the sky, growing at an incredible rate.

The young woman stood, both arms stretched out toward the trees, one growing and reaching for the sky, the other shriveling and fading, its life force drained as the other bloomed. Xander watched wide-eyed at the speed of her creation. He knew that they bred Halbrasse here, raising children with forms of magic unseen on Earthside but this girl was truly incredible.

"They call her Elf." A gruff voice came from the walkway behind him.

Xander looked around to see a soldier, the half-moon tattoo covering a web of burn scars.

"You should see what she can do with insects." The soldier shuddered. "Sir Douglas wants you in the library. Now."

The soldier didn't wait for an answer, just turned and stalked off, his message forgotten already.

Xander sat for a moment, his mind racing. At last, the chance he'd been waiting for. In a place where magic like Elf's was fostered and encouraged, his own talents would surely not be wasted. He couldn't help the grin that dawned on his face as he imagined what he'd find in the library, maybe even the secret books rumored to lie within.

He packed up his sketchbooks into the satchel by his side and jumped down from the wall, jogging into the cold shadows of the castle and winding his way through the corridors toward the library. It lay in the heart of the central tower, protected on all sides by thick walls and magical seals.

Xander stopped at the door to take a breath. This is what he had been promised. This is why he'd given up the Ministry.

He stepped inside and looked up at the soaring shelves around him, stacks of books of all sizes mingled with rolled parchment scrolls and carved stone blocks, metal plates and other forms of ancient knowledge. The border prevented modern technology from crossing over so books were the real treasure. As they were forgotten and discarded on Earthside, they ended up here, abandoned wisdom come to life again.

"Don't just stand there. Come in." Sir Douglas looked up from the armchair he sat in and Xander bit back the gasp that rose in his throat at the man's appearance.

Sir Douglas had been the epitome of English aristocracy, with a military bearing, salt and pepper hair swept back from an angular face, and three-piece tailored tweed suits that made him look as if he'd stepped out of a nineteenth-century painting. The vertical scar that ran down from his right eye to his short beard only served to hint at his rakish past.

But now Sir Douglas looked like a shell of his former self, his skin paper thin and dry as if all the moisture had been sucked from him. His hair and beard were entirely white and the scar looked like it had deepened, sinking into his skull. He still wore tweed but the suit was ill-fitting now, his skeletal limbs barely filling the sleeves. As Sir Douglas waved him in, Xander noticed the dark lines on his hands and wrists, the black marks that crept up his neck — and the tendrils of shadow that seemed to weave around him, obscuring his features before shifting again.

"You've never seen the transition to pure shadow, have you, Xander?"

"I'm ... sorry, sir. I didn't mean to stare."

Sir Douglas shook his head. "It's fine, it's not something many witness, but it is your future if you remain here with us, if you help us." He smiled. "To go from the physical body to the realm of pure shadow is the only way to make your power endless."

Xander couldn't speak, he couldn't move. Sir Douglas spoke as if this transformation was something to be desired but all he could see was the bitter and ugly end to a life.

Sir Douglas pushed himself up from the chair. "But you have much to prove and little time. Come with me."

He stalked over to a bookshelf filled with thick tomes with leather bindings and gold etching. The titles were obscure, arcane grimoires and ancient philosophies mingling alongside natural history and principles of engineering. There seemed no order to the chaos of books and Xander found himself leaning closer, trying to work out how they all related to each other.

Sir Douglas pressed against the spines of two volumes and something clicked behind the wall before part of it swung open, revealing a smaller room within.

The hidden library. At last.

"Can I go in?"

"Of course, this is what I promised you." Sir Douglas smiled but his eyes remained dark, the spark within them a black diamond that seemed to suck the life out of the surrounding air.

Xander stepped inside, his feet sinking into a plush carpet embroidered with scenes like a Hieronymus Bosch painting. Demons tortured sinners, their bodies torn on racks while others were burned alive or eaten by hideous misshapen creatures.

There were fewer shelves in here and only one desk in the center. A wooden box sat on one end.

Sir Douglas pointed to the books. "You will find much to occupy you here, many wonders to fill your sketchbook. It is yours to explore. But we have one task for you to accomplish first."

He walked to one of the shelves and pulled down a medieval book inscribed with two interlocking triangles on the leather cover. Sir Douglas opened it carefully revealing a diary of sorts within, handwritten words on fragile ivory paper turning yellow at the edges. He turned the pages until he reached one filled with images.

Rats. So many rats.

But not just any kind of rat. These were giant creatures gnawing on the bodies of the dead. One gazed out of the page, its beady eyes looking out from across the centuries.

Xander shuddered and then bent closer. There were fleas on the page, jumping from the bodies of the rats to gnaw at those who ran from the infestation. There were swollen lumps on the dead and suddenly, he knew what the images portrayed.

Sir Douglas turned the pages slowly, filling Xander's vision with drawings of death and suffering. Of mass annihilation.

"There was once a map that came with this book, but it was hidden, split apart so the island of the plague could never be found. But we will have it soon and these flea-infested rats will be our agents of change on Earthside."

Xander's heart pounded as the scale of possibility sank into his mind. He could only imagine the suffering, the millions who would die if a plague like this was released into the hyper-connected world he had left behind.

Sir Douglas reached over and opened the wooden box, lifting out a pile of skins, each perfectly prepared for the Illustrator's work.

"We need more of the creatures. You will illustrate them on these skins and we will bring them to life in the camps in readiness for the plague." He placed a hand on Xander's shoulder, pushing him down onto the seat. "You wanted to use your magic to create without limits. Well, here's your chance."

It seemed to Xander as if the chill of the shadow sank through his clothes and into his skin. Even as Sir Douglas turned to leave, tendrils of darkness snaked back to hover around the desk. Xander bit his lip and reached for his illustrating instruments with a shaking hand.

Something watched him, something began to insinuate into his brain and it seemed as if the first strokes of the pen were not even his own.

The rats that began to appear on the skins were more grotesque as his mind considered what would make them even more effective. They must run fast and spread wide, carrying the plague faster than ever before. He drew them with snake-like bodies so they could writhe through cracks, carrying their cargo of death into homes. He made them fierce with sharper teeth so predators would not be able to kill them off.

Some part of Xander watched his own hand with horror, a last vestige of his old self despairing at what he'd become. But as the shadow entwined itself around his drawing hand, he couldn't help but revel in his power of creation.

CHAPTER 12

THE PRIEST SHUFFLED BACK to the door, his belt of sea creatures rustling as he walked. "Bring them," he said, leaving without a backward glance.

"Wait, we're—"

One of the tribesmen cuffed Sienna around the head as she blurted out the words. She fell to the floor.

Finn surged forward but two other men held him back. The tribesmen laughed, talking to one another in a language Mila couldn't understand. But she got the gist of it. There was no way these people were letting them go.

The tribesmen pushed the Mapwalker team out onto the boardwalk in front of the hut. Dusk had fallen and the sound of bullfrogs echoed over the lake in the balmy evening. Clouds of insects hovered above the water and fish jumped to catch them from below while swifts darted down to pluck them from the air. Boardwalks stretched into the distance, a labyrinth of walkways between the islands of huts. Some had red or blue tin roofs, others were thatched with straw and mud.

Villagers paddled canoes through the channels, some glanced in their direction, others deliberately avoided a look as they headed home with vegetables and freshly caught fish.

A little boy poked his head out one of the windows,

gazing at the newcomers with curiosity as they passed. Mila smiled at him and he ducked back inside, shy or perhaps afraid of the priest who walked by with such authority toward the rocky shore.

"The topography is strange here," Perry whispered from behind. "Ganvié on Earthside is on a lake but it looks like this place is within a protected bay on the edge of an ocean drop-off. Check out the waves beyond the break-water."

Mila looked past the village huts to the shades of blue fading into the horizon. White-caps dusted the waves out there and her water aspect sensed the resonance of the deep. It called to her and she almost gasped as the need rose inside her.

The priest led the procession all the way across the village to a final walkway that led to a cave entrance where the rising tide lapped against the lip of a platform tethered to the rock. It had shackles embedded within, each pair rusty with age. Crabs scuttled around the edge, some with huge bodies as big as watermelons with long legs that probed the rocks as they passed. These were carrion eaters with sharp pincers that ripped and devoured flesh.

"This is where the children of Requin Géant feed. Perhaps your offering will bring the god himself." The priest clutched the shark's teeth in his belt, crushing his meaty hand against sharp edges until blood dripped down into the water, staining it red. He smiled. "Sharks can smell blood from across the bay, so they will be waiting when the tide floods the cave. But they will need something special to send them into the feeding frenzy that pleases our god the most." He pointed at Jari. "Bring that one."

Two of the tribesmen hauled Jari to the front of the cave where a single pair of shackles lay against a prominent rock. She struggled against them. "The Warlord of Aleppo will have your skin for this."

The priest laughed. "He owes me much for the slaves

we have sent to the Shadow mines and it is Requin Géant that I must appease now. He has not fed of human flesh for too long so you are all a welcome respite before I must offer from my own tribe again."

Finn frowned. "I've heard of this offering, my father does the same at the Tophet, offering children to a god who can never have enough blood. It does no good. It keeps us all in the dark."

The priest shook his head. "The balance must be kept. As Earthside pushes out those who honor human sacrifice, they end up here. We have no choice. If I do not offer, they will take whoever they choose and the village suffers."

Two tribesmen shackled Jari to the rocks at the entrance to the cave, right on the edge of a deeper drop-off while the others shackled the rest of the Mapwalker team to the platform beyond.

The priest took a shark tooth from his belt, chanted a prayer, then slashed Jari's arm. The deep cut began to bleed immediately, scarlet drops pooling in the water around her. The warrior woman already had to crane her neck to keep her face out of the surf. She was panting and gasping for breath in fear and pain and Mila knew it wouldn't be long until she went under. The only question was whether she would drown before the sharks ripped her flesh apart.

Mila could sense the creatures out in the waters of the bay, gathering for their feast. Beyond them, somewhere in the deep, she could sense the giant creature they all worshipped.

They needed to get out of here but Mila had to rein in her power while the team were outnumbered. She could whip the sea into weapons and turn her own body into water, but the others would be injured or worse if she acted too soon. Better to wait until at least some of the tribesmen had gone.

But the priest remained silent alongside his team of men, eager eyes fixed on the water outside the cave, waiting for the sharks they served to come for the feast.

They weren't leaving.

A wave washed over Jari's face and she spluttered and coughed, straining to lift her mouth and nose above water.

"Please," Finn whispered. "Help her."

Mila knew his words were for her. He had seen her wield her water magic before when they had been cornered by the Warlord's men. But they were still outnumbered — she had to wait just a little longer.

A dorsal fin of a shark broke the surface just outside the cave, moving quickly toward the bleeding figure on the rocks.

The priest raised his hands to the heavens. "Take this sacrifice in the name of Requin Géant." His voice echoed around the cave.

"Move, Jari!" Finn shouted.

The shark lunged out of the water just as Jari arched her body backward, pulling her wrist and ankle shackles as far as they would go.

The shark's jaws snapped shut only an inch from her stomach, then it slid back off the rocks into the water circling around to swim back and forth just a few meters away.

The priest clapped his hands in delight. "Next time the water will be higher. We will witness the sacrifice."

Mila couldn't wait any longer. As the waves washed over her feet, she summoned her magic, becoming one with the liquid. Her skin shimmered, expanded and the shackles broke around her ankles.

The priest turned, shock on his face. The tribesmen by his side raised their spears and charged.

Mila reached down to gather handfuls of the sea and spun it into two whips of water in the air. She snapped them at the legs of the men, knocking them off balance so they stumbled and fell into the rising waters.

As they tried to scramble to their feet, Mila spun her whips again, snapping off the shackles that held Perry and

Finn captive. They each turned to the guards nearest them, pushing them under water. The drowning men writhed as they tried to escape but Finn forced one into his shackles, snapped them shut, then turned to help Sienna out of her bonds as Perry wrestled with the other.

Mila turned back to the priest.

He pulled the shark's tooth blade from his belt once more, advancing with eyes blazing. "You dare challenge the priest of Requin Géant? You will pay with the salt of your blood, Waterwalker."

The priest rushed forward, surprisingly fleet-footed for a man so big. He thrust the blade at Mila. As she whipped the air before him, he cut through the water droplets with no hesitation, laughing maniacally as he bore down upon her.

"Help!" Jari's voice was desperate as the shark fin rose in the water before her, the dark grey of its great body visible beneath the waves.

A flash of white teeth.

The priest turned his head in triumph, eager to witness the devouring of his latest sacrifice. Mila charged at him, propelling the fleshy man across the cave so he tripped and fell back over Jari's shackled body, his head dangling right over the water.

Just as the shark rose and bit down with its terrible jaws.

Blood spurted from the priest's decapitated corpse, soaking the warrior woman beneath, pooling in the water by her side. Mila bent down and used the expanding water to snap the shackles from Jari's wrists and ankles.

Jari sprang to her feet, her clothes covered in blood. She kicked at the body of the priest, rolling him into the water. "Go feed your precious sharks, you bastard."

Out in the bay, more shark fins appeared, drawn by the gore. The two tribesmen, now shackled further back in the cave, began to beg.

"Please, we were just doing our duty. Let us go."

Mila turned to see Sienna reaching for the closest one, her friend was ever the forgiving type. But this was no ordinary place, and Mila had the sense that there was more to this hidden city than they knew as yet.

She walked over to stand in front of them, the rising waters now thigh deep. She looked them both in the eyes.

"One chance. Is there an older temple here? A temple for those with my kind of magic?"

One guard looked blank but Mila saw a flash of recognition in the other's eyes. She bent closer to him. "Do you know of it?"

He shook his head. "I've heard of it, but only rumors. The Waterwalkers are said to be extinct but—"

"We're not." The voice came from behind, near the entrance to the cave.

Mila spun around to see a young man pull himself out of the ocean. Water dripped from his body as he stood tall, wearing only a pair of shorts that did nothing to hide his muscular physique. His skin was the color of earth after warm rain and Mila couldn't help but want to run her hands across it. His black hair was cropped short, his eyes wide above angular cheekbones marked with wavy lines tattooed in tiny dots. Mila had read of this scarification, the markings made to honor the water gods.

The young man walked closer, his eyes fixed on Mila. "I'm Ekon, the last Waterwalker left in Ganvié." He reached out a hand and Mila stretched out hers in return. As their palms touched, she felt an electric spark between them, conducted by the water that bound them together.

"I'm Mila. These are my friends — Sienna and Perry, Finn and Jari."

Ekon looked at the group, his eyes resting on the half-moon tattoo on Jari's face. "Do you vouch for them all?" He half turned to indicate the sharks drawing ever closer in the lagoon, a pack of fins breaking the surface as the predators circled. "They still require sacrifice."

Mila took a deep breath, part of her wishing she could just ditch Jari here and now, let her be devoured by the sharks, be rid of her for good. But Finn wouldn't allow that, and they needed Finn.

"I vouch for them all."

Ekon nodded. "You've come a long way and you are of my blood, Mila Waterwalker, so I will show you the temple." He walked to the entrance of the cave, the waves now almost waist-deep. "We must hurry or your friends here will be shark bait." His face hardened as he looked at the tribesmen. "Leave those two. I've seen them watch enough people die down here. This time it's their turn."

He slipped around the pillar at the entrance. Mila hurried after him, Jari and the others right behind as the shouts of the doomed tribesmen faded in the distance.

Holes and crevices pitted the rock wall outside the cave where the water had eaten away at it over time. Giant ferns hung down, casting shadows over the water, the sound of waves against the rock beating time.

There were plenty of places to hold onto as Mila clambered along, trying to keep Ekon in sight as he scrambled sideways along the water's edge. She knew that he climbed instead of waterwalking to enable her friends to follow but she longed to see him slip into the water, his dark skin rippling alongside her own. She had never swum with anyone of her blood before, and now, here he was. Questions filled Mila's mind about whether she could be from this region, whether she once had a home here — and could there still be one?

Ekon turned to make sure she was watching. He gave a cheeky grin and ducked into a narrow entranceway just above the waterline. Mila followed him down a tunnel that soon opened out into a large cavern. Stalagmites climbed toward the roof, glistening with milky white crystals. It was cool and smelled of salt water and the earthy scent of minerals leached from the rocks around.

One wall was carved with wave patterns, similar to the scars on Ekon's cheeks.

"This was once the Temple of the Waterwalkers," he explained. "Our people were abundant, happy. They lived in union with the sea and its creatures." He turned and looked at Mila. "But the Shadow grew strong in our ruler and he traded many of the women for more power. Young men escaped rather than be forced into slavery. Our magic was lost and our people faded into history."

Mila reached for his hand. "Not all of us."

He smiled and Mila felt the moment stretch on, lost in the dark pools of his eyes.

Sienna broke the silence. "We're all facing a threat now, regardless of race or magic or which side of the border we stand on. We need to find the Map of Plagues and we think a knight came here hundreds of years ago. He may have buried something here."

Ekon nodded. "I know of this knight. Follow me."

He led them toward the back of the cave, through a winding passage between dripping walls of rock, emerging into a hollowed-out cavern. A rock in the shape of an anvil sat in the center covered with tiny sculptures made from carved driftwood and dried seaweed. Some were desiccated, shriveled with age and others were juicy and wet, recent offerings from one who still honored the ancestors.

Mila stepped up to the altar, feeling an urge to kneel here and pray to those whose blood ran in her veins. She reached for one of the sculptures and brushed the seaweed gently. This place felt so familiar.

Ekon pointed to the rocky wall behind the altar. "Is that your knight?"

It showed a mural of a man in unusual armor and a helmet painted in the natural colors of kelp and coral, faded by time. Next to him, a Waterwalker stood with a crown on his dark curls, his black skin shiny with new paint, the colors renewed over time in a sign of respect. The men stood shoulder to shoulder against a backdrop of a city that was nothing like Ganvié, a pyramid in pride of place marked with the black lines of a death's head skull.

Sienna walked closer to the wall. "He certainly looks like a medieval knight, and that image on the pyramid was also in the library. Perhaps he hid another piece here with the help of a Waterwalker?"

Mila examined the city behind the men. "It looks almost Egyptian, but how can that be?"

Ekon circled the altar to stand by her side. "As land is pushed over from Earthside, forming new places in the Borderlands, the same happens underwater but not at the same rate. This city is beneath us, an ancient place of mystery buried by the ocean perhaps thousands of years ago. Our ancestors worshipped at its altar but it is unreachable by any except our kind." He pointed at the Waterwalker king. "If he had to keep something safe, it would be in the city below."

Mila turned to face him, her eyes bright. "Will you take me?"

CHAPTER 13

Mila and Ekon sat on the edge of a pool at the back of the cave. It had clearly been formed by ancient tools, each inch of hard-won stone carved by those who spent their lives in the dark, the sound of metal on stone ringing in their ears.

"Have you been down there before?" Mila asked.

"Many times." Ekon ran his hand over the stone and into the water, his flesh shimmering, turning to liquid as he touched it. There was evident pleasure on his face, a sense of longing for the deep that Mila recognized. On Earthside, she fought the urge to swim, to call on her water magic and sink into the canal or the river or the ocean, because each time she used it, she exchanged a piece of herself with the shadow. But now, she could give in to her desire, sink into the blue, become one with the waves with no guilt. The penalty was still the same, but somehow, it didn't matter any longer.

Something changed along with her body when she became water. Sometimes she wondered whether she might turn into a sea creature if she remained underneath long enough. Her magic made her part of the water, and she didn't know how long she could stay down for. She had never tried it for too long, aware of the seconds ticking away and the drops of shadow turning in her blood.

Mila glanced sideways at Ekon. He didn't seem bothered by fear of what might happen. He seemed entirely at ease with his magic. His dark skin was several shades deeper black than her own, his body sculpted with well-used muscles. She couldn't take her eyes off him.

Ekon met her gaze. "My ancestors came from Africa on Earthside, you know." He shrugged. "At least that's what they told me when I was growing up in the camp. Perhaps we're related."

Mila turned her face away to hide her blush. *I hope not.*

Sienna came to kneel next to Mila at the edge of the pool. "Are you sure you want to do this? We don't know what's down there."

"But I do." Ekon's voice was confident, sure of himself. "I've been down to the ruined city many times." He looked at Mila, his glance hesitant. "We should be fine. I mean there are creatures down there, things that came over from Earthside. They should be as extinct as this city but they still survive here. Don't worry, I'll keep an eye out for them."

Sienna put her hand on Mila's arm. "You don't have to go."

Mila looked down into the deep blue pool. All she wanted was to swim away, to lose herself in the depths — and some time alone with Ekon would be good, too. But Sienna didn't need to know that. She sighed. "We need this piece of the map."

Sienna nodded. "But we don't know for sure that it's down there."

Finn stepped forward, his deep voice resonating in the chamber. "The mark on the pyramid matches the Librarian's map piece. All the signs point to it being down there and we have no way of exploring the city without you two. It must have remained untouched for so long because there are so few of your kind."

Your kind. Finn's words echoed in the chamber and Mila caught a tightening in Ekon's jaw at the implication.

They were the 'others' here. She and Ekon were outsiders and in a small way, it thrilled her. Mila had always felt like the odd one out and usually, in the Borderlands, she was lumped in with the rest of the Mapwalker team. But suddenly, she had kin. There was another of her kind here. Was this her true home?

Mila swung her legs around and put her feet into the water. The shimmer of blue washed up her legs as they became fluid, edges blurring into the pool. She caught Ekon's eye as he looked at her, his eyes darkening as he followed her curves into the water. Men had looked at her body with desire before, but never like this. Ekon saw her true self.

She looked up at Sienna and Finn. "We'll just go and have a look, then report back. We won't be long."

Ekon pushed himself off the edge of the stone rim into the pool, sinking quickly, his body quicksilver flashing beneath. Mila pushed herself off to join him, leaving her friends behind.

The water was clear turquoise and as they descended, the outline of the sunken city became clearer. It was nearly ten kilometers long and half as wide, bisected by a grand causeway lined with statues and a colonnade that led to the looming pyramid in the center.

Ekon darted in front of Mila, his features obscured by the water as if a layer of silk had been laid across his flesh. She had never seen herself in a mirror underwater after the change but she imagined that she must look the same way. Smooth lines gliding through the water like a water sprite. She wanted to touch him, to see what his body felt like down here.

"Isn't it incredible that this was built nearly ten thousand years ago?"

Mila froze, hanging in the water, stunned that she could hear Ekon's voice.

He frowned. "You can hear me, right?"

Mila nodded. "I didn't ... I didn't know you could speak underwater. There's never been anyone for me to talk to before."

Ekon laughed, the sound muted, pressed down by the weight of the water above them. "It seems there are a lot of things you didn't know about *our kind*."

He said the last words in an approximation of Finn's voice and Mila giggled.

A giant manta ray suddenly flew out of the blue toward them, black wings gliding on the current, gaping mouth open to filter feed. Ekon flipped over on his back, letting the wash move over him as it passed, then gliding in its wake. Mila loved to see him enjoy his watery body. She had spent so much time in denial of her true nature, it was refreshing to see someone so at home in his. There was a sinuous beauty in the way he moved and she wondered if she could ever be as graceful.

Ekon gave a cheeky grin as he turned in the water, catching her eye. He swept his arm over the drowned city before them.

"Some say it was buried under water when the ice caps melted, thousands of years before known civilization. After the memory of this city faded on Earthside, when it was written out of your history, it ended up here."

"But we've been told that the border was only drawn a few hundred years ago."

Ekon raised an eyebrow, a ripple in the water as he shook his head. "It may be your Mapwalkers strengthened what already existed, but there are things in the Borderlands that you haven't seen on Earthside for many generations. There are many levels to history — and to truth."

They swam down to the grand entrance gate, flanked by statues of ferocious warrior gods, swords held high in multiple hands reminiscent of the Hindu god, Kali.

As Mila swam closer to examine the weapons, a huge

shadow passed overhead, blocking out all light, turning the water to inky black.

Ekon grabbed Mila's hand and pulled her quickly behind the pillars of the colonnade. She peered out, wondering what could make such a shadow in the water.

A massive shark cruised by above them, at least four times as big as a Great White. Its colossal tail caused a current as it swept back and forth through the water and Mila had to hold onto the pillar to stop herself being washed away.

They had been in its way only seconds before. Mila's heart pounded as she considered the near miss. She had mostly waterwalked in the canals and inland rivers of modern England, threatened only by discarded metal or entanglement in fishing lines, as well as dealing with the occasional Feral Borderlander who crossed over. But she had never even considered the hierarchy of the deep.

Perhaps she didn't belong down here after all.

As the massive shark faded into the deeper blue, Ekon swam out from behind the pillar into the main causeway again and hovered above the huge cobblestones. "I'm not sure if the shark could even sense the signals we give off down here. I don't know anyone who's ever studied us, do you?"

Mila thought of the Castle of the Shadow and how they probably tested people like her and Ekon. Perhaps there might be children there with water magic, too. She pushed down a shudder at the thought of what studying them might mean.

She shook her head. "No, but let's not start now. We need to get out of here before dark."

They swam on past ornate columns, each decorated with a statue of a giant beast, some recognizable on Earthside, some strange hybrids she had only seen in mythological books. Mila floated beneath the statue of a lion, its paw resting on a globe, its mane eroded by time. Tiny fish swam in and out of its mouth, open in a roar, darting between its teeth with no fear. It looked as if it could step down from its pedestal and prowl this ancient city again.

They passed over mosaics, intricate tiles of brilliant color revealing scenes of city life — market stalls filled with produce, and busy street vendors with skin colors from all over the world. A huge octopus dominated one tableau, its tentacles reaching out, spiraling to the edge of the design. As they swam on, the mosaic displayed a scene from what must have been a brothel, naked bodies entwined with lust in all kinds of positions. Mila swam a little faster, trying to control her rising blush which of course, Ekon wouldn't even see down here.

He looked over at her, his smile cheeky once more. "I think you have this kind of thing on Earthside, right?"

"Umm, of course. But not usually displayed as a mosaic on the high street."

Ekon laughed. "Some say the city was destroyed because of sin. The people loved pleasure too much and they paid for it eventually."

"Like Sodom and Gomorrah?"

Ekon shrugged. "I've never heard of that. Remember, our histories differ even though we share common ancestry."

They swam on until the central pyramid loomed high above them. It was more imposing as they approached and light filtered down from above cast an eerie gloom over the place. It exuded dark energy, as if it pulsed with something inside. Mila had seen pictures of the Egyptian pyramids and those in South America, but somehow this was different. A wave of apprehension swept over her and she edged closer to Ekon. He had been down here many times and he had returned safely. She would be fine as long as they were together.

Toward the bottom of the pyramid, the density of the city increased, as if people crowded closer to the object of their worship. Temples crammed up against tiny dwellings and shops that must have once teemed with people.

In front of the pyramid there was an open area with huge stones in the shape of a circle, a magical symbol in so many cultures. Mila thought of The Circus back in Bath, a long way from here, for sure, but perhaps this pyramid had once been a powerful gate.

Two giant stele flanked the final approach to the pyramid, stone slabs covered in strange writing, somewhere between cuneiform and Egyptian hieroglyphics, a hybrid language lost along with the city.

Mila ducked down to look at it more closely and traced the lines with watery fingertips, wishing she could read the script. What would it tell of the history of this place? Would it warn of future destruction? She hoped the Mapwalker archaeologists could come down here and find out more at some point.

Ekon pointed toward the peak high above them. "There's a ceremonial entrance at the top of the pyramid, but that was blocked up a long time ago. I found another round the back. There are rocks barring the way, but I think we could get in there together."

A shiver ran down Mila's spine. Strange, because she was never aware of the temperature of the water once she swam within it, her flesh altering to become part of the liquid, but his words made it suddenly cold.

She followed Ekon around the side of the pyramid — straight into an army of statues. Some carried spears, others knives, others curved throwing implements. Some stepped forward with menace, others stood to attention waiting for command. They were of varying sizes, some little more than children, others taller than the tallest man on Earthside. They gazed up the slopes of the pyramid with empty eyes.

The statues were green with algae in places and fish darted in to eat from their flesh, picking pieces from their skin. A sea star crawled across the face of one soldier, questing tentacles poking into the nasal cavity as it traveled across the dead stone.

A group of statues stood in their own battalion with wings folded on their backs like dark angels ready to take flight. Mila called back to Ekon. "Are there winged people in the Borderlands?"

Ekon shook his head. "I've never seen them, but that doesn't mean there aren't any. I haven't traveled much, to be honest. Not like you."

"We don't have them on Earthside, at least not anymore. Only in stories and myth." Mila looked closely at the angels, searing them into her memory. These were real once, perhaps they still were.

No matter how many times she came into the Borderlands, there was always a surprise to look forward to. On Earthside, everything had been mapped. There was little of the wild left and technology meant that you could find anything on the Internet. It was a miracle, enabling people to see into worlds they would never visit on their own, but it also meant there was no mystery left.

The things down here had been lost to Earthside before technology could capture them, before cameras, before anything more than oral storytelling. These creatures had been passed down in the tales of myth, but to see even statues of them was a thrill.

Mila swam between the ranks of statues, looking up into their faces. They were all individually sculpted, each with a slightly different expression. The level of craftsmanship was incredible, further evidence of this advanced civilization.

She turned in the water to look up at the pyramid from the perspective of the soldiers. The dark lines of the stylized death's head stood out in different colored stone and at its center, a pile of rocks where the entrance must be.

Ekon followed her gaze and nodded. "That's where we need to go next. Are you ready?"

Mila looked up at the symbol of death, the entrance at its center. What choice did she have? They couldn't go back without investigating further. She nodded and together, they swam toward the entrance.

CHAPTER 14

MILA KICKED AND SWAM ahead of Ekon, trying to ignore the looming symbol that surrounded the entrance. The boulders had clearly been placed there to stop people entering and over the years, the rocks had fused together with coral and layers of silt. Together, Mila and Ekon generated small whirlpools of water to lift the detritus of years away and once the rocks were revealed, they began to shift those too. Mila was fascinated to see how differently Ekon lifted. She used her watery hands just as she would her solid flesh on the surface, whereas he floated a tiny wave underneath the rock and then brushed it to one side with a sweep of his hand.

He caught her watching him and shrugged. "I guess neither of us was taught the proper way to use our skills."

"I like your way better." Mila copied Ekon's actions and together they moved the rocks with little effort.

Mila swam through the narrow entranceway first, suddenly aware of the tonnes of rock above her, wondering if this was such a good idea after all. The sound of the ocean faded away as she went deeper within, the clicks of fish feeding on the coral, the call of whale song all muted now. It was as if the atmosphere of the ancient culture still remained, sucking all sound within as panic rose inside her.

Just as she was about to turn and swim out again, the small entranceway opened out into a chamber big enough to park a huge truck. It was dark with only a glimmer of light seeping in through the tiny entrance.

The chamber tapered away into blackness and Mila stopped in the water column, all her senses telling her to flee. It was too dark, as if the dead pyramid sucked all living things into it.

She felt a cool touch on her arm, like the fingers of a corpse. She yelped in fear.

"It's only me," Ekon said. "You're jumpy as hell."

"It's too dark." Mila's tone was annoyed, but mainly with herself. "We'll never find anything in here."

Ekon opened his hand and a green glow rose up from his palm, a whirling mini tornado of sparkling emerald and silver.

Mila couldn't help but smile. "Bioluminescence. How did you do that?"

Ekon shrugged. "I've always been able to do this. Try it yourself."

Mila opened her palm, conjuring the water with its microorganisms, drawing it to her. She could spin rain into whips, so why shouldn't she be able to spin water down here into a bioluminescent torch?

She concentrated on whirling it above her palm, drawing in particles until it began to pull light from Ekon's own.

"Hey! Enough already."

They laughed together and for a moment it felt less cold, less like a tomb.

They swam deeper into the pyramid, holding their bioluminescent lights up high. The chamber narrowed and then narrowed more until it was a slender tube heading into the depths of the pyramid. Mila swam slowly, remembering that Egyptian pyramids were full of traps and dead ends to confuse robbers, and tombs the world over had curses guarding what lay inside.

They finally reached the grand inner chamber, green light reflecting off statues of many-handed gods in each corner.

A stone sarcophagus sat in the center. Mila darted to it, brushing layers of silt from the surface. A six-pointed star was carved into the top, more like an occult hexagram than a Jewish Star of David. Curious. Mila frowned.

"This looks similar to the one in London, but how could that be? This city is thousands of years older."

Ekon moved around the other side, examining the edges of the lid. "Time moves differently here, you know that. As Earthside pushes things out, our world shifts."

Mila nodded. "And Mapwalkers can walk through gates that link to different times. Perhaps one of the plague knights ended up here."

"I guess he couldn't get back home."

"Or perhaps he found a reason to stay." Mila couldn't help the blush that rose up her cheeks.

Ekon broke the moment and used a whirlwind of water to widen a crack. "Help me open it."

"What if it's dry inside and we flood it after so long?"

Ekon shook his head. "I think whatever is in here is long gone."

Together they inserted watery fingers underneath the edges of the lid and lifted it with a waft of their hands, floating it down beside the sarcophagus.

A soup of deep reddish-brown rose from its stony interior. Mila couldn't smell underwater but she darted away, not wanting to touch the fetid remains of whoever had lain here so long.

Ekon created a series of little whirlwinds in the water to corral the foul substance into one corner, keeping the particles separate but leaving the heavier, more dense material inside.

They both peered into the sarcophagus. On the bottom lay pieces of what may once have been bone, some jewelry, brooches ... and a lead box marked with the same stylized death's head skull.

Mila looked at Ekon. "This has to be it."

As she lifted the box from inside, the sound of rushing waters came from above.

Ekon looked up, confusion on his face. Then realization dawned.

He grabbed Mila's hand. "We have to go — now."

As they swam for the exit, stone blocks moved above them releasing a huge dump of sand from the roof. It just missed them but it swirled up in the water, making it impossible to see.

Mila clutched the box in her watery hand as Ekon urged her on, confident in his sense of direction. But as they reached the final chamber, a massive rock fell from the ceiling and pinned Mila's leg to the ground.

She screamed in pain, pushing at the immense rock with futile hands as agony blazed through her. She pushed the box at Ekon. "You need to go before we're both trapped here. Take this."

Ekon knelt next to her and brushed a hand over her forehead, soothing her. "Think water," he whispered. "You *are* water. You cannot be pinned down. No rock can trap you."

His words cut through her pain, shifting perspective as she understood. Mila closed her eyes and visualized her body like Ekon's, liquid in motion. The weight shifted from her leg and she opened her eyes to see that she had slithered out from beneath it. The pain was gone.

She couldn't believe it. It was amazing what she had learned from Ekon in such a short time. Part of her was angry that no one had shown her this before, and a part of her wondered how much more she had to learn.

They swam out of the pyramid into the open water above the city as rocks tumbled down in front of the entrance, covering it once more, blocking the way into the tomb within.

Mila took a deep breath and shook her head. "That was close. How did you learn about your skills?"

Ekon smiled but there was an edge of regret in his eyes. "I was pinned once, just like that, but with no one to help me, no one to tell me what I should do. I lay alone for three days, and it was only in the depths of delirium that my perspective shifted. Perhaps one of our ancestors whispered it across the veil. It worked and now you know, too."

"I wonder what else we can do."

They smiled at each other, suddenly aware of their potential.

Mila looked back across the city and up to where they needed to go next. Back to the surface, back to her friends, back to responsibility.

They began to swim back up, keeping an eye out for sharks, and as they lifted away from the city gates Ekon reached for Mila's hand, their watery fingers entwined as they swam back to the entrance.

* * *

Sienna paced back and forth next to the pool of water, looking down into the darkness every few seconds, wishing for Mila's return.

"She's going to be okay." Perry sat by the edge of the cave, leaning back against the stone, his lanky frame relaxed as they waited. "Mila wouldn't follow him into danger. She knows better than that."

Sienna stopped and knelt by the pool. "But she's never met anyone like Ekon. She doesn't know how far she would go for him." She couldn't help but glance over at Finn. They still hadn't been able to find time alone to talk about whether there was anything between them, anything more than an unrequited mission romance. Jari kept close to him, and she was certainly more than just a fellow traveler.

Finn smiled. "Ekon will look after her. She's special and he knows that."

Jari snorted. "We can do without them both. We just have to—"

"Look!" Sienna shouted with excitement, as twin shadows appeared in the dark blue waters below, growing larger as they rose to the surface.

Mila's head broke first and a moment later, Ekon surfaced beside her. They beamed at each other, hands still entwined until they realized the others were crowded round the pool. They broke apart and quickly clambered out, their shimmering outlines solidifying once more into smooth skin.

"Did you find anything down there?" Sienna asked.

Mila held out a metal box. "This was within the pyramid in a stone sarcophagus that looked just like the one in London."

Sienna lifted the box and placed it down on one of the rocks. "How do we open it?"

Perry walked over. "Let me have a look." He cupped his hands around the metal, summoning a subtle flame, an exploratory spark. He closed his eyes for a moment, then frowned. "I just need to soften the metal a little without burning whatever is inside."

A moment later, he took his hands away, smiling with triumph. Two of the rivets had loosened in their sockets, the metal sides collapsing in on themselves revealing a piece of map within.

Sienna prised it loose and unfolded it with gentle fingers, sensing the same vibrations as the other piece from the library. She pulled it from her inner pocket and fitted the two pieces together. The ripped edges matched and she imagined the long-dead knight pulling it apart, hoping that he was doing the right thing.

What was the right thing now? Find the other pieces of the map or destroy these two here and now? Burn them to cinders and brush the ashes into the water to sink into the deep. No one could find the plague island then, no one could find a way to send the disease back to Earthside.

But something held Sienna back. Something about the way Finn looked at the pieces she held, as if his life depended on them. She had to find out what was going on and the only way was forward. Find the next fragment, the final piece of the map, and then face whatever came next.

There was no way the Shadow Cartographers would stop now. The final piece lay ahead and that is where the real battle would begin. She hoped Finn would be by her side.

The others gathered close to look at the pieces.

"Where next?" Jari asked, her no-nonsense tone breaking the silence. "Where's the final piece?"

Perry checked the inside of the metal box. "There's nothing in here, no indication of where it might be hidden." He looked at Sienna. "So where do we go?"

Mila cut in. "I saw something down there on the sarcophagus that might help. A six-pointed star, but not a Star of David. It was more like a hexagram, an occult symbol." She dipped her finger in the water and drew a star with droplets of liquid. "I've seen it before in a translation of the Emerald Tablet, popular in medieval times as a Hermetic text. It means 'as above, so below.'"

Finn frowned. "But how does that help us know where to go next?"

"Perhaps it's the other way: as below, so above." Mila drew the symbol again, reversing the triangles.

Jari stepped closer, biting her lip as she examined the marks. "There is a city of air, built into the hanging rocks of a lost canyon, a place so far out in the Uncharted that few dare to travel there."

Sienna could see the apprehension on her face. They didn't have any other clues for the next location, but what could possibly scare the warrior woman so much?

CHAPTER 15

As Finn sketched a map on the ground of how they might travel to the city of air, Ekon reached for Mila's hand and led her to the corner of the cave.

"You could stay." His voice was soft, tentative. "You've only just arrived and I know we've just met, but … I want more time and I know you do, too. Imagine what we could discover about our magic together."

His words echoed deep inside Mila, calling to a part of her that longed for home. Perhaps home was not a place, after all, but a person. Someone who understood her dual self, someone who saw beyond her magic to the woman beneath.

Part of her longed to say yes, to give in to this heady feeling, but if she stayed, if she used her magic the way Ekon did, she would soon be lost in shadow. They would be together, but they would also change into who knew what. The Waterwalkers had all but disappeared, living beneath the waves perhaps, or lost down there in the deep. Was it worth the risk for such a short time together?

* * *

"Mila, what do you think of this?" Sienna called over, frowning as she saw how close her friend stood to Ekon, how she could barely tear her eyes from the young man.

She looked at Finn that way sometimes, although he could barely look at her at the moment. He was hiding something, but she still didn't know what.

Mila turned, her fingers still entwined with Ekon's. "What is it?"

Sienna pointed down at Finn's rough map showing Ganvié surrounded by water and then the trader city, the approximate location of the library and a mountain further east. "Does this look like any of the maps you've seen back at the Ministry?"

Mila walked over and bent closer. "The distances are more spaced out on our version but it looks about right. Is it enough for you to travel through?"

Sienna gazed at the rough lines, letting her magic probe at the edges of it as she imagined the map as three-dimensional, a world she could walk upon, a land she could travel across — or fly over.

Mapwalking was still a mystery, but with every journey she learned more. She had sketched a map like this in the abandoned asylum of Poveglia and traveled through it, but she had been alone, and it was only a short journey. This was some heavy lifting and the more magic she used, the more the shadow entwined within her — and she was beginning to hear it call her name. The sound was a long way off but when she traveled it became louder, as if the shadow flew beside her. The drops of darkness in her blood expanded like the headiness of alcohol, as if she was intoxicated by it and all she needed to do was let it wash over her and she would be free.

"Sienna?" Mila's voice broke into her thoughts.

"Yes." Sienna nodded. "It's enough. I can take us through, I'm sure of it."

Finn and Jari gathered up the packs while Perry carefully wrapped the box to take with them. Sienna slipped the pieces of the map inside her jacket and pulled out her ritual knife. She cut into the still-healing wound on her palm, letting her blood drip onto the stones and mingle with the salt water. She placed her hand on the sketched map, becoming one with the contours of the earth.

She reached out her other hand for the others.

Finn, Perry and Jari gathered around, laying their palms on top but Mila stood apart. She stepped closer to Ekon and wrapped her arms around him. He pulled her into an embrace and for a moment, they clung to each other.

Then Mila stepped away. "I'm sorry. I have to go, but I'll come back. I promise."

Ekon nodded, disappointment in his eyes. "Travel safe, Mila Waterwalker." He turned and dived back into the pool, disappearing into the deep blue, leaving only ripples in his wake.

Mila took a step toward the pool as if she would follow him down there, her fists clenched. She sighed and turned back to the team, reaching out a hand to place it on top of theirs.

Before she could change her mind, Sienna closed her eyes and leaned into the map, pulling the others with her. A second later, she was flying above the floating city of Ganvié, the silhouettes of sharks circling below. As she rose higher, she could see the shimmering border and then the plains of the Borderlands stretching away before her, mountains in the distance.

She focused on the city of air that Finn had drawn for her on the ground and described for them all. A place built high above a tropical forest, with soaring pinnacles of rock. Her focus changed and the passage of time and space below shifted.

Suddenly, the air chilled around her.

Sienna shivered as dark clouds gathered, obscuring the land below. Wind buffeted from all sides and she lost her sense of direction. Panic rose within and her breath came fast. If she traveled accidentally over the border, Finn and Jari would be lost into the mists between the worlds, a place that no one returned from.

She spun around, desperately trying to see through the gathered fog, but all she could see were shadows twisting through the grey, black streaks that drew closer every second.

Then the voice called her name, the one she feared above all else because she longed for it.

Sienna.

The mist swirled clear in one direction, opening a path to the Castle of the Shadow below. Its twisted turrets spiraled high into the sky and at the top of one, a ruby light glowed like a welcoming hearth or a drop of blood.

She could dive down there right now.

Sienna wanted to and if she had been on her own, perhaps she would have gone. But the weight of the others pressed down upon her and Sienna knew she had to take them as far from here as she could. The Castle of the Shadow offered only death for them, or perhaps something worse.

She turned away and the mist closed around her again, cutting off the route down, leaving behind a sense of desolation, that she had missed a chance for something just beyond her reach. The voice grew softer as Sienna dived down through the mist, unsure as to whether she was falling or flying until suddenly the world around her was all shades of green and the shadows withdrew.

Pillars of limestone rose up toward the sky, rope bridges swung between them and on the edge of one pillar, hanging out over the forest, Sienna saw the ruins of a temple that Finn had suggested as their landing point. She dived down toward it and as her feet touched rock, she let the others go and collapsed to the ground, sinking into the welcoming darkness.

* * *

As the world stopped spinning, Perry opened his eyes. He couldn't focus at first, vertigo and nausea making him dizzy, his stomach clenching in protest at the rough trip. Something had happened as they traveled. Following Sienna through a map was usually like stepping through a waterfall, briefly violent and then another place, but that journey — Perry took a deep breath — that journey was like standing under the drowning water and being hammered into rock.

Shades of vibrant green shimmered and slowly came into focus as he sat up. The others lay around him on a stone platform, some kind of ritual circle on the edge of a cliff. Towering pinnacles of rock rose around them with trees growing on different levels, thick foliage obscuring what looked like cave dwellings. Mist gathered in the spaces between the pinnacles, obscuring how far up they must be. A strange cry echoed through the mist, the call of a predator hunting.

A groan then retching sounds behind him. Perry turned to see Finn on his hands and knees coughing and Jari beside him, both almost green with nausea but otherwise okay. Mila leaned against a huge stone statue of an eagle taking flight, rubbing her forehead as she tried to breathe deeply, the fastest way to get through the travel sickness.

Where was Sienna?

Perry stood on shaky legs, turning slowly, heart pounding as he remembered a voice in the mist calling for her. Could she have possibly—

Then he saw her, lying prone behind what looked like an altar on the very edge of the cliff. He stumbled over and knelt by her side.

"Sienna!" He shook her shoulder, turned her over and couldn't help the gasp that escaped his lips. Beneath the skin of her neck and up onto her face, tendrils of black wound through her veins, evidence of the shadow. But Perry had never seen it this bad, except on those who lay in the wards of the Ministry, lost in a shadow coma until they passed beyond the edges of the world.

He pulled up her right sleeve, then the left. Darkness coiled through her skin, whorls of blood corrupted with shadow. He had to tell Mila. They had to get her back to the Ministry.

He began to rise but Sienna gripped his arm, her eyes now wide open.

"Don't," she whispered. "Wait a moment."

As Perry watched, the black marks faded away and moments later, only her pale skin remained.

"How did you do that?"

Sienna shook her head. "I don't really know—" Her eyes widened in fear. "Down!"

She pulled Perry toward her as huge talons swooshed over his head, the cry of a giant eagle echoing around the pinnacle as it swooped back up to the sky above. A sky that was suddenly filled with a convocation of giant birds.

They dived, one after another, talons as large and sharp as scythes.

Perry and Sienna pulled themselves flat against the altar, using the stone to shield themselves against the plunging birds. Perry peered around the edge to check on the others.

Mila huddled behind the statue, but Finn and Jari were out in the open, still on the ground. Finn rolled to his front as one dived for him. The creature couldn't pierce his protective leather coat and flew away.

As another dived for Jari, she rose, twin swords in her hands, shouting at the sky. "Come get me, you bastards!"

An eagle dived for her, talons aimed at her eyes.

She slashed at it, swords tangling in its feathers as she went down under the weight of the creature. It pecked and slashed at her and she screamed as a warrior in battle as they rolled across the flagstones toward the edge of the cliff.

CHAPTER 16

Finn grabbed Jari's boot, pulling her back, even as she fought the creature on top of her.

Another eagle dived for Finn, its cry that of a predator who knows it has won. As the talons struck him, he was driven away from Jari, fighting his own battle even as she struggled under the weight of the eagle as it dragged her toward the rim of the sacred area where mist obscured the drop below.

"Enough." Perry stood up and raised his hands.

The black tendrils in Sienna's flesh reminded him of the cost of their magic, but Finn — and even Jari — were part of the team now and they had only mortal weapons to defend themselves. He didn't have to like them, but he did have to save them.

He summoned fire from within, the burning sensation rising inside until it burst out of his palms into white hot balls of flame.

Perry ran toward the warrior woman, catching her outstretched hand and pulling her away from the edge even as he threw the fireball into the side of the eagle. It caught fire, its feathers burning as it shrieked in pain, freeing its talons from Jari's clothes. It tumbled off the edge of the cliff, a three-meter-wide fiery death.

He spun around and hurled another fireball at the eagle attacking Finn, the blow driving the creature off its prey momentarily. Finn rolled away and ran quickly back to Jari, huddling over her as Perry stood protecting them both, hands raised to the sky, palms burning with almost blue flame.

The gigantic eagles circled above, wary now. Perry watched them, turning as he noted the passage of the largest. It dived once more, then another came from the opposite direction.

Perry waited, his muscles taut as he held himself in check, waiting, waiting …

When he could feel the wind of their descent on his face, he spun around, whipping his flames into a burning pillar then thrusting his arms out wide, creating a towering vortex of fire. The second eagle burned up almost immediately, plunging down to dash onto the stone beneath.

For a moment the largest eagle appeared more like a phoenix, its whole body alive with flame, its beak open to tear apart its prey. Then it too dropped to the flagstones, feathers burned and body roasted, the smell of scorched flesh in the air.

As the flames died down and the smoke from their bodies swept over the side to join the mists below, Perry stood once more, arms raised to the sky, challenging the flying eagles above. Those that were left, circled and then flew away, their cries echoing across the pinnacled valley until it was quiet again.

Perry dropped his arms and sat down heavily on the flagstones, a wave of exhaustion flooding him as the magic dissipated, leaving an emptiness that almost brought tears to his eyes. His shoulders slumped, his mind whirled. He would have fought on until he had been consumed by the flames. Part of him wished the eagles would come back, just so he could feel that surge of power again. In that moment, he understood why Xander had chosen the shadow side.

"Come on, Jari." Finn's voice was desperate.

Perry turned to see him wiping blood from the warrior woman's face, but her wounds were deep, gouges from the talons across her chest, through her armor, along her arms. Her eyelids fluttered and she tried to get up, hand reaching for her sword.

"Rest now. It's okay. They're gone." Finn calmed her and Jari lay back, her breathing a harsh rattle.

"We need medical help." Mila walked over from behind the statue. As she reached them, she squeezed Perry's hand, gratitude in her eyes.

Sienna stumbled over from the altar and sat down next to Perry. They were weakened, but they were still together.

The sound of a slow clap echoed across the sacred ground.

Perry tried to stand but his legs were too frail. The others could barely move either. They were helpless.

The slow clap grew louder and an old man stepped out onto the sacred ground, his face grim and set in craggy features. He wore a feathered cloak that dragged along the stones as he walked toward them. Behind him, a group of soldiers emerged from the trees, each one wearing a helmet in the shape of an eagle's head with a cruel beak spiking from the front.

The man stopped clapping. "No one has killed three of our sacred birds at one time for a generation. No one has ever killed the alpha male." He pointed at the still smoldering body of the biggest bird. "These are Haast's eagles, extinct many centuries ago on Earthside. There are a few left here." He looked pointedly at Perry. "Even fewer now."

Mila stood and faced the man. "They attacked us. We only defended ourselves."

The man pointed at Perry. "No, he defended you all."

Perry noted a strange look in the man's eyes, the look of someone starving who had finally found a good meal.

The man smiled, the stony expression on his face

dissolving into friendship. He held his arms out wide. "Welcome to Aetofolia, the eagle's nest. I am Aguila, ruler of this eyrie. You have passed the test of entry even before you were challenged, so come inside. Rest." Aguila nodded toward Jari. "We have medical help for your friend." He gestured for the soldiers to come forward.

Perry felt Finn tense beside him, a coiled spring ready to explode into action, but there was nowhere for them to go. In one direction there was only sky and mist. In the other, soldiers and perhaps help. Perry noticed the way Aguila looked over at his hands, scanned his body for evidence of magic, and he knew a reckoning must come. He glanced over at Sienna who had shrunk behind Mila. As long as they didn't realize what magic she had, they might be alright. At least for a while.

As Finn relaxed behind him, opening his hands in a sign of surrender, Perry nodded. "Thank you. We gladly accept your help."

* * *

Sienna watched Perry walk forward and clasp Aguila's hand, assuming leadership of the team with the natural confidence she had seen before in his father. But then she noticed the slight delay in his step, a halting stride that spoke of the weakness that came after using magic.

They were all fragile right now.

Jari and Finn were both wounded by the giant birds, Mila was exhausted after Ganvié, and her own mapwalking sucked the energy from her. Sienna knew she faced a challenge ahead, too. Somehow she had managed to dampen down the shadow inside, but Perry had seen the black lines on her skin. He would have to tell Bridget and her father, and she needed him to, because she couldn't do it herself. It might mean the end of her mapwalking before it had even really begun and she wouldn't give up the heady experience easily. But something was different with her. Somehow the shadow leached inside her at a faster rate than the others. Sienna remembered the voice in the mist that wanted to keep her inside the map.

Perhaps that had been its goal all along.

She pulled her sleeves further down over her hands, praying that the black lines would not re-emerge.

Mila took her arm. "You okay?" she whispered, as they walked behind Perry and Aguila toward the rock face carved with a giant eagle. The soldiers jogged behind, one carrying Jari and two others flanking Finn with careful respect, instinctively noting his ability to fight even when injured.

Sienna nodded. "Just a little fatigued after traveling." But as she took another step, she felt the world spin, her stomach clench with something like vertigo and her vision begin to narrow.

As Perry and Aguila stepped up to the rock face, the carving of the eagle split open revealing stone steps leading down into darkness. Sienna thought she saw the mist of the shadow curling out from the depths, undulating toward her with the head of a serpent. Panic rose inside, her breath coming faster and faster as she tried to control the dread rising inside.

They could not go down there.

The world turned to mist and Sienna fell to her knees as the serpent reached her, jaws gaping, fangs bared, swallowing her into the dark.

* * *

Sienna sat bolt upright, heart pounding as she imagined the jaws of the snake closing around her throat. But she found herself sitting up in a soft bed, luxuriant covers around her, a lamp casting a golden glow around the room.

"It's okay. You're safe."

His voice was soft, gentle and Sienna turned to see Finn sitting in a padded chair by her side. He wore a new shirt, no longer ripped and stained with blood. He had a dressing across his right collarbone, just visible as it wound up his neck. Sienna was suddenly aware of how close he was, how his lips were only inches from her own, how she just wanted to be in his arms. But there was so much unsaid between them now.

He reached for her hand and squeezed gently. "How are you feeling?"

"What happened?"

"You fainted just as we entered the eyrie." Finn got up and poured some water from a jug into a glass and handed it to her. Sienna drank deeply, suddenly parched, as he continued.

"You gave us quite a scare, but I know it takes it out of you to—"

Sienna put a finger on her lips and he stopped. They didn't know who was listening down here and if anyone found out about her own blood magic, they might as well give up their quest right now.

"I know it takes it out of you to — travel." Finn sat down again in the chair. "Perry has told of how *he* mapwalked us here, after Aguila enquired as to how we arrived on the sacred platform."

Sienna raised an eyebrow. "Perry's magic is truly all-encompassing."

"Indeed. Mila's sleeping next door and Jari is in their medical wing. They have special balm for eagle talon injuries, so she's going to be alright."

"And Perry?"

Finn sighed and leaned forward, chin resting in his

hands. "We haven't seen him since they led us in here nearly twenty-four hours ago."

"I slept that long?" Sienna shook her head. "We need to get moving. The last piece of the map must be here somewhere. We'll find Perry on the way out but we have to complete that map before the Shadow Cartographers find it."

Finn frowned. "Sienna, there's something I need to—"

A creak from the corner and the large door opened.

Mila walked in, her stride strong again. "About time you were up. Guess what I found out?" She sat on the end of the bed, eyes bright with the thrill of discovery. "The eyrie perches on the top of one of the pinnacles but there's a staircase down to the forest floor below."

"That must be hundreds of meters down?"

"Further than that." Mila grinned. "There's a tomb at the base, a tomb they say the ancestor lives in, a tomb marked with a special symbol." She drew the two interlocking triangles on the covers.

"As above, so below." Sienna smiled. "So we just need to get to that tomb. The final piece of the map must be there. Then we can go home." Her voice trailed off as she caught Finn's gaze, his eyes serious. Going home meant they would be apart again. But there was more distance between them this time than mere geography.

Jari.

Sienna still didn't know what the warrior woman was to Finn but she certainly complicated what had once seemed simple.

"You'll go as soon as you have that third piece?" Finn's voice was halting, his question more of a statement. "You'll just take them all back to Earthside?"

Mila nodded. "That's the plan. There's no way the Shadow Cartographers can find the island with only one quarter of the map, while we might be able to stitch together some options, find the island and destroy it or at least remove all traces of the way to get there."

The door creaked again. Jari stood there, her arm in a sling, her head bandaged, her face still bruised and puffy. She looked every inch the warrior and Sienna was suddenly aware of her own slim frame, sitting in a soft bed with nothing more than tenuous magic. No wonder Finn didn't look at her the way he used to.

"We'll help you finish your mission." Jari stared straight at Finn as she spoke, her eyes a silent challenge. As Finn hung his head, Sienna wondered once more what he was hiding.

Suddenly the deep base sound of drums beat through the air, the vibrations shaking the lamp beside the bed.

Finn looked up, his eyes wide with concern. "It's a call to worship, a call to sacrifice."

Mila and Sienna looked at each other as realization dawned. There was only one of their team missing, the one person who would be considered a powerful sacrifice to the gods.

Perry.

CHAPTER 17

As the drums beat a rhythmic pulse, Mila paced the room. "We don't have much time. We need to split up." She looked at the others in their weakened state. "We're going to have to fight to get to Perry so Finn and I will go up to the sacred area. Sienna, you and Jari go down to the tomb, find that piece of the map and we'll meet you down there with Perry."

"I can fight," Jari said, her jaw clenched with barely restrained anger.

Finn stood up and walked over to her. He grabbed her wounded arm, pressed into the bandage. She exhaled sharply, the pain making her almost double over.

"No, you can't. But you can protect Sienna." Finn adjusted his sword. "I trust you two will manage to get along?"

Sienna hesitated. She didn't want to be alone with the warrior woman. If she was honest, she was scared of her. The half-moon tattoo on her face was a permanent reminder of the side she worked for, and the fragile peace that held their little team together would be over as soon as they had that final map fragment.

Jari nodded. "Of course, we're not children." She took a breath. "And Perry saved my life, so you need to get him out of there." She looked over at Sienna. "You good with that?"

Sienna nodded.

The drums began to speed up, the beat now double time.

"Let's go." Mila grabbed the jug of water as she headed out the door, closely followed by Finn. He glanced back one more time and Sienna met his gaze, seeing concern in his eyes. He turned away and the sound of their footsteps heading upstairs was lost in the beating of the drum.

Sienna pulled off the bedcovers and dressed quickly while Jari gathered their packs. Then together, they headed into the corridor and down the staircase into the dark.

* * *

It was busy on the stone staircase that wound back up to the sacred ground as people from all over the eyrie hurried to witness the sacrifice. Mila kept her head down as she ran up the stairs with Finn close behind, no one paying them any heed. They blended in here, the color of their skin making them part of the mix of races that made a home in the heights of the pinnacle.

People streamed in from corridors that led out from the central staircase and Mila wondered how deep into the rock this city of the air penetrated. As they ascended, she noticed carvings on the walls, intricate designs of eagles soaring over treetops, plunging gorges and waterfalls beneath the towers of stone. Then pictures of sacrifice, figures of men and women, even children, pegged out on the sacred ground while eagles pecked at their soft bellies, dragging out their entrails while the crowd cheered around them. Nausea washed over her and Mila redoubled her pace.

At the top of the staircase, a wide doorway stood open with a vista out over the flagstones to the horizon beyond. The giant eagles once more circled overhead, their cries filling the air even as the gathered crowd clapped along with the drums, faces eager for spectacle.

Mila and Finn pushed their way through to the front of the pack, standing on the edge of the stone circle as a phalanx of soldiers marched Perry forward, chains around his ankles, his hands wrapped in some kind of fireproof material.

They had taken his only weapon.

Aguila, priest of the eagles, stepped out onto a ledge above the crowd and held his hands up to the sky. The drums stopped.

"This man killed three of our sacred birds with the gift of Prometheus. Now, he must pay the same price."

Mila gasped at the reference. Prometheus had stolen fire from the gods and as a punishment, he had been chained to a rock where an eagle pecked out and devoured his liver every day, and every night, it was renewed so he could suffer once again. Now Perry would face the same fate.

* * *

The staircase grew colder as Sienna and Jari descended, the flagstones less worn and older looking as the torchlight faded. Clearly, few people came down here, preferring to live their days up in the towering city of the eagles. There were only a few lamps and the steps between them were shrouded with shadow. The drums faded after a while and soon, the only sounds were their footsteps and their breathing.

Jari had led the way at first, but Sienna noted that her breath came faster now, her breaks longer on the ledges where they rested on the way down. Clearly, she was in great pain, but she wouldn't admit it.

Sienna counted the stairs for the first three hundred or so but then she'd lost count, unable to concentrate as the pain in her leg muscles burned and she clenched her teeth with every stride. Clearly the Mapwalkers needed step classes in preparation for missions, and the thought of Perry trying such a thing made her smile. She pushed aside the pain and concentrated on their task. Find the map fragment and be ready to travel when the others arrived at the tomb.

If they made it back.

After what seemed like an age, the light began to change in the dark of the staircase. A natural green permeated the golden glow of the lamps and as they descended further, it lightened more until they reached a ceremonial archway that opened up to the forest floor.

Jari leaned against a pillar carved with vines, berries and birds. "Just … a minute." Her face was pallid, her skin slick with sweat.

Sienna pulled a flask of water from her bag and offered it to her. Jari took it and drank deep, then handed it back. Sienna took a sip herself and looked around the grove before them. Clearly the people of the eyrie didn't fear whatever lay below, only what flew above. The grove was well-tended with patches of wildflowers dancing in the breeze. The sun lanced through the tall trees around them, dappling on the grass.

A path of stones studded with precious gems of many colors wound into the forest. Metal torch holders stood either side shaped like the heads of eagles. It was clearly a ceremonial way.

Leaving Jari resting behind her, Sienna followed the path into the shadow of the trees. Birds sang in the boughs overhead and the forest smelled of pine and sandalwood with a faint hint of apples. It should have been tranquil and peaceful but Sienna had a sense of foreboding, perhaps worry for the others, perhaps an overriding concern about what the Map of Plagues could bring down on them all.

She turned a corner to find an ancient chapel nestled amongst the trees. It was simple, built of the same stone as the pinnacle itself and as sunlight danced across its timber roof, Sienna caught a glimpse of flowers and limbs of trees entwined into the structure itself. It must have been here a long time, maintained by the people of the eyrie.

As she walked closer, Sienna noticed that the wide oak door was marked with the symbol of two interlocking triangles. She heard a scuff of boots on stone behind her and turned quickly, expecting to see Jari walk around the corner. But the forest fell silent again.

A cloud passed overhead and the chapel was cast into shadow. The stones, which only moments before had seemed welcoming, were now the cold blocks of a prison. Limbs from the trees above loomed like a threat as Sienna walked to the old door and pushed it open with a creak.

It took a moment for her eyes to adjust to the gloom. The old timbers let only a glimmer of light inside but as the room became clearer, Sienna could make out a sarcophagus carved from the same stone as the pinnacle and the chapel itself. It had some similarities to the one she had seen on the video footage of the London plague pit, but this one was carved with swooping eagles and the entwined branches of the forest. There was a stark beauty to the place, giving her a sense of perspective, as if only the bigger things mattered. Not the minutiae of daily life, but the questions that impacted humankind — on both sides of the border.

Sienna stepped closer to the sarcophagus, well aware of how far the knights had traveled to split the map apart. If the third piece was truly here, she would be responsible for bringing it almost back together again.

Could she really trust those in the Ministry with the fragments?

If the plague island really did hold what they thought it did, a weapon of such power could be used by either side to wreak havoc on their enemy. The Borderlanders were people, just as much as those on Earthside. But those on this side of the border still remembered their homes, and that drive could be more powerful than anything else.

She put a hand on the stone lid of the sarcophagus, trying to sense whether she should open it or just run from this place and forget it ever existed.

A creak made her jump and turn in haste.

Jari stood in the doorway, her twin swords silhouetted against the sun, blocking the path out again. "I'll help you with that." Her voice was a dark promise and Sienna couldn't help but shiver as the cold of the chapel pierced her heart.

* * *

"Chain him." Aguila pointed to the sacrificial altar and the guards dragged Perry to it, lifting him kicking and shouting onto the stone, securing the shackles to each corner. The cry of an eagle pierced the air, a hunter spying its prey.

Mila assessed the scene quickly, counting the guards, checking for where other soldiers might be. Behind them, the crowd continuing to surge from the staircase, more and more people blocking the route back down. She clenched her fists, her right hand holding tight to the jug of water.

"This is hopeless," Finn whispered, his face crestfallen.

They were completely outnumbered. There was no way to fight their way out of here and escape down the staircase, especially with Perry so weak and unable to use his magic.

No way out behind them and before them, only sky.

Mila looked out at the blue horizon and remembered one of the carvings on the wall of the staircase. A river, winding through the valley below the mist. It was a long way down — perhaps it wasn't even there at all — but it looked like their only chance.

"Do you trust me?" she whispered back.

Finn nodded. "Of course. I've seen you fight before."

"Then trust me to hold the guards off while you free Perry, and jump when I say jump."

Confusion flashed across Finn's face as Mila gave a wicked grin, her heart pounding with excitement as she ran full tilt into the center of the sacred area straight toward the guards.

They turned with swords raised, ready to fight.

As Mila ran, she summoned her magic from within. She threw the jug of water into the air. It rained down droplets of water which she spun toward the guards like a hail of bullets.

Two fell to the ground, wounds already bleeding. The others were driven back, leaving Perry exposed on the altar.

"Stop them!" Aguila's voice rose high above the cacophony of the crowd, who shouted with excitement at the expectation of a bloody fight beyond the usual sacrifice.

Mila pulled the drops of water back into a whip, spinning and whirling, driving back the other soldiers as Finn rushed to cut Perry from the altar and drag him behind the stone.

As soon as she saw they were free, Mila stepped carefully back toward the edge of the cliff. She found herself laughing as she spun the whips of water out and around the advancing soldiers. This was possibly her craziest idea ever and Sienna wasn't even here to witness it.

"Drive them from the edge and the eagles will have their fill!" Aguila raised his arms to the sky, calling to the giant birds. "Dive, my lords, and claim your sacrifice."

The soldiers pushed forward, swords outstretched. Mila whirled her whips just enough to keep them from moving too fast, while she stretched out her left hand over the edge of the cliff.

"What are you doing?" Finn shouted. "Are you crazy?"

Mila ignored him, sensing the water below. There was a river down there, a powerful rushing body of liquid and it called to her, reflecting back the magic she held inside. Like called to like and her power could be far more than she ever thought it could be. Ekon's face came to mind and what he had taught her in such a short time. He would laugh with her at this, he would join hands and dance in the water too.

For now, she would have to do it alone.

Mila summoned the water from the river below, calling up a towering pillar of spinning blue and white froth. It didn't quite reach the edge of the platform. She spun the whips faster, then risked a glance down. It would have to be enough.

"Jump!" she shouted at Perry and Finn.

Finn frowned and shook his head. "No way."

Perry stumbled away from him to the edge of the cliff, knocking little stones out into the abyss. "I've had enough of this place."

He leaned forward and threw himself out into the blue as two of the great eagles dive-bombed after him.

CHAPTER 18

As the eagles' cry echoed around them, Mila channeled her magic into the pillar of water, hoping it would be enough. Moments later, she sensed Perry's weight land upon it, but the water level dropped immediately lower and she could feel her magic start to weaken.

Mila spun her whips one final time, then used the water to provide a cushion as she jumped off the edge. "Now, Finn!"

She saw Finn's look of panic just before she fell beneath the level of the platform, then his tumbling figure above her as he jumped after, his cry a curse she hadn't heard for a long time.

They landed either side of Perry who lay cradled in the white water, his eyes fixed on the eagles that circled just above them, wary of their strange passage.

"I've had enough of being captured and tortured for my magic," he said. "Once we get that final piece, we're going home and I'm retiring to become some kind of archivist."

Mila snorted. "Yeah, right. Just as you've finally worked out how to use your fire to such effect?" She nudged Perry in the ribs. "You're tired, that's all."

"Can you get us out of here, please?" Finn's voice was clipped and Mila could see his skin was pale. Then she remembered how much he hated water as memories of the sea serpent under the volcanic city on their last mission flooded back.

Mila tuned into the flow of the water, using her magic to lower them gently toward the river below. The cliff beside them was hung with ferns, and wild purple orchids poked out from the greenery. She picked one as they passed by, its colors a reminder of beauty in the moments before they had to get moving again.

Further down, a graveyard of coffins hung from the rock face supported by woven liana. Each was painted with symbols of the sky and birds and Mila wondered what happened when the wood rotted away. Would the bodies fall to the river beneath or did the eagles come and take their share? Sky burial was part of Buddhist and Zoroastrian tradition on Earthside, so it made sense for it to be practiced here in the eyrie.

When they reached the bottom of the cliff, Mila used the water to deposit them carefully on the bank before returning the liquid to the rushing river. She dipped her hand back in, watching as her skin turned translucent. She sensed that this tributary flowed to the sea and some part of her wanted to dive in and just go with the current. Perhaps she would find her way back to Ekon again.

"I can't see the main gate, or anything that looks like the tomb of an ancestor."

Finn's words broke through Mila's reverie and she pulled her hand from the water, remembering Sienna and the map. She shook her head to clear the thoughts, exhaustion creeping up on her as the adrenalin of magic dissipated.

"We can walk around the base of the pinnacle. We're bound to hit it at some point." Mila looked over at Perry. He stared glassy eyed at the rock face, his body slumped. She frowned. He looked like a broken man. The Borderlands could do that, but she needed him to find his strength again, or they would be in trouble.

***

As Jari walked inside the chapel, Sienna turned back to the sarcophagus and touched its rough surface. It was pitted with age, discolored by years of the faithful running their hands over it, perhaps seeking a blessing, perhaps calling down a curse. Which would she find here?

"Help me lift the lid off." Jari positioned herself next to Sienna and together they heaved, thrusting the heavy stone away. It opened a few inches before they had to drop it.

"Let's wait for the others," Sienna said with a sigh, rolling her shoulders, trying to loosen the tight muscles. She could still feel residual tiredness from her mapwalking.

"No," Jari snapped back. "Try again."

Jari seemed on edge so Sienna tried again and this time, they managed to open it a few more inches. The gap was wide enough for an arm to fit through. Jari didn't wait, she stuck her hand down into the darkness and felt around. The sound of scraping nails over stone, the rustle of some kind of material as Jari grimaced with disgust at what she raked through.

Then she smiled with satisfaction and pulled out a small lead box with a hinged lid.

Sienna held out her hand. "Let me look at it."

Jari held it close to her chest, eyes flashing a warning as she clutched the box tightly.

Sienna shrugged. "We can wait until Finn comes if you like. But I need to verify the piece of the map against the others at some point before we leave this place."

"You have the other two pieces here?"

Sienna nodded. "Of course." She pulled the waterproof packet from her inner pocket, fingers brushing against the hilt of the ritual knife. While it was reassuring to have a weapon of sorts, she knew she was no match for the warrior woman, trained and experienced in warfare of all kinds. She could only hope that the fragile bond of their ramshackle team held just a little longer and that Finn, Mila and Perry made it here soon.

"Lay them out on the lid." Jari pointed to the top of the sarcophagus.

Sienna opened the packet and gently eased the two other fragments out, unfolding them and smoothing them down onto the stone.

Jari jiggled the lid of the box, tugging the two edges apart until they began to separate. She pulled it completely open to reveal a folded piece of patchwork skin inside.

"It looks like a match," Sienna said, barely able to contain her excitement.

Jari tipped the box so the piece of the map lay with the others. Sienna carefully opened it out, eyes widening as she saw the detail upon the skin. An island infested with giant rats feasting on its human prey as bulbous sores erupted from their skin.

Jari reached out and edged the piece closer to the others. It was clearly part of the whole and the map was only missing one final fragment now, which lay in the hands of the Shadow Cartographers.

"We've done it." Sienna smiled. "Now we can just wait for the others and get out of here."

"Is that them now?" Jari looked toward the door, head cocked as if she had heard something.

Sienna looked in the same direction, confused at first and then aware in that last millisecond that Jari reached for her sword.

The warrior woman swung the pommel of the weapon at the back of Sienna's head. A dark pain exploded.

As she sank into blackness, Sienna heard Jari whisper, "You're just as much of a prize as those plague pieces, Mapwalker."

* * *

Mila jogged into the clearing. Dark clouds scudded overhead and the entwined limbs of the trees above made it a realm of shadow with the ancient chapel at its center. An oak door lay open a few inches.

"Sienna!" Mila called out as she ran to the door, aware that Finn and Perry were only a few steps behind.

She pushed it open but even as she entered, Mila knew that it was empty. The atmosphere was charged, like the aftermath of a thunderstorm, but there was only dust and old bones here now.

A dark scowl marred Finn's handsome features as he walked carefully around the stone sarcophagus, noting patterns in the dust on the floor. Drag marks. A few specks of blood. His expression changed to something like recognition.

"What is it?" Mila tried to push down the fear rising inside. "Where are they?"

"I'm so sorry." Finn shook his head. "I thought she would wait for me, that I'd be able to—"

"To what?" Perry grabbed Finn's arm, knuckles white with tension. "You knew she was going to take the map pieces?"

Finn shook him off, strode to the other side of the room and turned to face both of them. "I offered to trade the map pieces for my niece, born in the Castle of the Shadow. You remember that hellhole?"

Mila took a deep breath. Of course, how could any of them forget that place of blood and suffering?

Finn continued. "I promised to get the map pieces but I also made my help conditional on you all being safe, crossing back over to Earthside with no harm."

Mila kicked at the door, slamming it into the stone with a shudder. "Now that bitch has all the map pieces *and* Sienna, a powerful Mapwalker whose blood they'll harvest and use to reshape the border. Nice one, Romeo."

Finn sank to the ground and knelt in the dirt, his face a mask of despair. "I know where Jari is taking her."

* * *

The sound of rushing water dragged Sienna out of a nightmare of screaming eagles with bloody talons. Her head thumped with pain. She opened her eyes to see the river running clear beside the hull of a little wooden boat. In the center, Jari paddled with her good arm, first one side, then the other, keeping the vessel in the middle of the stream. The air smelled sweet and pink cherry blossom rained down in a gentle breeze. It should have been idyllic.

Then Sienna remembered.

She lunged for the warrior woman, rage driving her forward. But ropes pulled her up tight and Sienna slumped back into the curve of the hull.

Jari turned her head, her expression closed and cold. "I never understood what Finn saw in you."

"Where are you taking me?"

Jari nodded toward a bend in the river ahead. "You'll see soon enough. We're almost there."

The water swept them on and as they rounded the end of the gorge, the river opened out into a wider channel, slowing its pace to a lazy stream. Women gathered on the northern bank, slapping clothes on rocks as they hunkered down in groups, chatting as they worked. Children played in the shallows, the sun dappling their skin, droplets of water sparkling as they splashed each other. It could have been the Ganges in India or the Yangtze in China, or anywhere across either world where people lived near the banks of a river.

But as the water swept them on, the sound grew louder

from the bank — the noise of a huge population gathered in one place. The smell of burning rubbish and human waste overpowered the scent of blossom and as Jari paddled the boat toward the shallows, Sienna caught a glimpse of what lay beyond.

Rows of tents laid out in a grid system stretched as far as she could see. Hundreds of thousands of refugees crammed into a makeshift city. They escaped danger in their homelands only to be rejected by the countries they thought were safe haven. So they ended up here in the Borderlands.

Sienna frowned. The Shadow Cartographers and the Warlord's men were no kind-hearted saviors happy to provide refuge. So what were these people doing here?

The boat bumped up against the shoreline. Jari jumped out and dragged it further up the pebbled beach. She pulled a knife from her belt and bent to Sienna, holding the blade close to her throat.

"Don't try to run. There's no one to help you here." She slowly eased the knife down until it rested on the ropes that held Sienna. Jari cut through them and stepped back.

Sienna stood on wobbly legs and clambered from the boat. She reached back to touch the side of her head where pain still throbbed. Her hand came back red with blood from the open wound.

"You'll be fine." Jari nodded up the beach and slowly they walked up the bank.

A group of soldiers spotted them as they crested the top of the embankment, two of them with the half-moon tattoo of the Warlord. Jari raised a hand in the air as she came to stand next to Sienna, her own tattoo now their passport into the tent city.

As the soldiers approached, Jari pulled a coin from her pocket, a wolf's head imprinted on the side. The lead soldier looked surprised and his face shifted to one of respect, even a touch of fear.

Jari spun the coin between her fingers. "He's expecting me. Take us to him — now."

CHAPTER 19

Sienna followed Jari through the refugee camp flanked by soldiers on either side. There was no point trying to run, and even if she did manage to get away she'd soon be lost in this labyrinth. She glanced to either side as they walked. Groups of people sat around small fires, the scent of herbs mingling with smoke in the air as they brewed tea and cooked meager rations. The sound of coughing and crying came from inside the tents as they passed — children in distress or those who couldn't hold onto hope any longer. It was a desperate place filled with people on the edge of the abyss.

They turned into a causeway that ran the length of the camp with makeshift stalls and food vendors either side. People exchanged what little they had for a bowl of soup or another blanket. The refugees were thin, malnourished, and Sienna still couldn't work out why the Shadow Cartographers had herded them here. She knew of the mines on the edge of the Uncharted, a place where those who entered never returned, worked to death as they dug resources from the ground even as it shifted. But why were these people not taken there to work when they arrived over the border?

At the end of the causeway, a large tent stood in pride of place marked by the half-moon of the Warlord, surrounded by flaming torches. The soldiers marched toward it and despite the foreboding in her heart, Sienna went with them.

The flap of the tent opened as they approached and while several of the soldiers waited outside, two escorted her and Jari inside.

The tent was warm with braziers giving off heat and light around a large wooden table in the center. Platters of meat, fruit and fresh bread sat next to cups and a flagon of wine, the abundance all the more shocking next to the privations of the refugee camp. A man stood in front of the table, his back to them, wearing a cloak of wolf pelts around his broad shoulders.

Jari fell to her knees, head bent in respect. "I have the pieces of the map, my Lord."

The man turned, his rugged features criss-crossed with scars, his muscled frame taut and always ready for battle.

Kosai. Warlord of Old Aleppo. High Priest of Moloch, devourer of children — and Finn's father.

His piercing blue eyes met Sienna's as she stood, chin raised high. She would not kneel, not to him.

Sienna remembered Finn's words about his father's love of books, his staunch leadership in battle, his devotion to his soldiers. But all she could see was a man who had sent his daughter to the Fertility Halls to die in a bloody dungeon, her child cut from her belly.

Kosai laughed, his smile transforming his face into that of a handsome man. Sienna saw then where Finn had inherited his grace and perhaps even his charm.

He bent and lifted Jari's chin, raising her up to stand before him. "You bring me more than the map, I see." He nodded at Sienna. "Is she the one?"

"She can walk through maps, my Lord. I've even traveled with her." Jari pulled the pieces of the map from inside her jacket pocket and handed them to Kosai. "These are the fragments we found at the library, in the under-sea pyramid, and in the city of the air."

Kosai took them, his powerful hands holding them with the gentlest touch. He laid the three pieces on the wooden table, arranging them until it was clear where the final piece would fit.

"Finally, they are together once more." The cut-glass British accent came from behind her and Sienna turned to see Sir Douglas Mercator step into the tent.

He was a shade of the man who had entered her map shop not so long ago wanting to purchase her grandfather's legacy. His flesh hugged tight against his skull, his limbs were wasted, he looked as inconsequential as … a shadow.

Suddenly, Sienna realized the word was exactly right. This was what a Shadow Cartographer eventually became. Soon he would be only ethereal mist, magic with no physicality to hold it together, magic that became one with the Shadow itself.

"After more than six hundred years, the fragments of the map remain intact. And I have the final piece." Sir Douglas strode forward and it seemed to Sienna as if tendrils of shade writhed around his limbs as he moved.

He pulled a folded fragment from his pocket, and laid it on the desk with the others, unraveling and turning it until the edges matched up.

As he smoothed out the corners, Sienna sensed a tug from the map. A pulse ran through her veins, a quickening, an energy that drew her in. She took a step forward.

Sir Douglas beckoned her closer. "I know you're curious, Sienna. It calls to you, doesn't it? As every map calls to those with cartography in their blood."

Sienna couldn't speak, she could hardly breathe as she bent over the ancient skin reaching out for the lines etched upon it with gentle fingers. It depicted an island jungle ringed by jagged mountains to the coast, then hidden by miles of ocean, accessible only through this map. Trails criss-crossed the jungle centering on a habitation of sorts, perhaps a village, perhaps a city, it was unclear from the scale of the drawing how big it might be. The knights must have opened a portal and taken the worst of the infected through all those years ago. Perhaps the survivors lived on.

She noted a strange symbol on the side of the piece that Sir Douglas had retrieved, like an hourglass resting on its side. "What's that?"

"Time shifts in the Borderlands and even slows in parts of the Uncharted. This symbol indicates a place where time has slowed to almost nothing. It may have only been weeks since the knights left the island if there is anyone left to remember."

"How can that be?" Sienna shook her head. "It doesn't make sense. The knights would have wanted the plague to disappear completely, so why would they stop time when time itself could destroy it?"

"How do you know the knights wanted it gone for good?" Sir Douglas traced the symbol with one finger. "They were as much of the Shadow as they were of Earthside. Why do you think three of them ended up staying here, hiding their pieces of the map in the Borderlands? Perhaps they always knew it would be needed later."

"Needed for what?"

Sir Douglas shrugged. "What knights have always fought for. Kingdoms, justice … borders." He looked at her. "And now you will help me resurrect what they left behind."

Sienna shook her head. "I won't do it. You can kill me, sacrifice me to your bloodthirsty god. I don't care. But I won't travel through that map. I won't bring back the plague."

Sir Douglas arched one perfect eyebrow. "Not even to save your precious friends?"

"What do you mean?" Sienna stammered. "You know where Mila and Perry are?" Her eyes darted to Kosai. "And Finn?"

The Warlord laughed. "My errant son comes for you, despite knowing the fate that awaits him. His die is cast, but the other two." He shrugged. "They're on the river heading here right now. My scouts along the bank follow their every move. You can still save them."

Sir Douglas put his hand on Sienna's arm, his bony fingers a freezing imprint on her skin. "Give in to your curiosity. Be the Mapwalker I know you are. Go to the island, see what is left of the plague and bring us back something that will save your friends."

"But what if I get attacked, what if I die of the plague?"

"Oh, don't worry. You won't be going alone." Sir Douglas beckoned to the entrance of the tent.

Sienna turned, her eyes widening as she saw who it was.

* * *

Mila and Perry stood with Finn looking down at the refugee camp. Rows of tents stretched into the distance, the glow of tiny fires interspersing the darkness as cries of children mingled with the barking of dogs and the sound of a fiddle. Music brought hope no matter how dark the night and somewhere down there, someone still believed in a future.

They had traveled by day on the river, propelled by the current and Mila's magic pushing them ever faster but now it looked as if finding Sienna in this labyrinth would be almost impossible.

Perry gazed out at the tent city. "How many people do you think there are down there?"

Finn's expression hardened. "I've heard this camp has over one hundred thousand, and the same again by the western gate, with rumors of more camps." He spun to face Perry. "These people are only here because they were rejected from Earthside. They fled their own cities for fear of being slaughtered and you turned them away at your borders. It's the fault of your kind that they are here."

Perry nodded. "You're right, but our people were just protecting their homes, their way of life."

Finn looked out again, his face wistful. "All these people want is to go home. They don't want your way of life. They want their own."

"And they'll do anything to get it back," Mila whispered, sudden realization dawning as she looked out at the tent city crammed full of refugees who only had one goal.

She spun around and grabbed Finn's arm. "You mentioned more camps by the other gates back into Earthside, right?"

Finn nodded. "Yes, there could be as many as fifteen more, all stationed at portal crossing points. But the gates are closed."

"For now," Perry stated. "But if all the gates are opened at the same time, these people will swarm through, desperate to get to their homes again."

"It's more than that," Mila said. "Disease doesn't respect borders. You can't reason with it, you can't pen it up in a refugee camp and banish it from your land." She swept her arm out over the camp, taking in the expanse of people below. "This is why the Shadow Cartographers want the Map of Plagues. These people are the invasion. When the gates open, they will stream back over, infected with the plague. The numbers will overwhelm Earthside cities, especially if they're all released at the same time."

Perry looked aghast. "It will devastate Earthside and there will be few left who could stop the borders shifting further after that."

Mila nodded. "The Shadow Cartographers will get their land back, but at what cost?"

Finn sighed. "You don't get it. They don't care for you. They will wipe you out as your people used disease to wipe out those conquered before you. Aboriginal Australians, Native Americans, African nations. The remnant of those people are here with a cultural memory of genocide bestowed on their ancestors. Do you think they care if Earthside is devastated by plague now?"

Mila reached for his hand. "Do *you* care, Finn? You've seen where we come from, you stood in The Circus and we fought your father together for the ordinary people in the streets of Earthside. Will you fight with us now?"

Finn pointed to the tents below. "I'll fight for them."

"We still have time," Perry said. "The Shadow Cartographers won't send people through the portals until they're infected. And they won't risk releasing bubonic plague through the gates. It won't spread fast enough. It has to go pneumonic and it takes time to infect the lungs and go airborne."

Finn shook his head. "You're in the Borderlands now and everything changes when it crosses over from your world. Don't think you know this plague anymore. It may have mutated into something new. We have to find Sienna before it's too late."

CHAPTER 20

Xander stepped through the doorway, his dark mop of loose curls longer now, a short beard outlining his jaw. His hazel-green eyes gazed at her with a touch of his old languid self but Sienna could see lines at the corners of his full mouth and he had an air of exhaustion, as if he had been draining his magic too fast. He had given up everything on Earthside to be here, but it didn't look like Xander was thriving in the Borderlands.

"It's about time we traveled together again," he said, his wry smile reminding her of old times.

Sienna pointedly turned her back on him and looked at Sir Douglas. "Why him?"

"His magic is useful and his lion will protect you both." He looked at his watch. "Besides, you know each other well enough to deal with whatever you find and he will bring us back the samples we need. Now, it's time to go."

Sienna took a deep breath as her mind whirled with possibilities. There was nowhere to run and if she refused, her friends would die. She knew what the Warlord was capable of and it seemed Sir Douglas was more shadow than man now. There would be no mercy.

Then there was the map itself. It pulled her in, she felt its tug deep inside like an undertow that threatened to drag her down to the depths. It whispered of mystery and secrets revealed after hundreds of years, secrets the knights had died to protect. She wanted to know where it led to.

"I'll go but I need your word that my friends won't be harmed."

The Warlord nodded. Sir Douglas waved his hand as if swatting a fly. "Of course. They mean nothing. Now, go."

Sienna stepped closer to the map, placing her hand over the center where the four pieces joined. She held out her other hand for Xander. His palm was warm, his fingers strong as they wrapped around hers.

She closed her eyes and dived into the map. At first the sensation of flying made her heart soar with joy. This was where she felt free, in this place between the pages of the world — but then the air grew chill and a dense mist swirled around her. Strange sounds came from the eddies of cloud, the crackling of burnt skin, the low moans of an animal in pain. Sienna hoped that the mist stayed around them. She didn't want to see what lay beyond.

She tried to travel faster but Xander's weight lay heavy on her. Even though his betrayal still stung, she would not let him go. She would not abandon him in this in-between world.

The plague island must be below them now and in her mind, Sienna imagined the hourglass tipping, the sand running out. She surfed down upon the grains, descending through the clouds.

They parted and there it was. The island, dense with jungle, the city at its heart hemmed in by jagged mountains. And it was a city, at least the size of one, albeit without the grand structures of Earthside or even the ramshackle growth of a long-term settlement. But as Sienna descended, she realized it was silent. There were no people in the streets, no animals wandering around. Even the surrounding jungle was quiet.

Could Sir Douglas have been wrong about the meaning of the hourglass? Were they six hundred years too late to find any evidence of the plague?

She chose a landing place in the middle of what looked like a public square, a clearing surrounded by stone buildings. One was larger than the rest, marked with a cross.

Xander rolled to his hands and knees, coughing and retching as his body adapted to the strange journey.

"That was awful," he groaned. "Now I remember why I never wanted to do that again."

"Happy to leave you here when I go back." Sienna scanned the hushed buildings with a sense that something was out there watching. "Get up quickly. We need to get out of the open."

She looked up at the church. Something about it drew her in. It was a simple structure but the stones of its walls had been selected and placed with care. It was testament to human faith that even at the end of the world, some could still look for God. Sienna hoped they had found him even here.

She walked toward the door, carved from what looked like dark oily wood from the surrounding jungle. As she approached, the smell of decay rose up around her. She stumbled back, hand to her face.

"What is it?" Xander stood to his feet, a little unsteady at first but soon gaining strength.

"In there." She pointed at the church. "I think we're too late."

* * *

Xander followed Sienna's gaze to the church, the cross on its wall a reminder of the simple country chapels in the Cotswolds near his home. No, he couldn't think of it as home anymore. That was Earthside, a land stolen from those he now served. He sighed. Perhaps Sienna should leave him here. Life might be simpler.

He walked toward the door, the stench rising as he drew closer. He pinched his nose and tried to breathe in a shallow manner, his heart pounding as he pushed at the entranceway. The door was jammed, something pressing against it from inside.

"Hello, is anyone there?" But even as Xander called out, he knew there was nothing alive inside the church.

He thrust his shoulder against the door. A crack rang out and he fell inward. A broken plank lay on the floor as if someone had forced it against the door, a barrier against what lay beyond.

Xander stepped inside, Sienna close behind. He heard her gasp as he tried to process the scene.

A huge pile of bodies stacked against the walls, as high as the church itself and several rows deep. In front of them, two men and a woman lay curled together. They must have been the last to die as the plague ravaged the place. It couldn't have been that long ago because decomposition was still in process. Time must have shifted here as Sir Douglas promised but Xander doubted if there would be anything he could take back as evidence of the plague. He grimaced as he looked at the bodies. He really didn't want to lug one of those back.

He turned around slowly to examine the church itself. Why had they holed up in here? They should have buried those bodies in the jungle, away from the rest of the population. Some of them might have made it if they hadn't kept the disease so close.

"Xander!"

He spun around to see Sienna desperately trying to shut the door, leaning her weight against it. He ran back to help her push — and caught a glimpse through a crack to the outside.

A sea of rats, overgrown and mutated, snarling with teeth bared, their silent surge a perversion of natural behavior. Somehow this island had turned the rats into the dominant predator, destroying the population with plague and presumably devouring any bodies left outside until there was nothing left to eat.

Until fresh blood arrived just minutes ago.

Xander shuddered and thrust the door closed. He and Sienna sank to the ground, their backs against the door as the rodents scratched and banged their heads against the wood. The pile of rotting corpses loomed ahead and Xander wondered whether taking a body would be a better idea than trying to wrestle one of those rats back to the camp.

"What now?" Sienna asked, her face pale as she looked up at him. "I can get us back out of here as soon as you're ready to go."

Xander shook his head, imagining his fate — and Sienna's — if he returned with empty hands. "I can't go back without a sample." He pulled two waterproof sacks out of his jacket pocket. "Sir Douglas gave me these. If we can get a rat and — something — from that pile, then we can go."

He edged away from the door, keeping pressure on it with one hand while reaching for the broken plank with the other. "We just need to block this shut while we figure everything out."

Xander hooked the plank and used it to pull one of the old pews closer, blocking the entranceway with its weight. "That will hold them at bay for a little while."

Sienna touched his hand, her eyes soft. "What happened, Xander? Why betray us back in the castle that day? Why work for the Shadow side?"

Her words echoed deep inside him and for a moment, he wondered whether she might help him return to his old life. He shook his head and gave a wry smile. "You haven't been working with the Ministry long. You don't know how little we're allowed to use our magic. They're more concerned with protecting those on Earthside from the knowledge of what lies beyond the border. Hell, most don't even know the Borderlands exist."

He stood up and pulled the ragged leather scrap from his pocket, his creatures etched around the edges. "I felt like half of me was trapped inside, and over here, despite the difficulties, I can be myself. I can do what I was born to do. I am an Illustrator."

Xander threw the leather on the floor and Asada, his lion, stepped out, shaking his magnificent mane. The beast nuzzled into Xander and then turned to look at Sienna, golden eyes acknowledging her presence.

"He's part of me," Xander said. "I understand that now. Asada is not some separate being that I conjure from the edges of the map, but an extension of my magic. Back on Earthside, it was like I functioned underwater, hardly able to move at all. But here, I'm free." He sighed. "Do you understand what I mean?"

To his surprise, Sienna nodded. "I can't say anything to the others but when I'm between the lines of the map, when I travel, I hear a whisper that I want to follow. The Shadow calls to me, Xander, and part of me wants to give in."

Xander couldn't believe what he heard and all at once, possibilities tumbled through his mind. "If you want to stay here, then there's hope, can you see that? You're powerful, Sienna. We could join the Resistance together, we could change things here in the Borderlands. Really change them, not just use all our energy trying to get back land on Earthside. We could make a new start."

Sienna gave a shy smile. "I could be with Finn. Be part of building a new way of life here, just as I promised."

Xander laughed. "Whatever you want. It's all possible now." A screech of wood on stone came from the door as the scratching and squeaking of rats grew louder. "Well, it's all possible once we get out of here."

"What about the plague?" Sienna said. "We have to take back samples and I can't leave Mila, Perry and Finn at the Warlord's mercy."

Xander took her hand. "We'll figure that out once we get back there. We have each other now."

She smiled. "Okay, let's do it." She grabbed one of the waterproof bags and looked at the pile of corpses, her face a mask of revulsion. "Which one of these do we take?"

Xander steeled himself and walked over to the pile of corpses — old men, young women, children, even babies, all lying together, equal in death.

One of the babies caught his eye, black lumps under its arms with grey veins spreading out like a sunburst of ash.

Sienna followed his gaze. "Oh no. You can't be serious?"

Xander raised the bag. "It fits." He pulled the bloated corpse from the pile, turning his face away as the stench rose up, making him gag. His stomach twitched and he almost hurled but he managed to hold it in. Sienna helped him close the bag, her face twisted in revulsion. Then together, they turned back toward the door.

"Maybe we can open it a little, let one in, then bag it quickly?"

Xander shrugged. "I don't have any other ideas."

They positioned themselves behind the door with Asada standing in the center of the room. He growled and pawed at the floor, ready to fight.

"Just pin it, boy, don't kill it," Xander called back, sensing the lion's understanding. He looked at Sienna. "Ready?"

"As I'll ever be."

Xander pulled the pew back a little and inched the door open. A thick grey muzzle pushed against the gap, nose sniffing the air, whiskers twitching. He let out the door a little more.

As the smell of the dead wafted out, the rats went wild, screeching and clambering over one another to try and reach the door. The swarm pushed forward, beady eyes fixed on the pile of corpses as they forced their way into the chapel.

Sienna fell backward as the mass of grey bodies surged in and Xander couldn't hold it alone. The door gaped open and a flurry of rodents raced inside.

"Quick, stop them!" Xander pushed hard against the door, Sienna rolled back to join him and they managed to get it closed again.

But it was too late.

Six of the giant mutated rats had made it inside. The creatures dashed toward the dead, thrusting their heads into the pile of bodies, the crack of bones filling the air as the stench intensified.

Sienna and Xander sat with their backs against the door, frozen still. Xander held a palm out to Asada to try and keep him calm — but the lion couldn't help his animal nature.

He swiped at one of the rats, batting it sideways then lunging to rip at its neck, shaking the beast in his jaws until its squeaking stopped.

The others turned from the pile of the dead, black beady eyes assessing the scene. Xander could almost sense their excitement as they spied fresh meat.

CHAPTER 21

As the rats began to advance on their prey, Sienna picked up one of the huge Bibles from the back of the pew, handing another to Xander. They moved slowly, eyes fixed on the rodents. Xander could see the individual hairs on one of the rats as it drew closer, each as thick and spiny as a porcupine quill. It bared its teeth ready to charge.

Asada pounced from behind, his huge legs crushing the beast's back with a crunch.

The other rats attacked.

One rodent dashed toward Sienna, its yellow teeth in a grimace, its thick pink tail lashing behind. She stood, brandishing the Bible like a baseball bat. It was almost upon her when she swung the heavy book, thwacking the beast on the side of its head, knocking it into the wall. She followed it down, beating it with the Lord's book, while she screamed her anger.

Xander turned as three giant rats lunged at Asada.

He swiped at one, knocking it into the wall, but another jumped on the lion's back, worrying at his neck. The last latched its teeth onto his forelegs, biting down and shaking its head to dig deeper.

Blood welled and Asada roared, ripping the rat from his leg, crunching it between his jaws before spitting it to the ground, a broken husk.

Xander swung the great Bible at the rat on the lion's back, connecting with a dull thud and knocking the creature to the floor. It writhed, spine broken, mewling with pain.

Asada suddenly dropped to his haunches, licking his foreleg as a black stain spread across the limb from the bite mark. Xander rushed to his side, his arms around the great mane. "Hold on. You're going to be alright, boy. I promise."

But even as he spoke, Xander saw a mark appear on his own arm. A sudden pain lanced through him as the black spread over Asada's skin and his own flesh.

Xander looked at Sienna. "I can feel it in my veins." His voice broke as he tried to hold back tears. "The plague has mutated. It's fast moving now."

He leaned against Asada, sensing the lion's strength falter even as his own began to fade.

* * *

Sienna quickly looked around for anything she could use to slow the disease. She pulled a shirt from one of the bodies and tied it as tight as she could around Xander's arm above the spreading black. Maybe the tourniquet would slow the movement of poison.

She thought about doing the same to Asada but he growled softly as he sank his huge head onto his paws, nuzzling against Xander. The lion might be an extension of Xander somehow, but he was still a wild animal. She needed to get them both out of here.

Sienna picked up the remaining sack and gingerly pushed the mewling rat into it, avoiding the jaws with those lethal teeth. She gathered up the other bag with its gruesome contents then pulled the ritual knife from inside her jacket. She nicked the side of her palm and as her blood dripped on the floor, mingling with Asada's, she hesitated.

She could take Xander and Asada straight back to the Ministry. He would have a chance at surviving and the Borderlanders would not have the plague.

But then she thought of Mila and Perry — and Finn. Their survival depended on her returning with the samples.

She sighed. Who's to say what the Ministry would do with the plague anyway? Since discovering the Mapwalkers, she had been torn as to who was right about the border, whose side she should fight on, or whether there could be any resolution to the question of who the land belonged to. Would those on Earthside be any better if they were handed this biological weapon?

She trusted her friends and together, they would figure out the next step.

Sienna drew a map with the scarlet drops, a map of a refugee camp with a grand tent at its center marked with the head of a wolf. She closed her eyes and traveled through.

* * *

When the smell of woodsmoke overpowered the stench of the bloated dead, Sienna opened her eyes. Xander and Asada lay before her, both unconscious, the two sacks by her side, one moving as the dying rat shifted inside.

Sir Douglas stood over her with a triumphant smile. He clicked his fingers at the guards on the door. "Bring the stretchers. We need to transport them to the pens."

His words echoed through Sienna's mind as she struggled to get her bearings. She was still woozy from traveling so fast, carrying the weight of the sick and the dying, the heavy load of the plague virus dragging her down in some unknown way. She couldn't stand up, she could barely breathe properly.

Sir Douglas ignored her as he opened the two sacks, his smile widening at what lay within.

The Warlord, Kosai, peered in at the rat, his nose wrinkling at the smell. "I'm getting my men out of here before you release those creatures into the camp."

Sir Douglas nodded. "Go now, take your best soldiers and start incursions into Earthside. Be ready when I open the gates fully." He laughed and shook his head. "They won't know what's coming until it's too late."

Sienna thought of her father and Bridget back in Bath. She needed to warn them of what was coming but she could barely move, let alone get herself and the others out of there. Her limbs felt weighed down as if she was smothered under a thick blanket and she could almost feel the spread of shadow in her veins.

A group of soldiers stepped into the tent and bundled them all onto stretchers, tying them down with strips of cloth. Xander and Asada didn't surface from oblivion as they were manhandled. Sienna tried to resist, but she was helpless against the strength of the men. She gave up, pretending to be woozy even as she began to feel her mind return to its former sharpness. Where were Mila, Perry and Finn?

The soldiers carried the stretchers double time back down the causeway toward a row of tents at the bottom of the hill nearer the river. As they approached, the stink of animal bodies grew stronger and Sienna heard the sound of squeaking — just like the plague island.

More rats. And they sounded hungry.

The soldiers carried the stretchers inside one of the biggest tents and laid them down on a dais in the middle of a series of pens each containing hundreds of rats trapped in wooden crates. Sienna tried to calculate how many there were in the tent and then multiplied it by the other similar tents nearby. There must be tens of thousands of the creatures. But how would they all be infected?

Sir Douglas stalked into the tent, his presence even more

spectral than it had been before. A young woman with short silver hair skipped along by his side, her face angelic but something about her made Sienna's skin crawl and her blood turn to ice. She feigned exhaustion, relaxing her body as if still semi-conscious even as she wanted to cry out in fear.

They approached the dais and the young woman ran to Asada, her slender fingers stroking the lion's fur. She bit her lip and clenched her fists with excitement. "This one first."

Sir Douglas nodded. "Of course, Elf." He waved across the sea of rats. "You know what to do."

The girl placed her hand on the lion's flank and stretched out the other over the first pen of rodents. Her body tensed and then an almost ecstatic look came over her face, as if she was touched by some unseen force. The rats squeaked wildly as Asada's body began to wither, his muscles dissolving under his tawny skin. Xander moaned and writhed on his stretcher, still unconscious but deeply connected to his lion through the magic that bound them together.

"No!" Sienna couldn't help herself. "Stop it. You're killing him."

Elf looked down at her with eyes like a pool of ice. There was no regard for life in those depths, no love for her fellow creatures, just pure joy at the thrill of power that ran through her veins.

Sienna knew then that she had tasted a glimmer of that joy when she traveled and if she gave in to it, she would be like Elf, a creature completely of the shadow.

Asada's body deflated, a bag of skin with dead bone inside, his life force and the plague that infected him now within the rats in the pen before them.

Sir Douglas gestured to a group of soldiers. "Take those crates to the other camps at the far gates and release them there. Be ready for the Warlord's signal."

The soldiers raced forward, lifted the crates and headed out the door. Sienna watched them go, dread rising within her at what they planned.

Elf walked to Xander's side and looked down on the young man. She stroked the hair from his pale face, sweating now as the black nodules of plague covered both arms and rose up his neck. "He must have been beautiful once," she whispered.

"Please, help him," Sienna sobbed.

Elf placed her hand on Xander's chest and stretched out the other over the next pen of rats. Her body tensed again as dark power surged through her. Xander convulsed under her touch, his body withering as the life was sucked from him.

Sienna wept for her friend's passing.

It was only a matter of minutes to reduce another life to dust and Elf seemed to grow in stature as she radiated the plague out to the rats gathered below. Another phalanx of soldiers picked up the next set of crates and ran with them into the night.

Then Elf turned to look at Sienna, her eyes alive with blue fire as she assessed her next victim.

CHAPTER 22

SIR DOUGLAS STEPPED IN front of Sienna, arms stretched wide to protect his possession. "Not this one. She's a Blood Mapwalker and she's not infected anyway." He gestured at the sacks. "There are diseased remains in there. Use those for the rest."

Elf stared back, challenging him, raising her hands as if she would use them against even her own. Sienna recognized that she was on the edge of her control and yet her power was barely yet grown. It was terrifying in one so young. If these were the children of the Shadow Cartographers, the future would bring far more terrors than the Ministry realized.

If there was a future after the plague of rats had stormed the gates into Earthside, of course.

Sir Douglas opened his palm and curled a pillar of flame into the air, spinning it into shapes of sharp-toothed rodents feeding on bloated corpses. Elf smiled at the fiery tableau and took a step back, acknowledging his superior power — at least for now. He had some kind of hold over her, Sienna realized, and as she looked closer, she saw a faint resemblance between them. The patrician nose, even the arrogant stance. Could Elf be Sir Douglas's daughter — and Perry's sister?

* * *

Perry watched in horror as a boiling mass of rats streamed out of white tents at the bottom of the hill. From their vantage point high on the hill, he could see the bristly bodies writhing as they fought to find a way out of the pack and into the wider camp. The high-pitched squeaking was soon drowned out by the sound of screams.

The sound of drums beating suddenly echoed across the camp, slow at first but with a rising tempo.

"My father's war drums," Finn said, looking out to the source of the sound. "They must be about to open the gate and let those people through along with the plague. We have to stop them."

Mila pointed at the soldiers herding people forward. "There are too many, and you said there were other gates, too." She shook her head. "We have to find Sienna. We have to get back to Earthside and close the gates from the inside."

* * *

In the tent of rats, Sir Douglas untied Sienna from the stretcher and pulled her to her feet. "Don't fight me now," he whispered. "Leave Elf to her magic before she turns it on you."

Sienna nodded her agreement but he did not let her wrist go as they walked to the door, his bony fingers tight and cold against her skin. With every step, Sienna expected the sudden wrench of magic draining her life energy but it never came and when they stepped out into the night air, she found herself almost breathless with relief.

Then the sound of squealing rats and crying children surrounded her, the shouts of people trying to fight the creatures and the screams of those bitten and infected.

"How can you do this?" Sienna whispered. "These people came to you for help."

Sir Douglas dragged her up the hill back to the main tent, his hand like a vise around her wrist. "These are your people, not mine. Their fate is the fault of Earthside and their death will be the instrument of justice."

They reached the tent, guarded by two soldiers who held their ground even as mayhem broke out around them. Their eyes were wide with fear but they stood to attention as Sir Douglas approached. He pushed Sienna forward and followed her in.

"There is one more thing I must do tonight. You'll stay here for now, but after this is over, you'll return with me to the tower in the Castle of the Shadow."

Sienna gasped as the vision of the turrets came to her mind, the place that called to her when she traveled. It promised dark joy, a sense of purpose, a future where she could live within her magic.

But that was also the training ground for Elf and those of her kind.

Sienna shook her head. "Never."

Sir Douglas smiled and opened his palm. This time, instead of flame, he conjured a ball of shadow, its surface like the shimmering waters of a deep pool. There were creatures inside, flying through the pearly depths with wings of gossamer.

"You'll change your mind once you see the possibilities." Sir Douglas let the ball go and it floated toward Sienna. She reached out a hand in wonder to touch it and as she did, the orb turned ashen and grew bigger until it surrounded her with a bubble of silver shadow.

She fought its power but her shouts were like those in a tomb, echoing back to her, bouncing off the walls of her shadow prison. She couldn't hear the screams of the infected now, she could only hear her own heartbeat. The creatures flying in the clouds drew closer until she could see their teeth and feel their claws. Sienna fell to the ground, hands wrapped around her head as they attacked.

* * *

Sir Douglas watched Sienna curl up within her shadowed cocoon. The creatures were all in her mind, but the torture would keep her occupied while he completed his own mission.

This was the last time he would have to cross over, the Shadow had promised him that, but it was critical to the success of the plan. He sighed. The mission was dangerous and somewhere deep inside, the part of him that was still a man wondered if it was the right choice. Then the Shadow rose within him, darkness suffusing his blood. He gasped as a thousand thousand pinpricks of shade pierced his heart, shuddering as the ecstasy of pain and pleasure possessed him.

As the convulsions passed, Sir Douglas strode out of the tent toward the gate, his eyes dark with shadow, his skin more shade than flesh. It was time for the reckoning.

* * *

Deep within the Ministry of Maps below Bath Abbey, the Illuminated Cartographer sensed the borders shift, then he heard the blaring alarm that warned of a breach. The sounds of the Mapwalker team running for the War Room echoed through the corridors beyond, a flurry of activity that seemed ever more frequent these days.

He stirred in his nest of maps, the rustling around him intensified by his movement. His own heartbeat pulsed ink through the living borders, but he was old and it was weaker now, the ink thinner in his veins, the magic diminished by his own fragility.

The library was bright with rays from the moon. Even though it was deep beneath the earth, a series of mirrors reflected light down into the darkest corners. A sheen of pale blue spread across the piles of maps, some rolled and stacked, others spilling over buried furniture. It smelled of rosewater, spice and incense, reminiscent of the souk in Istanbul where cultures crossed in an ever-moving melting pot. This was his home. Once upon a time, he had known where to find every map, he could summon the details of each drawing, each line, but now memory slipped away like the moonlight shifting with every passing minute.

The sound of shouting came from the corridors beyond, the clash of steel, a moan of pain. Then footsteps coming to his door.

The Illuminated Cartographer shifted his great bulk behind one of the giant bookcases, pulling the maps about him, their spiraling mass keeping him hidden in a pile of contours and symbols of the land.

The door burst open.

Two huge Feral Borderlanders stalked in, faces marked by the half-moon, sharp swords clenched in meaty fists. They stood either side of the door as Sir Douglas Mercator walked through, his aristocratic features more wolf-like than human now, his skin etched with shadow, his eyes as dark as the void.

The Illuminated Cartographer gathered his maps closer still, winding them about his body, protecting his heart with their pages. They would protect him for a while, but even as death stalked him in this realm, he could feel every hammering blow against the many gates of the border. His weakness was more than physical now and it threatened all of Earthside.

"It's time," Sir Douglas said softly, his voice as cold and

sharp as a blade. "You have sought peace all these years and now I will give it to you. But no one said peace would be on your terms." He raised his arms and opened his hands, conjuring balls of fire. The heat of the center burned blue surrounded by a penumbra of bright orange, its edges the scarlet red of blood.

The Illuminated Cartographer shrank back from the flame, every fiber of his entwined being recoiling from the element of destruction.

"You can't burn this place," the Illuminated Cartographer called out. "It's the beating heart of the maps. The borders will crumble if they are all destroyed. The ancient magic will dissolve and there will be nothing holding the two worlds apart."

"Exactly." Sir Douglas hurled the balls of flame into the thickest part of the pile of maps. The dry paper caught and the fire spread quickly even as Sir Douglas cast more heat into the blaze, his face alive with power.

Agony seared through the Illuminated Cartographer as he reeled back from the burning bookcase, pain suffusing his body even as the fire devoured the maps, each page like a piece of his own flesh. He wept for the destruction in the library even as he desperately tried to keep the border intact between the worlds.

One of the bookcases crashed to the floor, sending up a plume of sparks before spreading the fire further into the library. Sir Douglas laughed with the mania of destruction as he burned the ancient maps, pieces of ash rising in the updraft, whirling in the flame.

The Illuminated Cartographer crawled deeper into his warren of burning paper, coughing and retching as he struggled to breathe. He didn't have much time. He could sense the holes in the borders widening, the gates pushed open, every second weakening what remained of the ancient magic.

It was almost too late.

CHAPTER 23

The sound of fighting came from the corridor beyond and this time, gunshots. As the two Feral Borderlanders ran out of the room, Sir Douglas lowered his hands.

"Give up now and I'll spare this city the worst of the plague."

The Illuminated Cartographer remained silent as he gathered the last of his strength, tugging on ancient pathways that wound through the maps and into his veins. He pulled the vellum closer, huddling deeper inside layers of projection and elevation. Smoke enveloped the library now, the smell of burning like a pyre of the damned.

In the corner, a painted celestial globe mounted on wooden legs sat just out of reach of the fire, behind the line of Sir Douglas's sight. The Illuminated Cartographer sent his magic out through the tangle of maps, reaching crumpled paper tendrils out to grasp and wrap around the legs.

Sir Douglas raised his hands again. "So be it." He unleashed a hail of fire that swept over the remaining maps, his face transformed by the leaping flames.

As the lick of extreme heat reached the Illuminated Cartographer, he curled his hands and lifted the globe with the edges of his magic, wielding it as a giant club to beat at his enemy.

Sir Douglas fell to the floor under the weight of the globe, his fire extinguished as he smashed his head on the ground.

Then he rolled free, dark blood dripping from his forehead, face distorted by fury. He kicked the globe away and directed his stream of flame at what remained of the twisted paper.

Then he turned back to the remains of the library. "That will be the end of you."

He raised his hands once more.

The door burst open and the two Feral Borderlander guards stumbled in, bleeding from multiple wounds as they fought the Mapwalkers who chased them. Sir Douglas spun around, backing away into the flaming library. His little team was outnumbered but they had achieved their purpose. This place was finished.

The Illuminated Cartographer sensed the truth of it and as his vision blurred with smoke and ash, he saw Sir Douglas leave his guards to their death and dart out the back of the library toward a door that led to the Gallery of Geographical Maps where he could slip back into the Borderlands. No doubt he would return with an invading force through the holes in the border.

The future rose before the Illuminated Cartographer's eyes, a vision of plague devastation and a land laid waste before the Shadow claimed it in an orgy of destruction.

There was only one way to stop it, but he didn't have the strength left. After so many generations, he had failed Earthside. He closed his eyes, tears of ink rolling down his cheeks, as the darkness overtook him.

* * *

Bridget let the Mapwalker team subdue the Borderlander soldiers before she entered the library. John Farren limped in alongside her, his bleak expression matching her own. He reached for her hand and they stood for a minute, taking in the ruined desolation, words failing them both.

Sir Douglas had almost destroyed the library and then escaped in the smoke and chaos, but perhaps there was still a glimmer of hope.

"He has to be in here somewhere." Bridget put her sleeve over her mouth and pulled out her torch as John did the same. They began sweeping the wreckage for the Illuminated Cartographer.

He couldn't be dead yet or they would be overrun with invading Borderlanders, but he must be deeply wounded. The monitoring systems were in meltdown in the War Room, alarms blaring from gates all over the world as the border weakened. Few understood that the blood magic of this one man maintained the borders, a secret handed down to only a few over the hundreds of years of the Ministry's existence.

Even fewer understood that this was still the same man who had dwelled within the library for hundreds of years, his own longevity bound up in the long life of the maps around him, a mutual preservation of creator and created. Some annals said that the origin of the Shadow was a family feud that left twin brothers on either side of the border. Whatever the truth, no one had ever thought the Illuminated Cartographer could be laid low this way.

But the world had changed.

In her lifetime, Bridget had seen the Borderlanders go from being a ragtag bunch of mercenaries with occasional incursions into their world, to detailed invasion plans to retake what they saw as their lands on Earthside. Their magic grew stronger with their aggressive breeding programs while those on this side of the border only weakened as bloodlines were lost. Now it seemed like the Shadow Cartographers had the upper hand.

Tears welled as Bridget surveyed the destruction in front of her, piles of ash where once precious manuscripts lay, smoldering remains of vellum masterpieces, maps of places that had been lost over the years, places they could never find again now.

In the corner, she noticed a bigger pile, the outer layers burned but inside there might be a hollow of protection.

"Over here!" she called out.

John rushed over and together they pulled off the outer layers of maps until the body of the old man lay curled in what remained of his cocoon. His face was covered with ash, his skin no longer pulsing with the dark ink that sustained the magic of the Ministry.

Bridget's heart pounded with fear as she looked down at him. It was over, it had to be. She imagined the borders crumbling and Borderlanders streaming through as they knelt here in the remains of a once great place.

Then his eyes flickered and opened.

Bridget looked down and saw a world of star maps within them, a kaleidoscope of deep blue sky filled with possible futures.

He lifted one hand, the map fragments around him curling with his movement, wrapping themselves around Bridget's wrist. She felt his pulse — faint, but still there.

"You are the only hope now," he whispered. "I am finished but you're young and vibrant. You must be the new Illuminated Cartographer."

Bridget's eyes widened at his words. Fresh blood poured into the veins of the maps would strengthen the border and renew the power of the Ministry, but she had never considered that she might be the source. She looked around the burnt library, the broken shelves, the devastation of the place. If she took his mantle, she would have to stay here until her own lifespan ended. She would never walk in the sun again, never have the freedom to roam.

John reached out a hand to cup her cheek. "You don't have to do this, Bridget. Think of all you would have to give up. There must be another way."

In his eyes, Bridget saw a future filled with love, a second chance for them both. But if the borders failed, there would be little future for any of them.

"You … must … choose," the Illuminated Cartographer said as his eyes flickered closed once more. As Bridget felt his pulse fade, she knew she was out of time.

* * *

Mila led the others down the hill, her pace quickening until they reached the edge of the terrified crowds. As the rats spread out from the main tent, people tried to flee but the Warlord's soldiers blocked the perimeter, keeping the masses within the camp. Sounds of screams and shouts filled the air as parents gathered children into their arms, climbing where they could to get away from the rats but the relentless horde infiltrated even the furthest corners.

A river of rodents flowed up the hill toward them. There was no time to go around.

Mila heard the metal slide of Finn drawing his sword, the whoosh of Perry's flame. She reached out to the sense of water around her, pulling it from barrels and troughs nearby, curling it into spinning whips of shining droplets. They strode through the horde of creatures, cutting and burning, whipping them away.

But those around them were not so lucky.

A man cowered against a tent pole as they passed. Mila saw a rat sink its teeth into his flesh and watched in horror as the man's skin quickly turned mottled shades of blue and black. This was no longer any kind of plague seen before in the history of humanity. This was a Shadow plague now, hybrid death magic, fast and unstoppable. It would decimate Earthside and there was only a faint hope to hold it back now.

The border that had held for so many generations weakened as the seconds passed, she could feel it in the way her magic called to her darker self. Mila understood that if they were trapped here, she would lose herself in this midnight realm. She thought of Zippy, his happy spaniel face snuffling in the reeds at the edge of the canal. She conjured home to her mind, birdsong in the trees above the waters, the cheep of ducklings in spring, the smell of woodsmoke from the canal boats. All threatened by this invasion.

Mila started to run, suddenly aware of the sands of time rushing through the hourglass ever faster. Perry and Finn ran with her, the three of them racing toward the grand tent at the center of the causeway.

Two soldiers stood outside, distracted by the craziness around them and Finn despatched one with a few cuts of his blade and knocked the other out with the pommel of his sword.

They raced into the tent.

"Sienna!" Mila shouted, looking around in desperation for her friend.

There was a shape on the floor wrapped in spun silver like a giant cocoon. The surface was opaque, like clouds scudding across a stormy sky. Mila frowned and then realization rose within her, certainty of what — of who — lay within.

"What have they done to you?" Mila fell to her knees next to the cocoon, reaching out a hand to press through the surface.

Perry snatched her hand away. "Don't touch it. It's shadow-weave and it'll stick to your skin, too. You'll end up in there with her." Mila looked up in surprise at his knowledge. Perry shrugged. "It's one of my father's favorite tricks. He used to punish me with it back when I was young." His eyes darkened with the memory.

Finn walked around Sienna's encased form, frowning as he tried to find an opening, anything to lever his way inside. "How do we get her out?"

Perry smiled. "The shadow-weave needs form to cluster around. I think we might have a volunteer."

He darted outside and dragged in the body of the soldier that Finn had knocked unconscious, moving it close to Sienna's cocoon. He pushed the soldier's leg with his own, careful not to touch the shadow-weave as the man's limb sank inside the grey. Spindles of weave reached out, moving up the limb as it crawled over the soldier's body, receding a little from Sienna, leaving one of her arms outside its orbit.

Finn grasped her wrist and slowly pulled her body further away as the shadow-weave settled over the soldier until Sienna was finally free.

Her eyes were closed, her breathing shallow and Mila could see dark curls of shadow beneath her pale skin. She had used her magic too much recently. Could her blood be polluted beyond hope of return?

"Sienna," Finn whispered, as he knelt by her side and stroked her titian hair away from her forehead. "Wake up now. It's okay. We're here." He kissed her lips softly with the gentlest touch.

Sienna's eyes flickered open and for a moment, Mila could see the blue was tinged with silver, edged with dark storm clouds and flashing with lightning. Then Sienna blinked and the clouds cleared as she wrapped her arms around Finn.

He hugged her close, rocking her back and forth. "You're safe now."

Sienna leaned back, her face stricken with fear. "No, none of us are safe. I've seen what they can do, what power they have now. There's only one way to stop this."

CHAPTER 24

Sienna looked up at Finn, tears welling in her eyes. "We have to close the borders. For good this time. We have to shut the gates and stop the worlds bleeding into each other. It's the only way."

Finn reeled back and stood up, pacing the tent. "But then the plague will be trapped here. What if it spreads amongst my people?"

Visions of the creatures she had seen within the shadow-weave filled Sienna's mind, taunting her with the promise of more pain. But now she could see that pain reflected on Finn's face. She had crossed the border thinking that somehow they could find a way to be together, to save his world, and now her only plan was to shut the door and leave him behind in the path of destruction.

"They can stop the plague as surely as they're spreading it. But they won't if it reaches Earthside, and I have to protect my home."

Finn spun round, his eyes blazing with anger, fists clenched. "Your home? What about mine? You leave us all to die from a plague resurrected to destroy *your* people." He shook his head. "But what else would you do? Jari was right, you'll always be Earthsiders and like the rest of your unwanted and forgotten, you will keep pushing us out, denying our right to live."

Sienna wept at his words, tears streaming down her face. "No, Finn. I want to help. I—"

"We don't want it. Your help just makes everything worse." Finn stalked out of the tent into the maelstrom beyond.

"Wait! Please!" Sienna tried to get to her feet but her legs were weak and her body ached from deep inside.

Mila helped her up and as they stood together looking at the empty doorway, Sienna remembered Mila's face as they left Ekon behind at the rim of the pool in Ganvié. This was what her father tried to save her from when he hid her Mapwalker heritage. Love across borders could split a soul apart.

She wanted to run after Finn, fall into his arms, kiss him and stay in that moment forever. Yet every moment they stood here meant Earthside was one step closer to a plague that would shatter her home.

Sienna took a deep breath. "We have to go. Right now."

She turned to the table and pulled her ritual knife from inside her jacket. She held it against the side of her palm where the last cut had barely healed. The blood around it looked almost black and Sienna could see tendrils of shadow that ran deeper through her veins. She was so close to the edge now and part of her wondered what Sir Douglas would have shown her in the room at the top of the mysterious tower. Could she have saved the Borderlands from within? If she became a Shadow Cartographer, could she reshape this side of the world?

"Are you strong enough for this?" Perry's voice was gentle and Sienna knew he understood. His body and soul were battered from this trip, and Mila's, too. It had taken a toll on them all.

"Let's go home." Sienna opened the cut and drew the lines of a map on the wooden table with her blood. Bath Abbey bound by the lines of the river, the canal and the streets of the ancient city. She reached out her hand for her friends and closed her eyes, shutting out the cries of the damned as she traveled back home.

* * *

As the Illuminated Cartographer's pulse slowed, Bridget looked around at the library. On the surface, it was burned to ash, hundreds of years of history charred and blistered beyond recognition. Maps they could no longer travel through, precious tomes they could no longer go to for ancient wisdom, the past now turned to embers.

But as she looked closer, Bridget could see that not all was lost. There were layers of maps under the burnt ones, where the chaos of the Illuminated Cartographer's room had protected what lay beneath. Not all the books were ruined in the fallen shelves and even the globe lay on its side, dented, but not broken.

This was not the end. Not on her watch.

She pulled away from John's hand and her heart almost broke to see the pain in his eyes. He would understand one day but right now, there was no time for debate or argument.

"I have to do this."

John backed away. "Then you must do it alone. You've chosen a path I can't follow." He turned and walked out the door, leaving Bridget in the library alone with the dying Illuminated Cartographer.

She leaned down and whispered in his ear, "I choose this path. For Galileo."

For a moment, she thought she was too late. His eyes remained closed and his skin cooled under her touch.

But then the map fragments that curled around her wrist tightened and more of them began to wind around her limbs until she was pinned beneath the vellum and paper, the lines on them pulsing as if they searched for something in her, something that they could call home.

A sharp piercing pain in her right wrist and then her left.

Bridget screamed in agony as the ink from the maps merged with her blood and the maps transferred themselves from the Illuminated Cartographer over to her own body. They delved deeper into her veins until her heartbeat began to pulse through them.

The pain was still intense but suddenly Bridget could see into the maps themselves, and sense that she could fly into them in a new way. She could travel out through their portals in her mind even though her physical self would remain here, tethered to the library until her own end came.

It was at once terrifying and breathtaking and she desperately wanted to tell John.

But he was gone and she was here alone. Trapped here in the depths of the Abbey, shackled to the maps. The realization struck her. What had she done? Could she undo it?

Bridget began to pull at the maps surrounding her, tugging at their entwined fibers, desperately trying to rip them out of her skin. She sobbed in frustration, blood and ink dripping down her arms as she tried to escape her fate.

* * *

Sienna opened her eyes in the Gallery of Geographical Maps. It was still the same place that they had left from not so long ago, but she felt a deep sense of loss this time. Everything had changed but it wasn't over yet.

Perry and Mila lay at her feet, slowly sitting up as they revived from the vertigo of traveling through the blood map.

Alarms rang through the Ministry, the sharp sound a warning of attack, or perhaps an indication that it had already begun. The smell of burning hung in the air.

The library. The Illuminated Cartographer.

All at once, Sienna understood what Sir Douglas had left

to do while she lay in the shadow-weave. Were they too late?

"Quick, we have to get to the library." Sienna dragged Mila and Perry to their feet and together they hurried down the corridors.

The door to the library was wide open, a scene of devastation within. Her father sat outside, his back against the wall, his head in his hands as he wept.

"Dad?"

John looked up, relief washing over his face. "Sienna, you made it back."

"Are we too late?"

John shook his head. "I don't know. But I can't go in there. I know what she must do but I will lose her forever if she chooses that path."

Sienna frowned at his words. They didn't make any sense.

But as she walked into the library, the pieces suddenly fell into place.

The sound of sobbing came from the corner and behind a pile of burnt maps, Bridget sat next to the body of what had been the Illuminated Cartographer. The maps now wound themselves into Bridget's body even as she tried to scratch them out with bloody fingers, her face puffy with weeping.

"Help me," Bridget begged. "Get them out of my skin. I want to be free. Please."

Perry rushed forward to help, but Sienna grabbed his arm and held him back. She shook her head, resolve strengthening inside.

"There's no time, Bridget. You are the Illuminated Cartographer now. Your blood strengthens the borders. If you reject the maps, we are all lost. Earthside is lost."

Sienna knelt by Bridget's side and placed her hands over the wounds on her wrists where the maps entered her body. "I've seen the plague, and what the Shadow Cartographers can do now. They've bred magic like we have never seen before. We can't win this right now. We need time to regroup, rebuild, and figure this out." Sienna took a deep breath. "Close the borders now, Bridget. Seal them shut and stop the plague from devastating our world."

* * *

Bridget heard Sienna's words as if she was under a swimming pool, the sounds muffled and dense. She felt the young woman's hands on her wounds and the mingling of their blood from a wound on Sienna's palm. She was a powerful Blood Mapwalker, only just beginning to know her powers, but there was a darkness, too. The Shadow had its hooks in her and Bridget knew how good that felt.

But it would not win here today.

For in the mingling of their blood, Bridget saw the camp in the Borderlands, she witnessed the plague rats and Elf's power, the death of Xander and his lion — and Finn's face as he turned his back on love. Just like John as he walked out the library.

This Mapwalker life had taken everything from them both, but they couldn't stop now. Sienna was right. Closing the border was the only choice until the plague burned itself out in the Borderlands and they had the magic on Earthside to stop the Shadow.

From all her study in the annals of the Mapwalkers, Bridget knew that the border had only been closed once before centuries ago. She had read the annals about that occasion once but the details were hazy. There were great risks to both worlds in closing the borders but there was no time to review them now.

Bridget took a deep breath and relaxed into the pile of maps, letting their bulk take her weight. They softened around her in welcome and she sensed the possibilities in her new life.

"I'll do it," she whispered.

Bridget closed her eyes and reached out with her mind through the loops and byways and mountain ranges of the cartographic world. She sensed the line of the border between worlds battered by the plague-infested hordes and on the other side, Earthsiders walked unaware of the danger. Perhaps it was time they knew of what lay beyond. But for now, the Mapwalkers would uphold the ancient pledge — For Galileo.

Bridget poured her blood magic into the border, strengthening the line until it pulsed a deep scarlet, rising up to new heights and thickening to a huge wall as the border slammed shut.

In the far distance, she heard a howl of rage, a thousand thousand tormented souls trapped inside the Shadow, lost in the darkness. There would be a reckoning, but not today.

CHAPTER 25

Two weeks later.

Sienna lay on her back on the polished wooden floor of her grandfather's flat above the map shop. The sun streamed in through the high windows and lit her skin with the warmth of summer. Bath was blooming, the blossoms lay thick on the trees, birds sung in nearby Victoria Park and tourists strolled the streets with no inkling of what had almost befallen this land.

After such an intense mission, time apart from her friends was strange but necessary. Mila worked on her canal boat, repainting the decorative lines of the winding waterways as her spaniel, Zippy, lay ever watchful by her side.

Perry helped Sienna's father and others from the Ministry repair the damage to the library. They worked around Bridget who was still getting used to being tethered to the maps. She kept trying to walk out the door only to be pulled back into the scrolls. Sienna had caught her weeping more than once since the day she had made her choice and closed the border.

She sighed as she thought of Finn and the last time they had spoken, his rage at her justified, of course, but the pain still lingered. This was her home and she had saved it — but at what cost?

They had no way of knowing what was happening in the Borderlands now. Had the plague decimated the innocent? Had Sir Douglas stopped it with the help of Elf, or had her dark magic turned to creating even worse horrors?

And where was Finn? In the arms of Jari, the warrior woman, or sacrificed at the hands of his father, the Warlord?

Sienna had to get back over there. Somehow, she had to find a way without jeopardizing Earthside. She looked up at the shelves above, her grandfather's journals stacked in neat rows, full of diagrams and his thoughts over a lifetime of mapwalking. She thought of the Nubian woman, the Librarian, a love lost over the border, just like her own. It was time to get to know her grandfather better and perhaps she would find the answers to her own problems in his journals.

As she lay back, she noticed another book on the floor beneath the shelves. Sienna turned over and reached as far as she could underneath the bookcase and pulled it out. She dusted it off and noticed the number on the spine: 24.

The missing journal.

She opened the first page and began to read about something called the Map of the Impossible …

AUTHOR'S NOTE

Thanks for reading *Map of Plagues*. I hope you enjoyed the adventure. I always like to include an Author's Note in my novels as I love the research process as much as the creative part of writing.

You can find images used in my research on my Pinterest board: www.pinterest.com/jfpenn/map-of-plagues

Bath and finding home

When I wrote the previous book, *Map of Shadows*, we had just moved to Bath in the South West of England. I found it difficult at first and struggled with a place that seemed almost too perfect, a heritage city of Roman and Georgian grandeur as well as natural beauty. I'm a happy person but as a fan of Stephen King's books, I can't help but think that everywhere has a dark side! After all, Mary Shelley wrote most of *Frankenstein* here in Bath, so it definitely has a shadow element.

Writing *Map of Shadows* helped me understand Bath in a deeper way and I found my dark side again, then as I wrote the first draft of *Map of Plagues* we bought a house here. In a reflection of my own journey, this book shows Sienna settling on her own home in Bath and Mila questioning where her true place might lie.

At the same time, I also started a new podcast, *Books and Travel*, which is all about my search for a home and the places I have traveled along the way, as well as interviews with other authors about the places that inspire their stories. Check it out on your favorite podcast app or at www.BooksAndTravel.page.

Other places that inspired the story

The prologue describes a plague pit behind the Tower of London near the Royal Mint. This is a real site as documented on the London Plague Pits Map and excavations date the bones to 1348–1350.

Like many bibliophiles, the ancient Library of Alexandria is one of those places that I long to visit. I couldn't help but write it in. The Scryers are influenced by *The Dark Crystal* film, which I saw when I was seven years old and remains one of my recurrent nightmares. My little brother used to chase me with his hands like claws shouting, "I'll suck the life out of you." I hadn't thought of it for years but a new film, *The Dark Crystal: Age of Resistance*, is being released in 2019, and I happened to see a trailer and those nightmares emerged once more.

Ganvié Island is a real village built on Lake Nokoué in Benin but, as with Aleppo, I had it straddle the border between worlds. I wanted Mila to discover a glimpse of her possible ancestry and maybe she will even return to Ekon in another story …

The city under the waves was based on an underwater city found in the Gulf of Cambay in India, thought to be from 9000 BCE, which would make it the oldest civilization on earth. I recently narrated my own audiobook of *The Dark Queen* short story and found myself immersed in underwater archaeology once more.

Aetofolia, the eagle's nest, is based on Meteora, a Greek monastery perched on the side of the cliff, and also the landscape of the Zhangjiajie National Forest Park in China which was used as the inspiration for Pandora in *Avatar*.

Themes

I wrote the previous book, *Map of Shadows* after the Brexit vote in the UK. The theme of borders and being denied access runs through that story.

In a similar way, the news since has been filled with stories of refugees from war, climate change or those just searching for a new life with more opportunities. As countries build walls and strengthen borders, many refugees are turned away and it's not too much of a stretch to think of them ending up in the Borderlands. Perhaps there is an answer in *Map of the Impossible*?

MAP of the IMPOSSIBLE

A MAPWALKER NOVEL

J.F. PENN

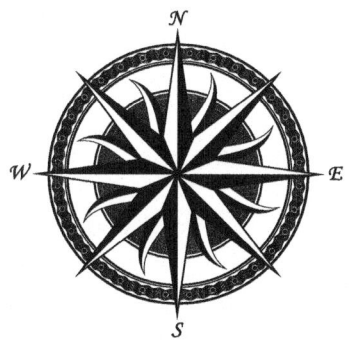

"Pulvis et umbra sumus.
We are but dust and shadow."

Horace, The Odes

"There is nothing impossible to him who will try."

Alexander the Great

PROLOGUE

Fongafale, Tuvalu, South Pacific

The earth shook once more, a tremor more powerful than the last. A deep rumble sounded from beneath the ground as if the gods wakened in anger, and Meihani clutched a nearby palm tree with gnarled fingers to hold herself steady. The rough bark scraped against her skin as she tried to stay upright. She was old but a lifetime of walking the island had strengthened her limbs and as she braced herself, the shudder passed beneath her.

It would not be the last.

Something had changed in recent weeks, a shift in the cycles she had seen in her long life. The earth was broken — and they would all pay the price.

Meihani looked out over the waves to the horizon across the tiny cove. She stood just around the bay from where fishermen launched their boats, hoping that today would bring enough food for their families and maybe even some to sell at the market. She walked here each morning as first light struck the water and every day, she thanked the gods she was still alive. At her age, there was no guarantee she would greet the dawn once more.

Meihani breathed in the salty air, relishing every inhale

and exhale. She had witnessed the final moments of so many as an elder of the village. The wracking coughs of the old, the tiny sighs of the too-early born and too soon to pass. So many souls ahead of her on the ancient path and still each day she rose once more to greet the dawn. She said a prayer to the god of the ocean, her lips moving as she whispered words of thanks and supplication.

The waves were grey green, reflecting the thick clouds gathering above, and the sun hid behind a storm front, its light and power dimmed by a force that would sweep over the island before midday. Meihani could read the signs as easily as others read the newspapers that came over from the mainland. She understood the moods of the ocean and from this vantage point each morning, she could judge her daily walk.

On soft days, when the waves were gentle, she shuffled off her shoes and paddled in the water, sinking into the sand and wiggling her toes like she had done since she was a girl, delighting in the pleasure of sensation. On wild days, she would stand here by the thick palm, both of them grown strong over the years they dwelled on the coast. The wind could howl and the waves pound down, but she was safe up here as rain pelted the green leaves above her. On those days, she would remember how wild she had once been, surfing on a hand-carved board, diving amongst the rocks, almost made of seawater. The ocean was in her veins and Meihani knew it more intimately than any lover.

Today, something was very wrong.

The ground shook again with a deep rumbling under the earth. A horde of tiny crabs emerged from the sand, shaken loose from the golden grains. They scuttled for shelter under the palms up the beach, their skittering legs leaving tiny marks in the sand that were quickly shuffled away by movement from the depths beneath.

Meihani frowned. That was odd. The creatures should

have run for the waterline and sunk beneath the wet sand once more. Out in the open, they would be easy prey for the gulls, flipped over, legs wriggling while sharp beaks tore the soft flesh from their undersides as they were eaten alive.

She looked up, expecting to see eager birds wheeling toward the ready feast. But the flocks overhead flew inland to the hills, calling to one another with shrill notes on the edge of a scream. When birds and beasts fled inland away from the water, the danger was out to sea. This ancient wisdom had never failed her ancestors and Meihani knew she should hurry back to the village, tell them all to run for higher ground. She looked again to the horizon. Perhaps it was only a storm and besides, warnings from the old were rarely heeded unless danger was imminent. She would wait a little longer.

The tremors had been coming for days, some sharp blows that knocked her off her feet like the fist of her husband on nights when he had drunk his weight in beer. Others had been soft and gentle, like the arms of her loving mama. Both dead many years now, but neither forgotten. Meihani could still remember everything from back then, even though these days she often forgot where she put her glasses, or the names of her various grandchildren when they came so infrequently to visit from Fiji, a world away from her quiet life. Her body may be stooped and wrinkled, folded by time, but this physical frame would not cage her mind — and on this beach every day, she was briefly free. A spirit of the ocean once more.

Another rumbling deep below the earth.

A jolt. A dip as the ground seemed to fall away.

Meihani's stomach dropped, and she gasped as a terrible realization rose within. She looked back at the path to the village, knowing that her legs could not carry her fast enough now. It was too late.

The water receded with a wet sucking sound, leaving sea

creatures in its wake, like the ebb of the tide but so much faster. Parrotfish flopped on the sand and arched their spines in desperation for water, mouths gaping open. Jellyfish pulsed their last as they lay stranded next to coral-tinted cowrie shells. A turtle clawed at the sand, head poked out, eyes wide as it stared around in confusion.

The sea withdrew further, revealing sand and rocks that had never been uncovered before in Meihani's lifetime. Then the skeletal hull of a wooden boat, barnacles clustered on its spars, rainbow anemones dying as they met the air, colors fading quickly.

Still the water sucked back, further and further.

Words came on the wind, whispering to Meihani in her Mama's voice, spoken from her deathbed as she took her last breath. "If there is danger, child, cross over. The Borderlands will always welcome you."

Some thought the Borderlands were a myth, but Meihani knew there was a place off the edge of the map where displaced people could find a home. When she looked to the sea some days, she glimpsed what might be a shimmer of a veil between the worlds.

Many in her village could sense some kind of border out there, perhaps descendants of those who had crossed long ago, leaving some latent gift in generations to come. But in recent weeks, they had spoken in whispers of it closing, a sense that the barrier in the sky and in the ocean had become blocked. Some dismissed their words, others stored up provisions in case of disaster. But none had seen this coming.

Meihani gazed at the track toward the village. Her footprints still lingered in the dust, marks made every day for the span of a life. Times had changed, but the ocean remained her constant — and now she knew it would be her end. She turned away from the village, putting the past behind her, and looked out to the waves as they pulled back still further.

Their island was low-lying, one of many threatened by the rise of oceans and vulnerable to natural disaster. They had been encouraged to leave, but this was their home. There was nowhere else to go. Meihani had hoped to die before the end of the island, but it seemed like fate would entwine them in a lover's embrace.

She pushed away from the palm and walked slowly down the beach, kicking off her shoes and wriggling her toes in the wet sand. A smile transformed her features into those of a young girl once more. She relished each footstep, an imprint on the ocean floor that disappeared even as she walked on. Manoko fish died around her, flopping their last, as she picked a path through the arms of death.

She reached the ruins of the fishing boat and touched its spars. Her father had once sailed something like it, his face ever set to the sea. Sometimes he would let her go out with him and she would sit curled up in the bow and watch for dolphins, shouting with joy when they swam ahead, leaping before the wave. He always told her that the sea was their life and their death, and that was as it should be for an island people.

Meihani looked past the boat to where the water towered high against the horizon, sucked back into a giant wave the size of the American skyscrapers she saw on TV shows. Such a thing was incredible to behold, but those who saw it this close would never tell their tale. That was certain.

Part of her wanted to keep walking toward that wall of water, to welcome it with open arms like the wild teenager she had once been, screaming her fury into the storm. But the little girl inside was afraid.

Meihani reached up into the boat and pulled herself toward the bow. Her arms were weak but her old body was frail and light so it wasn't too difficult. The wood was wet and cold but she had spent much of her life that way, so it wasn't a hardship to curl up in the corner of the bow, her face toward the island that held so many memories.

The smell of salt and kelp filled the air as the roar of the ocean grew to a deafening sound. A rush of oncoming horses charging into battle, a hail of rain and thunder. The first drops of the tsunami fell upon her face. As it towered above, Meihani closed her eyes, her palms against the wooden hull beneath her as she waited for its final embrace.

* * *

BBC News Report

A tsunami struck the low-lying island of Fongafale in Tuvalu today in the aftermath of a deep-sea earthquake off the coast. The entire island remains underwater with several villages and a resort submerged by the flood. Casualties are reported to be in the thousands and no survivors have been found.

Military vessels from Australia and New Zealand converged on the area to help the Tuvaluan police recover bodies from the waves, but the operation has been hampered by ongoing tremors in the region and stormy weather conditions.

Geologists cannot explain why there has been such an increase in earthquakes and natural disasters in the last month.

"After the San Francisco Bay Area evacuation and now this South Pacific disaster, plans are underway to move people out of possible danger zones," Dr Willow Mackenzie said, speaking from James Cook University in Australia. "It's a daunting task on a global scale. Tectonic plates all over the globe seem to be rubbing up against a new barrier, shifting in ways we've never seen before. It's unprecedented, but we have a multi-disciplinary team working on mapping scenarios. We can say that this will not be the last natural disaster."

CHAPTER 1

SIENNA FARREN CLOSED HEAVY curtains over the tall Georgian windows, blocking out the light. It was raining and the buildings opposite were empty, but she didn't want any witnesses to what she was about to do.

The open-plan apartment above the map shop in Bath had been her grandfather's, handed down to her on his death, a casualty of the ongoing war between those who protected Earthside and the Shadow Cartographers of the Borderlands. Sienna hadn't been in the place long enough to make it her own, or perhaps she wanted to keep it intact in memory of the man she hadn't known well in life. She felt his presence in the bookshelves filled with his journals and art on the walls that reflected his passion for cartography. And of course, downstairs, in the collection of antique maps and globes, each a portal to those who could travel through. But the toll of magic tainted their promise, the stain of shadow in exchange for the gift of mapwalking — and that price concerned her now.

Sienna walked over to the full-length mirror in the corner of the room and pulled up her long-sleeved t-shirt to reveal her slim torso. She had inherited her grandfather's pale skin and titian hair and usually her stomach was lightly freckled, but now those subtle hues were lost in tendrils of black that formed patterns under her skin like tattoos of some ancient tribe.

The marks didn't follow the lines of her veins, but curled into beautiful shapes, almost like ink swirling in water, shifting with the movement of her body and even her mood. Some days they were faint, like the last days of a bruise. She could even make them disappear if she concentrated hard enough. But after a night of restless dreams, the marks had etched themselves deeper into her skin and begun their journey along her arms toward her neckline. These t-shirts would not hide the stain for long and Sienna feared what would happen when Bridget or her father or one of the other Mapwalkers noticed. She didn't want to face the possibility of what it might mean.

But the dreams were becoming more vivid.

Last night, she had dreamed of soaring amongst the clouds above the Borderlands, darting like a bird into the blue. She heard her name called from the Tower of the Winds in a voice of a thousand thousand souls.

Sienna.

The pull was almost irresistible, a longing inside her that echoed some elemental need. But as she drew closer, the tattooed lines of the city of Bath on her arms burned, a reminder of her promise to safeguard Earthside. She shifted in the air, tried to dive down toward the land below, tried to escape from the voice, but mist gathered about her and skeletal shapes of winged creatures with razor talons swooped close to ward her away from safety, herding her back to the Tower of the Winds. Closer, closer, until she could almost see what lay inside. She had woken with a gasp, heart pounding, sheets damp with sweat, and the marks on her skin had spread.

Sienna traced one of the dark whorls with a fingertip, touching her own skin as if it was a stranger's body. The marks were beautiful and yet, if anyone knew how deeply she was entwined with the Shadow, she would be sent to the medical wing of the Ministry. There were rumors of it, whispers of a ward filled with Mapwalkers in shadow coma, their bodies etched in black ink. Some recovered, others were lost.

It was the price of Mapwalker magic, a drop of shadow for every use. Those with too much could turn and become a Shadow Cartographer, powerful on the other side of the border but a sworn enemy to those on Earthside.

Or they must remain here, banished from ever crossing again, denied the place that brought them alive, denied the use of their magic for fear of what they might become. Like her father, a broken man, bled of his magic, afraid of the Shadow turning him, scared of it taking what was left of his life, and yet, still, he craved its touch.

But perhaps she was different, perhaps she could remain on the knife edge — but only if she kept the marks hidden. At least long enough to get back over to the Borderlands.

Sienna thought of Finn's dark eyes, the soft touch of his lips as he woke her from the shadow weave when she had last seen him. What was he doing now? She didn't know if he was alive, safe but on the run with the Resistance, or dead at the hands of his father, the Warlord, Kosai. She had to go back to find out whether they might have a future together — and to face the voice that kept calling in her dreams.

She pulled down her t-shirt and turned away from the mirror, reaching up to the bookcase for one of her grandfather's journals. He had traveled widely in the Borderlands, with years of experience as a roaming Mapwalker. His skin had been tattooed with the lines of Bath, as her own was now, but perhaps he had never heard the call from the Tower of the Winds. Or things had changed somehow. The balance undone by the shifting wheel of time and circumstance.

Every day, she scoured the pages of his journals for some clue as to how they could undo what had been done. She kept coming back to journal 24. It mentioned the Map of the Impossible, a way through the space between the worlds. Her grandfather had learned of it during one of his sojourns in the Library of Alexandria, perhaps from the lips of his lost love, the Librarian, but there were no specifics as to what it was or where it might be.

Sienna turned another page of the journal, sensing the throb of shadow beneath her skin. Perhaps today she would find the way back.

* * *

Mila Wendell put another log into her tiny wood-burning stove, pushed it deeper into the flames with a poker, and then shut the grate once more. Rain hammered on the roof of the canal boat, making it a snug haven down here below. The smell of cedar wood hung in the air, mingled with the scent of freshly roasted coffee. Everything was as it should be — but Mila couldn't deny the sense of unease that curled in her stomach.

When Bridget closed the border, there had been a moment of rest, a beat of silence, almost a numb realization amongst the Mapwalkers. They had stopped the invasion, saved Earthside from a devastating plague — but the sense of loss took her breath away, as if they had chopped off a limb. Mila wanted to fling open the gates again and consequences be damned. She had an inkling she wasn't the only one who felt that way.

Zippy, her golden cocker spaniel, whined a little and nuzzled up to her leg before settling on the rug in front of the stove. He put his head on his paws and looked up at her with patient eyes. Mila knew he would love to be out there running along the towpath, splashing in the puddles. They would go out later, whatever the weather.

She reached down to stroke his soft ears, scratching the places he loved. "Good boy. You sleep there for a bit."

She stretched as much as she could in the tiny space, raising her arms up so they pressed against the ceiling. The sound of rain on the roof and the smell of wood smoke and Zippy's rhythmic breath could usually anchor her, but Mila couldn't escape her sense of restlessness.

Was this truly her home, or would she feel more at ease somewhere else … with someone else? She thought of Ekon, his lithe, muscular body slipping ahead of her through the waters beneath Ganvié Island. The touch of his liquid skin under the waves as they swam together to the sunken tomb with the buried map.

Mila smiled at the memory, a bubble of joy welling up at the knowledge that there was someone else like her out there. Perhaps there were more in other corners of the Borderlands. In discovering the Mapwalkers, she had found a family and a purpose to her life, but in finding another Waterwalker, Mila had glimpsed a possible future. She couldn't go to Ekon now, but there was something she could do to feel closer to him.

She bent to the woven rug in the middle of the canal boat and pulled it back, revealing a trapdoor surrounded by a waterproof seal. She tugged it open with a squelch of rubber and looked down into the dark water of the canal lapping beneath. Zippy put his head up at the sound, ears perked, eyes questioning.

Mila reached over to stroke him again. "It's okay, boy. I won't be long."

She slipped off her clothes and sat on the edge of the hatch, dangling her legs for a moment. The water was cool against her skin in the moment of change, but as her limbs shimmered, she became part of the liquid and pushed off to sink below the surface.

As a Waterwalker, she could travel in the spaces between ripples along the watercourses of this world and beyond, her magic turning her into almost another being. But every time she used it, Mila felt that drop of shadow remain. Even now, lying here under the canal boat, she could feel it seep further into her. Each time she turned, it was harder to emerge into the world of air above.

As she sank into the canal, Mila felt a sense of relief, a welcome coolness as her body changed. She was increasingly out of place in the world above and she wondered if perhaps her people had never disappeared, but merely stayed in the water, invisible to those above. Did they become pure liquid after a time?

She had no real knowledge of the bloodline from which she came, raised by a foster mum in the high-rise blocks of East London. There were hints that her father had been a student from war-torn Sierra Leone, her mother too young to keep her. In London, her mixed-race heritage was normal, but here in Bath, her dark skin and almond-shaped eyes stood out. Yet under the water, she shimmered and became all the colors of the rainbow and yet, no color at all.

Mila slipped out from beneath the shelter of the boat into the channel of the canal. She darted up toward the lock, her body reveling in the freedom to move, however brief her time could be here. She gazed up through the green light to the world above, watching as the rain dimpled the surface. It was a moment of beauty but the canal was a tame playground, protected and safe with only a short distance to roam. The only danger was the discovery of her true nature which she kept hidden by her daily routine as a resident of the canal.

But this dual existence was becoming harder to maintain. Should she embrace life on the edge of this elegant city of Bath and truly make her home here? Or was she really a Waterwalker, meant to live under the waves in a land on the other side of the map? She could not do both, for that way, madness would lie in the constant longing for a different life.

A choice loomed ahead, and it would come for Sienna, too. Something had shifted for both of them on the last mission, and Mila sensed her friend was even more torn than she was. They both had one foot on either side of the border and it was slowly tearing them apart.

CHAPTER 2

PERRY MERCATOR PULLED HIMSELF up once more, muscles bulging as he touched the lintel of the door with his chin.

"14 … 15 …"

Sweat ran down his back, his breath ragged as he counted the repetitions, embracing physical pain as the best way to dull the screaming in his mind.

"29 … 30."

He dropped to the floor and bent over with exhaustion as he fought to regain his breath. Nausea rose in his stomach as his body rebelled at the harsh treatment, hours every day, pushing himself to physical extremes.

For most of his life, Perry's fire magic had been out of control — sometimes a tiny flame, sometimes an inferno — and yet on the last mission, he had finally found a way to channel it. He had saved the Mapwalker team at the Eagle's Nest, and in those moments, he had felt most alive. But the stench of burned maps still hung in the air of the corridors of the Ministry, a reminder of how fire had destroyed the very heart of the Mapwalker domain. Fire started by his father, Sir Douglas Mercator, a Shadow Cartographer, a traitor — a murderer.

After the death of the Illuminated Cartographer, Perry

had helped John Farren take the body out to an ancient Somerset hill overlooking Glastonbury. Under the light of the full moon, they built a pyre of old English oak and piled up the tattered remains of the ruined vellum and paper maps and burned books, the scraps of what had once been his home.

Perry lifted the body of the old man onto the logs and placed him in the middle of a nest of map fragments, his frame so wasted and thin that there was hardly anything left before the flames devoured what little remained. The Illuminated had always seemed so vibrant, so strong, but clearly, the maps had sustained him. His blood ran with ink and when he relinquished their hold, there was nothing left but a husk of flesh. He had lived many generations For Galileo, his name lost to time, but whoever he had once been, his legacy was certain in the strength of the remaining Mapwalkers.

Perry had started the fire with his magic, kindling the remaining pieces of the maps around the corpse. As the flames rose, he contained its heat and strength, making sure everything was destroyed. The stars shone brightly overhead, the air crisp and chill, and the smoke formed symbols and pathways as it rose, as if the old man traveled through a new map toward the heavens.

Now, weeks later, Perry ached to get back to the fight. The Mapwalkers had stopped the invasion and won the battle, but they had lost so much. Earthside itself was wounded and Perry knew the time ticked away until he would cross the border again. There was no way to regain what they had lost, only a path forward to a different future.

He jumped and hung on the doorframe once more before pulling himself up to start the next set.

"1 … 2 … 3 …"

When he faced his father again, he would be ready.

* * *

Bridget Ronan sat at her desk in the library surrounded by a billowing sea of maps. As she reached for the next volume of the Mapwalker annals, the vellum and paper moved with her. She could feel their weight on her body — pressing down against the mercurial flights of her mind.

An anchor some days. A prison on others.

Some days her new role as the Illuminated Cartographer didn't seem real, and she tried to walk out the door of the library, striding toward freedom, only to be jolted back, held tightly by the maps that wound themselves into her flesh. The ink that now ran in her veins meant she could never leave this place again. She had traveled the world and the lands beyond and yet, she could now only sense it through the maps here in this room. Her world was at once constrained and yet also of unlimited possibility.

After the night of the fire, Bridget wondered if the Ministry was wounded beyond repair. But not all the maps had been destroyed in the flames that Sir Douglas had set, and the memory of many more ran through the ink that now mingled in her veins. In the weeks since, she had questioned her choice many times. But had there really been a choice? The maps could not live without an Illuminated, a Blood Mapwalker, and the death of the old could only mean a new one must be bound to the cause.

John had told her of the pyre he and Perry built under the stars for the old man. How the smoke had carried his spirit away. Bridget wondered if one day someone would do the same for her, whether she would last as long, and whether her name would also be lost over the generations ahead.

It wasn't clear how long the old man had been the Illuminated, but the line was unbroken, the position assumed and lived with no record of who each had been before. Eventually her own name would be erased. She would only be the Illuminated, tied to the maps for generations to come. Perhaps she would even forget what she had once been.

Memories came to her through the ink, memories held by the Illuminated Cartographers before her, remnants of what they had seen. Bridget understood that each time she accessed them, part of her own life crumbled away, dissolving into the ink.

Some days she raged against her captivity, wishing she had a flame so she could finish what Sir Douglas had started. Other days, she closed her eyes and roamed into the maps, traveling in her mind further than she had ever been able to do in person.

Over the last weeks, Bridget had called for a renewal of the map library. She sent requests to the other Ministries around the world, asking for copies of everything they had. She had used funds to buy originals from antique map houses in Istanbul and Amsterdam, needing to build the library back up but also to expand her world once more.

Truthfully, she did not know what she was doing, but she trusted that the maps of the world held everything she needed. There was wisdom in the maps and a vestige of magic in the ink that flowed through her. She just didn't know how to wield it yet.

Had the old man learned his role from a previous incarnation of the Illuminated? Or did he have to learn as she did from the very beginning? Perhaps her predecessor had not chosen this path either. Perhaps it was only ever unwillingly pressed upon the next.

Bridget sighed and opened the volume of annals, turning the pages and scanning the text as she continued her search for a way to open the border once more.

Suddenly, she stopped, her attention caught by a drawing sketched on the ivory paper. Its bold lines portrayed a figure whirling within a vortex of shadow and light, the face obscured by a silver mist surrounded by drops of scarlet.

A faint scent wafted up, a memory of flame. Bridget bent closer to the page to examine the medium and then drew back with a frown.

Ash and blood. Smoke and magic. But what did it mean?

"Look what I found." John's voice interrupted her from the outer room of the library and Bridget turned in greeting.

He pulled out a rolled map as he walked around the corner, still limping and bowed, his injuries a permanent reminder of how the Mapwalkers had failed once before.

"It's Buondelmonti's Constantinople from 1422. The only surviving map predating the Turkish conquest." John placed the scroll down on the desk and gently unrolled it. "The Bibliothèque Nationale in Paris sent it over. On loan, of course, but I thought it might brighten your day."

He smiled at her and in his blue eyes, Bridget saw a glimmer of the man he had once been, his head thrown back in laughter as they danced on the edge of a silver lake in the Uncharted, together for a brief magical moment. She smiled at the memory, bittersweet with the knowledge that they would never again walk those trails together. She was trapped here and the man he once was had been bled out of him, cut away by a Shadow Cartographer in the dungeon of a dark castle.

John had lost more than his blood down there and he could never cross the border again. Even if he could, Bridget didn't think he would go. He once had the confidence of the true Blood Mapwalker, one who could wield his power against the Shadow and win — but no longer. She only hoped his daughter could find her way to true power.

Bridget bent down to examine the map more closely, the waters of the Bosphorus in a faded green with ramparts of the walled city of Constantinople ringing its shores in shades of umber.

"It's beautiful, thank you." She gestured toward the racks of newly built shelving. "Put it on the third shelf down.

That's my to read pile — once we get through the rest of the annals." She pointed to the stack of thick books by her desk. "We've still got hundreds of years to trawl through."

John carefully rolled the map up with gentle fingers and laid it on the rack. He sat down next to the desk and pulled the next volume off the pile of annals.

"We'll find something. The answer has to be in these somewhere." He dusted the cover off, opened the front page and began to read.

Bridget watched him in companionable silence. John came every day to sit in the library and read by her side as they scoured the archives for anything that might help with the border. When it closed, they had not realized the ramifications. But the world beyond deteriorated, earthquakes, tsunamis and people dying because they couldn't cross over. The Borderlands were home to many; they were an escape to many more. Now they knew that Earthside needed an escape valve, a way to release the pressure — and neither world could exist in isolation.

Bridget stared down at the figure sketch in ash and blood. John had barely glanced at it in the excitement of the rare Constantinople find, so perhaps it was nothing. But blood had always been at the heart of Mapwalker history.

There were family trees in the scrolls, but over time, many of the bloodlines had dwindled in power. Those on Earthside truly had nothing to compete with what the Shadow Cartographers did on the other side of the border: forcible breeding across magical lines to create original forms of magic. There were also tales of a drug given to pregnant women to encourage mutation in children born away from the Fertility Halls, in the hope that nature would produce new kinds of power.

As abhorrent as the practices were, Bridget understood why they did it. Every day more children of magic were born over there, some powerful, some destined to work the mines or fight as soldiers, some discarded as worthless. It was relentless and if things didn't change, those on Earthside would be outnumbered within a generation.

But the border was the most immediate problem. They closed it to stop the plague coming over in a wave of refugees, but now that seemed like a terrible mistake. In closing the border, they doomed Earthside to an acceleration of natural disasters. They had to find a way to open it again.

Bridget pulled the next volume from the stack and began to read once more.

CHAPTER 3

Finn Page pulled his cloak tighter against his body, wrapping the black material around his sword to hide any glint of metal. He stood motionless in the shelter of a temple wall as a band of soldiers ran past through the narrow streets, the half-moon of the Shadow Cartographers tattooed on their faces, the banner of the wolf's head held high above them. As they rounded the corner of the street and their footsteps faded into the noise of the trader town, Finn shook his head and sighed. That had been much too close.

The price on his head was so high now that he had started to doubt even close members of the Resistance. His father, the Warlord, Kosai, offered riches and status to anyone who would turn him in, alive or dead, so he had to remain vigilant, only walking the streets when he really needed to.

Finn pulled out the vial of blue liquid from within his shirt pocket and swirled it around, inky darkness mixing with a lighter teal within. He hoped this had been worth the risk.

He set off through the warren of dirt streets, staying away from the thoroughfare of the trader town. The city was said to have no name because no one stayed long enough to call it home. Refugees arrived on its stinking shore, drifting across the ocean from Earthside to be swept up by the slave traders and sold to the mines or sent to the Fertility Halls — at least, they had arrived that way until the border closed a month ago. The trader town had emptied after days of watching the becalmed sea and now only a few slavers waited by the beach just in case, while the rest had gone to raid villages on the outer edges of the Uncharted. The tide of new arrivals had stopped altogether on that fateful day.

The last time he had seen Sienna.

Finn remembered her face that night, bruised and muddied but still beautiful, her titian hair streaming down behind her as she told him of her plan. The only way to stop the plague crossing over to Earthside was to close the border.

He had not believed it possible, but she had surprised him once again. Just as she had in the dungeons of the Fertility Halls where she had helped him find his sister moments before her bloody end. It was possible that Sienna's magic was much stronger than even she knew, and as much as he wanted more, Finn felt the distance between them might now be too wide a gulf.

He had fled the camp that night, guilt chasing him even as he ran through the sea of rats, leaving behind thousands of refugees to die of the plague. There was nothing he could do for them and it was better to live another day than die from the bites of plague-ridden rodents or under the swords of his father's men.

Flashes of memory from that night still haunted his dreams. Hordes of rats gnawing on the half-dead. A silver-haired girl with arms raised high, clawing life energy from those around her while mutants from the Shadow roamed the corpse-strewn camp, finishing any left alive. There was powerful magic on both sides of the border, but he was one of the majority who were merely human. Finn could only think that his role was to stand against the darkness as much as he could. The Borderlands were his world and he could not wait for the Mapwalkers or anyone else to save his people.

The Resistance had grown in the wake of the plague and mass murder of those in the camps. News had spread of the culling of infected refugees, the indiscriminate destruction of those considered useless once the invasion proved impossible.

Ordinary Borderlanders, those with no magic, had always known of the Shadow Cartographers and those who followed the dark path. It had been a minor part of life, but now, bands of mutants roamed the land, taking women and girls back to the Fertility Halls, increasingly spread across multiple locations. Those who protested, who went to try to get their wives or daughters or sisters back, were taken to Elf, the silver-haired banshee Finn had seen stalking the plague field that night. Her magical ability was like a battery, draining, storing and transforming life energy. It was said that those who faced her were dragged away afterward as a husk of skin and bone, mouths open in a last terrible scream.

Finn turned the last corner into a dirt street a few blocks back from the central slave market. The stench of fish hung in the air from the drying racks nearby, a staple food for those in the trader town, but even that was under threat now. The closing of the border had impacted the giant shoals of herring that once darted through the porous line between the worlds. Nature was out of balance and Finn was sure that those on Earthside must be suffering, too. He could only hope that Sienna was okay.

He ducked between rows of huts and stood for a moment watching the area, alert for any who might track the Resistance. A dirty tarpaulin flapped at the door of a nearby shack, drawing his eyes, but it was just the wind. Children played with a misshapen ball near a pile of rubbish, but they didn't even glance in his direction. Those who lived here learned to turn a blind eye almost as soon as they could walk. Better not to notice what went on in these streets.

Finn hurried to a ramshackle hut, pushed the wooden

door open and ducked inside. The point of a sharp blade against his throat stopped him, the cold metal tight against his skin.

A beat of silence, then the knife dropped.

"You're meant to whistle, you idiot." Titus O'Byrne stepped forward into the light, sandy curls tied roughly back from his face. "I could have cut your throat."

Finn smiled. "Just making sure you're staying vigilant." He walked further inside. The tiny shack was barely large enough for the two of them, both sizeable men used to more generous quarters. It smelled of yesterday's soup, old sweat and the reek of the open sewers only meters outside but it was only a place to lie low while they investigated the latest abhorrent attempt by the Shadow Cartographers to shape the destiny of the Borderlands.

Finn placed the vial gently on the wooden tabletop. "There were soldiers everywhere and this cost us most of the gold we had left. I hope it was enough to keep the man from betraying our location, but I can't be sure. We need to move on."

Titus bent to look at the vial, his blue eyes reflecting the hues of the liquid within. "It's worth it, brother. This might be the key."

Finn smiled at his words. They were brothers in the war against the Shadow, but no one could mistake them for blood relations. Finn's heritage was evident in his black skin and the regal bearing of an Ethiopian king. Titus was stocky and muscular, with the body of a boxer and a face to match, with mixed Irish and South African blood. They had served together several years ago in the Warlord's army, but Titus had deserted to join the Resistance in the wake of the atrocities against the refugees, many of whom he counted amongst his kin. Titus had knowledge of the mines and training in chemistry, primarily for warfare, and now he used his talents to fight against the Shadow. He was a brother in every way that mattered.

Titus ran a fingertip along the edge of the glass vial. "There's a midwife who lives on the other side of town near the soup kitchen. She helps women infected with this stuff. The … babies they deliver." He shivered, as if shaking off a bad dream. "She keeps them hidden from the soldiers, but I'm not sure they're better off …" His words trailed away.

Finn nodded. "We'll figure out an antidote. There has to be one. But first, we have to change locations. I know somewhere that might have what you need to analyze this." He put his hand on Titus's shoulder. "One step at a time."

They packed up their meager belongings, pulled cloaks around to hide their weapons and headed out into the night.

Finn led the way, cutting through narrow walkways between the shacks, navigating the warren of the shanty town on the outskirts. He had come this way many times, the makeshift city a perfect place to lie low.

Most people here were just passing through, forced on to work the mines or serve in the Warlord's army, others for the Fertility Halls, and still more to the farmlands. There were many mouths to feed in the Borderlands, many who went hungry and took handouts from the soldiers who controlled the food supply. The blue poison was an addictive liquid that the destitute begged for, that dulled their minds and took the edge off their hunger. It was added to food in the trader town and handed out on street corners, sometimes in exchange for pleasure quickly taken.

A giggle came from the shadows as they passed by. A young woman sat with her back against a dirt wall, filthy and stinking clothes stretched over a swollen belly. Maybe only a few weeks until she gave birth. She might have been pretty once, but now she looked ravaged, her skin taking on the hue of a corpse. Yet she smiled coquettishly, as if she wandered through fields of poppies without a care in the world.

"Take your pleasure for some blue, why don't you, boys?"

The sweet smell of something like marijuana hung in the

air but it was nothing so mundane as that form of escape. The blue drug was known by many names. Some even called it Liberation because those who took it were finally free from their enslavement, no longer caring about death — or those they left behind. The women who took it gave birth to mutants, many taken to the Castle of the Shadow, most never seen again.

Titus stopped and bent down to the young woman. He pulled half a loaf of bread from his pack and gave it to her. "Eat this. You'll feel better."

She looked confused, as if she hadn't seen real food in a long time and didn't know what to do with it. Then she tore at the bread with both hands, stuffing pieces quickly into her mouth. Titus turned away, his shoulders stooped as if he carried the weight of her suffering away, but Finn knew the young woman and her unborn child were already lost. They walked on through the streets, leaving her behind. One more life consumed by the Shadow.

Finn heard trickles of information from his Resistance sources, some undercover in the castle itself, risking their lives to reveal the truth. The blue drug twisted the genetics of the unborn, adding a dash of chaos into the mix so new mutations emerged. On Earthside, the numbers of those with magic dwindled, but here in the Borderlands, their numbers grew every day, cultivated as part of a new order dedicated to the dark plans of the Shadow Cartographers. The children were tested for their magic and many were found wanting. They were taken for sacrifice at the Tophet, or shoveled into the plague pits. Those with a touch of magic were siphoned, drained of what little they had. Finn had heard tales of the silver-haired Elf sapping newborns dry, leaving their tiny corpses as husks to blow away in the wind.

Finn's sister, Isabel, had died in the Castle of the Shadow, his baby niece lost to him when the traitor, Jari, had betrayed him in the hunt for the Map of Plagues. Titus, too, was driven by love to find an antidote to the blue, but Finn knew it went deeper for both of them. There were rumors that the drug was made in a camp by a lake out east and for the sake of all the sisters and daughters of the Borderlands, they were determined to find the source and destroy it.

The edge of the city soon bled into the desert, ever encroaching sand that claimed more dwellings by the day. Finn and Titus trudged out into the dunes, the way made harder as their feet sank down with every step. Far ahead, the stark lines of a ruined temple cut a line through the cliff at the base of an escarpment. As they drew closer, Finn remembered the last time he had come here — with Sienna and the Mapwalker team, on the way to the forgotten city of Alexandria and the library at its heart. But this time, the temple was a waypoint for a different reason and Finn could only hope that the sanctuary still held its long-forgotten treasure.

By the time Finn and Titus made it to the entrance of the ruined temple, clouds hid the face of the moon. Statues of the old gods stood in alcoves around the walls, some with faces smashed in by followers of Moloch, devourer of children, and others painted with curses in languages from foreign shores. Finn walked slowly to the stone altar, his footsteps echoing in the empty space. Dried garlands of marigolds and lilies bound with ivy hung from its edge, evidence of believers who still honored the lost religion. The temple might be empty now, but its power still lingered.

Finn knelt in front of the altar, holding his sword in front of him as he had knelt so long ago back when he entered his father's service as a soldier in the Shadow Guard. But now he pledged allegiance not to the half-moon, but to the people of the Borderlands, and to the Resistance. He prayed for guidance and for strength in the inevitable battle to come.

A minute later, Finn stood up, leaning on his sword with a scrape of metal on stone.

Titus emerged from the shadows. "We need to get out of here before dawn. Patrols come here all the time."

Finn nodded toward the back of the temple where stone steps led down into darkness. "This way."

He pulled a metal torch from a bracket on the wall. It had a small patch of oil left inside. Finn lit it and carried the flame down the stairs.

A ritual bathing pool filled the chamber below, empty of water except for a few brackish puddles. A mosaic of cavorting gods in faded colors hinted at the temple pleasures in earlier times, but now it was only a breeding ground for mosquitoes.

At the opposite end of the room, an arched doorway led into darkness topped with a carving of heaped bones.

Finn walked on, through the arch and down a spiral staircase into the halls of the dead below the temple. Torchlight flickered across alcoves in the walls, some with linen-wrapped desiccated corpses, others with piles of bones.

"Only the most powerful were buried down here," Finn said, his voice echoing through the chamber. "There is one who was buried with everything he worked on, so no one could continue his quest. Superstition keeps people away even now."

He stopped in front of a massive boulder roughly hewn into an oval shape and rolled in front of an opening. There were symbols carved into the rock — triangles of fire and water, the circle of the golden sun, and curved lines representing the metals of the alchemist.

In the center, a roughly carved skull, eyes of pitted rock that seemed to stare out from the abyss. A warning in every culture. Death lies within.

CHAPTER 4

THE DOOR TO THE Antiquities department of the Ministry of Maps was suitably ancient. Some said it was made of wood from the cedars of Lebanon that King Solomon spoke of in his Song of Songs. Others that it was hewn from the spars of Greek warships after the sack of Troy. Love and war, appropriate reminders of the inevitability of history. Zoe Saroyan pushed open the door and stepped into what had become her world in the last month.

She had transferred from the Ministry office attached to the British Library in London, a promotion of sorts since the corridors of Bath were hallowed ground and most ancient maps now rested here. Zoe could sense the difference in power. The earth almost throbbed with it, amplified by the magic of those who worked within. But it had been thrown off balance, wounded by the Borderlander attack. The fire destroyed so much, and now it was all hands on deck to restore what remained.

Zoe was early as usual, but there were a few familiar faces already working, heads bent over vellum, cloth or paper, all diligent in trying to trace the lines on the maps, some burned beyond recognition, others salvageable to those who knew their craft, both worldly and magical.

Her own magic was muddled, a touch of this and that, but

Zoe had found her life's work in restoration. She could lose herself in the maps, her light touch turning a broken thing into something those with real magic could travel through once more. She was a little in awe of the Blood Mapwalkers, those who could travel through maps, even create their own, whose very essence could transform the boundaries of the world. Her abilities seemed paltry in comparison, but she did what she could.

At the British Library, Zoe had been responsible for tracing the provenance of older maps, finding those with magic imbued within them so they could be separated from purely Earthside cartography. The collection held in excess of four million individual maps, and even with her touch of weaver magic, Zoe couldn't work fast enough. But she must have done something right because now she was here, in the Ministry at Bath, part of the Antiquities team drafted in to help Restoration after the fire.

Each of the workers had a private area shielded by high panels so they could work in the way that best suited their gifts. Magic had a hierarchy, just as any part of society, and the Mapwalkers were no different. Blood Mapwalkers were the most revered — but they also took the most risk, and when they died, their skin became the maps that others traveled in their turn.

Below them were those with strong fire or water magic, and then those with other kinds of gifts, many of whom found their way to the Ministry over time. Zoe had heard a rumor that those in the Borderlands deliberately bred children of mixed magic, trying to encourage new forms to emerge. But here on Earthside, such things were forbidden and Zoe's own gift was considered a lesser form. But she could still be useful in her quiet way, and to be honest, she was perfectly happy here in the quiet of Antiquities. She could dampen down the desire for something more — at least, most of the time.

Zoe primarily worked with the tools of every map restorer. De-acidification and removal of caustic adhesives from incorrect backing materials. Preparation and flattening, bleaching and cleaning, cutting where necessary, re-backing with linen. But she specialized in fixing rips and tears both physical and magical, and she suspected that this was why she had been asked to come to Bath.

She circled behind her desk, placing her bag underneath as she looked down at the map pinned gently to the surface. The Egyptian papyrus depicted a fifteen-kilometer stretch of Wadi Hammamat in the Eastern Desert made for Pharaoh Ramesses IV on a quarrying expedition. Although initially thought to show only rock formations, a magical imprint had been overlaid in generations past, now disturbed by the degradation of the map. Unless it was restored, the ancient paths would be lost forever. Zoe had studied Egyptology and ancient Egyptian hieroglyphics as part of her degree. If she could restore the papyrus, perhaps she could also restore the Mapwalker magic that lay interwoven with its strands.

She walked to the coffee machine in the corner, a filter system that seemed as ancient as the room itself. She poured herself a generous mug and went back to her desk. In the last few days, she had been preparing the map in traditional ways as she had learned in her degree in Conservation and Restoration from Lincoln University, home to the largest center for such work in the UK. She had already placed re-moistenable repair paper over the worst of the cracks. It was made from high-grade Japanese paper coated with a cellulose gum that would not degrade the papyrus, one of the best ways to both protect what was left and repair the map. But as Zoe looked down at the lines depicting the Wadi, she knew she had done everything traditionally possible as a restorer. It was time to move to the next step.

Her white gloves lay next to the map, and usually, reaching for them was her first task of the day. But now she left them to the side and concentrated on the map itself. Zoe softened her gaze into the space above the lines and curves and colors of ancient Egypt. As her focus shifted, contours appeared in the air, suspended as if woven from motes of dust and glimmers of sunlight. Tears and fissures cracked through the dimensions, breaking the perfection of the original magical lines and weakening its fabric.

Zoe raised her hands and began to gently tease the contours back into shape, weaving the magic together as if she stitched an intricate pattern in the air. The room fell away around her as she concentrated, barely breathing as she sensed the holes and gaps and filled them with little drops of her gift.

As the minutes passed, she began to comprehend the unseen undulations of the magical map. She had worked on enough of these multi-layered papyri to learn the conventions of how early Mapwalkers structured their cartography, but this one was different. Zoe frowned as she considered a particular layer over the quarry. As much as she tried to weave the contours together, it resisted her magic; the tendrils coming undone even as she repeated her actions. It was strange, something she had never encountered before, but she was sure her mother would have.

Her mother's family had been Christian refugees from Armenia, fleeing the Ottoman Empire in the wake of genocide. Three generations had passed but the pain of persecution and the loss of their homeland persisted, a shared legacy that permeated songs and stories told over and over to keep the memory alive.

Many of the women of her mother's bloodline had been renowned weavers — both of cloth and of magic. Her father was a British accountant, a straight-backed man of impeccable manners, a port in the emotional storm that was her mother's intensity. Zoe was their only child, and whenever she went home to the terraced house in Clapham, south

London, they wanted to know everything, all the details of her life. She left London partly to escape their constrictive orbit, but her mother had taught her everything about weaving, and she could use the help now.

Zoe took a deep breath. She did not want to call her mother and explain why she needed help. She had left London for a reason, and she could work this out herself. She just needed to go back to first principles.

The first step in untangling a bad weave was to step back and look at it from a fresh angle, to try and work out what could be released elsewhere to free tension from the knots. Brute strength made a tangle worse, whereas gentle easing could solve the problem and leave the strands unbroken. Zoe took a step backward to shift her perspective on the contours that hung in the air. But there was nothing new to see, and she bit her lip in frustration.

She hunkered down, squatting on the ground to look up from below and there, suddenly, she saw it. A golden thread hung from the underside of the deep quarry lines, a shimmering cord of magic that implied … another layer.

Zoe couldn't help the gasp that escaped her lips at the realization. She had read so many maps where there was only one layer of magic woven into the threads; she had never considered that there might be more below that. She reached for the golden thread and as she touched it, a jolt of energy passed through her. The scent of sandalwood filled the air and as she caressed the length of cord, she saw another dimension, another layer of magic, woven beneath the first.

She blinked, shaking her head a little, trying to adjust her focus so she could see what lay below. But it was as if she had only stitched a tiny part of the whole and much was left to be revealed. Perhaps fixing the upper layer further would uncover more.

Zoe stood again and worked faster, her fingers darting

in and out of silver contours, motes of light dancing around her as stitch by stitch, she remade the map.

It seemed as if time slowed while Zoe dwelled within and between the layers, fingers flashing faster, a smile playing around her lips. For so long, she had held her weaver magic in check, not daring to use it much for fear of discovery amongst those who knew not of Mapwalkers, but also for fear of the drops of shadow that all exchanged for the use of their gift. But now, Zoe glimpsed the possibilities. How many more maps had these layers, hidden magical paths below what was obvious? What else could she discover?

She made the final stitch in the upper layer of magic and the Egyptian papyrus seemed renewed, at least through her eyes. The physical cracks disappeared as the magical ones closed, and then it was as if the entire thing became a three-dimensional puzzle. She bent down to look on the underside, her eyes sparkling at what lay below outlined in threads of golden light.

Zoe carefully examined the network of underground caverns. What had been a plain quarry on the surface was clearly a funerary complex of great riches, a hidden treasure trove undiscovered by Egyptologists. An area of barren desert may well harbor the greatest wealth.

She traced a path through the chambers, glimpsing golden hieroglyphics on the walls, woven into the magical fabric. She frowned as she recognized symbols from the Book of the Dead, markers on the path to the afterlife.

Warnings and curses. A forbidden place.

What could possibly be down there that needed so much protection?

CHAPTER 5

SIENNA STEPPED INTO THE library, a bag over her shoulder containing her grandfather's journal. She stood in the doorway for a moment, gazing around at what was left. The fire had carved a swathe through the dry paper and ancient vellum once stacked on the English oak shelves that now stood bowed and blackened — but not completely ravaged. Perhaps nothing could really destroy the heart of the Ministry.

A rustle came from deeper within the room.

Sienna walked further in and rounded the shelves to the annex where once the Illuminated Cartographer could be found at study. At first glance, it was as if nothing had changed.

The area had been partially protected by the sheer density of maps and more had been brought from other departments to replace them. Rolled sheets of vellum painted with routes to distant places lined the walls. Tiny fragments of papyrus lay pinned within frames next to a grand print of an ancient sea map with a tentacled monster nestled in one corner. Glimpses of what it had once been — but the smell of burned paper still hung in the air, a reminder of recent desolation.

A figure stood at a desk piled high with books and for

a moment, Sienna thought she saw the craggy features of the Illuminated emerging from the maps. She blinked, and the image faded as Bridget turned. Her close-cropped dark hair still curled around fine features and piercing blue eyes. She still had laughter lines and an air of mischief, but it was tempered now with a darker stain, and her shoulders hung heavy as if she bore a great weight upon them. Where once she had worn multi-colored dresses of patchwork stitching, she now clothed herself in maps. They wound about her, wrapping her body in layers of lines and symbols, overlaying the tattoos she had etched on her skin. At her wrists, ink merged with blood, a pulsing of life and magic that sustained the border at a cost beyond imagining.

"Did we do the right thing when we closed the border?" Sienna said softly.

"We did what we could." Bridget shrugged, the maps rustling around her at the movement. "But I still don't know. It's impossible to tell." She turned back to the desk, indicating the books stacked high around her. "The reports of natural disasters keep coming, and the annals of the Mapwalkers have little of help. This has never been done before."

Sienna walked to the desk and touched the leather spine of one book. Words of those long dead meant nothing as people continued to die every day in the here and now.

"You can open the border again though, right?"

Bridget sighed. "It's hard to tell. When my blood mingled with the maps that day, I used significant power to close it. It would take much more to reverse that action." She hung her head. "I don't know if I can do it alone, or if I have the strength to maintain it without letting in a tide of Borderlanders."

Sienna put a hand out to touch the edge of the maps that curled around Bridget's arm. "You're not alone. There are still Blood Mapwalkers who stand alongside you, those who will fight for Earthside."

Bridget turned her palms upward and Sienna looked

down to see where the maps entered her veins at the wrists. Her blood turned to a deep indigo — not the dark blue of the Shadow but more the cobalt of Chinese porcelain or the hood of a saint in the stained glass of a medieval cathedral.

"You can still walk away," Bridget said. "It's too late for me. I decided to give my life For Galileo a long time ago, but you have a chance to get away from here."

Sienna took Bridget's hand in her own. She could feel the blood and ink pulsing between them and something called to the magic within her. Like calling to like. "This is my life now, too. I had no direction before coming here, no idea why I felt so restless. Now I know my place in this world and the one beyond." For a moment, Sienna hesitated, unsure of the next step. She bit her lip and then sighed. "But there is something I need to show you."

She pulled up her t-shirt with her other hand, revealing the whorls of shadow that patterned her torso.

Bridget gasped, her eyes widening. She dropped Sienna's hand in shock, the connection of ink and blood severed once more. "How did it happen?"

Sienna shook her head. "I don't know exactly. It ebbs and flows as I use my magic, but something is different now. I think I might be able to sustain a balance of shadow."

Bridget bent to look at the patterns more closely. "I've never seen marks as dense as this on someone still functioning. You have to see one of the doctors—"

"But—"

Bridget held up a hand. "Don't even try to argue. You'll see Dr Rachel Tabib. She's younger than most of the other Ministry doctors, more open-minded about possibilities. Please, Sienna. Your father will be so worried."

Sienna nodded. "Alright, but just to ease his mind. I'm not being confined to some ward while I have time left to find this." She opened the bag and pulled out her grandfather's journal.

Bridget moved a heavy tome to one side and Sienna glimpsed a figure sketched in black lines spinning in a vortex of shadow and blood on its ivory pages.

"Show me," Bridget said.

Sienna placed the journal on the desk and opened it to a page marked with a purple silk ribbon. Intricate drawings covered the paper, sketches of giant stones at the base of a pyramid, a boy lounging against a palm tree eating dates next to a sleeping camel, the triangular sail of a felucca on the waters of the Nile beyond.

Bridget bent to look closer. "Michael traveled often to Egypt on Earthside when he worked with the Antiquities department. Sometimes he would cross over to the Borderlands to fetch artifacts pushed over in ancient times. Why do you think this is unusual?"

Sienna turned the page. "He sketched a lot of tombs and because he saw so many, he noted when they were different, when they stood out somehow." She pointed to a set of hieroglyphics and the scrawled handwriting underneath. *Map of the Impossible.*

Sienna flicked through the subsequent pages. "Look here and here. He found these marks in several tombs but never discovered what it referred to. They were all etched with funerary texts and paths through the underworld to the land beyond."

Bridget traced the lines with a gentle fingertip. "You think the land beyond might be the Borderlands?"

"It's possible. We have to at least consider it as an option."

Bridget nodded. "Even if I could open the border once more, it would allow the invasion of the Shadow Cartographers and the forces of the Warlord. The best option is for you and the Mapwalker team to find another way through and see if you can work with the Resistance to change things over there before we open it again."

"We need someone who knows hieroglyphics with us."

The sound of hurried footsteps came from outside, then the door to the library banged open.

John rushed in, his face etched with concern as he rounded the corner of the annex. "You both have to see this."

He carried a tablet computer with the news playing on mute. He turned it to face Sienna and Bridget as he switched on the sound.

"The evacuation of San Francisco is continuing under almost impossible conditions this morning as earthquakes intensify. Emergency sirens sound throughout the downtown area and residents have been asked to calmly leave as fast as possible."

John muted the sound again even as horrific images of the aftermath of the Pacific Island disaster played on the screen, followed by footage of cars streaming east away from the coast of California, people running from what was on its way. The news cut to photographs from the 1906 earthquake that devastated San Francisco. Thousands of people dead, buildings destroyed and hundreds of thousands left homeless. Images of the stricken city seared on the memory of those who thought this day would never come in their lifetime.

"We could not have foreseen the impact of closing the border," John said. "But more people will die from natural disasters than might have died from invasion or the plague if we don't get it open again. We're running out of time."

* * *

Zoe felt a touch on her shoulder. She jumped, the vision of the golden underworld dropping away, the veil of magic dissipating as her focus shifted.

The Head of the Antiquities department stood by her side, the woman's gnomish face crinkled in curiosity. "Found something interesting?" She bent to look more closely at the map on the desk.

Her words made Zoe hesitate. She didn't really know what she'd found, but she didn't want to share anything yet. Not until she was sure.

"Perhaps, but I need more time."

"Well, you won't have it today. You're needed in the library."

Zoe's heart beat faster at the prospect of going to the center of the Ministry, the soul of the maps. She had visited the place briefly when she arrived as part of her induction tour, but it was a mess of charred ruins and everyone had ignored her, consumed as they were by cleanup tasks. She could only hope it was better now.

"What for?"

"Something Egyptian, right up your alley. Get going. Don't keep the Illuminated waiting."

Zoe grabbed her notebook and pen, as much for something to clutch onto as anything else, something to anchor her hammering heart.

She hurried through the corridors of the Ministry, winding her way toward the library. Thoughts ran through her mind, possibilities about how she could help. Perhaps she might become an important part of the team, or maybe she would just disappoint them and have to leave Bath almost as soon as she had arrived, slinking back to her parents in shame and failure. This was such an important moment in her career. She couldn't mess it up. But what if she did?

With her mind teeming, Zoe paused at the doorway to the library and took a deep breath. There was only one way to discover what came next. She stepped inside.

Rolled maps lined the walls of the first chamber alongside what was left of the ancient books that had survived the fire. A large framed photo took pride of place near the door, an image of what the library had been only months before — and what might be again with time and care.

"Come on through."

The voice came from the other side of the shelving and Zoe rounded the end to find herself in a smaller annex. This was much cozier than the grand entrance, clearly where the Illuminated worked. The woman clothed in maps turned around. She was beautiful in the way of the Pre-Raphaelite painters, women of ivory skin frozen in time, captured in the moment before their inevitable death. Something about her made Zoe want to curtsey.

"Welcome." The Illuminated stepped forward, maps rustling around her as she held out a hand. "I'm Bridget. This is Sienna and John."

Zoe shook Bridget's hand, shocked into silence. She stood with those considered royalty amongst the Mapwalkers. John Farren was a legend of many explorations and the Antiquities department had much he had collected on his travels. He was marked by scars, bowed with the pain of torture, but his eyes were still a steely blue.

Sienna's reputation was new, an estranged daughter who turned out to be far more than expected, with powerful blood magic that both empowered the Mapwalkers and endangered their future. Many within the Ministry considered her arrogant, given too much responsibility before she was ready purely because of her heritage. But Zoe saw doubt in Sienna's eyes, a fragility she had not expected. There was also a palpable sense of misgiving in the room.

"Hi, thanks for inviting me over." Zoe cursed the words almost as soon as they were out. She needed something better to impress the magical elite.

"We're hoping you can help us." Sienna pointed to the desk.

An old book lay to one side with a figure sketched in ash on its ivory pages, turning in a vortex of shadow and light. Next to it, a journal open to a page of hieroglyphics etched between the lines of a hand-drawn sketch.

Zoe found herself drawn closer, her love of Egyptology quashing the nerves that skittered through her veins. She bent to the page and examined the finely drawn images, translating the symbols in her mind. They were well-known passages from the Book of the Dead, and time slowed as she let the words wash over her.

She turned the page and a scent of cedar wood rose as if she were with the man who wrote these words, copying them from the walls of a chill tomb surrounded by the dust of the long dead. These were no common symbols. They were reflections of what she had seen in the golden layer of Wadi Hammamat. Zoe couldn't help the gasp that escaped her lips.

"What is it?" Bridget came closer as the others gathered round. "What do you see?"

Zoe pointed to a set of glyphs on the page. "These symbols are incredibly rare, a form of Mapwalker magic used to place maps within maps within maps."

John frowned. "A third layer of cartography? I've heard rumors of this, but I've met no one who could make or decipher them. A bloodline lost in the genocide of the east, perhaps."

His words echoed through Zoe, a call to her ancestral past. "My mother's family are from Armenia originally. We're Weavers."

"Weavers?" Sienna sounded curious. "You mean you weave cloth?"

"And magic," Bridget said, her eyes piercing as she looked at Zoe with new interest. "Weavers can layer objects with a magical thread and some can even manipulate the cords of the world." She placed a hand on Zoe's arm. "Where have you seen these glyphs before?"

Her touch was gentle, encouraging, but Zoe also felt an edge in the hard lines of the maps that encased her body. There was only one authority here.

"I'm restoring a map down in Antiquities. On one plane, it's an ancient quarry, but as I stitched, I found a layer below, that of a treasure house hidden under the rock. Then I found a golden thread to a third layer, a set of tombs. This glyph marks the door implying it is a way through the border in the realm between the living and the dead. There is no exact translation that I can find, but it means something like 'impossible.'" Zoe pointed to the journal. "This person knew something of Egyptology to translate such a word. Perhaps he was in the tomb, perhaps he found a way inside."

"Could you find such a place if you were in that quarry?" John asked. His words made Zoe's heart beat faster again. Something within her wanted this so very much.

"I don't know. Perhaps." She whispered the last word, like a prayer.

Bridget nodded. "Sienna, get Perry and Mila down here. You'll go together with Zoe, find these golden chambers, and see if the Map of the Impossible leads you to the Borderlands. In the meantime, John and I will continue searching for answers."

A decision made, a page turned, a life changed.

Zoe took a deep breath. She was ready.

CHAPTER 6

Titus couldn't tear his eyes away from the skull. It was clearly a warning, but death had already come for the people of the Borderlands and they had little left to lose.

Finn put the torch into a metal bracket on one side. "Help me move this."

Together, they put their shoulders against the rock and with a scrape of stone; they pushed it aside.

The tomb was hacked into the mountain itself, each cut made by hand to honor one so greatly revered. A stone sarcophagus stood in the center, adorned with alchemical symbols and around the casket, the implements and tools of the alchemist himself.

Titus took a deep breath as he gazed around at the tomb. It smelled musty with a metallic edge, like dried blood on a sword after battle. Thick benches of black wood lined the walls, piled with brass implements mottled with age. Bottles of varying sizes stoppered with beeswax lay in boxes, thrown together hastily in a mosaic of colored glass each containing mysterious liquid or powder. If only they had more time. He could spend a generation studying what lay here.

"Who was this guy?"

Finn ran a fingertip across the top of the sarcophagus, tracing lines in the dust. "Some accounts say it's Nicolas

Flamel, a fifteenth-century scribe and seller of rare manuscripts who discovered the philosopher's stone. It is said that two hundred years after his death, he learned the steps to immortality from a *converso* on the road to Santiago, a pilgrimage town on Earthside." He shrugged. "Clearly, it didn't help him much. His corpse still lies here. But this place has been used by other chemists over time, so perhaps something lies here for you now."

Titus hunkered down by one of the boxes, his eye caught by spidery writing on the labels. Hemlock, deadly nightshade, snakeroot and rosary pea. All deadly poisons in the right dosage. Sometimes, the same compound could be used in small measure for the good of the patient and where there was poison, there was often an antidote.

The alchemical symbols covering the central stone sarcophagus brought back memories of studying books in the Warlord's forbidden library back in Old Aleppo. He would creep in at night to read after a day of hard training and no matter how tired he was, Titus always made time to learn. He was muscular and physically powerful, even as a teenager, so it was assumed he was more brawn than brains. But his mother encouraged him to read from an early age and above all, Titus valued knowledge.

When the Warlord caught him one night with a chemistry book and tested him on his knowledge, Kosai directed him into munitions, helping to research new compounds for war. But Titus had learned enough to understand the balance in nature — that what can destroy can sometimes heal, and perhaps that applied to people as well as plants. After he joined the Resistance, he swore that he would only use his knowledge to help the people of the Borderlands from then on.

Titus knew that the drug Liberation had a natural plant base, grown in vast fields on the plains out east. Perhaps lupine or locoweed, known to cause birth defects in animals, but not strong enough to bring on miscarriage. It was mutated with magic, imbued with something that encouraged the genetic makeup of the fetus to develop new powers, some never seen before. Every day it was used in the population meant more children born under the veil of shadow.

Enough. He would not let it continue any longer.

Titus turned to Finn. "We need a still. Look for glass flasks of different sizes." He pointed to the benches and boxes on the far side. "Search those — but be gentle. This stuff is fragile and you don't want to break open one of those bottles. Who knows what we might breathe in?"

Finn hunted through the boxes, and Titus searched his side of the room. He needed to distill the liquid down to understand what it was made of. Perhaps that way he might discover some method to neutralize it. But of course, that would only reverse the natural element of the drug. The magical part could only be stopped by destroying the manufacturing plant. Perhaps his munitions expertise might come in handy, after all.

He pulled out another box and picked through the vials, carefully examining each before laying them gently aside. His fingers were soon covered in the dust of years, but he kept going at a steady pace. As every minute passed, time ticked away for his wife and the baby that grew inside her.

Maria had trained alongside him in the Shadow Guards, a lithe athlete with a ready laugh who pulled him out of the library on sunny days to dance in the water fountains and make love in the dappled olive groves. But he had not known that the women of the guards were encouraged to take Liberation, and if they rejected the drug, it was dosed in their food, anyway. When Maria found herself pregnant, they rejoiced — until the moment she found herself craving the drug, then demanding it, a slave to the blue addiction. That's when Titus had turned to the Resistance for help.

Now Maria lay tied to a bed in the rebel base in the

mountains, screaming as she went through never-ending withdrawal, her mind lost to the drug. The child growing within would likely be mutated and if discovered, it would be sent for evaluation. The Resistance camps were full of such children now, born in secret, some physically altered, others with anomalous abilities, others still completely normal — or so it seemed.

If Titus could find an antidote for Maria in time, maybe their child would be one of the lucky ones. He could only do what lay within his power — and he knew chemistry. He could not hide in the mountains listening to her scream when his action might save her and so many others.

"Is this it?" Finn's voice broke into his thoughts and Titus spun around.

Finn held a glass alembic, an alchemical still made from two glass vessels connected by a downward-sloping tube. It was dusty, but it would be enough.

Titus cleared a space on the bench top. "Put it here, gently now." Finn placed it down with care and wiped the glass with the edge of his shirt.

Titus searched in the same box and found an iron tripod, dulled to a dusty grey, to hold the alembic above a flame. He set up the equipment, part of him wishing he had lived in the mysterious time when the alchemists searched for the secrets of transformation. In another life, perhaps Titus could have joined the search for the philosopher's stone or the perilous route to immortality. For alchemists did not merely seek to turn base metal to gold. That was mere camouflage for their real mission, the true metamorphosis of nature itself.

With the alembic in place, Titus poured the blue liquid inside, hoping that whatever had been in it last was long evaporated and would not contaminate the sample. Finn lit the tiny pool of oil underneath the flask and within seconds, it began to bubble.

The first drop of liquid appeared at the top of the connecting pipe and slid down into the receiving beaker, with another following. Titus caught the next on his fingertip, its color now faint blue, like the reflection of water in ice. He sniffed it first — only a slight hint of sweetness, like honeysuckle in a far-off hedgerow. He touched a tiny amount to his tongue, closed his eyes and concentrated on the sensation. Chemists down the ages had relied on this most basic of tests and there was no time for anything much more sophisticated right now.

A definite sweetness followed by a dry mouth, his heart beating faster almost immediately. Signs of one of the most deadly plants, easily grown in terrains throughout the Borderlands. Laced with magic, certainly, but the base was a common noxious weed. Titus opened his eyes.

"It's mostly belladonna, sometimes called deadly nightshade. I'm sure of it. The antidote can be extracted from the seeds of the Calabar bean, which in itself is a poison, so it must be used carefully. The alchemist must have had some." He searched the bench, rifling through bottles of multi-hued powders.

Finn investigated the opposite side of the tomb. "What does it look like?"

"Black, small like a coffee bean. Maybe ground powder or perhaps in pods about six inches long."

After a few minutes, Titus unearthed an ebony box and opened the lid to find a black powder inside. A hand-written label pasted on the inside noted the danger of the Calabar. "Found it."

"How do we know it will work?" Finn asked.

Titus sighed. "We can't know for sure. The only way is to take it back to the trader town and test it. The midwife I know is ready to try anything to save the women and children in her care. She'll help us."

Titus held the box in his hand, knowing that the powder

was just as much a poison as Liberation itself. But in the chemistry of plants, this was often true. Dosage was everything and what could save one might kill another.

It was a step in the right direction and he had to do something practical or he would go crazy with thoughts of Maria's torment. Every night he dreamed of mutated babies thrown into blood pits at the Castle of the Shadow, their tiny faces contorted in screams. Action was the only way he knew how to deal with it all — and he would keep going until Liberation was ended, or until he was.

"Check the boxes for any more of it," Titus said. "And anything labeled with Manchineel. But whatever you do, don't get it on your skin. In tiny doses, Manchineel can counteract belladonna, but it is one of the most toxic plants, known as the little apple of death."

Finn gave a rueful smile. "And I thought my sword was the best weapon."

After an inch by inch search of the place, they collected up five boxes of powder, three of Calabar and two of Manchineel. Titus wrapped them carefully with lengths of rag found in piles beneath the benches so the boxes wouldn't leak and then loaded them carefully into backpacks.

At the door to the tomb, he looked back at the cornucopia of alchemy. He could only hope to amass such a heritage by the time he left this earth. Perhaps there would be time after they had ended the Liberation addiction for him to pursue the knowledge he craved. But not today.

Together, Finn and Titus rolled back the stone and left the ruined temple. As they hiked back through the desert, energy renewed by their find, Titus outlined his plan.

"This will be enough for initial tests in the trader town. Once we know what works, we can source more antidote ingredients. They're tropical plants, so we'd need to go inland."

Finn nodded. "I know of such a place where we might

find them. It has giant beasts and the produce of the rainforest might be just as bountiful."

"We can send a team out there to find more." Titus couldn't help the grin on his face, encouraged by their find and its potential. "While you manage that, I'll take a tiny batch to the mountains for Maria. She'll be well again, the baby will be perfect. This will work, Finn, I know it."

As they walked on through the night, Titus thought three steps ahead, planning the mechanism by which they might harvest the drugs, how long it might take to produce a batch of antidote, and how they could get it to the farthest reaches of the Borderlands. He carried hope on his back and for now, that was enough.

CHAPTER 7

Sienna couldn't have walked much more slowly to the door of the medical wing of the Ministry, but since Bridget wouldn't let her leave with the team until a doctor had cleared her, she forced herself to go. She tried to think of it as a positive step, valuable preparation before what could be an arduous journey, but her limbs were heavy as if her very being rejected the idea of such help.

Like all the doors of the Ministry, this one was solid wood. A dark grained ebony embedded with a carved Rod of Asclepius, a serpent entwined around a staff, representing the Greek god of healing and medicine. The rod was made from willow bark, used in many cultures as a pain reliever. All of this should have made Sienna feel better, but a sense of foreboding rose inside as she raised a hand to push at the door. There were stories of those who entered here and never emerged again. But there was nothing she could do but face whatever would come. She braced herself and walked inside.

The ancient wooden door disguised ultra-modern facilities within. A waiting room with comfy chairs decorated in shades of sage green, the relaxing scent of lavender. But underneath the calm, Sienna could make out the beep of medical devices in the ward beyond and the smell of antiseptic that betrayed the true nature of this place.

Her pulse raced at the possibility of being trapped here. She would not be entombed in the bowels of the earth. She turned to duck back out the door.

"Welcome!" The voice was warm and sweet, like peppermint tea served to guests as hospitality. An open gesture that promised no harm.

Sienna stopped, took a deep breath and turned round.

Dr Rachel Tabib was rounded and bespectacled, short and plump with a wide smile. Her straight dark hair was tied back in a no-nonsense ponytail and her Middle Eastern origins were clear in her darker skin and slight accent.

Rachel smiled. "Were you leaving?"

A beat of silence as Sienna considered her options. She could leave now, avoid all of this. Would Bridget really stop her from traveling to the Borderlands? She might want to, but Sienna knew her magic was necessary, so she'd probably be allowed to go, anyway.

But as she looked into Rachel's eyes, she sensed no threat, only gentleness and a desire to help. There was almost a hum of healing magic around the doctor, as if she had a hive of golden bees inside, producing honey to soothe those in need.

Sienna shook her head. "I'm staying."

Rachel indicated an open door behind her. "Please come this way."

The smell of antiseptic grew stronger as they walked together down a corridor to a suite of examination rooms. A nurse walked past and glanced down at Sienna's arms, his eyes widening in concern. Sienna pulled the sleeves of her t-shirt down, covering the tendrils of black that grew more intense as her anxiety rose. She tried to dampen them down, breathing deeply to calm her fear. The Shadow fed on such emotion and she could only keep it in check if she controlled herself.

Once inside the examination room, Rachel closed the door. "I saw what you did out there. Can I see your arms now?"

Sienna pulled up her sleeves again to reveal the marks already fading to grey.

Rachel reached out a hand. "May I?"

Sienna nodded.

The doctor's touch was feather light as she traced the whorls, her gaze following the patterns. "I've never seen them fade so quickly."

"I have more." Sienna's voice wavered a little, and she felt the prick of tears. She realized how much concern she had been holding inside and how worried she really was about the marks.

Rachel stepped back and Sienna pulled off her t-shirt to stand in her bra. Her skin prickled in the cool air and she was acutely aware that she must look diseased or infected. Tainted by darkness.

But the doctor's eyes brightened. "They're beautiful, Sienna. Truly, I've never seen anyone like this, not here in the wards or in any of the Ministry records."

"What is it usually like?"

Rachel sighed and shook her head, as if seeing the faces of lost patients before her. "The Shadow usually presents as a stain through the blood and blooms on the skin like a bruise. Once it reaches a certain point, the individual is overwhelmed and slips into a coma of nightmares."

Sienna remembered the horror of the shadow weave and felt her chest constrict. The whorls darkened and swirled across her skin, moving like constellations, their power held in check until an inevitable explosive end. They spun faster, obscuring the freckles on her pale skin.

Rachel reached behind her to press the emergency call button, her eyes wide with panic.

"Wait," Sienna said. She closed her eyes and thought of her grandfather's map shop, the rustle of paper like stalks of corn in a summer field edged with poppies, the smell of elderflower as she walked along the canal and the sound of birdsong. As her breath returned to an even cadence, tension releasing from her body, she sensed the marks fade. She opened her eyes.

Rachel stood in stunned silence. "You can control it?"

Sienna nodded. "I think so. I just don't know how much I can take, or how long I could do it for, or under what conditions. I have so many questions and no one to talk to."

Rachel held out a hand and took Sienna's. "You can talk to me, but I can't possibly understand what you're going through. Nobody can."

Sienna pulled her long-sleeved t-shirt back on. "I don't want Bridget or my father to know how extensive this is. They'll stop me going to the Borderlands again."

"They want to protect you."

Sienna nodded. "Yes, but I need to discover what this means. Something draws me back there. I have dreams …"

Rachel froze. "Dreams?"

"Of the Tower of the Winds, voices calling my name. I'm flying with creatures who might tear me apart, but I long to soar with them between the worlds."

"That's more like the reports of those who slip into shadow coma. They talk of being called over there, of desperately wanting to go. Be careful, Sienna, the Shadow is not always what it seems."

"What could happen to me?" Sienna asked softly.

Rachel met her gaze without flinching. "Come to the ward. See for yourself."

Without waiting for a reply, Rachel walked to the door, and a second later, Sienna followed. Behind the examination rooms, there was another row of doors. Like much of the Ministry below the streets of Bath, it extended in unexpected directions. Sienna suspected magical layers to the geography as it was impossible to see how there was space for everything down here.

Rachel pushed open one of the doors to a darkened space

beyond, lit only by occasional lamps that cast golden pools of light onto faces of sleeping patients. She beckoned and together they stepped onto the ward, walking softly between the beds.

It was calm and quiet and for a moment, Sienna wondered why there were such dire stories about the place. The patients looked well cared for and at peace. Then she noticed the black lines running under their skin, the marks of shadow holding them in a netherworld from which they could not escape.

A moan came from one of the beds.

Monitors beeped faster and a distant alarm sounded from outside the ward. The sound of running footsteps.

A young woman thrashed against her padded shackles, terrified of something in her nightmare. She howled, an animal sound from the core of what remained of her humanity, the part of her that could still respond. The lines of her IV drip stretched as she arched her body off the mattress, straining to escape her bonds.

Sienna wanted to run, but she couldn't tear her eyes away. Thoughts of the shadow weave that Sir Douglas had trapped her in surfaced once more, memories of teeth and claws that ripped into soft flesh, devouring what was left of her. To be trapped in something like that was beyond terrible.

The nurse they had passed earlier jogged in, his concentration fixed on the patient. He nodded briefly at Rachel, then went to the woman's side. He pressed a button to increase the dose of sedative and after a moment, the terrified woman lapsed back into fitful unconsciousness. But her mouth still twisted in pain, her fingers clutching at the sheets.

"Can't you help her?" Sienna whispered. "She's still in distress."

Rachel shook her head. "We've tried so many things and continue to experiment with more. But the coma is powerful, and the Shadow has its hooks in deep. Each of these Mapwalkers invited it in, a drop for every use of magic. You know the dangers, Sienna, and even though you have some ability to control it, who knows where that may lead. The only way to wake these people up is to take them into the Borderlands."

"So why keep them here?"

Rachel frowned. "What would happen to them over there? Slaughtered by the Warlord, sucked dry of their magic in one of the dark chambers, or turned into Shadow Cartographers like Sir Douglas Mercator — perhaps the deepest cut of all. I have heard of what goes on over there."

"But there is also beauty, and good people fighting in the Resistance — and hope for a different future." Sienna walked over to the bed and looked down at the young woman, her body and mind ravaged by a nightmare. "Perhaps even a way to end all this."

Rachel came to stand next to her. "If you think there is a chance, I won't stop you — I'll tell Bridget you have time left before the stain is critical — but you have to understand the danger, Sienna. I don't want to see you in one of these beds."

* * *

As dawn turned the sky coral-pink, Titus and Finn reached the outskirts of the trader town. Early morning workers emerged from the doors of the shanty-town huts, eyes blearily assessing the strangers before turning away.

Titus led the way, weaving through narrow lanes until they reached the densely populated center of town. Larger buildings made of stone and brick lined these streets, designed to last longer than the outer camp dwellings. Wealthy merchants lived in the upper floors, a world away from the living conditions of those they enslaved. Their servants lived in warrens of underground rooms beneath.

Over the years, these basement dwellings had been sublet, knocked together and turned into enterprises for the working class. In one such subterranean cellar, deep down and heavily insulated, Kabila the midwife helped women give birth away from the prying eyes of the Shadow Guards, those who would take the babies or even the women themselves for the camps.

Titus paused at a small wooden hatch in the side of one house, more like a hurricane shelter than a proper door. He knocked once, twice, once again, then waited.

A minute later, the hatch opened slightly.

Kabila smiled up at him, the lines on her face deepening in a broad smile. "Come in, come in."

Titus clambered inside and Finn followed close behind, shutting the hatch behind him and bolting it securely.

Kabila walked ahead down a tunnel with a ceiling so low, both Titus and Finn had to bend down. The midwife was short and wide with ample curves draped in a faded red sari embroidered with silver thread, a remnant of her Indian heritage.

She had told Titus about her early memories one night as they sat waiting for the guards to pass by overhead, how she had been aboard one of the refugee boats escaping a flood. Her family had found themselves lost in the dark and woken to find themselves in the Borderlands. Titus would never forget the look on her face as she recounted the terror of being torn from her mother's arms, from seeing her father beaten to the ground, her older sister taken by the guards for the Fertility Halls.

Kabila had been sold as a child slave to the household of the wealthy merchant whose house she still lived beneath so many years later. When she had outlived her use for her master's pleasure, she worked in the kitchens, learning from women in the warrens all the ways she could help the girls of the trader town. Kabila had eventually taken on the mantle of underground midwife, while still maintaining her day job above ground. It was dangerous work. The soldiers of the Shadow would be only too happy to destroy the rebels helping women in trouble, but Kabila saw her lost sister in every young woman saved and she lived for the cause.

"Come and have tea." The midwife led them into a cozy kitchen with low stools around a small table. Everything down here was compact and basic, but somehow it felt welcoming and just as it should be. Titus glimpsed a room beyond with a simple bed over a stone floor, scrubbed clean of the blood shed in childbirth, but still bearing marks from the suffering within. He thought of Maria, tied to such a bed in the mountains, screaming his name. He shook his head to clear the image.

Kabila filled a rustic teapot with leaves and boiling water and let it steep on the table, steam rising from its spout in spirals. She placed cups down before it and then sat, hands folded in her lap, her eyes alive with curiosity.

"Now, tell me what you found."

Titus pulled the black boxes from the pack and explained what they had found in the alchemist's tomb.

"I'm sure the base of Liberation is made from belladonna. If we can try an antidote for that, perhaps the magic will not take in the womb."

As he explained the plan, Titus knew his words sounded farfetched. He saw doubt in Kabila's eyes. What had seemed possible under the moon faded away in the harsh light of day. His words trailed off ...

Finn continued for him. "You could test these compounds and find the best option, then I can source more of these ingredients from the rainforest. We can make more of it. Send it all over the Borderlands. It's possible, isn't it?"

Kabila picked up the teapot and poured the tea, the sound of liquid sloshing into the cups filling the silence.

"Even if you're right, an antidote for belladonna means nothing."

Titus began to protest, but she raised a hand to stop him. "I've worked with it for decades, that and all the other medicinal plants. I know when to use them and when to hold off. You're not telling me anything new. Believe me, I have tried everything. The magic is responsible for mutation. The belladonna might carry it, but magic is the key."

She fell silent and took a sip of her drink.

Titus sighed and shook his head. "I had hoped that somehow this might be new knowledge, that there was a simple way to stop the abomination."

Kabila smiled kindly. "Life is never simple." She put her cup down. "And now I have something for you." The midwife rose and bent to a low cupboard, opened it and pulled a package from within. She handed it to Titus. "This came late last night by messenger from the rebel base."

Kabila put her hand on his arm, squeezing gently, with an expression Titus had seen on her face before when she told families of a death. A deep sense of foreboding rose within him.

He took the package, recognizing the handwriting from one of the women who cared for Maria and other addicts in the rebel camp. He tore open the seal and unwrapped it, barely constraining the sob that rose within at what he saw.

The necklace he had given to Maria on their wedding day, a tiny silver hummingbird representing the grace and speed at which she moved and the pace of their love. A folded note lay alongside it.

Titus flattened it out with one trembling hand as cold fear spread through his limbs. His vision blurred as tears ran down his cheeks, dropping onto the ink. He wanted to wash away the terrible words and then perhaps they could not be true.

"She's dead," he gasped. "She died giving birth to a misshapen corpse. A monster."

As he sank to the floor, Finn knelt with him and Titus sobbed into his friend's embrace as he clutched the tiny hummingbird in one fist.

Images of their love flooded back to him — stolen kisses in the library, lazy hours entwined under the apple trees in the orchard, running together over the hills, the sound of Maria's laugh echoing across the valley. He would never touch her skin again, never feel safe in her embrace, never hear her say his name. His heart emptied, each tear wrung from his wretched soul.

After the wave of despair passed over, Titus let the rage come. He would avenge Maria's death. He had nothing left to lose.

He pulled away from Finn and wiped his eyes. "We go east to the camp where they make Liberation. There's a munitions store on the way. We'll get explosives and stop this thing at the source."

Finn nodded. "I'm with you, brother."

CHAPTER 8

SIENNA WALKED OUT OF the medical wing with Rachel's warning echoing through her mind and a vision of the young woman's hand clutching at the sheets, white-knuckled as she faced an unending nightmare. Would she end up that way if she crossed the border once more?

"Sienna, wait a moment."

Her father's voice made her turn and Sienna waited in the corridor for him to catch up.

John Farren's gait was hobbled, his back torn beyond repair from the tortures of the dungeon below the Castle of the Shadow. He kept the suffering from his face most of the time, but Sienna knew that chronic pain tormented him at night, and plagued his waking hours. She had once believed her father lost on an expedition many years ago, and perhaps it was best to think that was still true. She had not told her mother that he still lived, partly because those old wounds had healed and they had both moved on, but also because of Bridget. Sienna had glimpsed the love between her father and the new Illuminated, but there was little hope for them now to act upon those feelings. Sienna could only hope that she and Finn could transcend their different paths and find a way to be together.

As her father reached her, Sienna wrapped her arms

around him, clasping his shoulders, careful not to press against his back. John winced a little, then relaxed into her hug, putting his arms around her in his turn. They stood for a moment, breathing together. Sienna could hear his heartbeat, still strong in his chest, the magic that ran through both their veins part of a long line of Blood Mapwalkers. There were so few of them left now, and still so much to do on both sides of the border.

John pulled away. "Be careful over there." His blue eyes darkened, like waves upon a storm-borne sea. "The balance of power has shifted and there is nothing in the annals to help us navigate this new time."

"It will be okay, Dad. Mila and Perry will be with me, and I'm sure we'll get through, find Finn and the Resistance and work with them."

John shook his head. "A cross-border alliance has never worked. Our worlds are ever more divergent and the Borderlanders are right to want their share of wealth. I fear it is too late for compromise."

Sienna smiled. "Your generation tried one way, now let mine try another. The Ministry has survived much, and it will continue on, I promise."

John bent forward and kissed her forehead. "I'm proud of you," he whispered. "And I know your grandfather would be, too. Go safe."

* * *

A few hours later, Zoe joined the Mapwalker team in the Gallery of Geographical Maps. She looked around with fascination at the long corridor, its walls painted with bird's-eye scenes of distant lands. Each was a portal, a simple way to travel through space and time with minimal use of Mapwalker magic.

They stood in front of a map of modern Egypt, made notable by the disruption of the Nile by Lake Nasser, but Zoe could see traces of another layer beneath, a magical map that would allow them to travel through. Now she had learned to shift her vision, she could not unsee the contours of the world beneath the real. It gave her a mild sense of vertigo even at this level. How much more would she feel if she navigated the threads below? She tried to quash her fear, digging her nails into her palms. She was determined to be worthy of this assignment.

Mila and Perry stood with backpacks on, faces set with determination as they gazed into the desert land before them. Both were around her age, but they had an air of experience that Zoe lacked. Mila moved with a liquid grace, but Zoe had heard tales of her ability to hold her own in a fight. Perry was muscular, his arms bulging against the seams of his jacket, his face that of a young god. He looked over and gave a smile. Zoe blushed a little as their eyes locked. Perhaps this trip wouldn't be so bad, after all.

The door opened, and Sienna walked in with a palpable sense of purpose. She walked to the map of Egypt and then turned to face Zoe.

"Have you traveled this way before?"

Zoe shook her head.

Sienna smiled and held out a hand. "Just hold on and keep breathing."

Mila and Perry gathered round and laid their hands on Sienna's. She reached out with her other hand and entered the map.

Zoe watched the golden threads part and suddenly, they were inside the fabric itself. She tried to catch her breath, but the rush was like a wind tunnel. It was all she could do to keep her balance as nausea rose violently inside. Sounds of rushing water surrounded her, a cacophony that made her want to cover her ears, but she couldn't let go of Sienna for fear of being trapped here between the threads of the world.

Under the sound of the storm, Zoe heard a voice.
Sienna.

A voice made up of thousands of souls, a sound that made her both shiver in fear and want to run toward it. Something seductive and powerful, something that promised the world and only asked one thing in return.

A bump. A crash.

The ground rushed up to meet her and Zoe tumbled to the desert floor, retching and coughing, spitting up the bile that rose in her mouth. Her head throbbed, her muscles ached. If this was mapwalking, then she'd stick with an airplane next time.

Zoe groaned and rolled onto her back. The sky brooded with heavy rain clouds and a falcon hovered in the warm air currents high above; the bird representing Horus, the Egyptian god of the sky and protector of the realm. Its cry pierced the air, a haunting sound of melancholy.

"Here, drink this." Perry handed her a bottle of water. Zoe sat up and took a sip. "First time is rough. But you get used to it."

Mila gave a terse laugh as she dusted herself off. "Well, some people do."

Sienna stood a little way off, looking out over the lip of a quarry. She turned as they reached her and for a moment she caught Zoe's gaze, a question in her eyes. The voice — perhaps the others had never heard it — but now was not the time to speak of what it might mean. Zoe gave a slight nod and a look of understanding passed between them.

"Wow, look at this place." Perry gazed out across the valley, a deep scar in the earth pitted with excavation, as the others came to stand with him.

"The great monuments of ancient Egypt were built from this rock," Zoe said. "The land was barren outside the reaches of the Nile, the only place where human life could thrive, but this place made their construction possible."

Countless slaves toiled and died here, their blood soaking the earth, augmenting the coppery red of the layers below. In the millennia since, the quarry had been partially filled in by the sands of the desert. A ruined village on the southern edge showed evidence that man had tried to flourish here, but rumors of a cursed land and the inhospitable landscape kept people away for generations.

Mila shivered as a sharp wind blew across the desert, sending whirlwinds of sand and dust into the air. Clouds gathered overhead and a roll of thunder sounded in the distance. "We need to get moving. That storm's heading straight for us." She turned to Zoe. "So how do we get in?"

Zoe flushed a little, suddenly the center of attention. "Well, um, I think …" The words were heavy in her mouth and it seemed as if everything she knew dissolved to incoherence now they were in the field. She had only ever dealt with manuscripts and papyri, never the genuine thing. This place was three-dimensional, it had texture, it had weather, and the team looked to her to take control.

After a beat of silence, Sienna pointed down the valley. "It looks like there's a change in the rock strata down there. What do you think?"

Zoe knew Sienna was trying to help and the moment of respite allowed a shift in her perspective. As she looked down the valley, she called to mind the papyrus map back at her desk in the Ministry. It had been too fragile to carry with them, but she had committed every detail to memory. She thought of the golden threads and how she had to see differently to allow them to emerge.

She closed her eyes for a second and then opened them again, focusing not on the landscape but in the surrounding air, softening her gaze until … Zoe gasped, grinning in delight as the world shifted and suddenly she could see the warp and weft of threads that held the environment together. There was a knot of stitches in the valley below and filaments that stretched down into the earth. It must be the opening to the funerary complex.

"What is it? What can you see?"

Sienna's voice startled Zoe, and the threads dissolved as quickly as they had appeared.

"I ... I saw the complex down there. I know the way now."

Zoe stumbled a little, suddenly weak, her head spinning.

Sienna put a hand out to steady her. "Careful now, we don't want to lose you so soon." Her voice was gentle. "Do you know how to use your weaver magic?"

Zoe looked into her eyes, meeting the young woman's more experienced gaze. "I thought it was just for restoration, but I think there might be more to it. I can see threads running through the earth, binding the world."

Sienna smiled. "There are often surprising elements to our gifts. Don't worry. We've all been through it. Just trust that it will emerge at the right time." As she spoke, shadows darkened in her eyes, thunderclouds gathering in a reflection of the storm above. Zoe blinked, and they were gone.

The team set off down the edge of the quarry, slip-sliding on the scree, careful not to trip over the rocks. The wind picked up and funneled through the valley, whistling through piles of strewn boulders like a warning in this desolate place. But there was life even here, clumps of prickly shrubs with small leathery leaves and tiny succulents with sharp spines. Zoe caught sight of a small furry creature darting under a rock as they approached, maybe one of the desert gerbils endemic to the area. As she turned her head to watch it run, she skidded on the loose stones. Perry reached out a hand to steady her.

"Careful, we need you." He smiled and Zoe's heart beat a little faster. Did he hold her hand for just a second longer than was necessary?

Rain pattered down as the Mapwalkers reached the bottom of the valley. By the time they made it to where Zoe thought the entrance would be, it poured down in sheets of wind that slammed against the rocks as if nature itself tried to stop their progress. They were all soaked through, dripping wet, cold and desperate to get under shelter.

They hurried to a pile of enormous blocks of stone, each one carved from the quarry and discarded here — or perhaps placed specifically to camouflage the entrance. Zoe relaxed her gaze and once again, saw the golden thread weaving its way through.

"This is definitely it."

Perry frowned. "How do we get inside? There's no way we can move these blocks ourselves."

Sienna placed her hands on the stone pile. "Now we're here, I can draw a map and take us inside."

Mila shook her head. "No need. But you all need to stand way back if I'm going to do this."

The others walked up and away from the entrance, high enough to be out of range but still close enough to see. Zoe's skin tingled with the cold of the rain but also with the anticipation of what might happen, of the thrill of being here with the Mapwalker team.

As the storm raged above them, Mila lifted her hands, then her face to the rain. Her clothes were soaked through and it was as if her skin underneath became one with the water. Mila reached for the deluge and brought it down in a torrent, using it to sweep under one of the heavy stone blocks and move it to the side of the entrance, lifting and floating it away as if on flood waters. She directed the rain as a symphony, sweeping it down from the heavens above and swirling the rocks away from the entrance. Mila's face rippled with joy as the surge washed around her. This was her element, and Zoe felt a sense of privilege to see the Waterwalker so transformed. Would she ever be that confident in her magic?

Once she had uncovered the entrance, Mila swirled the

water away from the quarry floor, pinning her flood behind the barrier of rocks now placed like a dam to one side. But it didn't stop the rainfall that still poured down upon them, trickling down into the revealed mouth of the complex below.

Mila beckoned, and the team jogged back down to the entrance. "Let's get inside, then I'll seal it up behind us with some rocks. We don't want a flood following us down there."

Zoe stepped inside the rough-hewn tunnel, chisel marks still visible in the stone overhead. It was just big enough for them to walk upright, although Perry's head almost touched the ceiling. As they descended, torches in hand, she wondered about the forgotten people who had dug this place, whether they had died here, their bones becoming part of history.

As they rounded a corner out of sight of the entrance, Mila dropped back and a moment later, a resounding crash echoed through the tunnel. Flakes of rock dropped from the ceiling from thin fissures above that seemed to widen as they watched. Zoe held her breath, aware of the tons of rock above, suddenly conscious that they were now barricaded in an ancient tomb, their only way out now blocked by impenetrable slabs of stone. There was no turning back.

A thin stream of water trickled down the tunnel as Mila rounded the corner once more, her footsteps a little weary as the magic took its toll. But Zoe could see that the tattooed Waterwalker welcomed the price for the joy it gave her in the moment.

As the team came together again, Perry led them on. "Let's see what's down here."

He walked on with confident steps as the tunnel wound down into the earth. Zoe recalled that the chambers of the complex were several stories down, so they were probably entering from one of the side tunnels. Etchings marked the walls of the corridor and occasionally, a few crude paintings, but nothing of the skill or importance of the art in the Valley of the Kings. These were only rudimentary slashes and fragments of curses that Zoe recognized from funerary texts. Nothing remarkable. Could this really be the right place?

They turned a last corner and Perry stopped in surprise; the others halting quickly behind him.

The tunnel ended in a low doorway, a crawl space into blackness beyond. Above it, an ancient god looked down upon them with eyes of deep blue lapis lazuli, its hideous features a dire warning. The head of a Nile river crocodile, jagged teeth dripping with blood, its forelegs the powerful body of a lion and its rear, the thick hide of a hippopotamus. It was carved into the rock and outlined in precious stones, surrounded by curses etched deep into stone.

"Ammit, devourer of the dead," Zoe whispered. "Made up of the three dread creatures the Egyptians feared the most. He eats the hearts of the impure if they are weighed and found wanting."

Mila bent down and shone her torch into the black hole. "And we're meant to crawl into this?" She looked up at Zoe. "Are you sure this is the right way?"

Sienna stepped forward. "It's the Map of the Impossible, it's not going to be a walk in the park, is it?" She pointed up to a series of hieroglyphics. "I recognize these from my grandfather's journal. This has to be the right way."

She bent down and crawled into the dark, the light from her torch vanishing quickly. Zoe held her breath, part of her expecting to hear a scream, a crash, a moan.

A moment later, Sienna's excited voice came echoing back. "You guys need to come and see this."

CHAPTER 9

It was a relief to get away from the image of the devouring god and out of the constricting tunnel. The vault stretched away into the shadows, the far end out of sight, but the echo of their voices showed how large the space was. Perry stood up, looking around as Mila and Zoe brushed dust from their clothes. His gaze lingered on the restorer for a moment. Something about her made him want to know more. Perhaps this mission would give him the opportunity.

Sienna stood shining her torchlight ahead. "What is this place?"

Her words were clearly directed at Zoe, the only one of them who knew much about ancient Egypt, but Perry couldn't help but feel it was a broader question. They had thought this was some kind of entrance to the Borderlands, perhaps a simple portal like the gate in the Circus at Bath, but this was far more than a doorway.

It was some kind of antechamber and bundles of cloth covered every inch of the floor, discolored with age, dirty yellow-brown wrappings around a bulbous center.

"What are they?" Perry nudged one with his toe, grimacing as it rolled heavily to the side, crunching on a layer of loose stones beneath. "Ugh. There's definitely something in there."

He shivered a little, trying not to imagine what lay inside.

Zoe bent to look at the bundle more closely. "The Egyptians mummified all kinds of creatures. Cats, crocodiles, mice and ibis amongst them."

Mila shone her torch at the wall, illuminating paintings of hundreds of birds. Hooked bills like scythes, black eyes made of obsidian beads that flashed as the light touched them, as if they watched the intruders from centuries past.

"I guess they're ibis, but why so many?"

Zoe pulled out a pen from her pack and used the end to prod at the mummified creature, trying to ease the wrappings aside. "There might be amulets here, evidence of what they represent. I've read of sacrificial chambers at Sakkara with thousands of dead ibis inside, offerings to Thoth—"

"God of wisdom, writing and magic," Sienna finished for her.

Zoe looked up. "Yes, you know of him?"

"My grandfather's journal contains much about Thoth, postulating that the priests who served him were some of the earliest Mapwalkers. Those who combined writing and magic, who created living worlds with their inscriptions — and their paintings."

"Makes sense," Perry said as he took a tentative step forward, trying not to tread on any of the shrouded bodies. "But whatever the reason, we have to get through this chamber. Let's move on."

He took another step, holding out his arms for balance as he gingerly tiptoed around the ancient corpses. The thought of the dust and bones and feathers and dried blood of millennia made him want to get out of there fast. The others gathered their things and followed in his footsteps.

A crunch as Perry stepped on more of the loose stones. These were larger chunks, and he rolled a little on his ankle. Steadying himself, he looked down, the light from his head-torch reflecting off … what was that? He bent down to look more closely and then stood up sharply. The others stopped at his alarm.

"Bones. Human, by the look of them." He pointed down, not wanting to move for the unbearable crunch that would inevitably come.

Sienna crouched down and examined the detritus on the chamber floor. "You're right. Human bones, dismembered. They have weird patterns on them, like tiny slashes. I wonder …" She looked up at the wall paintings where the ibis stood on the banks of the Nile, their beaks like scythes.

As she spoke, Perry saw a movement in the darkness near the wall, as if a shudder passed through one of the bundles. Mila saw it too and shone her light toward it, just as the mummies began to twitch and shake. Perry frowned, a moment of confusion before he realized what was happening.

The things inside were trying to get out.

"Move!" Mila shouted as the shuddering spread across the floor, the bundles rolling and lurching. The thud of bodies hitting each other and bumping against the walls echoed about the chamber as clouds of dust rose into the air.

The Mapwalkers ran through the field of mummified creatures, covering their mouths as they coughed, eyes streaming as dust obscured the way.

Perry led them on, no longer caring where his feet landed, relishing the crunch of bodies under his stride, each one a broken beast that could no longer emerge from the grave.

A cry behind him.

Perry stopped and spun round.

Zoe had slipped and fallen amongst the mummies. As he bent to help her up, he felt the sudden weight of bodies on his back, the slash of tiny knives on his skin. He jerked up and shook himself, seeing for the first time the horror that emerged from the dusty haze.

The remains of mummified ibis, dried flesh hanging from their skeletons, eyes coal black holes in elongated skulls and beaks like sickles, slashing back and forth. They shrieked together, high-pitched calls over guttural grunts, the volume growing as more escaped the bonds of their ancient wrapping.

Two more leapt for him.

Perry pushed Zoe behind his back, shielding her as he opened his palm and released his fire magic. The remains of the two creatures fell to the bone-covered floor. Almost immediately, the burned parts twitched and began to reform into a semblance of a creature, parts of one subsumed into the other — a hybrid corpse.

Perry shuddered as he directed his flame down and finished it off, leaving only ash this time.

Sienna and Mila fought the creatures alongside, batting them away with torches and kicking the birds as they attacked from below. Zoe regained her balance and swung her pack like a mace, using it to beat the birds off.

Together, they could keep the ibis at bay for now ... but they kept coming.

There were so many in the chamber, waves of shrieking dead birds with thousands more to be born anew from the bundles of wrapping that shuddered as the Mapwalkers progressed through the cave. They had to get out of here.

"Follow me!" Perry stepped past Zoe and sent his flame into the darkness ahead, burning a path through the writhing bundles, turning them to ash before they could even emerge. He turned and hurled balls of flame either side of Sienna and Mila, freeing them enough so they could follow.

Together, the four Mapwalkers darted through the tomb, beating back any birds that made it through, pursued by inhuman shrieks.

The end of the chamber emerged through smoke and dust. A solid wall painted with images of ibis slaughtering worshippers of Thoth, bloody limbs hacked from torsos, heads rolling as the birds overran the temple grounds. An avian massacre dedicated to the god who ruled them.

"How do we get out of here?" Sienna shouted above the din of screeches, pounding on the wall with her fists.

"There must be a way." Zoe scanned the wall for anything that might help. "The priests of Thoth would have made a door. The god is often shown carrying an *ankh* symbol, the key to life. Look for that."

Perry stepped in front of them, forming a barricade of fire to keep the birds away as the others scoured the wall, searching for a way out. He could feel the slow creep of shadow seeping into his veins as he blasted the enlivened carcasses, the stink of burned feathers and desiccated flesh filling his senses. This place drained more of him than it should. Something in the atmosphere seemed to deaden his very life force. They had not considered what might rule this place between the worlds, or the risk in crossing it. But it was too late to turn back.

"Hurry, I can't keep this up for too much longer."

Perry understood the price of his magic, and he accepted the risk, even knowing what his father had become. Sir Douglas was one of the great Shadow Cartographers, but Perry was still haunted by the image Sienna had painted of him on their return from the refugee camp on the last mission. She said he was closer to shadow than man now, his material self more inconsequential every day. Perry only wished to reach his father before the end — and have enough flame to finish the man himself.

A skittering noise broke through the roar of the inferno.

The clatter of skeletal feet.

The ibis surged over the barrier of flame, running up the walls and across the ceiling in some perversion of gravity, scything their beaks back and forth as they dive-bombed Perry.

He swung one hand above, burning them with a lance of fire as they dropped. A stinking rain of ash fell in their wake.

Perry retched as it filled his mouth and nose and eyes, chunks of stinking cadaver collecting around his feet. As the birds continued to advance in an unrelenting wave, Perry knew they would drown here in the dust of the dead in this god-forsaken place.

CHAPTER 10

"Here!" Zoe shouted.

The clunk of levers and the sound of stone rasping over sand.

Perry surged his flame into the birds in a final blast of magic. As hands pulled him back into a dark cavity, he burned the last of the ibis, pushing them away as the door swung shut. He sank to the ground, retching and gagging as he spat out the remains of the dead creatures, the taste of the grave lingering in his mouth.

Perry explosively coughed up the last of the feathers, then sank back against the cool stone. "I really don't want to go through that again."

Sienna reached out and placed a finger on his lips, her eyes flashing a warning as she pointed into the chamber beyond.

They sat on a wide ledge above a gigantic cave, the cold of the rock and freezing air a welcome relief from the claustrophobic heat of the ibis chamber.

Mila shone her torchlight out over the expanse, illuminating a roiling, churning mass of serpents below, like an undulating sea. They were all different sizes and colors, writhing together, hissing and rattling at the disturbance above. The giant loop of a colossal snake rose from the mass, each black scale as tall as a man, the powerful musculature of its body pulsing as it moved, slithering beneath its kin. An ancient creature, formed from magic and nightmares.

"Apep," Zoe whispered, her eyes wide. "The giant serpent, embodiment of chaos, sworn enemy of light and truth, devourer of souls."

Perry slumped back against the wall and sighed. "Seriously?"

Sienna pulled her grandfather's journal from her pack and opened it to the pages of hieroglyphics and sketches of the underworld path.

"Here." She pointed to the hand-drawn map. "After the guardians of the gate, presumably the ibis, there is a path of snake charmers. A way through the chamber of serpents."

Zoe pointed at the page. "This also says there is a high path, past the watchers. Perhaps that could be the better way?"

Mila turned her torch toward the ceiling of the chamber. Stalactites dripped from the roof of the cave, some sharp as a blade, others bulbous and curved. They glistened in the light as crystals within flashed with colors of turquoise and emerald, opal and gold. Droplets of water ran down to splash on the serpents below.

Then the light caught what lay beyond and between the needles of rock. Leathery cocoons, over six feet in length, each hanging down over the space below. Each pulsing with life.

"The watchers," Zoe whispered.

Mila thought of the winged statues she had seen in front of the sunken pyramid beneath Ganvié, a battalion of dark angels ready to fight. Could these cocoons be their resting place? She had wished to see such miraculous creatures in the flesh, but down here in the realm of the dead, that suddenly seemed like a bad idea.

Sienna shone her torchlight below the cocoons, following

a scar in the wall, a narrow path between the serpents below and the unknown creatures above. "That way," she said. "As quietly and as carefully as possible."

* * *

Zoe saw the sense in Sienna's choice, but it didn't make it any less terrifying. The ledge curved around out of sight to the left of the cave, a precarious track, wet with dripping water. It looked slippery with only the rock to grasp onto and a precipitous drop to the pit of serpents below.

Perry's magic could be useful if they needed to fight, but he looked exhausted, drained from the battle with the ibis. He struggled to stand, pulling himself up from the wall as they prepared to leave the safety of the ledge. Zoe wanted to reach out and help him up, but she turned away. Perhaps he didn't want to be seen in a moment of weakness.

Mila had also used her magic recently, opening the tomb and controlling the flood, while Sienna had mapwalked them all here from the Ministry. Each of them weakened, drops of shadow pooling in their blood, while her own magic was but a faint glimmer, an almost useless gift.

For a moment, Zoe wished she were back in the calm, safe world of Antiquities, the smell of old books, ink and coffee with the occasional sound of a turning page. No reanimated corpses to fight, no ancient Egyptian nightmares to run from — but no miracles either, no friends with magic in their fingertips, no sense of wonder.

"Are you coming?" Sienna asked softly, as she stood at the edge of the way ahead.

Zoe nodded. "I'll follow you."

The Mapwalker team crept in single file along the trail, Sienna in the lead, then Zoe, with Perry and Mila behind. Zoe hugged the rock face, edging almost sideways to keep as much of her body weight away from the precipice as possible. They walked on in silence, their breath frosting in the air.

Suddenly, Sienna tripped on a rock.

She clutched at the wall and righted herself, but tiny stones skittered off the path, disappearing into the writhing serpents beneath.

Zoe held her breath as the giant snake paused in its movement at the sound. Its head was still buried under the sea of squirming creatures and she really didn't want to see what happened if it emerged.

She had read of Apep's battle with the sun god, Ra, his magical gaze freezing the deity, his undulating body creating earthquakes in the world above. His terrifying roar was said to cause the underworld to shake as he devoured those who trespassed in his realm. To banish chaos and evil, the priests of ancient Egypt would build an effigy of the serpent every year and burn it for protection against the darkness — but the snake would rise again once more.

After a beat of silence, they inched along the track, each halting footstep placed carefully to stay quiet, hands reaching for holes in the rock wall to help steady the way. Sienna turned a corner where the path narrowed even more, disappearing out of sight. Zoe reached a hand around the edge to balance herself—

Her fingers brushed against something hairy, something with thick legs. She gasped as a sharp pain pierced the back of her hand. She jerked her arm back from the rock, glimpsing the orbed body of a spider squatting in the hole as she took a step back — into nothing, falling, tumbling away from the path.

Perry reached for her, his fingers brushing hers, but he couldn't get a grip.

Zoe screamed, her cry echoing around the chamber.

Time slowed, her vision narrowing as she fell, the eyes of the Mapwalkers upon her, helpless to stop her descent.

In that moment of terror, Zoe shifted her vision, and the cave was at once patterned with strings of light and cords of shadow, both making up the weave of the underworld.

Zoe reached for the strands, spinning them into a net of star and shade with the liquidity of water and the strength of rock. It cushioned her fall and held her above the sea of serpents on a web of gold. She lay there, stunned, hardly able to believe what she had just done.

The hiss of the creatures below intensified at the disruption.

"Move!" Mila shouted down.

Perry and Sienna pointed in desperation at something behind her. "Get up here!"

Zoe turned on the web, leaning on its bonds, comfortable in its embrace, sure of her safety — to see the giant serpent rearing up from below.

Its head was flint grey with sharp angular scales, its mouth open as it lunged with bared fangs. Zoe rolled sideways across the weft of strands, the snake's head passing by her so closely that she could feel the rush of air and smell the sulfur stink of its breath.

A drop of its venom fell onto the web, dissolving the cords. The lattice collapsed beneath her.

Zoe clambered away, pulling herself up even as the snake turned to attack once more. Her breath came fast, her arms aching as she tried to haul her body weight up. The golden strings glimmered, flickering in and out as her vision narrowed, her magic fading as fear rose within. She scrambled faster, looking up to the Mapwalkers above. She had to get to them.

Mila stood on the edge of the path, her arms outstretched. She drew drops of water to her from the dripping rocks, spinning them into what looked like a whip.

As the snake lunged for Zoe, Mila lashed out, smashing the creature's head with a spear of icy water. It stopped and turned at the sting, giving Zoe a little more time to pull herself closer to the rock. She climbed, only meters from safety now.

"Come on!" Sienna called down.

Perry lay on the path and reached for her. "Just a few more meters. You can do it!"

Zoe could see the desperation in his eyes, the hope of safety in his outstretched hand.

The snake hissed and lunged again. Mila cracked the whip once more, but the serpent ignored the barb this time, charging at Zoe's dangling legs as she hung from the rock, exhausted and panting with fear. As she looked back, it was as if the Shadow came to life in the creature, knitted together from darkness and magic, its only purpose to protect the way between the worlds.

It opened its mouth wider, closer now. Zoe felt pinned by its stare, hypnotized by the black gleam of obsidian—

A crack of pain on her arm, a sting of water. Mila's lasso.

"Grab it!" Zoe snapped out of her reverie and wrapped the water noose around her, using the last of her magic to wrap golden strands around it, turning the liquid into golden threads strong enough to hold.

The Mapwalker team yanked her up and away as the serpent smashed into the wall where Zoe had been just seconds before. Its frustrated hiss filled the cavern, its writhing brethren joining the chorus in a cacophony of reptilian rage.

They lay panting on the narrow ledge. Zoe sat up, her body shaking with the aftermath of the encounter, her clothes wet from the lasso. She looked at Mila.

"Thank you."

Mila shook her head. "You did most of it. What happened down there anyway? We saw you suspended in thin air, and you did something to my water lasso to make it hold your weight."

Zoe frowned. "You mean you couldn't see the web?"

They all shook their heads. Sienna looked at Zoe with interest. "Your weaver magic seems to be far more than just mending maps."

Perry touched Zoe's arm. "Are you okay?" She looked up into his blue eyes and noted the genuine concern.

"I'm just a little shaky. I'll be okay."

Perry helped her up, his strong arms a welcome sanctuary. "We should get moving—"

A screech cut through the cavern, an inhuman sound like nails scratching on flint, like ice shearing off the face of a berg. Then the flap of giant wings in the dark.

CHAPTER 11

A GIANT BAT FLEW across the cavern toward the Mapwalker team. Its leathery wings were several meters across with ragged claws halfway along. Thick black fur covered its body but its face was hairless, pale skin, an abomination of ridges and scars, an upturned snout above a mouth of razor-sharp teeth. As it dived for the team, it raised its hind legs, each toe topped with a sharp blade to slash its prey to pieces.

The Mapwalkers pressed themselves against the rock, making as small a target as possible. The bat's claws scraped against the stone above, sending a shower of sparks down upon them.

As it flew past and wheeled up into the air, Sienna pushed off from the wall. "Run!"

A ripping sound echoed through the chamber, like flesh torn by a ravenous predator. The cocoons split apart and more giant bats emerged from their sleep, dropping into the black, screeching as they flocked together in a dark mass.

The sound of their cries thrummed through Zoe's body, the pulse of the underworld creating a rhythm along with their running feet. They darted along the path, each footstep on the edge of the precipice, but Zoe was no longer afraid of falling. Something had shifted when she fell, her confidence rising as she learned more about her magic.

The bats dived for them in waves, swiping with sharp claws as the Mapwalker team crouched and ducked and hid in crevices as they ran on. One creature caught Perry's pack, lifting him from the ground. He reached back and shot a ball of flame into the bat. It dropped him quickly, its cry of pain sending the others into a frenzy.

But Zoe could see the toll even this little bit of magic took on Perry. He was still exhausted from the battle with the ibis and they all needed to rest — but there was no respite from the attack.

Sienna ran on, shouting and waving her arms to attract the creatures. "Over here!"

They dive-bombed her, leaving the others alone for a moment, enough time for Perry to catch his breath. Zoe turned back to see Sienna crouching under an overhang, several of the bats scraping at it, trying to pull her out with long talons.

"How much further?" Mila asked in frustration. "This cave is never ending. It's like we're running in circles."

Her words echoed in Zoe's mind, reminding her of something she had seen in the three-dimensional map back in the Ministry, a cavern spiraling into darkness.

"You're right." She pointed down into the mass of snakes below. "It's a circle. The way out is through the bottom of the chamber."

Mila shook her head. "Might have been useful information a little earlier."

Zoe flushed. "I'm sorry, I—"

"A little help over here, guys!" Sienna shouted from beneath the overhang.

Mila spun her water whip, pulling down droplets from the stalactites. She lashed out at the bats, harder now, with a vortex of spinning liquid interspersed with particles of rock. She ripped into the wings of the bats, dark blood spurting from them as they screamed and wheeled away. But above them, the next wave of creatures prepared to dive.

Sienna ran back to where the others stood, her face red with effort, panting for breath. "What are you waiting for? We have to go on."

Mila pointed down. "Apparently it's that way."

Zoe nodded. "I'm so sorry. I only just remembered that the map had a chamber like the circles of hell. The way out is through the bottom."

Perry pointed ahead in the gloom. "She's right. Look, that's where we came in. We've almost run a circle of this damned place."

They gazed down into the mass of serpents, the giant one undulating at the center like an angry god.

"But how do we get down there?" Sienna wondered aloud.

"We jump," Zoe said, a plan forming in her mind even as she shifted her gaze in the cavern. Strings of light and shadow emerged from the darkness, forming a pattern that overlaid the creatures of nightmare. A well of power rose within and she reached out, fingers entwining strands in the air, creating a funnel down into the depths.

"You know we can't see anything, right?" Perry said, his voice doubtful. "You expect us to jump into nothing. Toward them." He pointed down at the pit of snakes.

"You have your magic, I have mine," Zoe said.

Sienna nodded. "We're a team. We trust each other."

Her words gave Zoe a flush of pride, a recognition that she was truly a Mapwalker. But there was no time to enjoy the feeling now. They still had to get out of here alive.

She wove the threads together and then opened them up, creating a space between the serpents below, a funnel of light patterned with shadow. Both needed to make up the underworld.

As she manipulated the strings, Zoe felt eyes upon her. Not the eyes of the team, but something behind the creatures that surrounded them. Something gazed through the deformed snakes and bats, a knowing presence. Zoe shuddered as she felt its icy chill and worked faster. They had to get out of here.

"It's done."

Mila looked into the darkness. "I still don't see anything."

"You won't, but it's there. A funnel of strings that will take us down to the exit below."

"Will it hold if those creatures attack?" Sienna asked.

Zoe shrugged. "I hope so." A screech from above. "But let's not wait around to find out." She looked at the team. "You trust Sienna to walk you through the map. Trust me now."

She stepped out into blackness, shimmering strands of the weave world around her. A sense of power thrummed in the cords as she slid down the funnel toward the rock wall below. The net shifted with the weight of the others as they followed Zoe down. She rested her hands on the strings, sending energy back up to them, cushioning her friends, surrounding them with light. The gleam reflected off the scales of the serpents as they pushed against the lattice, but Zoe knew they could not penetrate her magic — as long as she could hold it together.

She reached the bottom of the cave floor and stood, arms raised, as the others landed around her. Behind them, a round boulder blocked the way ahead.

Mila rolled up to stand. "That was pretty crazy."

"I can't hold the lattice for much longer." Zoe felt the push of the serpents increase behind the light, the weight of their bodies, their slithering presence and hissing sound permeating her net.

One tiny snake dropped through. Perry stamped on its head, crushing it to a pulp. "Then let's get out of here. Help me with this."

Together they pushed the boulder away from the tunnel mouth and eased inside. It was big enough for two abreast if they crouched away from the low ceiling. Mila and Sienna went in first, and Perry helped Zoe inside. She backed away, pulling her net closer and closer, until finally, she used it to pull the boulder back in front of them.

In the darkness beyond, thick bodies thudded against stone as the snakes tried to reach them. But the barrier held.

Perry opened his palm, holding a flicker of light aloft as the four of them cowered in the tunnel. Zoe saw her own exhaustion reflected in the faces of the others. They were physically drained and almost spent of magic. They couldn't fight another battle today.

Mila pulled Kendal Mint Cake from her pack, broke off some pieces and they ate in silence, letting the sugar sweetness return some energy.

"Where next?" Perry asked. "What's at the end of this tunnel? Please, not another creature cavern."

"From what I can remember, it's not much further," Zoe said softly. "We've almost made it through." Her words sounded convincing, but she still felt a presence in the caves, something watching them, something aware of their trespass.

Sienna nodded. "We need to get out of this cave system before we rest. Come on." She got up and walked on, half-crouched, along the tunnel. Mila slowly followed, stretching her limbs as if frozen from the chill of the cave.

Perry helped Zoe up. "That was impressive," he whispered. "Nicely done."

Zoe flushed, appreciating his words as she walked ahead of him in the tunnel, his tiny light a welcome warmth at her back.

* * *

Sienna kept her face toward the tunnel ahead, even as Perry's flame lit the way from behind. She didn't want the others to see her expression because she was terrible at hiding her thoughts and right now, they were dark indeed.

A Shadow presence watched them, she was sure of it, and she thought Zoe felt it, too. The Weaver was a wildcard and something in her magic called to Sienna's own, like the young woman was always meant to be part of the Mapwalker team. And yet, she seemed to know so little about her gift. Sienna smiled to herself in the darkness. She had been in that position herself not so long ago. Perhaps she was still testing the bounds of her own magic.

Their footsteps echoed in the passage as it looped around, each turn making it harder to sense where they were under the earth. Sienna shivered as the chill air touched her skin, turning her breath to frosted mist as she walked. She could smell minerals in the surrounding rock, metallic with a hint of moss and lichen. It was strange to feel so untethered, to have no place of physical reference. This place negated her own magic, because she needed to know where she was and where she was going in the world. Neither was clear right now.

"What's that?"

Mila's voice brought Sienna back to the rocky tunnel. There was a light ahead, brighter than the reach of Perry's flame. It glowed a warm orange, a welcoming glimmer in the dark and cold of this never-ending cave system. But the biting cold snaked into Sienna's blood as she sensed the Shadow strengthening with every step. This place was no sanctuary, but there was no choice. They had to keep moving onward.

Finally, she clambered out of the end of the tunnel, emerging into a hollowed cavern that stretched high above into darkness. Stone walls with arched doorways created a circular space and above them, hundreds, maybe thousands, of niches cut into the rock, like a mausoleum waiting for the remains of the dead.

The light came from an altar, an enormous slab of rock surrounded by thick beeswax candles. Clearly someone tended the place, but Sienna didn't want to find out who would venture down so far.

Mila walked over to a niche and picked up a sharp-edged rock.

Perry came closer to examine it with her. "Obsidian. Volcanic glass." He looked around at the other niches. "There are many different kinds of rock here. What is this place?"

"The map indicated a temple at the heart of the border," Zoe said. "A place between the worlds."

Sienna sensed a shift in the air, like a breeze from above or the last sigh of a dying soul. Perhaps there had been balance here once upon a time, but now it reeked of decay, withering every second their worlds were held apart.

Mila dropped the obsidian, her hold weakened by the toll of the journey. A crash of rock splintering.

"Sorry! I'm so tired." She shook her head and Perry bent to help as she tried to sweep up the fragments from the ground.

"Ow!" Mila jerked upright as a shard bit into her skin. She held up a finger, a drop of blood rolling down … dripping …

Sienna watched it fall toward the slivers of broken obsidian as it reflected the light like glass. A moment of dread rippled through her as blood touched stone.

A smoky haze rose up.

Mila and Perry stepped back as shadow billowed from the rock, a bloom of darkness that coalesced into the faint shape of a woman. With soft curves draped in folds of silk, her lips a perfect bow, her cheekbones high and aristocratic, she looked like an angel trapped in smoke. She spun around in the mausoleum; her face twisted in grief and madness.

Her eyes darted around the cave — a trapped, tormented soul, desperate for escape.

Her gaze alighted on Sienna, and her expression changed. She bared her teeth, growling like a wild animal, her delicate features dissolving into decaying flesh hanging off a skeletal frame. Her visage shifted to that of a demon as she opened a vast mouth with bloody chunks of flesh inside.

She rushed at Sienna with a howl of rage.

CHAPTER 12

FINN AND TITUS WAITED until night fell once more before leaving the safety of the underground hideout for the streets of the trader town. The sounds of raucous laughter came from the usually busy slave square, drunken merchants idling away the hours until their trade in human flesh began once more. While the flow of immigrants had died down when the border closed, they still sold slaves from Uncharted villages to work in the far reaches of the Borderlands. There was no end to the appetite for servants and with the breeding program ever expanding, girls were particularly sought after.

Finn pulled his cloak tighter and ducked into the alleyway behind the houses, heading away in the opposite direction, Titus right behind. They had no time for a fight, but Finn couldn't help but clench his fists in anticipation of such a confrontation. He knew that Titus would appreciate letting out some of his pent-up anger and there could be no more deserving group of self-serving bastards than the slave traders. But they could not attract the attention of the Shadow Guards tonight. They had to get out of town undetected.

They slipped one more time through the warren of streets, ducking and diving into the shelter of shacks, behind shadows cast by ruined walls, a broken place that somehow sustained a pulse of life. Titus took the lead as they emerged from the northern edge, heading away from the desert toward the mountain pass that would lead to the Resistance camp. But instead of heading up to the ridge, they turned into a line of thick forest.

Once they were out of sight of the road, Titus paused, his face turned toward the mountain pass. The air smelled of fresh pine after rain. The hoot of an owl came through the boughs of the trees above, and Finn looked up to see the silhouette of the hunter on the wing.

He waited in silence, watching emotion play over his friend's face as Titus fought the urge to return to the side of his beloved. He imagined Maria up there, her bloody corpse washed and laid beside what was left of the baby. Perhaps they had already been buried.

If Titus wanted to go and mourn them, Finn knew he would proceed alone. He thought of Sienna and wondered if he would ever have a chance to love as Titus did. Such love came at a price, but it was worth trying for. After he had left her in the plague camp that night, Finn's anger had been all-consuming. Sienna had saved her world at the expense of his, but would he have chosen any differently? In the end, we all choose our own tribe over others.

Besides, it was not for the Earthside Mapwalkers to save his people — Borderlanders must save their own. He and Titus were but two of the growing Resistance, but their mission would light a flame that others could follow. The future of the Borderlands did not have to rest with those of the Shadow anymore.

Titus turned, the tracks of tears down his cheeks shining in the moonlight. He took a deep breath and nodded once. "We go on, brother. I will write her name in the sky with the blue flames of the burning crop and honor her death with the end of that which killed her."

He reached out a hand, and they clasped arms, a bond

that went far beyond blood. Finn knew they would rather die together on the mission than return to this place without achieving their goal.

Titus walked on, Finn right behind, as they wove between the trees, their footsteps crunching on a bed of fallen pine needles. The sounds of night hunters came through the branches, the bark of a fox, the roar of a mountain lion in the distance.

When they reached a break in the trees, Titus checked the stars before leading the way once more. Finn hadn't served in this part of the Borderlands. He could navigate around Old Aleppo and its surrounding region with his eyes closed, but here in the mountains, Titus was the expert. He had been with a ranger troop, searching far and wide for resources that the Shadow Cartographers could use in their never-ending war.

As they went on, walking became more like a meditation, their footsteps in time as they marched under shelter of the forest until the fingers of dawn crept across the sky catching the snowcap of the mountain peak high above them.

* * *

As the demon enveloped her, Sienna reached for her magic in a desperate attempt to get away from its grip. But before she could travel, a suffocating mist descended, choking her, wrapping her limbs in a cold dense fog, pinning her arms to her sides. She could hear the cries of the others as they tried to find her, but she was somewhere else now, somewhere between the worlds.

The woman had disappeared, but Sienna could feel her imprint all around. A desperate melancholy. She had lost her child, her family, her home — and her soul. A deep sense of rage throbbed through the air, an anger that would rip flesh from bone to defend a loved one. At the same time, a hopelessness, a desire for oblivion, a need to extinguish life in order to end pain. Sienna doubled over as a wave of anguish washed over her. She cried out in understanding as the world went black.

* * *

"Sienna, Sienna, wake up, please."

The voice was insistent, but Sienna couldn't move. Cold deadened her limbs, heavy with ice, as hard as the obsidian in the surrounding walls, souls trapped within each one.

She opened her eyes. Mila bent over, relief on her face, Perry and Zoe behind, standing close together as if finding solace in one another.

"We couldn't get to you," Mila said. "We thought you were gone."

"It's okay. I know what this place is now," Sienna whispered, her voice croaking from the effort.

Mila helped her sit up, leaning back against the rock wall as Perry passed over a water bottle.

Sienna took several sips before speaking. "This place sits right under the border, at the place where the worlds meet. Sometimes people are lost between Earthside and the Borderlands — over water, in the air, sometimes when the border shifts by deliberate action or chance. These souls are trapped here in obsidian, locked into volcanic rock, creatures of neither world."

Mila looked around at the many thousands of niches, each with a captured soul inside. "Should we smash all the rocks? Set them free?"

Sienna shook her head. "No. They can't exist anymore. They are like flies in amber, captured at the moment of crossing. The woman you released is one with the Shadow now. I don't know if that's any better than where she was."

Sienna couldn't share what else she had experienced — kinship, an affinity within her blood for those between one world and the next. A sense that fate swirled ever closer.

"I'm okay, honestly." She stood up. "The good news is that this is the center of the border, so we're almost on the other side."

Zoe nodded. "Yes, it's not much further." She turned around, her arm outstretched as she pointed at the many arches surrounding them. "We just have to find the right way out."

Sienna found her gaze drawn to the altar. "Can you guys start looking? I need a minute to pull myself together."

Perry and Zoe went in one direction and Mila in the other, working their way around the base of the mausoleum, checking each door for any distinguishing features or a hint of the way forward.

Sienna walked to the altar, the smell of beeswax lingering in the air as the flicker of flame drew her in. The candles were as thick as the waist of a man with multiple wicks designed to burn for months on end. A constant light in the darkness. A representation of hope in every culture.

There was a mosaic above the altar, each tile a precious stone fixed to the rock behind. Its backdrop depicted a vortex of light and shadow, strings of silver and black twisting together in an everlasting web. A representation of balance, perhaps?

Sienna leaned over the altar to examine the mosaic more closely. There were more colors entwined within — a line of rubies scattered amongst the black and silver, behind and between the lines. In the foreground, a young woman clothed in robes of Marian blue stood with upturned palms in surrender, her face lifted to the heavens, her features obscured by silver mist. Scarlet gems streamed from slashes on her arms and with a start, Sienna realized what it showed.

Blood magic at the very heart of the border.

She stepped back, heart pounding, her gaze fixed on the woman whose blood maintained the border. She thought of Bridget back in the Ministry, maps entwined in her veins, ink mingled with her blood. The book on her desk with the sketch of the figure in a vortex of shadow. Could Bridget be the balance?

Or could the voice that called to her from the Tower of the Winds be such a creature? And if so, did that mean its power could never be vanquished?

"Come and look at this." Zoe's voice echoed through the vault. "I think it must be the way out."

Sienna took one last look at the mosaic figure, fixing the image in her mind, then turned away from the altar, pushing down her unease as she joined the others.

The door was thick oak, patterned with intricate carvings of a spiked mountain range. A massive keyhole, far bigger than any human lock, sat under a handle carved in the shape of a lemur.

"Each portal has a distinct image," Zoe explained. "But the map I saw suggested a forest of barbed stone like this image."

Perry shrugged. "It's as good a guess as any and I'm keen to get out of here as fast as possible." He pushed down on the handle. The door didn't budge. He pushed harder, slamming his body against the door, then raised his hands, conjuring his fire, ready to burn their way out.

Zoe placed a hand on his arm. "Wait. Let me try."

She walked to the door and lifted her hands, her fingers weaving in the air in front of the lock. Sienna watched her magic in action, wondering at how Zoe manipulated reality. The weaver magic was most akin to her own, shaping the world anew, gently encouraging a shift that others could only achieve with brute force.

The lock clicked.

Zoe pushed down on the handle, and the door opened.

Sienna smelled the tropical rainforest before she saw it, a heady scent of wet leaves and night flowers that swept into the dead cavern on a warm breeze. It was dark up ahead and as the team walked through the door and into the trees, a bright moon shone above in a field of stars.

The rhythmic chirp of cicadas greeted them as the call of a night bird rang out above and the hoop-hoop of a monkey echoed through the trees. The air was humid and Sienna could feel sweat pooling at the base of her spine as they stood in silence. Was this even the right way?

Between the trees, spiked shards of needle-shaped peaks surrounded them, moonlight reflecting off blades of rock. A narrow path wound through the forest, the way ahead marked by a cairn of stones left by previous travelers.

Mila turned with a smile on her face. "This is the Borderlands. I can feel it."

Sienna nodded. "I sense it, too, but we need to rest before we travel on." The exhaustion of the cave journey crept through her bones, fatigue from physical exertion and the use of magic draining the energy from her. The others must feel the same. She still had a faint unease, but the sense of being watched had dissipated a little. The sounds of the surrounding forest were curiously welcoming, as if they were all just animals seeking shelter for the night.

Perry pointed at a patch of soft ground beneath the canopy of trees with boulders for shelter and support. "This seems good enough." He sank to the forest floor, rolling onto his back, eyes beginning to close already. "Who's taking first watch?"

"I can," Zoe said. "I'm not sleepy right now."

Sienna didn't argue. Now they were out of the cave system, a wave of exhaustion broke over her. Her legs trembled with the aftermath of the soul's connection, her head aching from the intensity of the cavern adventure. Mila looked just as weary as she curled up beside Perry, tugging her coat around her shoulders.

Sienna turned to Zoe. "Wake me in a few hours. I'll take over from you."

Zoe nodded and clambered up onto one of the boulders. She sat cross-legged on the rock and looked up toward the stars shining brightly above. A moonbeam touched the young woman's hair with a silver sheen and Sienna caught the peaceful smile that spread across her face.

She turned away and lay down next to Mila, pulling her pack under her head as a pillow. A tendril of fear snaked into her mind as she closed her eyes. Would there be demons in her nightmares, creatures of smoke and claw? But this time, the wave of fatigue swept her into oblivion.

* * *

Zoe relished the time alone, her mind still circling around the events in the caves. She had entered the chambers as an outsider but she had emerged with a sense of connection with the Mapwalker team, a knowledge that her magic was just as useful as theirs — and dare she think it? Perhaps even more so.

She looked down at her sleeping friends; her gaze lingering on Perry. His fingers twitched as if he dreamed of wielding his magic, and Zoe remembered how he had looked in the cave of the ibis. His hands raised within a tower of flame, his muscular frame silhouetted against the blaze, every inch like a young god of fire. They were so different and yet, there was a connection between them.

Zoe smiled as she leaned back against the cool of the rock and looked up at the stars, shifting her gaze to let the weave of the world emerge once more. The strings appeared more quickly this time, shimmering strands of silver and shadow and hues of green from the forest. All life was woven together and Zoe wondered how much she could manipulate these filaments, creating new things. Perhaps destroying them, too.

A crack in the forest. The snap of a branch.

Zoe sat up sharply and peered around at the thick trees, suddenly less of a haven and more a forbidding place of hard wood and sharp spines.

She looked down at the sleeping Mapwalker team. They were all exhausted, slumbering deeply. She didn't want to wake them and it was most likely one of the forest creatures going about its nightly hunt. She was just jumpy. There was nothing to worry about.

But as she turned back, a flash of silver caught the moonlight. A shadowy figure loomed over her. She opened her mouth to scream a warning, but a sharp pain at her temple turned everything black.

* * *

A chorus of birdsong woke Sienna as the sky turned from inky blue to pastel shades, the stars fading as light returned to the forest. She had slept all night and missed her turn at the watch. For a moment, she was grateful for it. Her body had regained its strength, and the creatures of the cavern were only a memory now they were out in the fresh air. But someone else must have taken her turn.

She sat up, noting that Mila and Perry were only just waking up beside her.

"Zoe," Sienna called up to the top of the rock. "Are you there?"

No answer. Just the call of birds warbling and whistling above.

Sienna rolled to her feet, unease rising within as she walked around the boulder and then clambered up onto it. Zoe was nowhere to be seen, her pack left discarded on the top of the rock.

Mila sat up and rubbed her eyes. "What is it? Did we sleep through?"

Sienna jumped down, pack in hand. "Zoe's not here."

"I'm sure she's just in the trees somewhere. She can't have gone far." Perry got to his feet, shaking sleep from his limbs, and clambered up the rock. "Zoe!"

Birds flew from the treetops at his cry, winging across the ever-lightening sky toward the jagged peaks beyond. But there was no answering call, no footsteps from the forest.

Perry pointed to a gap in the trees. "What's that? It looks different from last night."

Sienna jogged over to where the treeline parted into a semblance of a path, Mila and Perry right behind her. The carefully piled cairn of stones was now strewn across the track and next to it, a huge footprint in the dust.

"What is that?" Perry hunkered down to look more closely. "It's more animal than human but like nothing I've seen before."

Sienna's stomach turned at the sight of it. They had not left the Shadow behind in the cave system. Perhaps their use of magic had even alerted whatever ruled this area of the Borderlands. Whatever it was, it had Zoe.

CHAPTER 13

Sienna crouched by Mila as they examined the footprint more carefully. "It could be a mutant," Mila said. "One of those bred by the Shadow Cartographers. But why take Zoe?"

Perry stood and looked down the path, his face etched with concern. "It doesn't matter why. We have to go after her. We can track it, follow its path."

Mila shook her head. "We have to get to the Tower of the Winds. Our mission is to help Bridget re-open the border. Every moment we delay, Earthside suffers further. Zoe knew the risks when she—"

"No," Sienna cut in sharply. "We go after Zoe. We need her." She stood and spun on her heel, walking back to where the packs lay, her face flushed as she thought of the Weaver. The way ahead wasn't clear, but she knew Zoe was important somehow. And besides, they couldn't leave her in the camp of the mutants. Sienna thought back to Xander's end, sucked dry of his magic and life force by the coldly beautiful Elf. She would not leave another of the team to die so far from home.

Sienna picked up her pack. "We need to get going. They're hours ahead of us already."

"I hope you know what you're doing," Mila said, shaking her head as she grabbed her pack.

Perry snatched his up, shouldering Zoe's as well and strode into the forest.

Together they walked under the trees as morning light broke through the canopy, dappling the way ahead. The path wound past thick trunks, torchwood and ebony amongst them, hard tropical trees no longer so densely packed on Earthside, cleared for timber and other crops. Sienna spotted orchids as they walked by, bright colors of purple and scarlet, a glimpse of beauty in a dangerous land.

She had heard of the camp of the mutants, new species cultivated by the Shadow Cartographers, bred from humans with different magical powers to enable new strains to emerge. She remembered the Fertility Halls in the Castle of the Shadow, Finn's face as his sister died in his arms, his niece taken for the cause. She wondered where he was now, whether he thought of her at all. Finn had made it clear that his path lay in the Borderlands, whereas her allegiance would always be to Earthside. She had thought they could somehow make a future together, but it seemed impossible right now.

The forest path emerged at the base of a rock face pitted with fissures as if gouged by giant talons. Jagged peaks spiked into the sky toward the sun. It burned hot now they were out of the shade of the forest, the air more humid. Sienna wiped her brow of sweat as she searched for the way ahead.

She had a sense of time ticking down to some imagined countdown, when Earthside would crumple into the hard border, triggering an unstoppable series of natural disasters that would devastate her home. Yet being here shifted her perspective and made her wonder whether it was time for such a dramatic change in fortunes. Time for a new power to rise.

Sienna shook her head, banishing the thought that seemed to come from nowhere. Her skin burned under her t-shirt, and she sensed the whorls of shadow spinning ever faster. Was she transforming now she grew closer to the source?

"Are you okay?" Mila asked, putting a hand on Sienna's arm.

Sienna gave a faint smile. "Just over-heating, I guess." She pointed ahead. "We need to hurry. I don't think we have much time."

* * *

Zoe woke to a jolting rhythm, a bump-bump stride that jerked her into consciousness. She half-wondered why the rock beneath her moved, then remembered the shadowy figure looming above before all went black. She opened her eyes and froze as she looked up at the thing that carried her.

A craggy face with skin cracked like dried mud, muscles heaped like sacks of rock under a tunic stretched tight over its colossal body. It smelled like moss and minerals leaching from a mountain stream. As Zoe shifted, it stopped walking and looked down at her. Something like a smile crossed its face, a wide mouth opening like a cleft in stone, eyes like tiny emeralds hidden in the crevices.

"He likes you."

Zoe turned in the creature's arms to see a young girl, perhaps ten years old, blonde hair in messy plaits tied with twine, wearing a tunic the color of ripe olives. She signed with her hands and the living rock placed Zoe gently on the ground. She found her legs a little unsteady, and it held an arm out for her to lean against. There was consideration in the gesture, but Zoe understood that its docile manner would change if she tried to run. She glanced around at the high cliffs surrounding them, serrated edges like flint knives spiked with cactus and thorny scrub. There was nowhere to run to, anyway.

The girl approached and examined Zoe, looking her up and down with a maturity far beyond her age. "You have a strange aura. I've never sensed it before. What magic can you do?"

Zoe frowned. "You can sense magic?"

The girl nodded. "I see colors and textures around those with ability and I can usually tell what they can do. We're scouts, me and Hashim." She reached out a small hand and stroked the creature's arm. It was a familiar gesture, a touch of connection between friends. But as much as Zoe found these two fascinating, she had to figure out a way to get back to the Mapwalker team.

"Who are you scouting for?"

The girl looked puzzled. "Who else? The silver-haired one and the old man. They offer good coin for such as you. We need to take supplies back for my family and your trade will mean we can return with food." Her eyes darted away. "Maybe even medicine. My little brother …"

As her words trailed off, Zoe wondered how it was possible that this young girl was the only way her family could get the supplies they needed. It was a glimpse into a side of the Borderlands she had never appreciated before. This was not some utopian world of magic and plenty. It was a land of desperately poor people ruled by an upper class of Shadow Cartographers whose obsession with reclaiming Earthside reduced all to poverty. If they would only spend their energy building and improving what they had, this side of the border could prosper.

"I sensed there were others with you," the girl continued. "Maybe one with greater power than yours, but I have seen her kind before. I've seen no one like you." She came closer, this time reaching out a hand to caress the air around Zoe's face, like a blind girl reading features with touch. "It's beautiful."

Zoe didn't sense any danger from the pair and yet she

knew their destination might lead to her end. They might not know what happened to those they delivered up — or they chose to ignore it — but Zoe understood loyalty to family above all else. Perhaps she would do the same in their position.

She shifted her vision to examine the strings of the world around, allowing the weave of nature to come into focus. After the cave, she knew her magic was strong enough to manipulate the strands. She could trap these two and then escape into the labyrinth of rocks — but the use of magic would sap her energy and exchange drops of shadow for its use, the toll greater if used here in the Borderlands. The Mapwalker team would surely look for her once they woke and would come in this direction. She would bide her time for now and wait a little longer.

"I'm a Weaver. My name is Zoe."

The girl's eyes widened. "A Weaver. Oh, my. You're worth so much." She skipped around in a tight circle, plaits flying, dancing with joy as she beamed with pleasure. The rocky hulk of Hashim shook and then a booming laugh rang out at his friend's delight. Zoe couldn't help but join in, giggling a little at the strange scene, even as she questioned why the hell she might be so valuable.

The girl stopped spinning. "I'm Callen." She held out a hand. "Pleased to meet you, Weaver Zoe."

Zoe shook her hand with appropriate solemnity, wondering if the pair treated all their captives so well.

Callen turned suddenly, looking back into the forest, as if hearing a far-off sound. "We need to get moving. Your friends are on the trail, but we will trade well before they arrive."

Zoe hadn't realized they were so close to the camp. She had to get away.

She raised her hands, focusing on the strands of light and shadow — but the giant Hashim folded his bulky arms around her, crushing her to his chest. She couldn't move, could barely breathe.

Callen stepped in closer, transformed from a charming little girl to the steely eyed bounty hunter once more.

"You don't have to do this," Zoe gasped. "I can help your family. Please don't—"

Hashim squeezed more tightly, cutting off her pleas.

Callen remained silent as she clambered up onto Hashim's back, riding his shoulders as if they were one creature, a strange pairing in a land of aberration.

The mutant lifted Zoe up, locking her into a vice of stone. He stood and strode on past the towering cliffs, each stride ten times that of a man. Zoe knew that the Mapwalker team would never reach her in time. She would face the mutant camp alone.

CHAPTER 14

"It's not far now." Titus pointed to the flank of the mountain, the blush of dawn painting it in shades of coral and amber. "The munitions dump is on the edge there, near the snow line to keep it cool and away from the major trade routes."

Finn hunkered down on a log and made a small fire, boiling up water for coffee while they both ate in silence from the supplies of meat and bread that Kabila had given them. Both men were used to marching on military rations, so they ate quickly and before long, they were heading up the side of the mountain.

Titus scanned the rocky escarpment above, pointing out features of the slope. "It's between three points — the summit, the woman's profile, and a dead tree struck by lightning. The cache is equidistant from each."

They zigzagged up the side, navigating the scree and patches of scrub where tiny wild flowers grew, purple against green. Finn found his breath ragged as they climbed, the slope becoming ever steeper.

Finally, a dead tree came into view, its stark white limbs reaching for blue sky as the sun burned down upon them. Titus turned to scan the surrounding area, then pointed at a rocky outcrop a little higher and to the east. "There."

Finn supposed it could be a woman's profile at a stretch, but Titus seemed sure and set off to climb higher, picking up his pace as they neared their goal. Finn turned to look back over the plain. They were high above the forest line now and below, the trader town stretched to the coastline, the sea shimmering beyond to the horizon. It looked so peaceful from up here, with no sense of the suffering that lay within its streets. But as much as this wild place had a stark beauty, Finn was a city boy, and his life blood beat to the pulse of a faster pace of life. If he survived this mission, he would return to Old Aleppo and liberate it from the iron grip of his father. Perhaps Sienna would even join him and they would eat oranges together in the market in a time of peace.

He shook his head and gave a rueful laugh. If only life could be so simple.

"Come and help me!" Titus shouted down from higher up. He was on his knees by a thorn bush, scrabbling at the ground.

Finn hurried up the slope and together, they cleared the rocks and dug down into the ground beneath.

"There should be enough explosives in here to destroy the main crop." Titus grinned in anticipation at what they would find. "It's been way too long since I've done some proper demolition, but I'm sure I'll get back into the swing of it."

They soon hit upon a metal trunk and as the sun rose high overhead, they levered the lid open and revealed what lay within.

Finn sat back on the hard ground, staring into the chest with despair. It was completely filled with rocks, hiding the fact that the explosives had been taken long ago.

Titus picked up one of the stones and hurled it down the slope with a violent shout. He picked up another, then another, throwing until he exhausted his frustration.

"We'll go on anyway," Finn said. "We don't know what

we'll find at the camp. Maybe fertilizer you can use. There will surely be something explosive."

Titus sat down heavily and sighed. "You're right. I just hoped this would give us some advantage. It's the two of us against whatever is out there. We have no chance."

Finn pulled out a flask of water and took a sip before passing it over to Titus. "There's always a chance. Besides, what else do you want to do now? We can at least scout the camp and if it's impossible to destroy the crop, we'll return to the Resistance for reinforcements." He pointed back to the trader town. "Think of all the people down there taking Liberation, addicts getting their fix, women carrying monsters. Every day that drug is loose it corrupts more Borderlanders and turns them to the Shadow."

"Or leaves them dead in its wake," Titus said quietly. "So we go on." He pointed up the face of the mountain. "It's faster to go up and over than around at lower altitude. If the weather holds, that is. The forest lower down ends in towering pinnacles of rock and a labyrinth of stone needles. It's hard to navigate. If we descend from above, we can at least figure out the best way into the camp."

They both stood and brushed down their clothes, then set off up the mountain, faces set toward the peak, footsteps even, breath panting as they rose higher.

To be honest, Finn had never wanted to climb a mountain and after this experience, he never wanted to climb one again. Titus kept up a grueling pace from years of experience on this kind of terrain, but Finn felt every single step of the hard ground, his leg muscles screaming in pain as they wound their way up toward the peak.

The weather held, sun baking down on them with no shelter from the heat even as the wind whipped their faces. But each step took them closer to the camp, so Finn gritted his teeth and kept walking.

Just another ten paces.

And another ten.

Finally, they skirted the summit in a haze of clouds, the valley before them obscured in mist. But Finn felt a change in the air and sensed a kind of shimmer in the gloom beyond. The way down was even harder on his leg muscles and his knees ached with every jolt on the rocky ground.

As they descended, the mist cleared, and the sun came out again. Suddenly, they saw the camp laid out below them.

A wide lake lay in the center with organized barracks, and before it, a central plaza with some kind of temple. Further out, a patchwork of crops in shades of green and fields of blue.

"All different stages of growth," Titus said. "They've got a year-round crop here. Enough to dose the whole of the Borderlands."

Finn marveled at the scope of the Liberation project, the drug an effective route to the ultimate goal of creating a superhuman army to take back Earthside. His father, the Warlord, Kosai, was a man of great cruelty with no love for Earthsiders, but Finn doubted that even he would countenance dosing his own people with such a drug. This was masterminded by those closely aligned with the Shadow.

Resolve hardened within him as they descended into the valley. Finn would not leave this place without burning those crops down.

As they approached the fields, they stopped behind a rocky outcrop to plan the next step. Workers tended the plants, immigrant slaves amongst the crops, while Shadow Guards patrolled the perimeter. The balmy evening made the guards relaxed and lazy, and at some command posts, they played cards and joked with each other. Clearly, tending fields was not a high-stress position, and they were not concerned about possible attack.

Piles of fertilizer lay at specific points amongst the fields and workers occasionally went into huts, so perhaps more lay within. It was peaceful, a deadly beauty with a malignant harvest. But as Finn watched the pastoral scene play out down below, he knew they couldn't possibly destroy this entire crop. They didn't have enough people to start fires at the same time, and both he and Titus would likely be caught trying to set the fields alight alone.

It was an impossible mission.

CHAPTER 15

Zoe smelled the camp before she saw it, a stench of too many people, cooking fires and the faint metallic scent left after an electrical storm, the residue of spent magic. Hashim had carried her for several hours, Callen on his back, never slowing, never stopping until they reached the end of the tangle of paths through the rocky chasm and emerged at the edge of a valley.

A river ran down from the mountains into a vast lake with a church submerged in the middle, perhaps drowned on Earthside and pushed through here by lack of belief. There were fields of some kind of crop with blue flowers in vast terraces up the slope, workers moving in channels between them.

Around the lake, the camp was divided into clear sections, more like military barracks than the ramshackle place Zoe had imagined. There were permanent structures built at strategic positions around the edge and open training grounds where groups of soldiers marched in formation. The sound of laughter echoed up from children out at play in a schoolyard. It looked just like any other small town—

A flash of blue light above a temple by the side of the lake.

The soldiers stopped marching. The children fell silent. Even the birds muted their song. Hashim and Callen froze, eyes fixed on the scene.

The light rose like a mushroom cloud from the vaulted roof and then dissipated into haze.

Zoe felt the tension drain from her captors as all evidence of the light disappeared.

"Let's go," Callen said. "It's a good time to trade." The girl's voice trembled a little, as if she had to convince herself to go on.

Hashim walked into the valley. He stepped more carefully now, covering the ground a little slower as he dodged the boulders on the way down.

"Why is it a good time to trade?" Zoe asked. "What was that light?"

Callen was silent a moment and then spoke softly. "They always need more resources after they use someone up." She looked down at the ground, her young face haunted. "They say it doesn't hurt when they take your magic. They say it's quick …" Her words trailed off, her gaze fixed on the camp ahead.

They soon reached the perimeter where two guards with the half-moon tattoo of the Warlord waved them through, clearly recognizing Callen and her strange partner. But as they moved into the camp itself, Zoe saw that Hashim was not so strange after all.

The path led directly toward the temple cut across by concentric circular routes that linked each area. Hashim or his kind were clearly unremarkable as no one gave him a second glance as they walked through, although Zoe noted a few people looked up at her with interest. A pair of twins, long-limbed with black skin and curious eyes, ran past and circled back for a second look. But no one challenged or even spoke to them. Guards on patrol walked by at regular intervals, keeping a tight grip on security.

Hashim strode down through the camp until they reached the back of the temple where two guards stood either side of a staircase that led up to a finely carved wooden door. As they approached, one guard ran up the stairs and knocked twice, then once again.

The door opened an inch and Zoe glimpsed a swirl of shadow inside and a hand with bony fingers. She felt eyes upon her, a chill creeping up her spine as if she had been plunged under ice, drowning in the depths under a thick layer of impenetrable blue.

The figure dropped back into darkness; the door left ajar.

The guard stepped forward to meet Hashim. Callen jumped down, her demeanor one of a trader far beyond her years.

"He'll take this one." The guard pulled a leather pouch of coins from his belt and handed it to Callen. She opened it, her eyes widening in appreciation. "And he'll take any more like her you can find."

Callen wouldn't meet Zoe's eyes as Hashim placed her gently on the ground. The giant patted her head in a friendly manner. He clearly did not understand what part he played in the demise of so many who carried magic in their veins.

Callen clambered up onto his shoulders and without even looking back, they began the long climb out of the camp.

The guard grabbed Zoe's arm and thrust her up the stairs toward the door.

"Please," she begged. "Don't do this."

The guard didn't acknowledge her words and as the door opened wider; he pushed her forward and darted away down the stairs without even a glance back.

Zoe stumbled inside the darkened room and blinked as her eyes adjusted to the dim light. It was starkly beautiful, like a forest transformed into architecture. Thick pillars of cedar wood stretched from the floor carved with vines and the faces of mutated woodland creatures, twisted into visages of horror. The delicate smell of cedar pervaded the space, refreshing and cool after the hot exterior. Oak beams stretched up into a coffered ceiling painted in shades of midnight and on the side facing the lake, an arched window stood covered by thick drapes. A sliver of light lanced across the wooden floor, empty except for a single chair — and the man who stood in the shadows behind it.

"You're a Weaver." His voice held the kind of interest that a predator has in a particularly tasty prey.

He walked toward her, avoiding the ray of light on the ground, and it seemed as if he merely skimmed the earth. Zoe blinked once more to try to focus on his figure, but his outline constantly shifted, as if smoke wreathed his flesh. She caught her breath as she realized this man was almost a creature of pure shadow. She had read of these powerful Mapwalkers who turned, but she had never wished to meet one.

He came closer, distinguished features betraying his nobility on Earthside and an old facial scar evidence of past battles.

"I'm Sir Douglas Mercator. What's your name?"

"Zoe." She blurted it out quickly, then clapped a hand over her mouth. It had been a reflex, a polite response to an unremarkable question, but she had totally failed interrogation 101.

Sir Douglas laughed. "Oh, don't worry. You're safe with me." He glanced toward the door to the lakeside. "At least for now. Come. Sit. You have nowhere else to be." He pointed at the chair.

Zoe's heart beat faster as she walked across the floor and sat, straight-backed. She needed to stall for time because there was no easy way out of here. Guards stood outside the doors and in here, a Shadow Cartographer who could wrap her in shadow weave or crush her lungs with a wave of his hand.

"How did you get here?"

"The bounty-hunter girl, Callen, and her giant friend, found me lost in the forest."

Sir Douglas took a step forward. "Try again. How did you get into the Borderlands? The border is closed and none have passed through it since the Ministry slammed it shut, damning us all." His features contorted with rage as he spat the final words.

He bent down until his angular nose almost touched hers and gripped her chin hard, turning her face up toward him. His grey eyes were the color of a wolf pelt, an old alpha male with sharp teeth covered in the blood of its prey.

"Tell me."

Zoe thought of her desk back at the Ministry, the calm, quiet atmosphere of the Antiquities department. She should have just stayed down there and told no one of what she had seen. Bridget had not prepared her for any of this. She was just a Weaver, after all, but she had to tell him something.

"We came through a path of the dead, one of the ancient Egyptian tombs full of creatures and traps and—"

"We?" Sir Douglas snarled as he cut off her words.

Zoe bit her lip as she realized her mistake, but she wouldn't give her friends up. Whatever he did to her.

Sir Douglas turned away, his robes a swirl of smoke. He strode across the floor, shaking his head as if deeply troubled. "The way has only been used in rare times," he muttered. "It cannot be crossed without …" He spun around. "A powerful Blood Mapwalker. You came with Sienna Farren. Perhaps he is with her …" Sir Douglas's voice trailed off and Zoe thought she saw something wistful in his gaze, an edge of vulnerability.

The door from the front of the temple banged open and his eyes turned cold once more, like a graveyard as storm clouds gathered overhead. The sound of a growing crowd came from outside, cheers of excitement mingling with the anticipation of carnival pleasure.

A young woman with pixie features entered, her silver hair reflecting the sun from outside, a white dress swirling around her slight figure. This must be Elf, but even though Sienna had described her, somehow, the girl was smaller than she expected.

"Oh, wonderful. You found me a fresh one. We just have time before the challenge." Elf reached out a hand.

Zoe felt a jerk inside, as if the girl reached inside her chest to tug on her heart. Her ribcage contracted and suddenly, she couldn't breathe. Something — her magic — seeped from her in tiny pulses. Like the death of a thousand cuts, Elf would drain her dry.

Zoe gasped for breath, tears running down her cheeks as she doubled over, clutching her hands to her aching chest.

Sir Douglas stepped in between them and the pain stopped. "Not yet," he said sharply. "She came with others more powerful. We need to know more."

Elf spun on her heel, her face like thunder as she marched to the window and threw back the drapes, letting light flood into the temple. Sir Douglas shrank back into the shadows, but not before Zoe saw the smoke at the edge of his robes disappearing in the sun, evaporating like clouds on a summer day.

The window had a view out over the vast lake and the ruined church at its center. Four huge vats of a deep blue liquid sat directly in front on the shore.

"She is enough for this batch of Liberation. You can't stop me." Elf turned around again and raised her hand. Zoe shrank back, waiting for the pain once more. They were both in sunlight now and Sir Douglas could not stop her again.

"Sienna came over the border," he said from the shadows.

Elf frowned and dropped her hand. "How? The border is closed." She shook her head, eyes narrowing in concern. "No matter. Her blood is the key. If I can siphon it at the Tower of the Winds, I can amplify my power and smash down the border for good. Earthside will be ours for the taking." She smiled triumphantly. "Where is she?"

Sir Douglas circled the edge of the temple, staying out of the light. "I was just about to find out. But your magic is of no use for — persuasion. Give me more time. I will find her."

Elf smiled in anticipation. "Then I will take whatever you leave behind of this one when you're finished." A cheer rose up from outside. "But hurry, the challenge begins soon."

She pulled the drapes closed, leaving the room in semi-darkness again, and swept out the door. Zoe watched her go, icy fear creeping through her veins as Sir Douglas circled behind her.

Chill fingers touched her neck, gently brushing her hair to one side.

"Tell me where they are," he whispered, the threat clear as his grip tightened, bone digging into flesh as if he might burrow within her.

CHAPTER 16

Forbidding shards of rock loomed above the Mapwalker team as they wound through the labyrinth of paths below the jagged peaks. Sienna no longer knew how she chose the forks ahead, only trusting that the pulse of shadow inside drew her on to her fate. It felt symbiotic now, a separate presence inside her, but one that belonged there. She couldn't talk about it with the others and she wondered whether all those who ended up in a shadow coma felt this way before succumbing to the darkness. Whatever it was, it pulled her on.

They reached the end of the path in the balmy early evening. A gentle breeze wafted over the valley before them as they crouched in the lee of a pile of boulders and looked out over the camp.

"It's huge," Perry said. "More like a small city. How will we find her?"

"And get out of there alive," Mila added. She tilted her head to one side as she stared down at the lake. "What is that?"

Within the blue waters, an electric storm churned, crackles of energy radiating out from thick serpentine bodies. They writhed together, then raced around the sunken church at the center.

"They look like electric eels but they must be gigantic."

Mila sounded both fascinated and appalled at the same time, and Sienna wondered if her friend longed to sink into those cool waters. Perhaps she understood the dichotomy of both longing for the Shadow and fighting against it? She remembered Mila's face in the caves under Ganvié as she left Ekon behind to finish the mission. Perhaps they both had regrets about what — and who — they had left behind.

A cry rang out overhead, a sound of desperate loss with a distinctly human quality. Sienna looked up to see the silhouette of a giant creature against the clouds, its body some kind of hybrid bird, its wings like monstrous sails criss-crossed with bones of human anatomy, talons like razor blades hanging below. She shuddered and looked away. She didn't want to see its face, didn't want to imagine how they could have created such a beast. It cried out again and winged its way across the valley, heading out over the lake.

"We need to get moving. We can't leave Zoe here any longer." Sienna tamped down the rising fear as she watched the creature fly away.

On Earthside, the theory of eugenics involved breeding the best of a species to create superior beings. But the dark side of the practice involved killing those considered inferior by the ruling class, no matter their true worth. Here in the Borderlands, they had taken the philosophy to extremes, breeding whatever they could in terms of magical ability and physical deformity with the aim of creating an overwhelming force that could take back the land they believed was rightfully theirs. If they were too late, Zoe would be the latest victim in an endless bloody war.

They walked down the side of the valley as quickly as they could over the rocky ground, approaching the camp from an oblique angle and staying away from the main entrance which bristled with guards. A rubbish tip spilled out from the side of the camp toward the cliff face, a deep crevice scarring the rock face behind.

Sienna pointed up to it as they approached. "If anything happens, if we get separated, we meet there. Wait one sunset and one sunrise." She hesitated a moment. "Then leave."

Perry and Mila both nodded and Sienna could only hope that they would all walk out of the camp together with Zoe by their side.

The stench of waste greeted them as they reached the edge of the tip, rotting produce underpinned by a copper tang of butchered flesh and spilled blood. Perry pulled up his t-shirt, holding it against his mouth and nose. Sienna tried to breathe shallowly through her mouth, but nothing kept the awful stink from them. At least it kept the guards away from this area and only a few scrawny children sifting through the rubbish at the edge of the tip witnessed their arrival, skeletal frames on the edge of survival unheeding of the passers-by.

Mila clambered up the pile of rubbish to where it spilled over a wall into the camp, Sienna and Perry close behind her. They dropped down into a warren of ramshackle shelters and weather-worn tents fortified by sheets of metal and planks of wood.

Like all shanty towns, this one was filled with desperate people, working however they could to feed their children. With no magic, they were worthless to the Shadow Cartographers, used only for manual labor in the mines and camps. Were they also used as pure life energy, transformed into darkness by the silver-haired Elf?

Grief jolted through Sienna as she remembered those terrifying last moments as Elf sucked the life from Xander and his lion, Asada, using it to power the infection and transformation of the mutant plague rats. Sienna had no direct evidence that the girl was here, but she sensed the presence of a powerful Shadow Cartographer, one who commanded the camp and directed the metamorphosis of the creatures within.

An old woman peered out from behind a ragged curtain, her features etched with deep lines betraying her years of suffering. She looked at them with bleary eyes, a flicker of interest quickly dying as they passed by.

The team walked in silence, alert for any sign of danger, but the streets seemed oddly deserted as they skirted a path leading downhill toward the lakeside.

The sounds of a crowd soon came from up ahead. There was a sense of excitement and festivity in the air, incongruous in a place that seemed so full of desperation.

A slow drumbeat began, booming out across the valley.

Perry shook his head and sighed. "Nothing good happens when the drum starts."

Sienna knew what he meant. They had heard the drums at the Tophet, the Warlord's place of child sacrifice, and again at the eyrie where Perry almost had his liver devoured by giant eagles.

The drum was the sound of death.

They ran toward it.

* * *

The drumbeat startled Finn, a sudden interruption to his concentrated study of the valley below.

Workers in the fields stopped pruning the plants and stood up to rub their backs and ease aches and pains. The guards gestured down the hill, giving permission to stop working. Groups of laborers set off toward the plaza, laughing together with a sudden sense of celebration.

Finn followed the lines of the paths as they walked down the slopes to the barracks at the bottom, neatly organized in ranks with dirt tracks between.

In the center of the camp, an open plaza lay in front of a lake with a sunken church at its heart. Finn could just make out black shadows undulating within the depths and he shuddered to think what monsters lay below the surface.

A sizeable building — a temple of some kind — stood in front of the lake and behind it, by the water's edge, sat deep vats of inky blue liquid. Finn narrowed his eyes as he focused on the unusual feature. Then he realized what they must be.

A great deal of water would be needed to turn the plant extract into liquid doses of Liberation that could be bottled and distributed. Someone needed to add the twisted magic to the belladonna before it was shipped and it made sense to store it centrally.

Finn pointed to the pools of blue. "We destroy those and it will disrupt the entire supply chain, at least for a time. Then we bring others from the Resistance to help finish the place."

Titus nodded and pointed at a roughly hewn hut on the edge of the plaza with more guards than the rest. "I'd say that's where they keep weapons, maybe explosives. We should duck in there on the way down."

The drum beat faster, its rhythm steadily increasing.

Finn stood up. "Come on. This is our chance. We'll join the workers and mingle with the crowd." He set off at a run down the hill between rows of deadly plants, Titus right behind. They tagged along at the back of a group of farmhands, laughing and joking as if they had come from plantations higher up the mountain.

"Good day for a sacrifice," one man said. "Helps the crops grow faster, see. Goddess be praised."

Finn nodded, the words bringing back memories of his father's sacrifices at the Tophet. Blood always drew a crowd. He pitied the victim, but the distraction would be perfect. He and Titus could proceed with their plan unseen.

As the crowd streamed into the plaza, they peeled off, skirting the edge of the barracks and circling around to the back of the guard's hut. Constructed of wood and raised on stilts, the hut had a 360 degree walkway around the perimeter and a central staircase up the middle. One way in, one way out.

Heavily armed guards walked the perimeter, but as the drum beat faster, those at the back edged forward so they could see the action.

Finn and Titus ducked underneath the walkway and ran to the staircase. The boom of the drum grew louder and faster, the resonance so deep it made Finn's heart beat in time. A neat trick to fire up the crowd and make the soldiers above want to join the party. He could only hope they stayed distracted.

Finn pulled his sword and ran up the stairs on light feet, eyes darting around for any guards. No one in sight. He beckoned Titus up and stood watch while the explosives expert ducked inside the building, leaving the door ajar as he searched for something they could use.

Seconds passed, and Finn counted his breaths. He stood motionless, listening for footsteps under the drum beat, but the soldiers stayed riveted to the scene in the plaza.

Then the drumbeat stopped.

A rustle inside and then silence as Titus must have frozen in his search, aware that the soldiers were only meters away.

The crowd erupted into a cheer, their shouts and applause a deafening roar.

Titus ducked out the hut, bag in hand, triumphant grin on his face. He ran down the steps and Finn dashed after him with no fear of being heard under the sound of celebration. They kept moving until they were well away from the guard's hut.

Behind one of the barracks, Titus stopped and opened his bag. Sticks of dynamite used for mining rock and a long roll of detonator cord lay inside. "I only wish I could have taken more."

Finn looked back at the raucous crowd. Working Borderlanders, some mutated, but most here as slaves.

"We should try to minimize the damage and only blow the Liberation vats. Maybe bring down that temple on whatever dark power is inside." He pointed at the building. "We just need to get around the back. We'll rig explosives while the crowd is fixated on whatever the hell is happening out there."

They ran on, skirting the edge of the crowd as a carnival atmosphere took hold. Couples reveled in the shadows, so engaged with each other that Finn and Titus passed unnoticed.

Four huge vats stood on the edge of the lake, giant wooden structures made from aged oak on tall stilts with lines of taps underneath for the bottling process. A ladder up one side led to a series of walkways between them.

Titus pointed up. "Take the detonator cord and wind it between the vats, then drop it down. I'll set the explosives underneath and then connect it together. Hurry now, we're running out of time."

CHAPTER 17

Mila pulled ahead of Perry and Sienna as the path narrowed on the hill, switch-backing between the shanty town structures to emerge between military style barracks. People thronged the street, heading down toward the central area. Street vendors hawked their wares in a carnival atmosphere, the smell of roasted nuts mingling with hops as revelers drank ale from barrels. Mila slowed down to walk next to a buxom young woman, who swayed a little as she swigged from a pewter mug.

"This should be exciting," Mila said, smiling in welcome.

"Oh yes," the woman said. "We haven't had such as these for a while. Some say they're true aberrations, powerful enough to make it through the challenge." She gave a sly grin. "But it will go better for me if they're ravaged or devoured."

Her words startled Mila with their violent intent, but she kept a smile plastered on her face. "Why's that?"

The woman thrust her ample figure forward. "Good for business. The soldiers spend more coin after savagery." She laughed and took another swig.

Mila fell back to walk alongside Sienna and Perry. "There's some kind of competition or tournament and it might not end well for whoever's involved."

"Do you think it's Zoe?" Perry asked with a frown of concern.

"Perhaps, but the woman mentioned 'they' as if there are multiple contenders. We have to get closer."

Mila wiggled through the crowd, flowing with the stream of people until she reached a low wall at the water's edge with a clear view. A ceremonial temple made from thick wooden pillars carved with magical symbols stood pride of place and before it, a wide open plaza. The sense of excitement was palpable, a thrum of energy from the gathered masses, eager for blood.

A flash of blue light came from out on the lake, then the buzz and snap of electrical force as something twisted toward the shore. It darted below the wall and Mila recognized its shape. An enormous electric eel, its body as thick as the wheel of a car, crackling with its own current. From the flashes of light further out, there were more of them waiting to be fed.

Sienna and Perry joined her by the wall as a hush fell over the crowd.

Two figures walked out from the wooden temple doorway, a silver-haired young girl with a willowy figure next to a tall man wrapped in a cloak of shadow, his face obscured by a hood. He stayed out of the sunlight, shielded by one of the pillars.

"Elf," Sienna whispered, and Mila remembered what her friend had told of Xander's death. The girl's power was not to be underestimated.

"And my father," Perry said, his voice hardening. "Or what's left of him."

Mila narrowed her eyes, trying to focus on the shape of Sir Douglas, but he was more a cloud of particles than a solid body now.

The transition to pure shadow was by all accounts a painful one, undertaken by only the most powerful Cartographers. It was unclear how much of the original man lay beneath that dusky blur, but while his physicality diminished, his magic grew.

These two were the central force powering the dark transformation of the Borderlands, and as the crowd cheered, raising their hands in salute, Mila wondered whether anyone could stop them.

Elf's sweet girlish voice rang out. "You are all welcome here tonight to witness the challenge. The reward for survival is great, but the risk is only undertaken by a chosen few." She pointed out to the lake. "Tonight, the challenge is something we have never seen before. A magic once thought lost has been reborn. If the challenge is won, we will have a new force to add to the army of the Borderlands."

She turned and beckoned to the side of the dais.

Two slight figures walked onto the stage, their steps hesitant as they emerged in front of the crowd.

Mila gasped at the sight of them. Twins with skin as black as Ekon's, limbs as long and slender as her own. A boy and a girl, twins, around eight or nine years old.

"Waterwalkers," Elf announced in triumph. "The first in a generation. They will face the challenge together." She pointed to the sunken church, its spire jutting out toward the night sky with a half-moon pennant flying from its peak. "Retrieve the flag and I will grant you the highest honor."

"They're only children," Sienna said softly. "How will they survive alone?"

Mila couldn't speak, could hardly breathe. She had thought for so long that she was the only one of her kind until she had met Ekon at Ganvié and seen evidence of their once great people. Now two more stood before her — about to go to their deaths.

Even if the children survived the electric eels, she didn't like the sound of the 'highest honor.' The challenge was clearly a way to find those who had the strongest magic, but what was their fate if they proved themselves?

The crowd parted before them as the children walked down the steps. There was no hesitation in their stride, their expressions determined as they faced the water. Waves lapped up on the shore, a surge generated by the powerful tails of the creatures below, their thick bodies undulating through the liquid, their blue light arcing out around them. The air hummed with anticipation as the twins reached the edge of the lake.

They stood for a moment on the shore, then dived in, bodies shimmering as they shifted into their magical form. The crowd gasped at the sight, unseen for so long.

Mila didn't hesitate.

She dived over the side of the wall into the water below, disappearing into the depths as she followed the Waterwalker twins.

* * *

Finn wound the explosive cord tightly around the barrels and then dropped it down through the center to Titus waiting below. As he emerged onto the walkway between the vats, he had an unobstructed view over the lake and the crowd beyond.

A splash caught his eye from the other side of the plaza where people gathered around a low wall.

Someone had dived in after the children.

Behind the wall, Finn saw the sun catch on bright titian hair before the figure ducked away into the crowd. Could it be Sienna? Was Mila the unknown swimmer?

His mind raced with the possibility of what it might mean. He had to find her and there was only one place they would all be heading for. He turned to peer around the vat to the temple. Surely, the Mapwalker team would head there next.

CHAPTER 18

As Mila sank into the lake, her body changed and she moved as one with the water, scanning around her for the Waterwalker children and keeping an eye out for the electric eels.

Other strange creatures moved in the gloom, the pulsating mass of globular jellyfish, their insides glowing with a bilious light, disfigured tentacles hanging down to catch passing prey. Shoals of silver-sided fish darted past with misshapen heads and tumors bulging from their spines. Even the rocks on the lake bed were contorted, as if twisted by some primeval force into submission. Whatever they did in this camp, it affected the environment as well as the people.

A flash in the black water ahead.

As her vision adjusted, Mila could just make out the thick body of one creature as it darted after the twins. These were no ordinary beasts, but mutants created by the Shadow. They were gigantic, hunting with high-voltage pulses like a radar to locate their quarry before crushing it in their coils and activating the electric charge.

A scream echoed through the water. "Daniel!"

The cry for help galvanized Mila into action and she darted through the water, accelerating past the eel. It lunged, snapping its jaws, sending a pulse of electricity through her.

A searing jolt of pain and her limbs softened. For a moment, Mila thought she would sink to the bottom of the lake, a broken thing ready to be devoured.

The eel twisted its coils, whipping its tail at her.

Mila summoned her strength and rolled, corkscrewing down and away before it could catch her — then hurtled toward where the sound had come from.

The sunken church emerged from the gloom, its once majestic windows covered with green algae, its graveyard now home to crawling, creeping things with poisonous spines and probing tentacles.

An eel lay wrapped around one of the Waterwalkers, the girl, her face flitting between water and skin as the creature pulsed with electricity. Her crumpled body was limp, her eyes closed.

Her brother tried in vain to pull the coils of the beast away, screaming as he tried to help her. "Dawn, wake up! You need to get out of there. Please!"

Their language was a different dialect to the one Ekon had spoken with her in the ruined world under Ganvié, but Mila understood his desperation.

As the eel pulsed once more, she dived down, remembering Ekon's words when she lay trapped under the boulder in the ancient pyramid.

You are water. You cannot be pinned down. No rock can trap you.

And no eel either. These children had no one to teach them the ways of their people. But she could show them now.

Mila swept past Daniel, surprise flashing over his face as she eased herself between the coils next to Dawn. She wrapped her arms around the girl, whispering to her. "You are water. Nothing can trap you."

Dawn shifted a little, her eyes flickering as she registered the strange presence. Then the little girl wrapped her arms around Mila, clutching her as a child needing protection. Mila felt the frail body turn into pure liquid and made herself the same, dissolving out from under the coils of the eel.

She darted into the nave of the church, Daniel following close behind.

The eel swam after them, crashing into the stone doorway, its body too thick to enter. They were safe — for now.

"Who are you?" the boy demanded as Mila laid his sister down on one pew.

"A friend," Mila said. "A Waterwalker."

Daniel crossed his arms, a frown on his face. "They told us there are no others. We're special, our magic is unique."

Mila smiled. "You're definitely special, more than you know, but there *are* more of us. I have a friend, Ekon. He lives where our people have always lived." She smoothed a hand over Dawn's forehead as the girl stirred. "I hope you can meet him."

"But we live here," Daniel said. "Elf is our friend. She said there'll be a party if we can bring back the flag."

I bet she did, Mila thought. But she didn't want to frighten the children.

"Have any of your other friends had parties with Elf?"

Daniel's frown deepened. "Some said they were having one, but they didn't come back to school, so maybe they didn't pass their challenge …" His voice faded away.

Dawn opened her eyes and tried to sit up. Daniel rushed to her side as Mila helped the girl and together, they sat side by side on the pew in the church. Water eddied around them from the circling of the eels beyond the stone walls. The faint sound of carnival from the shore echoed through the water. Bread and circuses indeed. The masses kept at bay with alcohol and sacrifice. But Mila would not see these children suffer the same fate as Xander.

"Did you come from Atlantis to save us?" Dawn asked hesitantly, the words unfamiliar in her mouth. "They told us you were all dead."

Mila shook her head, wondering what else the children had been told of their heritage. "I'm not from Atlantis, at least not that I know of. But I am here to help you."

Dawn curled inward, pulling her legs up to her chest as she looked at the door of the church, illuminated by flashes of light outside. The eels battered the surrounding stone, seeking a way in. "I don't want to go back out there."

Mila put her arm around the girl and Dawn leaned in, snuggling up as if desperate for the contact. Daniel sat up straight a little way off, still wary. Mila's heart ached for them both, knowing full well that they couldn't stay in this sanctuary for long. They had to leave this place — but they did not have to return to the camp.

Daniel stood up. "I will get the flag. I'll wave to shore, make it clear we won. Then we can work out how to get back safely." He smiled at Mila. "Elf will be pleased to meet you, too. Maybe you can come to our party?"

Dawn reached out a hand to her brother. "No," she whispered. "You haven't seen what she does."

Daniel snatched his arm away. "What do you mean? Elf is our friend."

Dawn shook her head. "She steals magic, she sucks it from you. When Jenny went for her party—" She turned to Mila to explain. "Jenny was my second best friend. She could make anything grow really big, insects and plants and animals." Her face crumpled and tears ran down her cheeks. "I followed them, Daniel. I saw Elf pull something out of Jenny, like a magical spark, and she sank to the ground as if she was just empty skin." The little girl shuddered. "I couldn't run in case they saw me. I watched them sweep up her remains. She was dead, Daniel. Elf killed her."

"Why didn't you tell me before?"

Dawn sighed. "You wouldn't have believed me, and anyhow, we couldn't get away from her. If she found out I knew, she would have killed me, I know it."

The eel outside smashed its tail into the door of the church once more, this time dislodging chunks of stone. A cloud of dust swirled through the water.

Mila looked up as a crack split one pillar to the side of the entrance, a fissure running up into the arch, dislodging the keystone. Another thump as the creatures outside battered their sanctuary. They didn't have long before the entire place came down around them.

CHAPTER 19

When Mila dived into the water, Sienna quickly took a step back. She pulled Perry away from the edge out of the line of sight from the main stage as people around them shouted and pointed in excitement.

"Another Waterwalker!"

It would only be minutes before the guards made it to this area of the crowd. They slipped into the mass of revelers, aware of suspicious stares as they retreated. Sienna slipped her arm around Perry's waist and he hugged her close to his side. They giggled and joked as they pushed through, trying not to draw attention. Just another pair of drunken young lovers on their way to find somewhere more private.

The crowd thinned out toward the barracks at the back of the plaza and they ducked behind one of the huts.

"What is she doing?" Perry whispered, his fists clenched in frustration. "Now they know we're here. What can she possibly hope to achieve?"

Sienna shook her head. "I don't know if she even considered her actions. She saw the children and went to help. We don't know how it feels to have her kind of magic. They are others like us, but she is—"

"A shifter," Perry finished for her, and Sienna heard resignation in his voice. "She belongs here, doesn't she?"

Sienna nodded. "Perhaps. But she might need our help to get the children out. We have to assume she'll go to the meeting place if she can. We'll get Zoe and wait for her at the cave."

Perry grinned. "Just like that?"

"Just like that." Sienna peered around the side of the barracks. "The crowd's attention is still on the water but the guards will be looking for us. Sir Douglas knows of Mila's gift. He must know we're here."

She looked toward the temple, its wooden beams over the ceremonial door urging her closer. An energy pulsed from within, something bound with stripes of shadow and flashes of light, a sickening mix that made her dizzy. Sienna closed her eyes, attraction and repulsion warring inside as the earth shifted beneath her. Nausea rose inside and she put her hand on the barracks wall to steady herself.

"You okay?" Perry asked.

Sienna nodded. "She's in there. I'm sure of it." Her heart thumped as she considered who else might be in there with Zoe, but they had no choice. The Weaver could not be left behind.

They darted between the huts, hiding as groups of guards ran past. Some revelers spilled out of the main plaza, drinking in groups around campfires as dusk turned to night. They shouted and sung together, drowning their miserable lives with cheap ale and the promise of human connection, even just for one evening.

As Sienna and Perry drew closer to the temple, the atmosphere changed. People clustered in groups to pray, prostrating themselves on the ground as they reached toward their imagined salvation. One woman beat herself with a flail tipped in glass, ripping open her tunic, blood flowing from her wounds and dripping onto the earth.

She swayed in ecstasy, her lips moving in a constant prayer. "Transform me, renew me, remake me."

This place was a magnet for those who desired to become one with the Shadow, who would knowingly give their life force to join with something beyond their understanding. Perhaps it was ever thus, Sienna thought. Was her own quest to the Tower of the Winds any different? Was she really going to save Earthside or did she pursue it because she needed to see whatever called in her nightmares? The promise of power and the threat of annihilation would be held in balance until the moment she stepped into that place.

She looked up at the temple looming ahead. They had to get there first.

"Where are they?" Elf's high-pitched peal of a voice came from the front of the building. "The children should have captured the flag by now. Get some guards out there on the water."

She was distracted by the scene on the lake. They had a chance to get inside.

* * *

Perry ducked around the back of the temple, Sienna close behind. Two guards stood either side of a staircase, their attention distracted as they talked amongst themselves, unaware of the threat approaching. Zoe was in there, he was sure of it, and the thought of what his father might do to her made him feel sick.

Perry made it within a few meters before the guards saw him, eyes widening as they opened their mouths to shout a warning. He opened his palms and fired two perfectly aimed fireballs — small enough to swallow, expanding into a fast-burning flare.

The guards slumped to the ground, helmets smoking from the heat within.

Perry crept up the steps, wood creaking under his feet,

the sound drowned out by the din of the celebratory crowd. He pushed open the door and slipped inside, hands raised at the ready. A dark blue flame flickered around his fingertips with barely restrained energy as Sienna followed him inside.

It was dark at first, and it took a second for Perry's eyes to adjust to the dim light.

Zoe sat tied to a chair, arms bound to her sides, her face bloody and bruised, head hanging down, maybe unconscious. Perry wanted to run to her, pull her into his arms — but by her side stood the insubstantial figure of his father, Sir Douglas Mercator, the once regal frame reduced to almost complete shadow.

Yet, he was stronger now than he had ever been in flesh.

"I've been expecting you." Sir Douglas stepped forward, although it seemed as if he glided more than walked across the floor. In the half-light of the lamps, Perry could see within the folds of his cloak to the shaded contours beneath. His body was almost completely gone, transformed into shadows that rippled and twisted in and out of what had once been flesh.

Perry raised his hands, turned his palms up and summoned his flame into writhing balls of fire. He lifted his chin, eyes fixed on his father as he channeled his magic, intensifying the flame until it burned hot as molten lava.

He had trained for this moment, summoning his father's face in the practice rooms under Bath Abbey, slamming fire into that gaunt visage over and over until it splintered into ash. But now he was here, he felt a heaviness in his limbs, a resistance to the one task he had set himself.

His father drew closer. "Join us, my son. There is much opportunity for you here." He reached out a hand toward Perry's cheek, gentle fingers outstretched.

In his eyes, Perry saw a flicker of the man he had known as a child. The man who had taken him to the woods and shown him the gift of fire, encouraging him to use his power in secret, to keep his Halbrasse status quiet in case he was chosen to fight for causes he did not believe in. A principled man — who had now given his life to the Shadow.

Perry stepped back and raised his hands again, causing flames to rise in pillars before him.

"We're here for Zoe."

Sir Douglas waved a dismissive hand. A curl of shadow extended out from his reach to swirl under Zoe's chin, lifting her face toward them, her skin marred from a beating.

"She is nothing." He snapped the shadow back and her head dropped again.

Perry heard Sienna's sharp intake of breath, instinctively knew that she would go to her friend. In that moment, he saw the trap.

Sir Douglas had always and only wanted Sienna. Perry's own power was nothing compared to that of a Blood Mapwalker, one who could be twisted to true darkness.

Sienna ran forward.

Sir Douglas wheeled toward her and opened his arms wide. He summoned a great veil of shadow that billowed high and wide, filling the air with dust and ash and the stink of the grave, obscuring the room with shade.

"No!" Perry cried. He shot his flames into the cloud of darkness, momentarily illuminating Sienna as she ran from Sir Douglas toward Zoe, her arms outstretched. But his fire crashed down into the floor, extinguished by the weight of particles in the air.

The Shadow Cartographer loomed tall above Sienna, his skeletal form suddenly filled out, as if darkness expanded his frame into some hybrid creature that straddled the realms of man. He stretched his arms wide and gathered her to him, enveloping her in shadow, their bodies shimmering as something rose in the darkness beyond.

A corridor. A portal. Back to the Tower of the Winds.

He couldn't let his father take Sienna.

Perry bellowed in rage, summoning flames to surround his entire body. He ran, a burning torch, head down into the cloud of dust and tackled the fading figure of Sir Douglas.

The three of them fell to the floor, writhing in a pile of ash. Perry grabbed tight, wrapping his arms around his father's chest, his knees latched on to what was left of the man's legs. He called forth the flames within, burning hotter than he had ever tried to burn before.

His father writhed beneath him, moaning in pain. The sound echoed through his very soul, his heart almost bursting — and yet Perry would not let go.

As he thrashed in agony, Sir Douglas released Sienna, his grip loosening as his fingers crackled in the heat. She rolled away, hair singed, her clothes burning as she crawled along the floor, coughing and retching in the smoke.

She looked back at him and Perry saw horror in her eyes, a reflection of two entwined still-living corpses, burned flesh oozing together, becoming one in their inevitable end. She reached out a hand, shaking her head as she begged him to stop.

But Perry didn't want to stop. This was his mission, the task he had come to complete. There would be no better chance to end the Shadow Cartographer. Flames roared in his ears, blood pounding in his head as the temperature rose. He gripped his father tighter, summoning all the power he had left, determined to burn them out of existence together.

The door burst open.

Brilliant white light shot through the cloud of ash, as sharp as a blade, throwing Perry off his father.

He pinwheeled across the floor, driven by the force of the light and slammed against the back wall of the temple, his flames quenched by the frosted silver that froze his skin instantly. The crushing pain of ice spread through his veins and Perry screamed as the shock of it rippled through him.

Sir Douglas lay moaning in a tattered heap of smoking

rags, his arms a patchwork of oozing burned flesh with shards of bone visible beneath. Tendrils of shadow entwined with curls of smoke above him as the stench of charred skin filled the room.

Elf stepped through the open door, two huge muscled mutants behind her. She held one hand outstretched to hold Perry in place with the silver light, her eyes flashing an icy blue as she stalked toward her prey.

CHAPTER 20

As Elf walked in, Sienna looked at the floor, her eyes fixed on the thick wooden boards, noticing the whorls within even as she tried to dampen down the magic that flowed inside, trying desperately to stop the eddies of shadow emerging on her skin.

Elf had only glimpsed her briefly in the refugee camp that night. Perhaps she would not recognize her now? Smoke and shadow shrouded the room, and the young woman's gaze was fixed on Perry. But would like call to like?

Some part of Sienna wanted to stand and show the darkness on her skin, share the ties that bound them together and embrace the way the young woman so freely explored her magic. But if Elf realized the power that sat so close, Sienna knew she might not make it to the Tower of the Winds. Elf would take all she was and use it for her own ends.

Perry groaned and Elf stalked toward him, the others forgotten as she concentrated on her prey. She twisted her hand into a fist, crushing the silver light into a pinpoint. Perry doubled over, hands clutched to his belly where the beam focused.

She opened her fist again, her fingers spreading like a flower. The brilliance expanded, licking across Perry's skin as his flame awakened once more.

But this time, it was not under his control.

Elf tore it from him as she pulled the magic out, her breath rapid, her face transfigured into something like ecstasy as she fed on his power.

Perry cried out, his tortured body shuddering as he convulsed in pain.

Sir Douglas raised himself up onto one elbow, weakened by the attack but not finished yet. His face was human now, less shadow, more burned flesh. One piercing blue eye remained while the other was swollen shut, the eyelid red and oozing.

"Leave him." His voice trembled, but Sienna heard the edge of steel in his tone.

Elf tightened her grip. "So, this is your son. The one who chose his Mapwalker friends over you."

She tugged harder on the silver cord and Perry jerked once, then collapsed into spasm, his body sagging in on itself as energy was sucked from him.

Sienna wept as she watched her friend suffer, with no way to stop his end as she could not have stopped Elf killing Xander and his lion, Asada. In that moment, she wished for a different type of magic, one that would enable her to fight back. She wished for Mila's water, for Perry's fire, for Zoe's ability to manipulate the strings of the world, for anything but her own blood. She could escape right now, mapwalk out of here, but that would leave her friends behind. And she was nothing without them.

Elf laughed as she tore into Perry with both hands, teeth bared, nails ripping into the air, as her silver light dug deep within his bones for the last vestiges of power. He was silent now, a husk of the man he had been, his face pallid, eyes closed. Sienna felt the beat of his magic slow.

He was almost finished.

"Enough." Sir Douglas reached out one blackened, twisted hand. A bolt of flame shot from his outstretched fingers, cutting off Elf's silver blade of light and blocking its path. Perry's body slumped to the floor, his chest rising and falling in a jerky manner. He still lived, but not for much longer.

Elf turned, her expression alive with cold anger but Sienna saw something else there. Excitement for a confrontation she had clearly wanted for too long.

Sir Douglas had reined the young woman in, his power too much for her to challenge. But now the old man lay crumpled on the floor, the shadows that normally writhed about him in powerful arcs were now merely shreds.

"Leave him. He's mine to finish." Sir Douglas stared at Elf, his one good eye meeting her piercing gaze.

She smiled and shook her head. "Not anymore."

Elf raised her hands and shot darts of white light toward Sir Douglas.

He thrust out one palm, flames erupting around it, pushing back the white light, burning it with his crimson blaze. The hiss of steam erupted into the air as fire met ice. Elf reared back as the force hit her, but then she leaned into the fight, redoubling her efforts. She seemed to grow taller in stature as she called forth her powerful magic.

The last remaining shreds of shadow shrank from Sir Douglas, curling away from him like snakes deserting a home that would soon burn them alive.

Elf's silver shard of light inched its way closer, forcing him back. Sienna watched as the last shadows left his body, his face contorted in pain as he became more like the man who had come to her in the map shop that first day. It seemed a lifetime away now.

Elf smiled in triumph. She walked across the still burning timbers of the floor, raising her hands higher. As her light broke through his wall of flame, Sir Douglas gasped in agony.

She tightened her grip and tore the last vestiges of magic

from him. "Your time is over, old man. The Shadow favors me now."

He convulsed as coils of magic shuddered from him. Elf threw back her head and screamed in pleasure as she drank in his power.

A sudden explosion rocked the building, a series of blasts from outside at the vats. A heavy beam jolted loose above.

Elf looked up, her eyes widening as it dropped.

* * *

Mila heard the explosions from inside the church, a series of deep booms that rippled through the water. A moment later, the attack on the door stopped and the giant eels darted away back to the shore. She didn't know what had happened, but she could imagine the chaos of the drunken revelers on the beach running for the water. Food for the eels, after all.

She urged the children to their feet. "Quick, we need to get out of here while they're distracted."

Dawn shrank back on the bench. "I don't want to go out there."

Mila hunkered down in front of her. "They're gone, but not for long. We can swim to the opposite side, get out the water there. I can take you to a safe place."

Dawn looked up at Daniel. After a moment, the boy nodded.

They swam to the opposite side of the sunken church and Mila peered out the little window into the murky water. There could be more creatures waiting, but they had no time to wait and see.

She held her hands out, and the children took them, trusting her. Their skin reminded her of Ekon, a dissolving of flesh to water, something only their kind could do. She had to take these children home.

They darted together out into the gloom. None of them looked back.

* * *

As the beam fell, Elf jerked her arms up, shielding herself with magic and pushing the heavy beam toward Sir Douglas. The weight of the wood crushed him to the floor, pinning what remained of his body under the smoldering shaft. Burning embers tumbled down around them as the flames took hold.

Two more booms shook the building.

Screams from the panicked crowd outside.

Another beam came loose and crashed down. It glanced off Elf's shoulder, sending her to the ground with a cry. The mutant bodyguards surged forward. One enormous brute picked the young woman up in his arms, shielding her as they ran from the building even as the beams tumbled down behind them.

Zoe's chair tipped over in the blast and Sienna dived to stop her head hitting the floor. She wrapped her arms around her friend; her face only inches from where Sir Douglas lay unmoving, half-crushed beneath the fallen beam. His remaining eyelid flickered, and he breathed in shallow gasps, his lungs clearly constricted by the weight.

Perry sprawled only meters away, his body broken, his magic siphoned away, his mind possibly damaged beyond repair.

The shouts of a frantic crowd came from outside through the roar of the flames that licked at the beams. The shifting sound of wood collapsing. It wouldn't be long until they were buried in here or burned alive.

But there was one way out.

"Perry!" Sienna shouted, weeping as she called for her friend. "Can you hear me?"

If she could get to him, she could mapwalk them all out of here.

The sound of running footsteps and the creak of wood.

Two figures entered the disintegrating building, big men with weapons at their sides, faces obscured by the smoke. Sienna ducked quickly back behind the burning beam, desperately hoping they wouldn't see her.

"Sienna?"

His voice was everything she had longed for. Sienna looked out under the beam and her heart leapt at seeing the regal profile silhouetted against the flames.

"Finn. Finn, I'm here."

He turned at her voice. Their eyes met, and the world melted away. For a second, Sienna could believe that everything would work out, that he would save her and they would escape this terrible place and be together.

Then the building shifted once more, flames crackled and another beam fractured above her head.

Finn and his companion darted forward, shouldering through the burning wood, sheltering Sienna as they untied Zoe from the chair.

"Titus, carry her outside. I'll be right behind you."

Titus nodded, hoisting Zoe into his arms and barreling back out into the chaos beyond.

Finn put his arms around Sienna, pulling her close to his chest, his hands tender on her skin.

He looked down at Sir Douglas. "What about him?"

Sienna shook her head. "Perry first, he's over there. He's hurt."

Together, they climbed over the beams and dug through the fallen wood. Perry lay on his back, his face pale and waxy, ash in his hair, soot smeared over his skin. His eyes fluttered open as they helped him up to a sitting position.

"My father?" His voice rasped from flame-cracked lips.

Sienna pointed to the fallen beam. "He's pinned. Elf took his magic and if he's not dead already, he will be soon."

Perry tried to get up, but his legs crumpled beneath him.

Finn took his weight. "We have to get out of here. The building could collapse at any minute."

"Please. I need to see him."

Sienna could see the conflict in Finn's expression, his jawline taut with tension. The rebel leader had faced his own father on a battlefield, a man who still held the power of life and death over him.

Finn nodded, swiftly lifting Perry to his feet and helping him around the back of the beam to where his father lay.

Sir Douglas looked dead, a crushed corpse, but as Perry knelt and rested a hand on his blackened brow, the man opened his one good eye.

His lips parted in a sigh. "Son," he whispered.

Perry leaned closer, tears spilling down his cheeks. "I'm so sorry, Dad."

Sir Douglas closed his eye a moment and then opened it again. "Inside my cloak. Reach in."

Perry frowned and bent to his father's chest, easing his hand inside the burned clothing. He couldn't help but touch the weeping, blistered flesh, coating his fingers in sticky blood. But Sir Douglas was beyond feeling anymore and Perry thrust his hand in further. A second later, he withdrew his hand and uncurled his bloody fingers.

Sienna gasped at the sight of her grandfather's silver compass. Stolen by the man who had murdered him one stormy night in Bath in the grove of sacred plane trees in the center of the Druid's circle.

Sir Douglas looked up at Sienna. "Use it once more," he whispered, his voice slowing. "For Galileo."

His eye drooped shut as he let out a final breath. His head lolled to one side and Perry let out a sob.

A beam cracked overhead, and the sound of trampling footsteps came from outside.

"We're out of time." Finn grabbed Perry with one arm,

pulling him to his feet while he helped Sienna with the other.

The floorboards creaked underfoot, weakening even as they darted between falling beams. Burning embers and ash rained down as smoke filled the building with choking fumes. Sienna could barely see what direction they should go in, but Finn dragged them on.

A light ahead. The back door gaped open, the staircase burning up from below.

"Jump!" Finn shouted, half-dragging Perry over the edge. Sienna followed close behind, rolling as she hit the hard ground behind the scorching temple.

The crackling sound of flames filled the air alongside the screams and shouts of the panicked crowd. They flowed like a river away from the plaza, back to the barracks and shacks at the edges of the camp. Sienna pushed herself up quickly as two men ran past, unheeding of her on the ground. Another inch closer and they would have trampled her.

She stood up and turned to find Finn helping Perry, and Titus waiting with Zoe over his shoulder in a fireman's carry. Sienna wanted to be the one in Finn's arms, but Perry's face was blanched with grief and the aftermath of whatever Elf had done to him. She didn't know whether he still had any magic left, but they couldn't wait to find out.

"This way," Titus shouted and headed away up the hill, joining the throng.

Finn nodded at Sienna. "I'll help Perry. Go. I'll be right behind you."

Whatever was unsaid between them could wait. She turned and jogged after Titus, merging with the crowd and ducking down as they passed the mutant guards. But the sentries were distracted and waved everyone on, eyes fixed on the burning temple and the ruins of the plaza beyond.

At the top of the hill, Sienna turned to see what had them so mesmerized. The waters ran red at the edge of the lake, bodies torn apart by the giant eels that writhed in the shallows, razor-sharp teeth slashing soft flesh in a feeding frenzy. The explosions must have driven some of the crowd into the water, only to be met by the monsters that lurked just below the surface.

Sienna stifled a sob as she thought of Mila down there with the children. "Please make it back," she whispered, then turned and ran once more.

She caught up with Titus on the edge of the shantytown as he easily carried Zoe's slight frame over his broad shoulders. He turned to greet her, and she noticed the stain of blue on his fingertips.

He noticed her look and raised an eyebrow. "I'm a chemist."

She smiled. "Useful skill. Was that—?"

Titus nodded. "Our explosions. Yes. We came to the camp to destroy the manufacture of the drug these bastards peddle in the trader towns, but then Finn saw your friend dive into the lake. He can recognize an Earthsider from a mile away and had an inkling you might be close by." Titus hesitated for a moment, then sighed. "To be honest, I haven't seen him this alive for so long."

Warmth spread through Sienna at his words. Finn had missed her just as much as she had longed for him and that gave her hope.

Zoe stirred. Titus gently lifted her off his shoulders and set her down on the ground. She rubbed her eyes, blinking as she took in her surroundings. "What happened?"

Sienna knelt next to her. "It's okay. You're safe now."

Zoe reached up and grasped her hand, eyes wide in desperation. "Elf. We have to stop her. She's found a way to drain and concentrate magical power."

"I know," Sienna said softly. "That's how she killed Xander. She almost killed Perry back there and who knows how many others."

Titus frowned. "She must be the one responsible for adding the mutation magic to the Liberation."

Zoe nodded. "Yes, but it's much more than that. I heard her telling the old man, Sir Douglas, how she could use the shadow portal in the Tower of the Winds to reach all the Borderlands at once. How she could somehow bleed power from everywhere, then use it to finally blow apart the border and retake Earthside. I saw the look on his face, Sienna. He was scared. It must be possible. We have to stop her."

CHAPTER 21

TOGETHER, THEY MADE THEIR way back to the cave. Titus helped Zoe and Sienna over the wall into the rubbish heap beyond and Finn half-carried Perry, who grew weaker with every passing minute.

No one tried to stop them. No one even paid any attention as they climbed away from the mutant camp into the sanctuary of the cave system.

As they approached, Sienna kept looking up at the opening, hoping that Mila might have already arrived. But there was no sign of the Waterwalker, and when they made it inside, Mila had not returned.

Finn helped Perry to rest against the back wall and Zoe curled up next to him, both exhausted. Titus pulled food from his pack and shared it out with water from his canteen.

Sienna sat at the lip of the cave entrance and scanned the hill below for any sign of Mila or approaching danger from the camp. Finn came to sit beside her and she leaned into his warmth.

"I'm so glad you're here," she whispered.

He put his arm around her and pulled her close, kissing her hair. "I'm sorry I didn't make it earlier. You should have told me you were coming."

Sienna closed her eyes, and they breathed the night air together. Whatever anger and misunderstanding had passed between them mattered little now. There was only the moment and in this crack of time, Sienna belonged to Finn alone.

She raised her head and looked up into his dark eyes, stroked his cheek. He leaned down and in their kiss lay the promise of possibility, the hope that Borderlander and Earthsider could live in peace. A world where the moon rose on all kinds alike.

Sienna wanted to stay in that moment forever, lost in his soft mouth, but the sound of scraping on stone came from below, then the tumble of loose rocks on scree.

They broke apart and looked over the lip of the cave.

Mila scrambled up the incline, two children behind her.

Sienna wanted to shout in excitement, but the sound would echo in the valley and might alert the guards. She restrained her happiness by kissing Finn once more, her smile reflected in his glad expression. The team was wounded, but they were not finished yet.

Mila soon made it to the lip of the cave. She hugged Sienna and Finn, but the children hung back, their faces curious but shy.

"It's okay." Mila beckoned them forward. "These are my friends. You're safe now."

She introduced them, and the children solemnly nodded in greeting.

Titus pulled out some more food, and the children were soon chattering away happily with the big chemist. Finn went to join them, leaving Mila and Sienna to talk.

They sat at the cave entrance under the light of the moon, the camp below them calm now as the night wore on, intoxicated revelers sleeping off the carnival and the stress of the day, blood and chaos chasing them through nightmares.

"I thought you might not make it back," Sienna said, taking her friend's hand. "I saw what those creatures did to bodies on the shoreline."

Mila squeezed her hand with a rueful smile. "It was pretty crazy down there." She shook her head. "I just had to go after them … And it's more than that." She paused, a moment of silence before a sigh of acceptance. "I need to take the children to Ganvié and to be honest, I want to go home. To my true home, that is."

Sienna heard the longing in Mila's voice and wished she could feel that certain about where she belonged.

Mila continued. "I felt something rare under the lake. An elemental joy that has always been out of reach on Earthside. I can't leave that behind again. I can't go back to living outside my true nature."

Sienna smiled. "I know that leaving Ekon was difficult for you. I saw how you transformed when you were with him."

"I think more of my kind still exist under the waves, but they've become one with the water somehow. Perhaps I can find them with Ekon and the twins by my side — after we finish this mission, of course. I'll come with you to the Tower of the Winds first. We'll finish this together."

Sienna sat silent for a moment. She thought of the woman in the mosaic on the cave wall under the impossible mountain. She had been alone — and perhaps that was the only way. Perry and Zoe were injured. Finn and Titus had no magic. Mila would be the only one who could stand with her — but the path ahead was dangerous and Sienna knew she had to face whatever it was alone. If Mila came to the Tower of the Winds, she might not make it out again. She had a chance for happiness, for a life fulfilled, and Sienna wanted that for her friend. Her own future was uncertain, but Mila and the twins could start anew.

"I don't want you to come," Sienna said, pushing down the tears that threatened. "I don't need you, anyway."

Mila frowned. "What do you mean? I can fight by your side. We're a team."

"Not anymore." Sienna looked into Mila's eyes. "I don't

want you to bring the children and they need you more than I do. We'll be fine, Mila, really. I want you to go to Ganvié. If we need you, I'll send word somehow."

"If you're sure."

"I am." Sienna put every ounce of confidence into her words, knowing that Mila would follow if she did not dissuade her.

"Then I'll go to Ganvié tomorrow." Mila turned to look back into the cave. The others were too far away to hear them. She leaned in close. "But be careful, Sienna. I know something calls you from the Tower of the Winds. I know the marks on your skin have spread."

Sienna flushed. "Is it obvious?"

"Not to everyone, but you and I … well, we've discovered a lot on these last missions. I've seen you change to become a powerful Blood Mapwalker. Your destiny draws you on, as does mine."

"But not together anymore," Sienna whispered as she leaned in and they hugged, clinging to each other for a moment, then they parted.

"I left Zippy with a friend who loves him," Mila said. "And a letter for Bridget in the canal boat explaining everything, but I won't go back this time. I am not of Earthside anymore. Perhaps I never really was."

Sienna hugged her friend again, hiding her tears against Mila's hair, smelling the fresh water of the lake on her skin. They sat for a moment, holding each other tight, both aware of an ending they hadn't expected to experience so soon.

Sienna pulled away and wiped her eyes. "How will you get to Ganvié?"

Mila shrugged. "The watercourses will guide us. We'll travel up river and find our way from there. I'm drawn back somehow, like a compass needle pointing true north." She looked out at the horizon. "I know Ekon will welcome us."

"He will." Sienna rose to her feet. "But I hate goodbyes so this is temporary. I'll come visit when I can."

Mila smiled and stood up to join her. "Of course." She gave a cheeky grin. "And bring Finn with you."

Sienna looked back into the cave where Finn sat by the fire, the light dancing off his angular cheekbones as he played a dice game with the children. They laughed, leaning on his legs, trusting him instinctively. With their dark skin, they could be his and Sienna was suddenly struck with a glimpse into a possible future.

Finn looked up at her, a question in his eyes.

She smiled and went to join him. They all needed to rest before the day to come.

* * *

The rays of dawn reached into the cave and touched Sienna's cheek. She opened her eyes to see coral light bathing the sleeping group, as if blessed by some heavenly benediction. She nestled back into Finn's embrace, trying to fix the moment in her mind.

Sienna thought of her father and Bridget back on Earthside, the same dawn rising over the Ministry. Mapwalking had broken their love apart, taken everything from them both. Her father was a crippled husk, his body and mind shattered by that final mission. Bridget had given her very blood to the service of the Ministry, trapped in the guise of the Illuminated for who knows how many generations. Her grandfather's skin lay in the Blood Gallery, his life sacrificed for a portal he couldn't even ultimately defend. Sienna pulled his compass from her pocket.

The silver gleamed in the morning light and she opened the case to reveal the five-pointed compass rose and the city of Bath etched in tiny lines within. The abbey, the map shop, the Circus, the river, the canal. Five places to anchor her back to Earthside.

Sienna clutched the compass tightly in her hand. If the border had been open, she could cut herself right now, map-walk through the power of her blood and take Perry and Zoe home. But she would have to leave Finn behind once more — and besides, the border was still closed, and her fight was here now.

Zoe's words about Elf ran through her mind. What did the young woman intend at the Tower of the Winds?

There was only one way to find out. It was time she faced whatever called in her nightmares.

"Morning," Finn whispered, his breath caressing her ear as he shifted position, wrapping his arms more tightly about her. As he pulled her closer. Sienna could feel his muscular body down the length of her back and she longed to stay right there, sheltered in his warmth. But the sun rose higher in the sky and every minute that passed was another minute that Elf traveled before them.

Titus sat up, yawned and stretched his arms. He looked over and smiled as he caught Sienna's gaze. "I'll make coffee. You lovebirds stay right there."

He set up a small fire near the entrance to the cave then pulled his pack over, scouring through it for matches.

"Damn, I must have dropped them when we set off the charges." He looked over at Finn. "You have any?"

"Let me do it." Perry's voice was weak but Sienna heard determination as he rocked up to his hands and knees and crawled to the pile of wood, Zoe helping him with a steady arm. Sienna sat up, Finn sitting with her, all of them willing him on.

Perry reached the pile of kindling as the rising sun caught his face with an orange glow, brightening his pale countenance. He reached a hand out, extended his fingers, looked down into his palm. His brow furrowed as he concentrated, curling and tensing his grip until his hand was almost a claw.

Sienna held her breath, willing him to find that spark, desperate to know what was left of his power.

CHAPTER 22

THE SECONDS TICKED PAST with not even a flicker.

Perry tightened his fist and slammed it down on the cave floor. He hung his head and then looked out to the horizon, biting his lip in frustration. Zoe wrapped her arms around his shoulders, silent in her support.

Sienna wondered whether his power was gone completely or just weakened. In such a state, should she really take him with her to the Tower of the Winds? With Mila leaving, she needed Perry — but he could be more of a liability in this state.

Finn rummaged in his bag and pulled out a box of matches. He tossed them to Titus, who lit the fire and soon had water boiling for coffee.

"What did I miss?" Mila sat up, her expression confused at the tense silence in the cave.

"Nothing," Perry whispered, a hint of bitterness in his tone. "Nothing at all."

The twins stirred, their small hands reaching for Mila as they awoke. Sienna smiled to see the way her friend gathered them to her, a Waterwalker family on its way home. At least something good had come out of the camp.

Titus made coffee, a thick brew in the Turkish style, a shot of caffeine to send them off suitably fired up. Sienna sipped at hers, trying to hold off the inevitable. But as the sun rose higher over the lip of the cave, she knew they had to go.

There were clouds on the horizon, a gathering storm that would sweep over the camp within hours. Mila could leave in the shelter of its rainfall and the rest of them would be long gone by then.

"Pack up," she said. "We need to leave."

It didn't take long to ready themselves, but it took longer for Mila to say goodbye to everyone. Perry clung to her the longest and Sienna had to turn away to hide the tears in her eyes. She had to believe that the team would be together again — sometime, somewhere.

She put her hands on the wall of the cave, cold stone anchoring her to this place in this moment. Once she took the team through the blood map, her path was set, but she could see no other way forward.

The border must open once more or Earthside would be wracked by increasing natural disaster. But the opening must be controlled otherwise the Borderlanders would stream over and take what they believed to be theirs. If Elf was truly going after whatever lay in the Tower of the Winds, Sienna had to get there first.

They had one advantage. Elf had to travel by road, and even with her mutant pack running at full pace, she would still be hours away. The rest had been worth it. Sleep in Finn's arms had renewed Sienna's strength and revived her sense of purpose. She was ready.

She drew on the stone wall with a fingertip, lightly etching a map over the rock. One that seemed carved on her heart. She had seen it so many times in her nightmares. It would be easy to travel there. All she had to do was follow the voice that called and drop down through the clouds to the tower. She could find the place easily. The only question was what waited there — and whether she could resist the pull of the Shadow once inside.

"Sienna?" Mila touched her arm gently.

Sienna turned to embrace her friend. "Go safe."

Mila nodded, her eyes betraying both her sadness but also excitement at the start of a new adventure. "One time of life ends, another begins."

Sienna smiled. "Perhaps for both of us."

Mila stood back by the cave entrance, the twins on either side, hands curled in hers, their faces curious but trusting. They had seen so much of magic, but perhaps never the strange exit of a Blood Mapwalker.

Sienna turned her back to them so they would not see her pull out the ritual knife, the sharp blade almost a friend to her now. She cut into the side of her palm, blood welling fast, and used it to sketch over the lines on the wall.

Her fingers moved with accuracy and speed, as if the map was carved inside her, just waiting to burst free. Sienna's skin itched, and she sensed the dark whorls eddy and throb as they drew closer to their home.

As she inscribed the last line, she reached out her other hand. Perry and Zoe, Finn and Titus grasped it, palm over palm, holding onto each other as Sienna drew them into the map. As the world shifted, she met Mila's gaze in one final goodbye.

The caves fell away. Below them, the expanse of the camp and beyond that, the lake of strange creatures, then the river heading off toward the coast where Mila would swim home. Sienna rose higher, reveling in the sensation of freedom as she reached out across the Borderlands with her magic.

She flew like one of the giant eagles they encountered in the eyrie back in the search for the Map of Plagues, with keen eyesight that could pick out detail in the expanse below. Beyond the towering sharp peaks, a track stretched out into an arid plain spiked with cactus and patches of scrub. A dust cloud headed east, thrown up by the running feet of a pack of mutants. Elf was amongst them, carried on the back of one beast and beyond, in the distance, the Tower of the Winds.

Sienna circled up into the clouds that obscured the sun. Without the distraction of the world below she could hear her name more clearly, a whisper that rippled down her spine, causing her to ache for some dark pleasure she could not quite name.

Sienna.

Did Elf hear her name called like this? Were they both summoned for the final reckoning? Sienna shivered as the clouds darkened and a sudden rainstorm blew across the sky, bringing with it rolls of thunder.

A flash of lightning caught a jagged outline above, the wings of a huge beast with talons raised like a hunter. She had seen something like it when imprisoned within the shadow weave, and she had no wish to encounter such a creature again.

Sienna dived back down through the clouds, emerging close to the Tower of the Winds. The fortress spiraled into the sky, a citadel of many levels. It was made from pieces of black stone locked together in intricate patterns with fragments of obsidian and black onyx mixed in with the pocked surface of volcanic lava and glossy agate. Polished to a sheen, the tower rose with curves as smooth as glass, impossible to climb from the outside even if someone were to brave its heights.

She soared around it, sensing the intensity of shadow in the highest part of the tower. Some part of her wanted to land right there, cast the others off into the space between the worlds and go alone to meet whatever waited. Her blood hammered through her veins, a pulse that demanded to be shed. For what was a Blood Mapwalker unless her power could be wielded?

Sienna.

The whisper grew louder now with the heady sensuality

of a lover's call. It promised gifts and pleasure, and the dark whorls of shadow on her skin wanted only to give in.

But the weight of her friends anchored her, and Sienna fought against the desire to rush to the summit. She swooped lower, spotting a library through arched windows with giant books chained to wooden lecterns and shelves full of ancient tomes. She plunged down in her mind's eye and when she could feel the solid floor under her feet and smell the faint musty vanilla scent of old books, Sienna opened her eyes.

The others lay on the floor around her. Titus coughed and retched, reeling from his first mapwalking experience. The others were more used to the nausea and lay still for a moment as they recovered. Sienna gazed down at them. They were weak, pitifully so.

The sudden thought was shocking. These were her friends. How could she think that way?

Finn sat up and looked at her, his eyes widening as he mouthed a prayer to the goddess. Sienna saw fear in his expression where such a short time ago, there had been only love. What was happening?

She gazed down at her bare arms, now deeply mottled with black symbols that writhed on her skin as if alive with dark magic. There was a mirror against one bookcase and she walked to it quickly. The same marks now covered her face and neck, signs of shadow whirling on her skin, winding in and out of her tattoos depicting the city of Bath. Sienna's entire body was now a fusion of light and dark, a battleground for the Shadow — and it felt good.

Sienna knew that Finn was right to be afraid. Her power was rising. She needed to ascend the tower but the others must not come with her. She didn't want them to see what she might become — or what she might do to them once she reached her goal.

* * *

Zoe rolled onto her hands and knees and pushed down the queasy sensation in her stomach. They should have a name for the travel sickness that came with mapwalking, but then naming it would only make it seem more normal, and there was nothing normal about traveling through a map made from the blood of a friend. She looked around for Perry, saw him lying near her, his face pale, no longer traveling with ease. She reached out a hand—

A gasp.

Zoe looked up to see Finn's horrified expression as Sienna gazed at herself in a mirror. Dark whorls of shadow eddied across her skin and in the reflection, Zoe saw Sienna transformed. The blood that ran through her veins now channeled the power of the Shadow and yet, her eyes were still clear and bright. Somehow, she managed to keep the darkness in some kind of balance — but for how long?

Zoe's vision shifted, and she saw the strings of the world bend around Sienna, warping away from her as if repelled by her aberration, then attracted back in. They hummed with increased power, charged by her very presence. Whatever was happening, it intensified the closer Sienna came to the peak of the tower.

It wasn't much further now, but this was a strange place to make their last stand. The vast library was round with a central staircase the only route up from below. A single narrow doorway with stairs of black stone wound up to the higher levels.

Mahogany bookshelves spread like spokes from the middle of the room, leading to arched windows at the end of each corridor, allowing light to illuminate the halls of knowledge within. There were books here that were rare on Earthside, heresies thought lost to history, but each found a place off the edge of the map. Vanished ideas melded into something new, every dark entreaty giving power to the Shadow. Some of the books had crumbled in place, their spines damaged by the years. In another time, Zoe would have taken them for restoration and granted the tomes a new life. But not today.

"They're almost here," Titus shouted, pointing out the window at a dust cloud approaching. Zoe could just make out figures on the wide open plain. A pack of mutants ran on thick limbs, Elf riding high on the shoulders of one colossal beast.

"They'll have to come this way to get up to the top." Finn leaned over the balustrade of the spiral staircase to look down to the levels below. "We need to block this as much as we can." He glanced over at Sienna. "We'll buy you time for whatever you need to do up there."

She nodded and without a second look, walked through the narrow doorway to ascend the black stone stairs.

Finn watched her go. As soon as she disappeared, his expression hardened. He dragged one of the huge lecterns toward the hole and put his back against it, muscles bulging, legs straining with the effort. Titus joined him and with a crash, the lectern fell down onto the intricate staircase.

It was a start, but they would need much more to stop anyone coming up.

Zoe dragged herself to her feet, pushing aside the leaden weight in her limbs as she helped Perry up. Together they all pulled piles of books off then shouldered the heavy shelves onto one side, sliding them over the holes left in the staircase, slowly forming a great pile of heavy wood blocking the only entrance.

A dull thud came from way below. The sound of a massive door opening.

"Keep going." Finn's chest heaved in great breaths as he pushed another bookcase onto the pile, now stacked three deep.

Heavy footsteps came from below, shouts in a guttural tongue and the high-pitched voice of Elf urging the mutants on.

A hammering sound thumped through the library. The bookcases shook, jolting up and down as if the heavy wood were nothing more than kindling.

Finn and Titus drew their swords, stepped back into a fighting stance as they faced the stairwell, bodies taut as the warriors took their last stand.

Perry retreated to one arched window, his back against the wall as he raised his hands, palms up. He closed his eyes and whispered something, a prayer or an entreaty, it didn't matter which. Zoe could see the frustration on his face as he desperately searched within himself for a tiny glimmer of the flame he once called easily to his bidding. But his palms remained empty. Not even a flicker of light left. She wanted to go to him, but Zoe knew she could offer nothing that would help. He had to face this moment alone.

The thumping came again.

The sound of cracking wood and splintering timber. The middle set of bookshelves crashed down, opening a hole big enough to climb through.

Two mutants surged up through the gap, faces contorted with rage. They looked similar to the giant Hashim, but where he had carried Zoe with gentle arms, these beasts now swung clenched fists like steel hammers.

One forced Finn back with a flurry of blows, oblivious to the cuts and slashes that the rebel Borderlander managed to land.

Titus went down under the blade of another, a deep gash on his forehead, his arms and torso quickly bloody and bruised. Finn rushed to stand over the body of his friend, sword flashing in the air, faster than ever, a warrior in his prime.

More mutants clambered out of the hole, hacking with their short swords. Finn parried and thrust, dancing around the lumbering creatures.

But they kept pouring from the hole. There were too many. They were almost out of time.

Perry tried desperately to rekindle his flame in the maelstrom of the library, but Zoe could see he was broken.

She stepped in front of him and shifted her vision. The weave of the world appeared in shades of gold and silver thread shot through with black. But now she understood that the Shadow was just one aspect of the whole and it could be manipulated just as other threads.

Zoe reached out and weaved the cords together, creating a net around the mutants. With one tug, she pulled them away from Finn.

They struggled and grunted, striking at the air as they tumbled over one another, clutching at nothing. The net was invisible but as strong as her magic, and Zoe clenched her fists as she entangled them further.

Finn fell to his knees, gasping for breath in a moment of welcome respite. Perhaps they could hold off the attack after all.

A sudden white light shot out of the well of the staircase, blowing the Mapwalker team backward and tearing the strings of the magic net apart.

The mutants rolled out of their entanglement, bellowing with rage.

Elf rose out of the staircase behind them in a blaze of silver light. The jagged edge of a bolt of lightning with as much fury as the oncoming storm. She looked down upon them, cold violence in her gaze. She raised her hands for the slaughter.

CHAPTER 23

SIENNA RAN UP THE stairs toward the top of the tower. The sound of fighting below soon faded to nothing as she climbed higher. The staircase narrowed, winding tighter as she rose. The walls seemed to suck in the light from the tiny arrow-slit windows, smothering it with pitch like a dying animal sucked to the bottom of a peat bog.

Her footsteps slowed as she reached an open wooden door carved with runes of power.

Sienna.

The voice she had heard high in the clouds was now a caress, inviting her in.

Sienna pulled her grandfather's compass from her pocket, holding it in her hands like a talisman, anchoring her to Bath. Her home, her family, her world.

She stepped inside.

The circular room had high ceilings with thick wooden beams that met in the middle, vaulted like a cathedral. Between each, arched windows hung with heavy drapes that must look out over the plains in every direction. Etchings covered every surface of the walls, the stone carved into tableaux of war and violence, plague and suffering, lust and cruelty. The shadow side of humanity's existence.

Sienna tore her eyes away from the depravity and stepped

further into the room. Shadows shifted around the walls, snaking behind the drapes, pooling around the corners of the beams.

The metallic stink of dried blood hung heavy in the air, evidence of recent sacrifice to the dark power that ruled here. The remains of an offering lay on a stone altar against one wall, a dismembered corpse the size of a child. Sienna gripped the compass tighter, her skin crawling with the sense of being watched.

A circle lay marked out in the middle of the room, bounded by a ring of skulls. They were all different sizes, some animal, some human, others of mutant origin, some hideously disfigured, others from creatures long extinct on Earthside.

Within the ring, a vortex of black energy spiraled up toward the roof and high above, an opening led out to the sky. Inside the whirlwind, a dark figure spun in slow spirals, features obscured by tendrils of mist, its shape concealed by folds of midnight cloth that merged with the eddies of shadow.

Sienna.

The voice was all-consuming now, and a longing rose inside her, the marks on her skin calling like to like.

Sienna reached out a hand. The edge of the whirlwind licked along her skin, tendrils of black mist emerging as if to join with her flesh. For a second, there was tension, a skin on the tornado — then it broke, like the surface of water parting. It pulled her inside, the silver compass falling unheeded to the floor.

She gasped at the chill, the cold of the depths below ice caps, darkness tinged by blue light from a world now out of reach above. Creatures swam just out of sight with scything teeth ready to tear her apart, scuttling legs and unseeing eyes waiting to devour what remained. The sound of her pulse pounded through the water and below that, the howling of trapped souls drowned in the pitch black below.

Sienna reached out for the surface, desperately clawing her way up, but her limbs were too heavy, her lungs tight to bursting.

She wouldn't make it.

A lithe figure dived in from the ice above and reached for her hand, soft skin but with a powerful strength. As her vision narrowed, Sienna grasped hold and let herself be dragged back up to the world above.

As her head broke the surface, she took huge gasps of life-giving air. Her rescuer helped her to shore — not a world of ice, but a meadow of green grass, cherry trees and dappled light. Pink blossom blew on a warm summer breeze and flowers spiraled around her as she lay on the bank, the touch of soft petals on her cheeks.

Sienna.

Her rescuer was a young woman, her features perfectly sculpted like a Renaissance portrait. A robe of Marian blue clung to her body, wet from the water, and a silver mist hung around her like an aura. The woman from the mosaic at the heart of the border.

Her eyes were the shifting shades of opal and Sienna thought she could see a touch of Xander, maybe a hint of Sir Douglas. The silver hair at her temples mirrored an echo of Elf, yet the woman seemed ageless and Sienna could sense her deep wisdom. How long had she been here sustaining the Borderlands? There was so much Sienna wanted to know.

Let me show you.

The woman reached out a hand, and Sienna took it gladly. Together they spun into the air, up into the sky above the meadow and into the clouds away from the tower. They flew across the realm of the Borderlands, rich and teeming with life. So much to explore and learn about. A beautiful chaos, so different to the cornered world of Earthside where everything was ordered and limited. Sienna knew she could never be her complete self there. She could never use her magic in the way she was born to if she went back.

All this can be yours, Sienna. Join us and we will bring down the border. One world, together at last.

* * *

As Elf rose on a pillar of blinding silver light, anger surged through Perry in a burning white-hot heat. She had taken his father from him. She would not take Zoe and Sienna and his friends.

Perry let his grief ignite and in that moment, the spark caught within. He raised his hands, opening his palms as fireballs formed and caught alight in blazing crimson dancing with flecks of electric blue. He tapped into the last of what remained of his magic, conjuring the words his father had spoken as he died. *For Galileo.*

Perry roared the cry of the phoenix who rises once more within the flame. His entire body flared into a blaze and he ran full-tilt across the library floor, fire catching the surrounding wood.

Elf turned in surprise and reached out in a blaze of light —

Perry leapt, spun in the air, and her beam glanced off his shoulder.

He slammed into her, a human pillar of flame. He wrapped his arms around her and as every cell of his body transformed into fire, Perry split open with metamorphosis, screaming in agony as he became more heat than skin, more flame than bone.

Within the ring of his grasp, Elf twisted and shuddered, her skin melting. He held her ever more tightly, burning through to the white of her bones, blood boiling, her hair on fire, eyes bulging as she screamed in torment.

Smoke rose around them, an offering to the ancient gods, those who had split the worlds apart so long ago. Perry felt

Elf sag in his arms and sensed her spirit burn up alongside their fused flesh.

With his last fiery breath, he spun into a pillar of flame, twisting down through the wooden staircase, burning a giant hole and pulling the last of the mutants down with him.

* * *

Zoe gasped for breath as the library burned. Smoke billowed out of the chasm in the center, embers dancing in the air like fireflies as ash rained down. The staircase had collapsed and only the roar of flames came from below. She clutched a hand to her mouth, tears streaming from her eyes, a sob erupting from her throat. Perry was truly gone.

In that last moment, she had witnessed his transformation from man to a creature of flame and burning wind, a fierce magic that ripped through his very flesh. He had become a master of his craft in those last moments — and it had cost him everything.

Zoe sat for a moment, her back against the stone of the tower. In the haze of smoke, it seemed as if she were here alone with the crackle of fire and the creak of burning wood. Was this really the end of the Mapwalker team at the top of the tower at the edge of the world? How could they have traveled so far and failed so badly?

But then she thought of Perry's face, his determination in those final moments. His sacrifice set a fire within Zoe's own soul. If he could summon so much in those last seconds, then she could, too.

She reached out and tested the strings of the world. Somehow, there was still balance. The Shadow had not won yet. Sienna was above in the tower and down here — she tested the cords — yes, Finn and Titus still lived.

Zoe pulled her sleeve down and held it over her mouth

and nose as she crawled through the wreckage of the library, coughing in the dense smoke. She sensed the heaviness of the men before she saw them. Broken bodies, unconscious from the pain of their wounds, barely breathing.

Finn lay face down over Titus, shielding his friend from the worst of the fire even as his own back lay scarred and ragged from mutant claws and embers from fallen beams.

Zoe grabbed Finn's arms and tugged him sideways off Titus's body and out along the corridor to the window. Muscles screaming, she dashed back through the smoke to do the same for Titus, laying him next to his friend.

Maybe the fresh air would revive them. Maybe together, they could help Sienna.

"Finn," Zoe croaked, her voice hoarse from the smoke. She stared down at the rebel leader's handsome face, sooty with ash and bloody from his wounds. "Wake up, please."

Finn stirred. His eyelids fluttered as he groaned and reached for Zoe's hand.

"Sienna," he gasped from his burned throat, his voice breaking with the effort. His face contorted with pain and Zoe could see how much it cost him to speak.

Zoe squeezed his hand. "It's okay. I'll go to her. Follow when you can."

She saw doubt in the rebel Borderlander's eyes, but Zoe knew he couldn't make it up those stairs right now, let alone face whatever lay in the tower above.

"It will be okay." She tried to hide the desperation in her voice. Finn and Titus were out of action, so she would have to go alone to face whatever was left in this dark place. Creatures of nightmare or Sienna herself, transformed.

Zoe left the men and crawled around the perimeter of the library, one hand on the rough wall to guide her. After a few meters, she turned back. Finn and Titus had already faded from view, obscured by the billowing smoke.

She was alone.

The black staircase emerged from the gloom. Zoe pulled herself to her feet and began to climb. She could hear something in the tower above, a cacophony of sound that drowned out the flames below. But she couldn't hear Sienna.

Zoe ran up the steps, driving herself on with every ounce of energy she had left. Was she already too late?

CHAPTER 24

Zoe reached the top of the stairs and rushed through the door, her breath ragged from running. Hideous figures carved on the walls around her seemed to move as she walked past, trapped in grotesque portraits of suffering, writhing in unending agony.

Smoke whirled in the air from the fire below, along with shadows that formed into tattered creatures of claw and fang. Zoe's heart hammered in fear, but she forced herself to step further into the room.

Sienna spun slowly in a vortex of shadow in the center of a circle of skulls. Her eyes were closed, but she smiled in delight as dusky mist contorted around her, bearing her up into the air like a celebratory offering. The patterns on her skin twisted in dizzy formation. The sound of many voices joined in a chorus. A harsh discord, like all the wrong notes played at once, and behind them, the fleshy sound of beating, whips hitting flesh, the thud of fists, the cries of the tortured.

The silver compass lay on the floor next to the skulls, its face sprung open to show the five-pointed design and the lines of Bath within.

Zoe bent to pick it up. One of the shadow creatures lunged at her, swiping with claws of rotted flesh, the stench of the grave rising up around them. Zoe rolled sideways, grabbing the compass as she did so, pulling it to her chest with one hand.

The specter leapt upon her back, its skeletal fingers freezing her flesh as it tried to wrest the compass away. It opened its maw and instead of rotting teeth; the thing had writhing maggots inside. They tumbled out over Zoe. She wriggled and screamed as the things burrowed into her skin, her breath coming in terrified gasps.

She threw up her hands and opened her eyes, allowing her vision to shift. The strings of the world appeared, and she saw that the ghoul of smoke was merely a creature of lies and deception, the maggots merely motes of dust on her skin. Zoe grasped the cords of shadow, her fingers darting through the air as she twisted the threads together, binding the creatures behind a lattice of their own substance. They moaned and twisted in desperation, clawing for her eyes, but the net held.

She crawled to the outside of the circle of skulls, clutching tightly to the compass. The dark well reached to the edge of the bony perimeter and something inside told her not to step into that vortex or she would be lost in the world between, trapped in the obsidian shards in the temple below the border.

"Sienna," she shouted, but the cacophony that whirled about her friend drowned her voice.

She held up the compass and called once more into the maelstrom. "For Galileo, Sienna. For your grandfather. For Earthside."

* * *

High above the clouds, Sienna heard someone call her name. A voice from home. Zoe.

The beautiful woman by her side tugged on her hand, distracting her. She pointed down at a giant creature below them just under the waves, scales like a dragon with a long neck and powerful jaws. It was terrifying and glorious all at once — and part of her domain if she would just become one with the Shadow. A promise of the world held out in exchange for what? Her blood, her life?

Zoe's voice came again. It was faint, but Sienna could just make out her words. *For Galileo.*

A flash of memory and the world darkened. Sienna saw her grandfather in the copse of plane trees in the Circus on a stormy night in Bath. A pack of wolves closed around him as he painted the sigil of the Illuminated on the earth with his blood, then gave his life to seal the border. Sir Douglas in the robes of a wolf reached down and took the compass, an offering to the darkness that ruled his life. But her grandfather had vanquished the Shadow that night and his blood called to her now.

Dr Rachel's voice came back to her from the clinic. *The Shadow is not always what it seems.*

Sienna looked over at the ageless young woman whose hand she held so tightly, then down at the Borderlands below. She could not be up here. There was no icy water, no drowning. She had stepped into the vortex — she must still be down there. This was all some kind of vision designed to distract her.

A howling rose up and the wind whipped them as lashes of rain descended. The woman gripped her hand more tightly, her eyes fixed on Sienna's, a triumphant smile on her lips. Was it too late?

They fell out of the sky, tumbling together through darkness and hail, the clash of lightning as if the gods raged about them.

But Sienna pushed it all aside and opened her eyes.

She spun within the vortex of shadow — and she held the

dried hand of a desiccated corpse made from mis-matched pieces of mangled cadavers, those lost to the Shadow over generations. A husk somehow sustained by dark blood magic.

Sienna desperately tried to thrust the hand away from her, but the shriveled flesh had fused to her own, their skin merging together. The symbols on her body spun ever faster as the silver mist crept up her arm, bringing with it flashes of memory.

A young woman in robes of Marian blue tied to an altar within a circle of skulls, surrounded by hooded figures. Mapwalkers from long ago — those of the Illuminated and those of the Shadow, joined in one moment to split the worlds. They slashed her skin and as her blood ran red; they bound her with a net of magic to this place — a vortex to hold the worlds in balance created by a Weaver.

The woman had held equilibrium in place for a time, but over generations, Earthside Mapwalkers withdrew, leaving the Borderlands to the Shadow. It had taken hold and slowly, slowly, turned the world toward darkness.

But it needed a host, and the withered corpse before her was finished.

As the silver mist receded from what was left, the body began to crumble, leaving only ash and dust in its wake. It was up to Sienna's elbow now and she knew that once it reached her heart, she would no longer be able to stop it.

A rush of wind from the opening high above in the vaulted ceiling. The storm was almost overhead. Lightning flashed from heavy clouds, creatures of winged terror flying within. If the Shadow could not take her alive, then Sienna knew it would destroy this tower and all within it. Her friends would die, the border would remain closed, perhaps forever, and Earthside would be wracked with disaster.

She thought of her father and her grandfather, how much they had given to uphold the secrets of the Mapwalkers

— and Bridget, tied to the maps themselves, her life blood pulsing with ink.

This path was her true heritage. She had been lost before the Ministry with no purpose, no direction. She had always longed for the world beyond the map — and now she stood at the heart of it. The young woman had held the worlds in balance for generations. Perhaps she could, too.

It was a chance to renew the worlds, save Earthside, and give the Borderlands a chance to thrive. It was everything she had wanted — for Finn, for Mila and Ekon, for those back on Earthside.

The Shadow was within her and on her skin in the writhing symbols and yet, a part of her still clung to Earthside, to her Mapwalker lineage. Her grandfather's blood had closed the border that night, perhaps her own would open it again. *Use the compass once more,* Sir Douglas had whispered in his dying words. *For Galileo.*

Tears spilled down her cheeks as Sienna desperately searched for a way she could make it work — but every path led her back to this place. There was no other way, but she would go on her own terms. The compass would be her anchor to Earthside.

The silver mist rose higher and cold crept over her skin. She was almost out of time.

Sienna turned to the edge of the vortex. Zoe stood on the lip of the circle of skulls, holding out the silver compass. Her lips moved, but the wind drowned her words.

Sienna remembered the moment in the winds as they descended into Egypt. Zoe had heard the voice that time. Perhaps she could hear through the wind now.

"I need your help."

At the words, Zoe stopped speaking and nodded.

"There's only one way to stop this. Throw the compass in and then bind me with cords of light and shadow."

Zoe shook her head, her eyes wide with horror.

"You must do it." Sienna nodded down at the rising mist. "If the Shadow takes me first, I may not be able to balance the worlds. But this way ... it gives us more time, Zoe. Do this and then go back to Bridget. Search the annals for another way. But now, I choose this path."

The desiccated corpse began to split into fragments, chunks of it breaking off to dissolve into the spinning wind.

"Hurry! We're out of time."

Sienna took the ritual knife from her pocket, the blade that her grandfather had used to shed his blood and save Earthside once before. As the wind whipped around her, she drew it down her arm, blood rising and spinning away, droplets joining the vortex.

Screams echoed from within the Shadow as the last of the corpse split into dark beads, joining with Sienna's blood. Like calling to like.

"Now!" Sienna shouted. She saw Zoe throw the compass as the mist rose to encompass her.

She sensed the expanse of the world outside, a blossoming of power within, that could rise up and spread across both lands. Sienna wanted to tear it all apart, ravage every last inch and absorb the power of those who thought they could stand against the Shadow.

The silver compass tumbled into the whirlwind.

It hung in the air, opening to reveal the lines of Bath, carved by her grandfather's hand. With the last of her strength, Sienna reached out and hugged it to her chest.

"For Galileo," she whispered as lines of silver, blood and shadow formed a net around her.

* * *

Zoe wept as she weaved the threads of the world together, her fingers flashing through the air as she created a lattice of magic, a net to hold Sienna within the Tower of the Winds. Tears ran down her cheeks as she trapped her friend within the vortex, Sienna's slender frame now obscured by swirling blood and ash.

She could only hope that she had done the right thing, that somehow Bridget would know how to undo it all, to set Sienna free once more. But deep within, Zoe knew this was the only way.

Fate had bound a Weaver to their journey for this purpose — and now that purpose was fulfilled. The path of her own heritage and Sienna's bloodline had always been entwined. Zoe understood the truth of that now. For Weavers had always known the lines of the world were spun by fate. They were only instruments of destiny, and now Zoe could see that her own path had always been laid out this way.

She stitched the final element of Sienna's bloody prison and stepped back from the edge, her hands dropping to her sides.

"No!" Finn limped into the tower, his hand clutched to his side, his clothes covered in ash. "What have you done?"

He staggered over and pushed Zoe roughly aside, then lunged at the vortex for Sienna. His hand bounced off the perimeter, leaving his knuckles bloody and bruised as if he had punched a wall. He tried again and again, every blow coming back at him until he fell to his knees, broken and exhausted.

He looked up with tears in his eyes as Sienna spun unseeing behind her cage of silver and crimson.

Zoe knelt down beside him. "It was her choice," she whispered.

Finn shook his head. "There was never anyone else. Your people sent her here for this, even if she didn't know it."

Zoe remembered the woman in the mosaic beneath the border and the book in the library that first day with the hand-sketched figure in ash. Perhaps he was right. Perhaps

Bridget had known all along. But had there been any other way?

The storm calmed outside, the sound of thunder rolling away to nothing. Blue sky opened up in the skylight above and the sound of birdsong filled the air.

Zoe stood up and pulled back the heavy drapes from one window, letting the light inside. A sunbeam struck the whirling vortex that surrounded Sienna and the remains of ash within dissolved. It shone with ruby and golden light, reflecting into every part of the room.

The altar with its grisly sacrifice crumbled to dust, and the shadow creatures dissolved in the light. The carved abominations in the walls turned into patterns of flowers and fruit, an abundance of nature.

Zoe turned around in wonder, a smile dawning on her face. Somehow Sienna had shifted the balance of power and the Shadow was no longer the dominant force in the Borderlands.

She turned to Finn. "Help me open them all."

Together, they pulled open the other drapes, allowing light to stream into every corner. As the tower brimmed full, the light rolled out the windows once more, down the sides of the building and out onto the plains beyond. Flowers bloomed in its wake, the air filled with the scent of summer as the golden hue spread into the distance, illuminating the Borderlands for the first time in generations.

CHAPTER 25

Finn stared out the window, Zoe beside him, as the land below bloomed under the golden light. There was a buoyancy in the air where there had only been heaviness before, a sense of the world pivoting.

"This is more than just the renewal of the border," he said. "It's the restoration of the land itself. The Borderlands can thrive again without the dominance of the Shadow." He spun around to look at the vortex where Sienna spun within. "She has changed everything. The Resistance can take back Old Aleppo, purge my father's forces. It's a new beginning."

He walked back to the edge of the circle of skulls and reached out a hand, holding it only a millimeter from the spinning vortex. It was as close as he could get to Sienna through the veil when just this morning he had woken with her in his arms. The warmth of her body, the smell of her hair, how she had fitted so perfectly against him. It was how he hoped to wake every day for the rest of his life, but now …

Finn bit his lip as he tried to hold back the tears that threatened. She had chosen to leave him for the final time and the blood of a Mapwalker was now the hope of the Borderlands. He would honor her sacrifice and live on for the land they both loved — but now he would do it alone.

* * *

In the library under the Ministry back in Bath, Bridget sensed a sudden tension in the maps, the pulsing of ink beat more strongly within her veins. The rustling around her grew louder as cartography began to shift and re-form, as if the very fabric of the world had shifted.

She turned to the desk and pulled out the volume of Mapwalker annals. She opened it to a page marked with a scarlet silk thread. A figure sketched in ash on its ivory pages, her features suddenly clear.

Sienna, wrapped in a shroud of shadow and light in the midst of a whirling vortex of blood. Her life force would sustain the border and keep the Shadow at bay — at least for a time. The border was renewed and the natural disasters would soon end on Earthside as the world moved freely once more.

Tears ran down Bridget's cheeks as she reached out a fingertip and touched the face of the young woman trapped within the Tower of the Winds. Sienna was bound to her Mapwalker destiny just as Bridget was herself shackled to the library, a balance of Blood Cartographers until their lifespans ended or someone else took their place.

A gasp came from behind her, then a low moan of despair. Bridget turned to see John staring down at the sketch of his daughter. He sank to his knees and Bridget knelt to embrace him as they mourned the end of one time and the beginning of another.

* * *

Mila felt a shift in the water as she darted between the ripples of the river heading west toward the coast. It was as if all sharp edges became smooth for a moment and then reset themselves, like an earthquake passing beneath the mantle of the earth, lifting and lowering everything in its wake.

She glanced behind to check on the twins and by the look on their faces; they felt it too. Something had changed in the Borderlands and somehow, Mila knew that Sienna had made it to the Tower of the Winds.

They swam fast over submerged boulders, translucent skin flashing in the sunlight that dappled down through the water. Mila led the twins on. No time for stopping, and no need to. They all reveled in the freedom of being one with the water.

Up ahead, Mila heard the thundering of a waterfall. The river frothed, churning as it became shallow in places, and carving deep in others. Eddies and whirlpools formed at the sides. Daniel slipped into one, laughing with delight as he spun around. Dawn joined him, and the twins flew in circles hand in hand, dancing in the water.

Mila smiled as she watched them play, remembering her own solitary life in the canals of London and later in Bath. No one understood her. No one laughed with her. But that would all change now.

The Mapwalker team had been her home for a time, but losing Xander had been a heavy blow. Sienna would always be a friend, but her powerful blood meant she stood apart and her choices were beyond reach now.

Finn's words in the cave at Ganvié echoed back to her: *There are so few of your kind.* And yet, here they were, three lost Waterwalkers heading for home.

"Come on, you two," Mila called out. "I'll show you what fun really is."

She beckoned and then turned in the water, darting ahead of them through the rapids as they followed her with whoops of delight.

Mila dived down into the depths before the waterfall met the edge of the cliff and then leapt like a dolphin up out of the froth and into the air.

She spun around, her body diaphanous in the sunlight, a figure of water droplets and air, her laugh the tinkle of rain on stone. The twins leapt just behind her, shrieking with joy. The three of them plunged down the falls into the pool below and then on — toward Ekon and Ganvié.

THE END

ENJOYED THE MAPWALKER TRILOGY?

Thanks for joining Sienna and the Mapwalker team in the Mapwalker Trilogy. If you enjoyed the book, a review would be much appreciated as it helps other readers discover the story.

Get a free copy of the bestselling thriller, *Day of the Vikings*, an ARKANE thriller, when you sign up to join my Reader's Group. You'll also be notified of giveaways, new releases, and receive personal updates from behind the scenes of my books.

Click here to get started:

www.JFPenn.com/free

Day of the Vikings, an ARKANE thriller

A ritual murder on a remote island under the shifting skies of the aurora borealis.

A staff of power that can summon Ragnarok, the Viking apocalypse.

When Neo-Viking terrorists invade the British Museum in London to reclaim the staff of Skara Brae, ARKANE agent Dr. Morgan Sierra is trapped in the building along with hostages under mortal threat.

As the slaughter begins, Morgan works alongside psychic Blake Daniel to discern the past of the staff, dating back to islands invaded by the Vikings generations ago.

Can Morgan and Blake uncover the truth before Ragnarok is unleashed, consuming all in its wake?

Day of the Vikings is a fast-paced, supernatural thriller set in London and the islands of Orkney, Lindisfarne and Iona. Set in the present day, it resonates with the history and myth of the Vikings.

If you love an action-packed thriller,
you can get Day of the Vikings for free now:

WWW.JFPENN.COM/FREE

Day of the Vikings features Dr. Morgan Sierra from the ARKANE thrillers, and Blake Daniel from the London Crime Thrillers, but it is also a stand-alone novella that can be read and enjoyed separately.

AUTHOR'S NOTE

Thanks for reading *Map of the Impossible*. I hope you enjoyed the adventure. This is the end of the trilogy that encompasses Sienna's Mapwalker journey, but I have some ideas for Mila and Zoe, so you never know, there may be more Mapwalker adventures to come.

I always like to include an Author's Note in my novels as I love the research process as much as the creative part of writing. You can find images used in my research on my Pinterest board: www.pinterest.com/jfpenn/map-of-the-impossible

Inspiration for the story

The Map of the Impossible was inspired by the oldest map of the underworld found inside an ancient Egyptian coffin inscribed 4000 years ago. It was intended to help the dead pass through a series of challenges including snake charmers, high paths, and the watchers.

https://egyptfwd.org/Article/6/712/Oldest-Map-of-The-Underworld-Found-Inside-An-Ancient-Egyptian

The ibis room was inspired by pictures of mummified ibis and an article that mentioned 4 million sacred ibis mummies found in the catacombs of Tuna el-Gebel and 1.75 million discovered in the ancient burial ground of Saqqara as votive offerings to the god Thoth. The thought of millions of mummified ibis coming to life is pretty terrifying!

https://www.theguardian.com/science/2019/nov/13/experts-crack-mystery-ancient-egypt-sacred-bird-mummies

The antidote to belladonna is Physostigmine which is found in the Calabar Bean and the manchineel tree.

The idea of Zoe's weaver magic was inspired by The Lady of Shalott poem by Alfred Lord Tennyson and the gorgeous painting by John William Waterhouse.

A note on strange times

I started the book in November 2019, so the idea of natural disaster impacting the world while the borders closed had nothing to do with the pandemic. But as it turned out, I wrote most of the story whilst in lockdown in Bath, UK, in the spring of 2020.

As I write this final note, we are still in the summer of coronavirus and while some borders are opening up, many remain closed, and I don't know when I will travel again. What a strange time in history, indeed.

ACKNOWLEDGMENTS

For Map of Shadows

Thanks to my editor, Jen Blood, for her help with the book, and my proofreader, Wendy Janes. Thanks to Jane Dixon-Smith for the cover and interior print design.

Thanks as ever to my readers, and especially the Pennfriends, for the supportive emails and enthusiastic reviews. You keep me writing!

For Map of Plagues

Thanks to Jen Blood, for continuing to make me laugh during edits. Thanks to Wendy Janes for proofreading, and to my Pennfriends for useful advanced reader comments.

Thanks to Jane Dixon Smith at JDSmith-Design.com for the great cover design and print formatting.

For Map of the Impossible

More than ever, a special thanks to my readers and my Pennfriends for continuing to support my books in what has turned out to be the wierdest year (2020 pandemic).

Thanks to Michaelbrent Collings, whose positive encouragement (and terrific stories!) helped me through a difficult time.

Thanks to Mark McGuinness whose creative coaching helped me get through a lockdown process block and finish the book.

Thanks to my editor, Jen Blood, for continuing to understand my crazy brain, and to Wendy Janes for proofreading.

Thanks to Jane Dixon Smith at JDSmith-Design.com for the great cover design and print formatting.

MORE BOOKS BY J.F.PENN

Sign up at www.JFPenn.com/free to be notified of the next book in the series and receive my monthly updates and giveaways.

* * *

Mapwalker Dark Fantasy Thrillers

Map of Shadows #1
Map of Plagues #2
Map of the Impossible #3

If you enjoy **Action Adventure Thrillers**, check out the **ARKANE** series as Morgan Sierra and Jake Timber solve supernatural mysteries around the world.

Stone of Fire #1
Crypt of Bone #2
Ark of Blood #3
One Day In Budapest #4
Day of the Vikings #5
Gates of Hell #6
One Day in New York #7
Destroyer of Worlds #8
End of Days #9
Valley of Dry Bones #10
Tree of Life #11

* * *

If you like **Psychological Thrillers**, join Detective Jamie Brooke and museum researcher Blake Daniel:

Desecration #1
Delirium #2
Deviance #3

* * *

For more **dark fantasy,** check out:

Risen Gods
The Dark Queen
A Thousand Fiendish Angels:
Short stories based on Dante's Inferno

More books coming soon.

You can sign up to be notified of new releases, giveaways and pre-release specials - plus, get a free book!

www.JFPenn.com/free

If you loved the book and have a moment to spare, I would really appreciate a short review on the page where you bought the book. Your help in spreading the word is gratefully appreciated and reviews make a huge difference to helping new readers find the series.

Thank you!

ABOUT J.F.PENN

J.F.Penn is the Award-nominated, New York Times and USA Today bestselling author of the ARKANE action adventure thrillers, Brooke & Daniel Psychological Thrillers, and the Mapwalker fantasy adventure series, as well as other stand-alone stories.

Her books weave together ancient artifacts, relics of power, international locations and adventure with an edge of the supernatural. Joanna lives in Bath, England and enjoys a nice G&T.

You can follow Joanna's travels on Instagram @jfpennauthor and also on her podcast at BooksAndTravel.page.

* * *

Sign up for your free thriller,
Day of the Vikings, and updates from behind the scenes, research, and giveaways at:

www.jfpenn.com/free

* * *

Connect with Joanna:
www.JFPenn.com
joanna@JFPenn.com
www.Facebook.com/JFPennAuthor
www.Instagram.com/JFPennAuthor

* * *

For writers:

Joanna's site, www.TheCreativePenn.com, helps people write, publish and market their books through articles, audio, video and online courses.

She writes non-fiction for authors under Joanna Penn and has an award-nominated podcast for writers, The Creative Penn Podcast.

Printed in Great Britain
by Amazon